EMERGENCE

EMERGENCE

GAJA J. KOS & BORIS KOS

EMERGENCE

Cover illustration © 2019 by Merwild (Coralie Jubénot)

Cover design by Morana Designs

ISBN 978-961-94501-4-7 (hardcover)

ISBN 978-961-94501-3-0 (paperback)

ISBN 978-961-94501-2-3 (eBook)

Published by Boris Kos

Celje

October, 2019

CHAPTER ONE

VIOLET FIRE REIGNED ABOVE. STREAKS OF PINK AND DARK blue tinted the wispy clouds strewn across the majestic sapphire and purple gradient of the sky; a multitude of hues that set the world alight, yet spoke of soothing darkness on the cusp of its departure.

I stood immobile, my fingers wrapped around Ada's blade and the hollow ache in my chest a constant presence—yet even *it* seemed to have quieted, as if taken by the beauty. I pressed my bloodied hand to my heart, the other clutching the dagger even tighter.

Svitanye. The land of dawn.

In the distance, the hazy arch of the sun spread its rays across the horizon and brushed the delicate contours of trees and wild fields.

Morning.

This was what true morning looked like.

It didn't matter how late the hour was, that it had been

evening when we had left Somraque behind. Gazing at this vibrant canvas...

I felt something in me awaken.

My head spun, and I forced some air into my too-tight lungs, though it did little to curb the wonder keeping me enthralled.

Something I hadn't thought myself capable of slipped into the tranquil atmosphere—a breathless, astonished laugh.

There had been a drawing in one of the books I'd stolen from those dusty crates years ago. A swirl of colors over a slumbering landscape my mind had recreated time and time again; a combination I had sought out at parties when I gazed at the lively gemstone-adorned dresses and silken tablecloths meant to reflect the vivacious revelry. But even my imagination, as elaborate and unburdened as it might have been, fell short in light of what spread above me now.

A blend of so many nuances, so many textured shades no fabric or living thing could ever hope to encompass. Not even Zaphine's skills that had stolen my breath away when I'd roamed through the back of her shop and had first laid eyes on her creations.

The thought of the raven-haired Illusionist, the memory of the tumultuous roll of events that had descended upon us all once I'd set foot in that alley behind the boutique shook me from the stupor—and reminded me why I was here. Why I was privy to this beauty at all.

A bitter taste coated my tongue, the wonder turning to venom.

I tore my gaze from the sky and whirled around. Ada stood a short distance away, right where gray rock gave way to grass, her profile sharp with her hair braided away from her face. Only she wasn't perusing the canvas of dawn as I'd expected, but the umbrella pines and cypress trees, the splash of lavender growing beneath them.

"They're not here," she whispered, so quietly the words barely carried over, yet I felt the impact of every single one.

Unease coiled in the pit of my stomach.

"What?" I asked, perhaps hoping the edges of truth protruding through the discordant mess that was my mind were false.

Ada kept her gaze trained on the landscape as I approached, and only when I stopped beside her, turned to face me. A slender ray of light fell on her drawn face and illuminated the stark jade of her eyes—as well as the turmoil raging within them. I handed her the dagger I'd still been clutching just to break the skin-prickling tension.

"The others." Ada accepted it with stiff fingers and stashed it into its respective sheath on the second try. A touch of my blood, darkened, dry, still marred the edge of the blade. "Zaphine, Eriyan, Dantos, Ivarr... I can't see them anywhere."

The final kernel of amazement still pulsing within me burned to ashes when my mind could no longer deny the meaning of Ada's words. I made a slow circle, observing every shadow pooling within the outcropping of rocks, every tree with branches fanned wide—

Ada was right. I didn't know how, but we were alone.

A soft melody rose in the distance, reminding me of the wind chimes I'd hung on my bedroom balcony back in Soltzen. Usually, I found the sound soothing. Now, it only set me on edge.

A crease formed between Ada's eyebrows. "You think they left?"

"If they did, they couldn't have gone far," I said, convincing myself more than anything else. The portal—it should have deposited them in the exact same location where we, too, had arrived. There was no reason for them to wander unless something happened that caused them to flee. Still— "I know we didn't go through *immediately* after Dantos, but we hadn't lingered *that* long in..."

The name stuck in my throat.

No, we truly hadn't lingered that long just outside Nysa—the town that had been teetering right on the verge of destruction that would, hopefully, birth salvation. The weight of what I had left behind, *who* I had left behind, turned my insides leaden. I schooled my expression and clamped down on the hurt before its talons would rip the remaining foundations still holding me together to shreds. A fragrant wind, utterly new in its texture, the richness of undertones, caressed my skin—a reminder.

Mordecai had gifted me this opportunity. He had reunited me with Ada and the others while he stayed behind, entrusting us to do what was right.

Personal grievances had no place here.

"Ember," Ada called out just as I banished Mordecai's image to the deep vaults of my mind. I hadn't even noticed her move. "I found footprints."

She followed the seam between the rocky, packed earth and grass, the faint sunlight haloing her black-clad form.

"Strange." She knelt and touched two fingers to the soil just before the grass line. "They...stop."

I carefully closed the distance and peered over her shoulder. Though I could barely make out the imprints meandering along the curved edge of the clearing, I certainly didn't fail to notice their glaring absence up ahead.

No, not just up ahead...

"Why does it look like they—"

"Disappear?" Ada rose and tossed her long braid back. Lines formed around her tight-set mouth. "Because they do."

"That...makes no sense." I narrowed my eyes and did another sweep of the landscape. I noticed a copse of olive trees I'd missed earlier, but nothing even remotely resembling a person. Let alone *four* of them. "You think they were taken?"

While it couldn't have been more than seconds separating our arrival to Svitanye, we knew so little of this land it would be foolish to dismiss even something that might seem improbable. After all—I grazed my fingertips over the relic secured behind the band of my stocking—the last time I'd traveled between the fractured worlds ended up with me unconscious. Maybe the pendant, when used for portals designed to bridge such distances, altered time, too.

I rubbed three fingers across my forehead and quieted the too-many thoughts vying for attention until all that remained was the indisputable fact that, somehow, the footprints ended.

"Maybe someone, I don't know, *flew* them away?" I suggested.

Ada pressed her lips together but didn't answer.

We retreated to the spot where the portal had temporarily fused the two lands, Ada's gaze on the ground while mine was turned to the sky. No winged beasts. Nothing in the air to indicate danger.

As far as I could tell, there wasn't even a single bird anywhere in the vicinity.

"Maybe the grass simply *hid* the tracks," Ada offered, though it was clear she didn't believe that any more than I did. At least some of the blades should have been damaged if they'd crossed there. "There are more footprints headed in that direction."

She gestured towards the lavender stretching beyond a pointed boulder.

Again, nothing resembling a person caught my eye.

"You want to see where they lead?" I asked. "Maybe there's something we're still missing."

Ada nodded, but there was a touch of hesitation, even censure on her face. I turned around to face her fully.

"What's wrong? Aside from the obvious, I mean." I motioned to the tracks.

Silence met my question.

I stepped closer. "Ada?"

She tugged on the band securing her braid, then finger-combed the fiery strands until they settled over her shoulders—shoulders that had lost their typical straight edge of determination.

"Just tell me. Whatever it is."

"I—" A tick worked in her jaw. She sighed, then met my gaze. "I tried sending a flame to Eriyan."

Their own little communication trick. I hadn't been around long enough to learn just what it truly was, but I suspected it had to be some long-distance illusion, signaling they should meet. If Eriyan wasn't answering...

Realization slammed into me, and I couldn't help but feel rotten that I had been so caught up in myself, in this land, that I hadn't even considered what coming here would mean for her. For *all* of them...

"You can't use your magic, can you?"

Ada shook her head and sank to the rocky ground right by the seam, her hands folded in her lap. So the theory about native magics had proven true. But as remarkable as it was, the influence of the respective lands on which magics were allowed to exist, not even a kernel of wonder rose within me.

I lowered myself by Ada's side on a flat slab of stone,

repositioned the long skirt of my dress, then slowly, tentatively, wrapped my arm around Ada's shoulders. She had been unexpectedly...amicable when we had reunited in the rocky desert outside Nysa, but I had no idea how much of that had derived purely from the blunt relief of having the Savior within reach again.

How much of it was because, if only momentarily, she had forgotten about the shadowfire coiling beneath my skin.

And I—

I would be lying if I said I wasn't hurt when faced with the memory of her reaction to my true self. Despite that part of me that yearned to mend the many bridges we had burned.

Or maybe because of it.

Ada's warmth bled through the velvet of my dress as she leaned into the embrace. As did her shudders. I held her tighter.

"I know I shouldn't worry about magic, not now, not when... when we have *this*"—she flicked a hand towards the cut-off footprints just to our right—"to deal with. But..." A groan wrenched itself free from her hunched form. She ripped a long blade of grass from the ground by her boots and started tearing it into pieces. "I understand, Ember." She yanked out another blade, sprinkling soil onto her ankles. "I understand what my mother meant. To be forced to live like this, so *empty*..." She sobbed and released the small green pieces to flutter onto the ground. "It's like I'm a shell. Useless. Broken."

Her words drifted across the serenity, fragile and raw.

I ran my fingers down her back, then shifted so I was kneeling before her. I took both her hands in mine. "You're neither broken nor useless, Ada. You lost something that was always yours, and that's terrifying, but *you* are still here. You're still you. And you have friends who are just as disoriented right now, struggling to adapt to the exact same absence."

The gentle chiming I'd picked up on earlier weaved through the air once more, then faded. Ada lifted her gaze to mine. A steely resolve gradually suffused the jade until she nodded and pushed off the ground. The loss of her magic still resonated in her posture, in the slight stiffness of her movement, but I was glad to see a hint of her usual fire return to her face.

"Why don't we take a better look around? You follow one set of tracks, and I'll do the same with the other," I offered as I rose. "Let's say we walk...a hundred steps, then meet back here and decide what to do next?"

The part of me that ran on instinct wanted to skip the search, but if there was even the tiniest chance one of us would find something, I couldn't bring myself to miss it based on a presumption.

Ada, apparently, thought the same.

"One hundred steps," she repeated. "Okay."

I observed the ramrod straight line of her spine as she stalked back towards the first line of footprints. Regardless of her struggles, Ada was a leader. I had faith she would do everything to get the crew back together. After all, it was her well-intended stubbornness and determination that had set me on this course in the first place. And I hadn't exactly been the easiest person to sway.

Again, the chiming sounded, this time appearing farther away than before. I set off towards the jagged boulder. The footprints indented in the soil and sparse grass here were visible even to my untrained eye, as was their abrupt stop right before the rock. I made sure the relic was secure under the band of my stocking, then moved forward, following the path I imagined whoever had walked here must have taken despite the lack of outward signs. Fragrant lavender encompassed me from both sides, the plants oblivious to the fact that we were in the middle of winter. Although with the mild, almost warm weather bestowing soothing caresses on my skin, I supposed seasons didn't have the kind of impact on Svitanye as I'd experienced in Somraque. Even Soltzen, for that matter.

Fifty footsteps.

Sixty.

A slight drizzle sprayed my face, the lavender fragrance becoming headier. But as I reached my eighty-sixth step, the rain cut off as if I'd crossed some invisible demarcation line.

I glanced up, then behind me, pausing for a moment. A light gray curtain separated dry land from the rain-touched part, but I could hardly focus on how sharp the cut was as my gaze caught on the twisted trunk of a lone olive tree just off the path.

Frowning, I padded closer.

With the gentle rain bringing out the colors and darkening the bark, its texture stood out. Gently, I traced my fingers across the rough surface, tracing the grooves that seemed like—

Like smudged sentences.

I lowered myself into a crouch and studied one of the bright green lavender leaves reaching up beside the tree. I sucked in a sharp inhale. The veins running down its length weren't veins at all, but inscriptions. Too minuscule for a person to read, but inscriptions nonetheless. I took the leaf between my index finger and thumb, half expecting to find... I wasn't sure what, exactly, but this utter normalcy was *not* it.

The structure, the feel of it as I traced my fingertips along the leaf's surface suggested there was nothing peculiar about it. And yet...

Something to do with words, Ada's voice resonated in my mind.

Svitanye's magic came from words. Was this it? Was their entire land built on them? Even the aspects of it that were *alive?*

I straightened and began to retrace my steps. I'd lingered long enough already. As I strode through the drizzle that kissed my cheeks, then beyond it, I mulled over what I'd seen. What I *continued* spotting with my gaze trained on the ground where blades of grass swayed in the soft breeze. The slender lines running up their center were just a touch too fuzzy to be anything but strung-together words my eyes alone weren't sufficient to decipher. I pursed my lips and walked on.

Even before Ada had explained the finer nuances of how Somraque and their blood magic worked, I had been on the right path of figuring most of it out through sheer observation. And eavesdropping. But here, with no people around, just nature and the wind chimes ruling beneath a dawn sky, every explanation I tried to come up with fell short. Svitanye was an enigma.

A breathtaking one, true, but I would have given anything for a detailed account from one of Ada's ancestors.

As I neared the jagged boulder, the chiming grew louder then faded once more. I let my fingers travel across the aromatic lavender, let the perfectly normal feel of the plant anchor me before I pushed past the rock.

My breath caught in my throat, the muscles in my shoulders knotting.

I glanced at the pointed boulder again, recognizing the jagged tip, the structure that exposed the various shades of stone. It was the same one I'd passed earlier. I knew it.

Only Ada wasn't waiting for me in the space up ahead.

And neither was the clearing.

CHAPTER TWO

THE CHIMING SANG IN STARK CONTRAST TO MY POUNDING heart.

I waded out on what should have been the clearing, but the rock and earth were now a green meadow, a touch of rain lingering in the air and perfuming the earth as if a storm had ebbed only minutes ago.

I cast a look over my shoulder.

Dry, untouched land.

A tightness clawed at my throat as I returned my attention to the meadow that could *only* be here if I'd stepped through a portal. My hand sought out the bump of the fragment on my thigh, the other finding anchor in the crescent pendant. Their power whisked against my skin, my very essence, but it was no more than an idle, low rumble. Surely, I would have felt crossing the, however brief, in-between; would have *seen* the gateway, had it truly been a portal.

Tremors skittered all the way to my fingertips.

I wasn't losing my mind. I *wasn't*. It was this damned world...

Something tugged on my insides. A heaviness that was neither pleasant nor unpleasant, but simply was. I squared my shoulders, forced out a shaky breath, and willed my scattered thoughts to prioritize.

Whatever it was that had altered my reality, here in the open, I was unprotected. I needed to find a safe place where I could hunker down and truly think this through. Any other course of action would only do harm with all the unknowns pressing down upon me.

I spun on my heels to head back towards the lavender that would offer at least moderate cover—

I froze.

What...

The boulder. The sea of violet.

It was *all* gone.

"Shit," I said softly.

There was nothing recognizable anywhere I looked. Not a single landmark my eyes had skimmed over when I'd ventured beyond the clearing now absent, just as the footprints—

It hit me then.

The inscriptions on the plants, the blurred lines...

Had I—had *we*—somehow activated the magic by coming here? Was this why there was no one waiting when Ada and I had emerged through the portal?

But no, the others couldn't have influenced the land. Their power wasn't viable in this slice of the world, which left only me as the possible culprit.

So why, then, had they vanished? Could it have been the portal itself, interacting with and influencing the environment?

I cursed myself for those final moments in Nysa. Maybe if I'd paid more attention, if I'd been more vigilant about what rested *beyond* the portal instead of saying my silent farewell, I might have seen the magic whisk them away.

A citrus-scented breeze played with my unbound hair as I walked to where the boulder should have been. The soil beneath my feet hardened, a stark contrast to the damp earth I'd just left behind. Wrong.

All of this was wrong.

My fingers curled into fists, and tension slithered down my spine. Even in Somraque, there was a rhyme and reason to everything. Including the shadowfire. Me.

I took a tentative step forward.

Here, I was grasping at straws that faded at my touch.

The only thing I was certain of was that I would only make things worse if I kept drifting around the countryside with no tether.

As fast as I could, I rushed over to one of the larger olive trees jutting towards the sky, and after a quick readjustment of my stocking to make sure the fragment would remain secure, painstakingly scaled its trunk. Despite my care, my lavish midnight dress tangled around my feet, the fabric catching on the rough structure of the bark. I had to pause several times to disentangle the velvet but eventually managed to climb up a branch that looked sturdy enough to hold my weight.

Briefly, I contemplated cutting the skirt and tying the strips into makeshift pants, but as I ran my hand across the star-sprinkled fabric, I simply couldn't bring myself to do it. Not when the dress had been one Mordecai had gifted me.

I snorted and shook my head.

Alone in a world that morphed in front of my very eyes with zero understanding of its magic, and here I was, fussing over a garment. Still, regardless of how ridiculous I sounded even to myself, I couldn't deny that the dress wrought of night also infused me with strength. With memories of all I had accomplished in the past hours, even if they did possess a dark edge—one I refused to succumb to.

I'd found a way to open a portal between lands.

I'd stepped onto a new plane.

I would learn to navigate it, too.

After I made myself as comfortable on the branch as I possibly could, I used the higher vantage point to monitor the diverse landscape. Though the wild, uncultivated fields—so at odds with what I'd seen during my rare ventures across Soltzen—and patches of shrub-ridden, rocky terrain struck me as haphazardly stitched together, they nonetheless carried a sense of unity.

I curved my fingers around the branch, legs dangling freely—as if this unexpected peace rising from the land had settled into my very flesh. No stirrings rippled across the icy lake of shadowfire within me, and for a moment, one no longer than a heartbeat or two, I allowed myself to forget about everything but the sight, grander than any painting gracing the Norcross manor walls.

The blend of morning colors blanketing the sloping terrain was vivid, but not aggressive, complementing the flora that was perfectly devoid of human and animal life alike. That odd pull inside me I'd shoved into the recesses of my mind grew stronger, clearer as I calmed. A presence I could no longer ignore, nor wanted to.

Squinting, I tilted my torso and strained to look past the treetops to the seam where land met sky. Though the outlines were hazy, hardly more than swishes and blotches of indeterminable color, it was impossible to mistake the dense cluster among the abundance of greenery for anything but what it was.

A city.

Thank the Stars.

And that foreign presence within my flesh seemed to tug me straight in its direction.

A smile curved up my lips. I had my destination. A goal. I only hoped that wherever they were, Ada, Eriyan, Zaphine, Dantos, and Ivarr were feeling the same thing.

The wind chimes sounded again, a stone's throw to my left, it seemed. I craned my neck, searching the land for any sign of what could be the source of the melody when the massive oaks dominating the slight depression beyond the shrubs vanished.

I dug my nails into the bark.

Vanished. Without as much as a single heartbeat separating the trees' disappearance and the sudden manifestation of a sunflower field in their stead.

I lingered on my branch, perfectly still, and listened.

Whisper-soft rustling carried on the breeze. The fragile murmurs of a pulse belonging to a land where no claws skittered across the rocks and no wings flapped in melodic flight. Somraque had been barren, but with the people's thrumming magic, it hadn't been quiet. Not like this.

Just as the eeriness of it threatened to slip beneath my skin, the chiming began once more. I twisted in the direction of the sound, the muscles in my back protesting the strain, and watched the land change. Then again. And again. And again— until the inconceivable exchanges became indisputable reality.

It was hard to tell how much time I spent on that branch, not only confirming that the melody was somehow linked to the shifts, but attempting to figure out a pattern. Proximity, size, frequency—a headache was starting to throb in my temples from all the information I fought to process, yet in the end, all I had to go on was that nothing remained stagnant in Svitanye. I suspected even *my* little island of nature was constantly moving around, although due to my fixed position and the endless changes happening on all possible sides, I was unable to sense it myself.

A nervous, maybe slightly hysterical laugh clawed up my throat.

Throughout the shifts that, as far as I could tell, caused no true damage to the land, the city was the only landmark I never lost sight of. Unfortunately, the direction of my path to it was *not* fixed. And neither was the distance. There were moments when, had I not known what to search for, I would have easily written it off as a faraway outcropping of rocks. Only to glimpse roofs and straight edges mere chimes later.

A mess—all of it was a dissonant mess of possibilities in a game logic wouldn't help me win.

The single comfort I had to fall back on was that tug inside me, a compass that always pointed out the right way. If I could figure out how to navigate the magic...

I chewed on my lower lip. Maybe there *was* something I could do.

With a long exhale, I reached into that Ancient core at the heart of me and tried to bring the ethereal tapestry to mind. In Somraque, every thread woven into its structure was a signature, indicating not only the person it belonged to, but the intensity of the power they were releasing into the atmosphere. Why shouldn't the same apply to magic originating from the land?

I grappled for this other sight with phantom fingers, with all the will and magic coursing through my veins—

My perception remained the same.

I sighed and slumped against the bark, chipped bits of it raining onto the ground. Shit.

If such a superimposed reality existed in Svitanye, I had yet to find the key. For now, the only thing I could do was hope the inner tugging would suffice.

I waited through the shifts until the city came closer, scrambled down the tree, and ran.

I DIDN'T GET FAR.

With the varying size of the shifting fragments, not always marked with contrasting flora, it was impossible to predict *where* the land would cut off once the chiming started. Or when.

I was running blind, exhaustion weighing down on my limbs and lungs caught in a perpetual burning scream. The volume of the irritably calming music notified me of an impending change in the landscape, but I could do little more than pray it wouldn't throw me somewhere even farther away.

The city grew nearer.

Then blurred in the distance.

A vicious, never-ending game I was losing even when I believed success loomed just beyond the next stretch.

More times than I could count, I wanted to collapse on my knees and release those tears of frustration that kept building behind my eyes, but I didn't want to accept surrender just yet. My growing hunger and thirst would catch up with me eventually. I might as well try to do my best until that blow came.

The change whisked me away again. The earth beneath my feet was suddenly softer, tall umbrella pines blanketing me from all sides. I didn't see the city, but I *felt* it—closer than ever before.

My spirits lifted, only the hopeful, gasping sound that left my lips was lost to a new surge of chimes, so loud it could only mean one thing.

My stretch of land was on the brink of moving.

"No," I whispered.

I ran forward even when I knew it was futile. My ever-weaker legs would never carry me fast enough to escape the change.

My foot hit a protruding root and sent me careening sideways into a gnarled trunk. The bark scraped my palms hard enough to peel skin and reopen the old wound, but as I steadied myself, I forgot all about the stinging pain shooting up my senses. A song far more beautiful than the chimes caressed my ears.

Stunned, I gazed to my left.

Dozens of birds watched me from the plush, leaf-bearing branches of the tree next to mine.

The magic gained volume, expanded, the change I was starting to doubt was limited only to *this* sector imminent. I couldn't—

I couldn't start all over again.

Not now.

With nothing to lose, I propelled myself towards the bird-favored oak. Behind it, the outlines of the city crystallized, a view I knew I would lose the instant the song ended.

Pastel-colored wings fluttered and frightened chirps

exploded through the air as I slammed into the wide trunk, bracing my entire weight against it. Unable to bear witness to my failure, I closed my eyes.

The chiming ceased.

Tremors skittered down my limbs, my every breath a ragged attempt to pull myself together, to not crash down to my knees as dizziness swirled through me.

I opened my eyes.

The world had changed. And the city...

I slid to the ground.

The city remained the same.

CHAPTER THREE

A CHOKED LAUGH ESCAPED MY LIPS. FROM ABOVE, THE vigorous chirping seemed to echo my joy, exploding into a boisterous melody.

I peered up at the birds tucked in the bright green canopy— birds I hadn't seen *anywhere* but here, on this *one* oak that had remained static when every inch of ground beyond its roots had transformed.

"Clever birds," I muttered, my words greeted by more chirps.

Afraid I would startle them, I didn't dare climb the tree all the way to its widespread top, but I did lift myself to the first branch that promised a view—which was no small feat to achieve with the abundance of thriving serrated leaves.

And the abundance of bird droppings I had to avoid.

I ignored the stinging protests of my already worn palms, and, as soon as I found a position that offered the most support while also granting me some freedom, checked the fragment tucked in my stocking. Thanks to the tight band, it had hardly moved during my disgustingly many sprints, though the jagged ends *were* beginning to chafe my skin.

Wincing, I shifted it a little, thanking the Stars, the Sun, and whatever else was out there, that the fractured hallow wasn't only small, but light. Still, I wouldn't have minded having a pocket to stuff it into.

I let the velvet fabric cover my legs again, brushed off the worst of the dust, then studied my newest perch. A bird drifted from one branch to another, but the delicate yellow-and-grass-green thing didn't move beyond the tree's reach.

In the distance, as another bout of chimes suffused the air, the cityscape continued to stand at a fixed distance.

I returned my attention to the oak.

This couldn't be a one-time thing. Maybe I'd passed similar occurrences before but had been too blinded by my need to *run* to actually take notice. Even atop that olive, I'd been preoccupied with studying the magic's influence on Svitanye to notice the details—regardless of what I might have believed of my observational skills at the time.

Too much—there had been too much to take in and make sense of. And once I started to move...

If the birds hadn't announced their presence through song, I would never have spotted their dainty forms nestled in the treetop.

My fingers skimmed the pendant's chain as I dragged my gaze from them to the intimidating distance still separating me from the city. I scrutinized every bit of landscape, every shadow, tree—

A pomegranate shrub.

Its spiny branches shifted as if a phantom wind that caressed nothing else played with it. There *had* to be animals hiding there, too, however small. Probably more birds that seemed content to lounge around instead of risking inessential flight in such unpredictable surroundings. Not that I could blame them after my own disorienting experience.

Unless you needed to go somewhere, staying put did seem like the wisest choice, if restrictive.

Unfortunately, it was also one I didn't have the luxury to afford.

A new wave of chimes swept through the air, comprised of three distinct threads. As I expected, several chunks switched around, painting an entirely different yet still harmonic view— with the pomegranate the sole survivor of the change.

I sank my teeth into my bottom lip and nibbled on it, excitement and caution warring within me. Finally, finally, I had something tangible—*tested*—to hold on to.

A graceful, dusty pink bird soared off a near branch and cut a straight line towards the shrub. I held my breath, marveling at the beauty of it in flight—then basking in the relief that surged through me when it landed atop the pomegranate, unscathed. The shrub swayed gently, as if beckoning me to come over.

I itched to do precisely that, make the leap that would bring me closer to my goal, but the chiming curved on the nearly imperceptible wind again and swept away the grass until all I saw was a vivid field of poppies. I squinted, clutching the branch hard enough to chip the bark.

I could no longer see the pomegranate.

I swore under my breath even as I crawled back to the trunk, then up, past the birds' curious glances and rustling wings. I scaled a branch thinner, younger than the one before, and strained my neck to see past the leaves.

There.

Just behind the line of red petals, the pomegranate remained.

My heart hammered against my ribs even as a labored exhale hollowed out my chest.

Not gone. Merely hidden.

I mentally marked the path as best as I could when I would be unable to rely on any other set points to guide me, then climbed down, and broke into a breakneck sprint. The poppies fluttered in my wake, utterly beautiful, but my sight was set on those narrow green leaves, the sprinkling of bright red among them, clearer with every stumbling, rushed step.

I hurtled myself forward—and crashed into the shrub just as the chimes whisked away the latest surroundings once more.

HAZY OUTLINES TURNED TO ROOFTOPS. Turrets. The details remained obscured, but as I rushed from point to point, always seeking out the wildlife I now spotted with far more ease, the distance separating me from the city lessened.

What had struck me as insurmountable became...possible.

Sadly, the hope sparking inside me wasn't sufficient to gloss over *all* of my problems. The exertion sinking its talons into my bones being the main one.

To keep myself occupied, trick my mind that I wasn't as ravenous and tired as my body let on, I cataloged my surroundings every step of the way. Although there was much I still didn't understand, I did glean that not every shifting fragment had one of these static points, as I'd taken to call them.

Twice it had been sheer luck that had prevented the chiming from spiriting me away as I dashed across the terrain, hardly maintaining my footing and thanking the Sun I hadn't paired high-heeled shoes with the dress back in Somraque. My ankles felt more like gelatin than bones as it was.

Though when I scaled the latest of the static points, my legs shook from more than just the exhaustion. Forked tongues licked the air as I edged past the numerous snakes lounging atop the bare rock. I controlled my every move, careful not to step on any of the slender, coiled bodies. The snakes didn't seem to truly mind my intrusion, but I'd seen back home how fast they were to strike if they felt threatened.

Stomping on them would certainly achieve that.

The wise thing would be to abandon the notion entirely, but I *had* to get to the top. The view from the ground had been abysmal throughout the three chime-shifts. I'd studied the land with zero success at locating the next point. Though the city had steadily grown before my eyes, I was still nowhere near close enough to reach it without waiting out the shift in-between.

So I climbed.

I'd tied the dress in an awkward creation that mimicked pants, but even with my newly found freedom of movement, my ascent was painstakingly slow. With all the fissures and ledges concealing the snakes from my sight, I had to tap the rock every time I sought new purchase, then wait for the telltale slithering sound. Or silence.

So far, none had sunk their fangs into me. The warnings seemed to suffice, though my pulse continued to pound in my ears.

I doubted anything but me *leaving* the rock would quiet it.

When I finally made it to the top, however, my heart plummeted. I dropped down, legs bent beneath me and hands splayed across the hard, dusty surface. A snake wriggled into a crevice, as if escaping the wave of desperation that poured from me.

The next post—

The next post was more than *three* times farther than any of the previous ones.

It was a stunning meadow, with deer feasting on blades of grass, though their shapes were fuzzy, almost blending with the background, the antlers next to indistinguishable. I hoped it was purely because of my tired eyes that I didn't see them clearly, but I couldn't bring myself to believe such a blatant lie.

They truly were that far away.

Without even realizing it, I ran my fingers along the velvet of my makeshift pants and traced the relic's form.

A week. A week since I'd come to under the Somraquian sky, alone in that rocky desert with no way back. Only forward.

I released the relic and balled my hand into a fist.

Only forward.

I crawled closer to the edge of the rock. One of the snakes occupying the left-hand side slithered away languidly, unaware of the turmoil raging within me. I watched its glistening blue-green scales slink over the ledge in a graceful, fluid motion, then trained my gaze back on the meadow. On the city rising behind it, as colorful and as lovely as the sky.

The chimes weaving through the land were no more than a faint echo at the back of my mind as a crooning, vicious voice edged its way to the forefront.

You'll never make it.

The doubts that had already been lurking like hungry shadows on the periphery descended upon me. Desperate, I pushed to my feet and wiped the sweat off my forehead, then made a full circle atop the flat, jutting tip of the rock the serpents had cleared. I fumbled my fingers absentmindedly with the pendant.

The meadow was in the direct line of the city, but maybe... maybe there was a detour somewhere. It seemed too cruel that just when I was a step away from escaping the wilderness, the land would trap me. Toy with me like I was some plaything meant to suffer.

Then again, perhaps I shouldn't have been so surprised.

The wicked, rotten voice purred its agreement.

There were no guarantees in anything I did. My time with Mordecai had certainly proven that.

A Savior who couldn't save Nysa.

A sentimental fool who believed in bridging differences to obtain a higher goal only to slam headfirst into rebuttal and repulsion.

I grimaced and rubbed the butt of my palm across the left side of my chest. With no one around me—and with the certainty of failing leaving an acrid taste in my mouth—thoughts I'd kept locked up surfaced.

Only the darkness that rose was not the bitter one I expected, stained with destruction and death. It was brilliance. Light. The soul-baring depths that do not strip you raw but cradle and highlight the concealed parts of you with devastatingly beautiful affection.

I closed my eyes and, as if outstretching my arms, dove into the obsidian river.

Mordecai's smile suffused my mind. How it curved up his mouth—as sharp as diamonds, yet never cold. Never a dispassionate decoration.

His touch, heady and soft and searing.

As much of a thrill as was the magnetic call of his argent

shadowfire.

I brought my fingers to my lips, almost believing I could still taste him there. The pitch-black ink of his wonderful soul.

The miniature renders with their deep, endless wells swept through me in a rush I didn't want to stop, painting impression after impression and reminding me of what I'd lost.

What I was fighting for, too.

To connect the three lands, yes. But not just that.

When the world is right, I'll find you again.

It was a promise I intended to keep, whatever the cost.

The snakes didn't bother flicking their tongues at me as I descended, as if sensing the purpose driving me on. The steel encasing my spine. I lingered as close to the rock as possible once my feet hit the ground, grinding shale into dust, and waited for the chiming to abate. For a fleeting moment, I surrendered to the sight of the dawn sky—the streak of sapphire arcing across the canvas—then broke into a run.

Packed earth, grass, roots, rocks... I felt more than saw the terrain roll from one texture into another, my gaze trained on the meadow gradually coming into sight. The ache in my feet built up, calves and thighs burning until an odd lightness settled inside me—almost as if I were on the verge of levitating. With horror, I realized what it meant.

My legs were about to give out.

Though I had no idea how, I pushed myself harder, faster, blatantly, perhaps recklessly, ignoring the feeling that I was a heartbeat away from becoming one huge mess of tangled limbs, completely at Svitanye's mercy. The deer watched me from their meadow. Close enough that I could see their faces—the large, round black eyes, a smattering of white around their noses. The blades of grass they had ceased chewing on still dangling from their mouths.

A series of chimes raked through the air.

No.

Knees wobbling, I sprinted towards the animals, but as hard as I tried, the chiming grew louder. And louder. I felt it in my bones, the impending shift. The surge of magic.

I wouldn't be spared.

Just a short stretch of land separated me from the meadow, but as the chimes resonated through my very essence, I knew I would never touch the lush grass.

A cry of frustration and anguish ripped free from my throat. I tugged on the chain to liberate the pendant from my dress, then wrapped my fingers around the crescent moon and linked myself with the power embedded in its core. Let it permeate me, use me as a conduit, a beacon that sent it soaring across the land caught in a shift—

That *slowed.*

THE WORLD WAS TRAPPED SOMEWHERE in-between, as if two canvases intersected.

Each its own image, neither I could make out fully—a medley of brushstrokes and notes and flavors that threatened to send my senses reeling if I attempted to focus too much. Or simply lingered too long.

As I crossed the fuzzy, uneven but solid ground, it was impossible *not* to look.

The two realities blended into one another, yet contrasted, the sight something I was fairly certain no being was meant to experience. My eyes watered from the strain.

I averted my gaze, then shut my eyelids altogether, my course set. It wasn't as if I could entertain any deviations now, with the pendant's magic issuing soft warnings that it would not last indefinitely.

Five seconds in, I opened my eyes and looked.

My breath hitched into a sob.

A flimsy, translucent veil of intersected realities still hung before me, but beyond it, the meadow was clear—untouched, though frozen.

Three steps.

Two.

I leaped right as my temporal magic couldn't maintain its hold any longer.

The grass softened the impact as I dropped into a clumsy roll. I ended up on my back, the dawn sky spanning wide above me. Laughter bubbled in my chest and rang across the meadow —undulating and expanding as the deer shot a generous amount of odd looks my way.

I couldn't help it.

I laughed until tears streamed down my dusty, sweaty cheeks and the cool touch of the grass seeped through my dress and whisked away the burning heat.

I influenced a shift.

I lifted the pendant above my face, the silver stunning against the violet and pink hues of the sky. I had no idea if he knew of the perils dominating Svitanye, but Mordecai had given me the only means that might help me survive this world.

I pressed my lips to the tip of the crescent moon, then tucked it beneath my neckline and rolled over. The world around me spun as I braced myself on my hands and eased onto my knees. The laughter I let loose anew only pronounced how dreadfully parched my mouth was.

Yet when I looked at the city, now able to make out the colorful facades clearly, the ailments bowed before the rush of determination.

I could do this.

My body could do this.

A doe padded closer on slender legs and nuzzled my mussed hair. I brought a tentative hand to its pelt, savoring the warmth, the *life* radiating from it, then rose. The doe didn't run. Merely observed me with its stunning dark eyes as I steeled myself for the final round.

When the land sang and transformed again, I said my goodbye.

Listening to the chimes, using the pendant, and pushing my body to its limits, I evaded shift after shift, jumping between the final static isles until the buildings were within reach. The facades formed an uninterrupted straight line, save for a narrow alley pressed between two houses—one a baby blue, the other a light pink that complemented the white shutters framing its windows.

I hurtled myself into the gap.

My right shoulder hit the corner.

I bit down to stifle the pain even as the momentum carried me forward, deeper into the alley and across the cobblestones—

Crap, crap, crap, crap.

My efforts to slow, to gain at least *some* control were in vain as my wobbling, exhausted legs seemed to take on a life of their own. I careened forward, the baby blue wall perilously close—

A firm hand gripped my forearm hard enough to bruise.

CHAPTER FOUR

I TENSED AT THE UNEXPECTED CONTACT EVEN WHEN IT softened almost immediately—when it *had* saved me from flattening my face against a rustic, white-painted door. But the curve of fingers still pressing into my skin, the disadvantaged position—

"I'm all right," I squeezed out, barely seeing anything beyond the door straight ahead of me, the edges dimmed—from exhaustion or panic, I wasn't sure. *Both*, my thunderous chest suggested.

"I'm all right now, thank you," I repeated, louder this time.

The hand retreated.

A shudder rippled through my body, and I braced a palm against the rough, baby blue facade. I didn't even bother to suck in a fair measure of air before I straightened. The urge to assess the situation overpowered my need for oxygen.

"Hello," I said, my hoarse voice more than reflecting the sorry state Svitanye's countryside had left me in.

But the tall man looking down at me with gold-speckled, vivid blue eyes didn't remark on it beyond a quick flicker of his gaze—probably making sure I was whole.

One arm still casually held out as if to catch me in case I stumbled, he smiled at me, his sun-kissed skin offset with a bright pink beard.

"Hello." The corners of his eyes crinkled. "Temperamental shifts today, eh?"

It was a struggle to force myself to relax. Whether he noticed my discomfort or not, the stranger's smile didn't falter, though his hands went down to smooth the bright fabric of his gossamer skirt—such a small, common gesture that hinted he might have picked up on my mood after all.

"Thank you," I said, "for catching me."

He inclined his head, gold-blue eyes turning a shade warmer, then motioned towards the street visible beyond the narrow alley just a few houses down. Drawn forward by the numerous voices and the sweet, entrancing aroma of ripe cherries that made my mouth water, I fell in step with him. Not that I had much of a choice, really.

Anything was better than going back into that ever-changing madness.

When we reached the last of the buildings, an elegant mint-green thing with white wrought-iron window boxes overflowing with greenery and the occasional blooming lily, the man chuckled and cast me a sideways glance. "You know, you're the second person I saved from splattering against a wall today..."

I let out a slightly breathless laugh that surprised even me. Although with how bizarre this entire situation was, it *did* seem easier to simply go along with it rather than to put up a struggle.

"The Council of Words should have sent out a warning that

the land is acting up." He frowned. "Good thing I went to check if things truly were getting worse like the townsfolk were saying..."

Or I would have rammed headfirst into the wall.

My lips pulled into a grateful—if a touch embarrassed—smile. Losing control over my own body was not a situation I was ever enthusiastic about.

"You look like you had a rough time out there." His gaze swept down my attire, lingering on the makeshift trousers I'd twisted the skirt into. "Though *that* looks practical."

Cursing, I quickly untied the fabric to release the skirt, then grumbled, "That's putting it mildly."

When he arched an amused eyebrow, I added, "The rough time, not the..." I gestured to the once more sweeping skirt, fervently ignoring the dirt stains I'd accumulated on the blue-black fabric. Mercifully, nothing seemed torn at first glance.

The man leaned against the corner of the building, his back to the street alive with so many people and colors it was easier, safer not to look at it at all. "Forgive me if I'm wrong or prying"—another easy, laid-back chuckle—"but I'm guessing you aren't local. Came here for the book fair?"

"Yes," I lied, although a part of me almost felt bad for doing so. "I got separated from my company—"

The second person.

I was the *second* person who'd stumbled ungracefully into the city. A long shot, perhaps, but maybe he'd run into Ada, too. Or one of the others before that. My heart sped up. I opened my mouth to ask him what his previous rescue looked like when a tug came alive in my chest.

Similar to what had guided me through the wilderness, yet of a different flavor.

33

A delicate crease adorned the stranger's forehead. "Where did you get separated?"

Before I could come up with a vague but valid answer, someone called out from the street.

"I'll be right there, Alryn!" the pink-bearded man shouted over his shoulder, then turned to me again, his face open and the corners of his mouth still tilted up.

I knew that if I asked, he'd offer his help without hesitation regardless of the company waiting for him. But the need to explore that silent pull overpowered my every other impulse. And being on my own...

Well, it would save me from whipping out more plausible half-truths.

"Go ahead," I said softly. "I'd hate to keep you from your friends. Now that I'm done getting thrown around"—I curved my lips into a wry, lopsided smile—"I'll find my own way back. Don't worry."

For a moment, the man hesitated. His fingers tangled with his beard, twirling it as he studied me, more than obviously torn.

I flashed him a reassuring smile. "Truly. I'll be fine."

A sliver of doubt still lingered in his eyes, but he dipped his chin nonetheless. "The fastest way to the fair is down this street." He motioned to the one running past us. "Then, once you hit the main square, go east. The fair is static, so you shouldn't have too much trouble, but in case you take a wrong turn... Just make sure you keep to the city."

"I will. And thank you again, for before."

"It was nothing." He waved a dismissive hand, though warmth suffused the blue-and-gold of his eyes. "Good luck finding your companions."

With a final concerned look that gave me time to change my

mind should I wish it, he strolled onto the boisterous street to where a small group of men and women stood before a vendor's stand, all sporting tops that ended just above the navel and pants that hugged their waists before they fanned out down the legs. I took a few heartbeats to drink in the local fashion as more and more people swished by, acutely aware of just how out of place I looked in my night-wrought gown.

Once again an outsider.

Feigning casualness I didn't feel, I stepped out of the secluded alley and made my way down the street in the direction the man had indicated. Groups of various sizes flitted up and down the smooth cobblestones with a few solitary figures like myself thrown into the mix. I kept to the naturally formed stream of pedestrians where I'd stick out far less than I would have had I chosen to hug the buildings. A medley of scents enveloped me as I progressed—perfume and food and those cherries that only grew headier. I pressed a hand to my growling stomach but didn't pause. Didn't yield even the tiniest fraction to the many aches plaguing my body.

Regardless of how things had turned out so far, I kept expecting for this initial normalcy to erupt in an onslaught of suspicious gazes that would oust me for the intruder I was. But none of the passersby seemed to pay me much attention beyond a few approving looks that held no edge of malice or wariness.

Definitely *not* the reaction I had anticipated.

The silent compliments weren't intrusive; they weren't leering, the kinds men and boys at home brazenly gave, nor did they harbor any concealed judgment. And the longer I walked among the locals, the more I realized why.

Unlike in Soltzen, or even Somraque for that matter, there appeared to be no rules, no guidelines dictating what one could or couldn't wear. There was no distinct style, no gender boundaries to adhere to, even the colors, while predominantly vivid, ranged across every possible hue the mind could conjure up.

Liberating, that's what it was.

I straightened my spine, tipped my chin up, then strode on as if I belonged among the crowd. No longer pretending, but entering it.

They accepted me.

Pink, orange, yellow, and lavender buildings lined the cobblestones, some bearing intricate wrought-iron window railings with matching semicircular balconies, while others boasted shutters—not the rundown ones I'd seen in Soltzenian towns outside estate walls, but a merger of decor and practicality. Boutiques and taverns with small round tables set out front dominated the ground floors I walked by, the upper levels dedicated to private residences. For the most part, at least. A few, I noticed, had shops spanning throughout the floors, some offering different wares sectioned within the buildings, some stocking up the entire space with their specialized items.

My gaze caught on one displaying a vast array of wrought-iron objects—lanterns, basket-like holders fashioned so they could be mounted on walls, even delicate bedside tables, far more stunning than the cumbersome wood in my room at home. A few of the items boasted intricate glass inserts, the colors echoing the vibrant warmth of the city.

Entranced by the beauty, the hunger and exhaustion hollowing me from the inside out lessened, dimmed to something manageable, if still present. But giving in to the atmosphere wasn't without its perils. With a kernel of misplaced regret, I forced myself to keep walking. To search the faces for one I recognized.

Despite this zeal that had ignited in my veins, I wouldn't be able to go on indefinitely.

The tug within me remained a constant guide—telling me I needed to reach the end of the street. Beyond the city, the draw had made sense. I wondered what could possibly carry the same importance here, where there were no shifts to interfere with people's paths. Maybe it was the fair the man had mentioned. According to his guidelines, the direction fit...

Just as I neared the square that opened up ahead, my feet stumbled.

Though I didn't know how, I caught my balance, one hand coming to rest just beneath my throat, the other skimming the fragment. The stream of people parted around me as I stood there, rooted to the spot and unable to do anything but breathe.

If they were frustrated by the obstacle I'd become, I didn't know. Couldn't know. Not when my entire attention was on the three-story building to my left, on the wicker baskets and round wrought-iron tables set out front, the white shelves dominating the gentle pink interior I had no difficulty seeing through the large, clear windows.

Books.

Stacks upon stacks, and rows upon rows, the tomes stood proudly on display that wasn't some empty, curated yet meaningless decoration, but a treasury open and accessible to all. Leather, cloth, with letters of varying colors stretching along the spines, they were utterly beautiful in their diversity. People pulled them off the shelves, thumbed through them...

All that knowledge available in exchange for a few coins

those with purchases in their hands handed over to the blue-haired girl manning the counter.

I craned my neck up, noting the upper two floors were the same.

My eyes teared.

It was a useless, out-of-place reaction, but as my gaze brushed over the simple sign hanging over the door that read Seline's Bookstore, it...it touched something deep inside me.

This was more than I'd ever dreamed of.

I didn't know whether it was so many books held in one public space or the people who took them in their arms with affection and excitement, perhaps even reverence, but it was without a doubt one of the most breathtaking sights I'd ever come across. Even children were running around a sector filled with shorter, sturdier stands, pulling out the thin volumes and taking them to their parents with pleading eyes.

They didn't leave the shop empty-handed.

It felt like an eternity had passed before I was able to move on.

Just to end up stunned once again.

The square, while filled with taverns, harbored even more stores. Some with those wrought-iron wares I was starting to believe were a Svitanye specialty, others with garments, jewelry —but most of all, my gaze always lingered on the ones displaying varieties of books. New. Used. Covering a vast array of subjects. There was even a shop full of quills and tomes with blank pages waiting to be filled by their prospective owners. Magnus would have loved this.

He might not have shared his mind openly, but I'd seen its brilliant depths. Knew he would cherish a personal, private means of shaping those thoughts and dreams into something more tangible, even if merely paper and ink.

Silently, I vowed to find him when everything was over and... not exactly make amends, as we hadn't parted on bad terms despite how unfavorable the situation had been, but extend the friendship he deserved. The one he always had in me, from me, but had no hopes of truly developing.

As the decision settled within me, I cast one last look at the shop, the bottled inks, then moved on.

Sweet vanilla twined with blackberries drifted through the crowd. A patisserie of some sorts I couldn't see but smelled distinctly as more hunger-inducing aromas joined the mix. I stuck close to the sides of the square, skirting the large, four-tiered white marble fountain just as the tug inside me dictated. Yet I never took my eyes off everything the city offered. The sensation within me intensified as I reached a welcoming tavern with round tables set on the slightly raised patio, nearly all of them occupied by people enjoying a glass of wine with their dinner.

I'd passed no clock to note the time, but I was fairly certain at least a couple of hours had passed since we'd entered Svitanye, which suggested the evening wasn't all that young any longer. Yet the patrons sporting smiles on their faces and basking in the visibly relaxed atmosphere revealed none of those typical shutting-down signs that often accompanied this kind of unwinding in the evening.

Yes, they seemed to have shed the cloaks of responsibility and slipped free from whatever drive pushed them on through the day, but they were definitely in no hurry to call it a night.

Perhaps it was only the book fair, bringing people out as the solstice celebrations had in Nysa. Perhaps. Deep down, I doubted this was a special occurrence.

The inner draw seemed to want me to go into the tavern, so I loped around a group of children playing with lavender-scented rag dolls on the edge of the patio and edged my way past the patrons and lush green plants sprinkled throughout towards the entrance flanked by two miniature potted figs. My stomach tightened as the smell of roasted meat and vegetables curled around me, the pleasant, full-bodied aroma of wine urging me to take a seat.

Sun, I was starving.

And thirsty.

And in desperate need to stop before the strings still holding me up snapped.

Coming back from that wouldn't be easy. Nor fast.

I glanced around the warm interior outfitted with rustic white wood and pastel blue accents that only further opened up the airy space. Gentle light seemed to disperse from the entire ceiling and blend with the natural one filtering through the large windows, but for the life of me I couldn't make out its source. Maybe I was even more exhausted than I dared to admit. I traced a finger along the back of the nearest chair, as if contemplating whether I wanted to sit here, and studied the interior in more detail.

There were fewer people here than outside, but soft chatter still ruled the aromatic air. A lean man in a basil green jacket and tousled blond hair sat alone at a table by one of the windows overlooking the square, a glass of something I couldn't make out set in front of him. For a moment, he reminded me of Eriyan— he would have certainly enjoyed this atmosphere. But for all his laid-back, perky nature, I knew he wouldn't be sitting so calmly, so content here. Not with the weight of all that had happened hovering overhead.

The thought was enough to set my mind straight.

I had to find him. Had to find everyone.

Yet the tug insisted I stayed *here*.

Lips pursed, I shifted to the side as a serving girl with colorful floral tattoos covering nearly every inch of her skin breezed towards the front door, a full tray of drinks balanced on one hand. My gaze followed, admiring her dexterity, then skimmed the brimming patio.

There *was* logic in choosing a tavern as a base. Especially if this town received a lot of travelers. What better way to regroup and replenish your strength before venturing on than a place like this?

A setup that ensured all parties were satisfied.

Unfortunately, I had no group *and* no money to spare.

I would have laughed at the pattern I seemed to become cursed with if a pang of hunger hadn't nearly doubled me in half —or at least if the mere act of standing wasn't becoming agony.

I made my way towards one of the free tables at the farthest, most secluded end of the room. Maybe I could convince the barkeep that I was waiting for my friends to arrive, buy myself some time to rest.

The blond man looked up as I strode past him, blue eyes falling on my face—

I blinked.

I knew now, why he'd reminded me of Eriyan.

My butt bumped into the chair behind me as I staggered.

He *was* him.

CHAPTER FIVE

"Ember, have you had the pleasure of trying *lumi* yet?" He lifted the glass in that utterly Eriyan way that dispelled any and all doubts about his authenticity.

Not an illusion.

Not a *de*lusion, either.

But *Eriyan.*

I stared at him.

His ruby-red drink swished.

Then I stared some more.

Only when I became aware I was on the verge of drawing more attention from the other patrons than was advisable did I take the empty seat opposite him. I set my palms flat against the white wood and snapped at him over the potted succulent at the very center of the table, "What are you doing?"

He took his sweet time sampling the drink he brought to his lips, a damn epitome of someone out to have a good time. My temper spiked.

Maybe it was the fatigue, maybe it was simply *knowing* the depths lurking under the surface I wasn't yet ready to touch, but his aloof attitude lacked its usual charming effect.

I clenched my jaw and, with both eyebrows arched, shot him a not-so-gentle prompt.

"Well," he drawled and swung his arm to the side, the ruby-red liquid almost sluicing over the rim, "I *did* plan to experience the local culinary,"—he tapped one finger against the glass—"but it seems like I'm about to get lectured by the One."

My head jerked back of its own volition as disbelief consumed me whole. Despite the obvious jab, there was nothing but...*amusement* on Eriyan's face. He threw one arm over the backrest of his chair, realigning his body into a nonchalant, casual position. He fit perfectly with the languid pool of people gathered on the patio beyond the window. As if he'd simply come to the tavern for a drink—or several, if the color staining his pronounced cheeks was any indication.

I slid my hands off the table and dropped them in my lap. "Eriyan..."

An easy grin spread across his face, mischief sparking in his eyes, now more green than blue. I opened my mouth, only what came out wasn't the string of curses I'd been prepared for.

It was a laugh.

The sound bubbled up and hit the air, a force similar to the one in the meadow. Only now there were no deer to side-eye me. Just Eriyan and that wicked, wicked grin, as if he'd known precisely the outlet I needed to free myself from the pressure building within.

"By the Sun, Eriyan, I was worried." I shook my head, then snatched the short-stemmed glass from him and took a long swallow. The drink reminded me of wine, only this was lighter, sweeter, and fruitier, with just a bit of a bite underneath. I groaned as the flavor exploded in my parched mouth, then went on. "Worried. Starving. Thirsty—"

"Well then, why didn't you say so?" Eriyan raised his hand, torso tilting dangerously to the side as he peered around me. He caught himself on the chair beside his with a *thud*. "A second portion of everything I ordered, please."

Elbow braced against the table, I glanced at the older man behind the counter whose age-white hair was bedecked with blooming flowers. He nodded, then promptly called over a woman with blonde-and-pink hair from the other side of the tavern.

I arched an eyebrow at Eriyan and dropped my voice. "How do you plan to pay for all this?"

It was a question that should have been a lot lower on my priority list, but apparently my mind refused to stick to the plan. More than likely because I *was* ravenous, and the last thing I wanted right now was to get into trouble for stealing a meal. My legs wouldn't be able to carry me far—even if I used the pendant to gain an edge.

Eriyan, from the looks of it, didn't seem too keen on moving anytime soon, either.

"Ember,"—he splayed his hand over his heart—"I'm wounded by your lack of faith in me." The mock hurt gave way to a wide, blinding smile—not unlike the one he wore when we'd first met at the sowhl stand. He flipped open his basil green jacket and revealed a heavy pouch attached to a thin but seemingly sturdy leather strap running across his tunic-clad chest. "I never leave the house without my drinking coins."

Of course he wouldn't. I shook my head, then drank more of

the sweet drink—lumi, he called it?—grateful not only for Eriyan's habits, but the fact that Svitanye didn't have a unique currency his coins wouldn't have been able to pass for.

I wondered whether he'd gleaned that fact through observation or if he'd outright attempted to purchase something —the latter, I was betting—but I really couldn't bring myself to care as long as the end result worked in our favor.

"Good, isn't it?" He looked pointedly at the rapidly diminishing drink.

I licked a droplet from my lips. "It really is. But I didn't peg you for the type to enjoy something so...fruity." I swirled the glass and locked eyes with him, permitting myself this tiny slice of normalcy I'd needed more than I'd thought.

Eriyan pursed his lips and kicked back in his chair. "*Llllluuummmiiii*," he drawled. Yes, definitely tipsy. "Lumi, lumi, lumi." He sighed and straightened, his eyes just slightly unfocused. "It's no sowhl, that's for sure, but I like a little diversity in life. Maybe"—he flicked a wrist—"once you do your Savior business, I'll travel the lands and create a culinary map. *Eriyan's Edibles and Alcohols.*"

He could, too. Eriyan would probably charm the whole of the united world if he was set loose upon it.

But as heartwarming as the image—the idea—was, it also pierced the blissful bubble I'd wrapped myself in.

My offtrack excursion needed to come to an end.

Right as I opened my mouth to ask him the one thing I should have straight from the very start, movement in the distance behind me caught his attention. I pressed my lips together, suddenly *seeing* him.

Past my initial shock and anger and relief.

Past this easiness he'd submerged me in.

This rendition was a wholly different one.

I'd caught glimpses of the true Eriyan back in Somraque—gleaned that while his nature *was* amicable and open, he also liked to hide behind his aloofness. Maybe this, returning to what he knew, was his way of coping with not only the uncertainty of where everyone was, but the absence of magic. Still, his state, this nonchalance... It truly didn't seem forced.

Like he knew something I didn't.

Then again, he was also *far* more comfortable than I had expected him to be around *me*, which I didn't doubt was thanks to the lumi—and whatever he'd had before that.

Drunk or concealing, there was only one way to find out.

"Have you seen the others?" I asked when he stopped observing the people in the tavern—in particular the server with pink-tipped blonde hair who was stacking plates onto one arm, hips swaying softly to the twelve-bar music drifting in from the square. "Do you know where they are?"

"Nope. Came straight here." He tapped the table with a lazy finger.

I had to stomp down hard on the anger threatening to rekindle. "Wait... You didn't think to even *look* for them?"

Eriyan shrugged, then grinned when the gorgeous woman brought over our meal. Mouthwatering meat that looked tender to the eye, with a generous portion of mashed potatoes on the side and a smattering of green beans to top it all. She placed down two more glasses of lumi from her tray and winked at Eriyan.

"Yours is on the house."

Eriyan's grin grew wider. "You're too kind."

A hint of a blush colored her plump cheekbones, but she tipped her head in acknowledgment and retreated back to the counter without another word.

I snorted at Eriyan's almost dreamy expression as he watched her leave, then cleared my throat. "Well?"

"Well what?"

"Weren't you worried where the others are?" *Aren't you still?*

He speared some of the green beans. "Of course I was." He tossed them in his mouth and chewed. "But I figured they would all follow that pesky yanking. *You* clearly did. Besides,"—his fork *clanked* against the ceramic—"even without it, the safest bet where Dantos might turn up is a tavern." He swallowed the last of the beans he'd been chewing and dropped his gaze to the still untouched plate before me. "Didn't you say you were hungry?"

Like a sleepwalker, I scooped some creamy mashed potatoes onto my fork, but didn't eat a bite. I couldn't deny there was sense in his logic. Eriyan and his cousin were two peas in a pod. I stuffed the potatoes in my mouth, then sliced the meat and threw that in, too. A groan reverberated in my chest. Shit, that was good. No, not just good. It was dreamy and divine and—

"Go on, tell me I made the wrong choice," Eriyan teased.

Clutching the knife tighter, I shot him a glare, but couldn't keep up the charade for long with the delicious food beckoning me to finish what I started. So I dug into my meal, and only after I wolfed down almost two-thirds of it, asked, "How did you get into the city?"

"Walked."

My fork clattered onto the plate. "Eriyan."

His answering sly grin had the desired effect.

I chuckled, then asked again, *"How?"*

"Well, one moment I was searching for Ivarr who was nowhere in sight when I came through the portal, and the next I was a few steps away from town. It seemed like a far better environment to get lost in than the wilderness, so I walked down the first alley I found."

"Wait. You just...*strode* into town?" I picked up the fork, tines hovering just above the tender beef.

"You didn't?"

A dry laugh slipped from my lips. "I had to make a few... detours along the way."

"What do you mean?" He sipped his lumi, appearing genuinely puzzled.

I heaved out a breath then, in-between bites, told him what happened. Although he maintained his easy demeanor throughout my recollection, he did blanch a little, probably realizing just how lucky he'd been. And what our different experiences might mean for the rest of the group.

If there was any way I could venture back out there and find them, I would. But it was an impossible task. The city was vast, the countryside vaster. Even without the shifts, combing through every inch would be a tedious, more than likely futile, process. Once I accepted that, Eriyan's decision to find a base and stay put made even more sense.

If they were in trouble, the two of us running around wouldn't help them. And if they weren't...

The tug would lead them here sooner or later.

Just as we finished our meals and I returned from the lavatory, face fresh and clean of smeared cosmetics, the two slender braids joined at the nape of my neck redone, the reasoning had proven true.

Dantos and Zaphine walked into the tavern, elbows linked

and both looking a little disheveled—hinting their path hadn't been quite as easy as Eriyan's. But I spied no injuries, nothing to indicate their time outside had been *too* rough. If anything, there was an air of calmness to them. I sagged in relief.

Eriyan, too, seemed struck by the sight, but recovered faster than I did. He raised his arm and bellowed out a greeting. The instant Zaphine and Dantos laid eyes on us, any and all traces of fatigue vanished from their faces. They hurried across the space to our isolated perch by the window, bringing with them the scent of almonds and crisp apples.

Wherever their path had taken them, it certainly hadn't followed the same route as mine.

"Hope you ordered us a round," Dantos said as he took the empty chair on Eriyan's side and slapped him on his back, while Zaphine eased herself down beside him. Our gazes met briefly—such a fleeting connection it could hardly be called a proper acknowledgment.

We might have come to a truce before venturing through the portal, but our seating arrangement made it clear I was the odd one out. No one wanted to be voluntarily stuck next to the girl with shadowfire coiling beneath her skin.

The thought stung a little, but I also understood where their already staggering reservations were coming from, so I let it be.

I suspected the differences between us were even worse here, where their magic was muted, though none of them seemed to have as much issue with the loss as Ada had. Maybe the magnitude of it was a Mage thing, directly proportionate to the power they'd wielded in Somraque...

Zaphine swept her gaze across the tavern as Dantos and Eriyan dove into a round of banter, then said to no one in particular, "Ada and Ivarr aren't here yet?"

GAJA J. KOS & BORIS KOS

"No," I said when it became clear Eriyan was too preoccupied to answer.

Zaphine didn't quite meet my eyes, but she didn't ignore me, either, so I went on, "Ada and I got separated shortly after we entered Svitanye. Eriyan said Ivarr was already nowhere in sight when he stepped through the portal."

At the sound of his name, Eriyan poked his head around Dantos's powerful form and peered at Zaphine.

"Zaphine, my dear, have you tried lumi yet?"

MORE FOOD ENDED up in front of us mere minutes after the lumi. Much to Eriyan's disappointment, it was the barkeep with flowers in his hair who'd delivered this round. Eriyan glanced towards the gorgeous server tending to other patrons with a wistful expression on his face, then sighed and dove into his own line of questioning—similar to what mine had been, though far lighter.

I let him take the lead, content to just sit back and listen while my body recovered. The lumi and food did wonders, but I was by no means in top shape.

Now that the most pressing issue was—at least partially— resolved, whispers of the past beyond the portal we'd stepped through crept up from the crevices. I couldn't leave myself unguarded. Couldn't risk letting them out when all of us seemed to be so, so careful not to touch the gaping maw of pain we shared, but looked at from different angles.

"We got thrown around a few times, yes," Dantos said and rested his arm on the back of Zaphine's chair, apparently in no hurry to eat. "But with her beside me,"—he tipped his head

50

towards Zaphine who blushed—"cursing and dragging me forward, the land didn't stand a chance. Sharp as one of her pins, this one." He huffed a laugh and winked, then grew a shade more serious. "The town doesn't seem to change though."

"You felt the pull, too, right?" Zaphine's gaze crossed mine before she focused on her food and scooped up a forkful of green beans.

"We did." Eriyan nodded. "Both of them. We're all thinking they're some sort of beacons, right?"

His question voiced my own theory and lured me back into the conversation. "It makes sense they would set up something out there to prevent people from getting lost."

Or wandering aimlessly, hopelessly until their bodies gave out.

I swallowed the tart memory of the chimes counting down the heartbeats to a complete reset. Encased in ever-tighter panic, my head nearly under the surface, I hadn't even considered using a portal to get me where I wanted to go. I chased away the taste with a swallow of lumi and a chocolate-dipped cherry.

Maybe that had been a good thing.

Temporal magic had been safer than opening a doorway between two segments when the segments themselves weren't stable. Though if it hadn't been for the tug—

"I'm just glad it brought us here." Dantos's rich, full-bodied voice washed over my pondering and what-ifs. Apparently I'd missed a part of the conversation since he was clearly referring to the second tug. "Whoever set it up is my kind of person."

He clinked glasses with Eriyan, earning an eye roll from Zaphine.

"But it's still a bit weird, though, isn't it?" Her brows knitted together, and this time, when our gazes connected, she didn't avert hers. "If the town is stable, fixed—why have this pull?"

"Maybe it's habit," I suggested, not really believing the words.

"Does make things easier to navigate," Dantos added, looking up from the food he'd finally devoted himself to. "We got turned around a lot before we decided to just go precisely where the pull told us."

"Huh." I plucked another cherry off the plate. When he put it so simply... "You could be right."

From what little I'd glimpsed on my short trek to the tavern, the streets *were* laid haphazardly. Far from the neat organization that had made Nysa so easy to navigate. I thought back to the children I'd seen.

The tug could also serve to keep them from wandering too close to the city's outskirts. With no walls, no barriers, I couldn't imagine how their parents could leave them unsupervised out in the streets. If they crossed into the countryside—

A tall figure dressed from head to toe in black strode through the doors, cutting my musings short. The few blades he'd left unsheathed on his belt glinted as he moved with liquid grace past the patrons and empty tables. I lost track of the conversation still swirling around me entirely, too absorbed in watching the flitting, puzzled reactions and inquiring glances that followed him across the space.

So there *was* something Svitanyians weren't used to.

Then again, the newcomer *did* look like a night-wrought blade himself in the perky, bright atmosphere. Attention trailed behind him like ripples in water.

Boisterous laughter I wasn't entirely sure belonged to Eriyan or Dantos redirected his focus. He spun on his heel, wavy black hair setting like an inky ocean around his handsome face.

A face I recognized from my final moments in Somraque— and gained a confirmed identity as Zaphine called out his name.

Ivarr.

CHAPTER SIX

THE MAGICIAN DIDN'T SAY ANYTHING, NOT EVEN A BRUSQUE hello. He simply sank into the chair beside me like a wisp of tenebrosity and eyed the food. I pushed one of the still untouched plates towards him.

The clanking of his cutlery seemed stark, and it took me a moment to realize our table had grown silent. No chatter. No movement at all, really. Only three pairs of eyes studying the new arrival. Four, if I counted mine.

But there was a vast difference in the texture of our gazes.

Snippets of an exchange I'd almost forgotten slithered through my mind.

The most notorious Magician. One drop of blood away from kicking the Crescent Prince off his evil throne.

Ivarr hated Mordecai. I remembered that now. But *he* was hated, too.

Despite Ada roping him in—and the others clearly honoring

her choice since they'd been together at the Whispers, then again outside Nysa—it was our side of the table versus theirs.

Ivarr and I were merely the opposite ends of the same darkness.

"Were the shifts hard on you?" I inquired sincerely, ignoring the tension coalescing in the air.

Ivarr stilled, his knife mid-slice, then looked at me. Deep lines I'd missed earlier curved around his green-brown eyes and wide mouth, a silent strain I suspected had a lot to do with his repressed magic. Like Ada, Ivarr was powerful. And the absence was taking a toll.

"I thought I had it figured out, but..." He cut through the beef then speared the piece and grabbed a slice of white bread from the basket to his left. "I was almost to the city when I got thrown back farther than where I started from."

His voice was clipped, holding back more information than he was sharing. Given the circumstances, it wasn't surprising. I didn't think any of us wanted to relive those desperate moments. Not when they were still so fresh.

"I'm glad you made it. You're Ivarr, yes?" When he dipped his chin, I offered him my hand. "Ember."

Zaphine, Dantos, and Eriyan scrambled to occupy themselves with anything but our exchange, though in the tavern, there was little to do but toss back their drinks. So they did.

Ivarr set down his cutlery and plucked a napkin from the wrought-iron holder, making quick work of cleaning his fingers. His hand was smooth in mine, although I detected a touch of calluses that hinted his assortment of knives wasn't reserved for his blood only. Lethal in more ways than just magic.

"Thank you for coming along," I said, then left him to his meal.

Only Ivarr surprised me by saying, "I'm fucking done with the oppression." His gaze bored into mine. "I want to set the world right."

I tipped my head. "Then our goals are aligned."

AFTER TWO HOURS and still no Ada, it became increasingly harder to sit idly in the tavern. We kept ordering snacks, and desserts, and drinks—for the most part of the non-alcoholic variety—that Eriyan and Dantos insisted they could pay for. And we'd all freshened up in the tiled lavatory, shedding the stains and marks of our travel.

Many patrons had drifted in while others left, though a generous number remained unchanged. It calmed my mind to know our prolonged presence wasn't suspicious in itself. Only that did little in light of the larger problem adhering to my every thought like pollen.

Shifts or not, Ada should have come here by now. She was too resourceful, too clever and inventive to get caught in the volatile nature of the landscape, which could only mean something else was going on.

A concern I voiced, curtailing the exchange between Eriyan and Dantos about introducing sowhl to the Svitanyians when the time came—a superfluous conversation at first glance, perhaps, but also a safe one. The deep, dark ravine we all knew existed was better left untouched.

For now.

"What do you propose?" Zaphine asked as she polished off

the last of her lumi, her gaze sharp despite the drink's soothing influence.

"We need a place to stay, right? The tavern is our meeting point, but we can't linger here indefinitely." I dealt Eriyan a silencing look when he raised his hand, his entire body buzzing in announcement of whatever protest wanted to leave his lips. Dantos grabbed him lightly by the wrist and lowered his arm. "We can search the town while we look for appropriate lodgings, talk to the locals. I know the plan is weak at best, but maybe someone has seen or heard something that will point us in Ada's direction if we're unable to find her outright."

When my words were met with puzzled countenances, I told them about the pink-bearded man who helped me after I all but literally crashed into town; how the people here seemed open and willing to help complete strangers. There was a chance, however small, that someone had crossed paths with Ada. Noticed her in the crowd. And with that book fair I had to stifle the burning impulse to steal a glimpse of taking place and attracting visitors, we wouldn't stand out as the only out-of-towners.

Or the only ones who had misplaced a friend, I hoped.

"Book fair," Ivarr muttered, then looked up, briefly meeting my gaze before he addressed the others. "I heard them talking about it, too. Some sort of bi-monthly market where people from all over Svitanye come to sell or exchange their goods."

"We can use it to our advantage," Dantos pitched in as he readjusted the rolled-up sleeves of his shirt. "Zaphine and I can track down a suitable place to stay so you three can focus solely on locating Ada."

Zaphine's eyes widened slightly, but she didn't argue the division of labor. Or the company she was to keep.

Despite myself, I had to bite down a smile.

"It might take us a while to track down something with vacancies," she said at last, regaining her composure. "If the situation is anything like the solstice celebrations in Nysa..."

Her words trailed into heavy silence that consumed our table. I wasn't entirely sure I was even breathing as every one of us made certain to look anywhere but at each other.

Too close.

This came too close to the maw of darkness.

Mercifully, Dantos broke the rising tension. "I'm sure we'll manage." He poured himself some water from the decanter. "This town looks big, and we passed quite a few inns already."

The lightness in his voice was forced, but in that moment, it was enough of an anchor for us to latch on. Dragging up the depths of our differences, our fears, would do none of us any good at the moment. Least of all Ada.

If too much of it surfaced, I feared the resounding landslide would be one none of us could stop.

"Excuse me," I said to the server who'd just whisked by to tend to the group of women sitting two tables over, "how long until you close?"

She let out a snorting laugh, but the sound carried a good-natured quality. "We never close, dear. With people coming here at all hours, it would be a shame to turn down their coin." She winked. "Can't leave the people hungry."

Another group called to her, and she breezed away—though not before tossing a smile Eriyan's way.

"I love this place," he drawled, chin propped on his palm, and earned himself a smack on the shoulder from Zaphine who'd reached around Dantos's back with the dexterity of a viper. He jerked up. "What?"

"We meet back here in two hours sharp," she said to everyone, then cut a pointed look at Eriyan. "But not *before*. Understood?"

"Are you *sure* one of us shouldn't stay here in case Ada shows up?" he asked, though the humor in his tone fell short.

"You know that if she hadn't until now, she won't, right?" Zaphine's voice broke a little towards the end, but she quickly patched up the chink in her armor—channeling the precise energy Ada used to whenever she took charge. A mesmerizing, admirable change that stirred something in my chest. "Stop thinking about yourself or your dick, Eriyan. We head out. All of us."

He waved his hand. "Fine, fine. But I *am* going over there to ask the beauty where a dashing young man might find a lost thorn-in-his-side Mage."

THE SQUARE WAS STILL alive when we emerged from the tavern, music drifting from beyond the fountain where three women played a guitar, a bass, and a harmonica respectively. The patios of the surrounding taverns, much smaller than ours, brimmed with Svitanyians—some sitting, some dancing. Yet despite the sheer number of people milling about, I didn't feel tension clawing up my throat as we navigated the cobblestones.

There was nothing oppressive about the swirl of colors and voices and movement. If anything, it filled me with a similar sensation as I'd experienced when I first strode into Nysa and allowed the excitement to wash over me.

Unlike then, however, it was merriment I felt, a connection

with the lives surrounding me instead of wonder that existed behind impenetrable walls.

Once we parted, taking different streets to cover as much ground as we could, the press of people lessened, but the pulse of the town didn't suffer for it. I walked past numerous establishments ranging from bakeries, specialty food stores, and small galleries with a stunning variety of styles I'd never encountered before to those that sold fabrics, fragrances, toys, and, my favorite of all, books. The sights I continued stealing glimpses of aided in making me forget about the aches plaguing my still-tired limbs.

As often as I could, I stopped and asked the people who looked particularly open for a discussion with a stranger if they'd seen a girl with dark hair gradually flowing into a fiery red walking about. Given how much attention they all seemed to devote to their colorful hairstyles, I suspected it was a trait they would least likely miss.

Unfortunately, none of the answers helped—unless I counted that one time a man offered some quick advice on how to blend various colors together without creating visible lines between hues. Not information I needed, exactly, but an interesting insight the knowledge-thirsty part of me cherished nonetheless.

I veered down another street that smelled of vanilla, raspberries, and chocolate—a mix reminiscent of one of the mousse desserts we'd tried out at the tavern—then cursed softly when I reached a dead-end. For a second, I allowed myself to lean against the stucco and rub my temples. The clock faces adorning a flower shop's display on the other side of the street reminded me that I was running out of time—and wasn't any closer to tracking Ada down.

If the others were as unsuccessful... I wasn't sure what the next step would be.

Except getting some sleep and hoping a fresh idea would come to us in the morning.

Retracing my steps, I decided to check one last quarter before I headed back to the tavern. But when I reached the intersection, a hollow laugh spilled from my lips.

We'd been wrong.

We'd been utterly, completely *wrong*.

The city *did* change.

Only it wasn't random parts of it, but entire streets that shifted around, leaving nothing but the structure and position of the intersections intact.

No wonder I hadn't noticed it before.

Though I'd paid attention to my path, I'd only ever gone forward—not once checking the streets I'd left behind. And I hadn't lingered at any of the intersections since finding people to talk to was a lot easier when they were studying the displays or sipping on their drinks as they lounged around the tables tucked close to the colorful walls.

By the Sun... If I hadn't doubled back now...

A sense of deep gratitude for the persistent tug in my core flooded me. At least I could get back to base without losing my nerves in the process. I doubted I could survive the ugly sense of helplessness a second time.

The longer I walked, noting the oddly constructed nature of the shifts, the more I understood my own oversight. Even now, when I knew they were happening, I was unable to actually *sense* the changes.

No unnerving chimes.

No bursts of disorientation.

And the people around me seemed to pay them no mind.

Unlike beyond the city limits, whatever was taking chunks of the world and placing them in different spots was kinder, not quite so disruptive to the rhythm of life. Normal—to them.

I let loose a breath and willed the last of the tension from my limbs. But before I could give myself over entirely to searching for Ada, I spotted a face I'd seen before. *Twice* now. In entirely different districts.

It could be a coincidence, but—

The orange-haired man appeared to be examining a clothbound book from the nearby display, posture wholly casual, but his gaze—his gaze was focused on a single point on the cover as if his true attention rested elsewhere.

As if he were looking at something out of the corner of his eye.

Feigning ignorance, I strolled farther down the street.

The man followed.

CHAPTER SEVEN

WITH THE MAN'S PRESENCE LICKING AT MY BACK AND SENDING pinpricks of awareness down my spine, keeping my steps unhurried proved to be a serious test of self-discipline.

Still, I didn't relent.

It was a false sense of control, perhaps, but I told myself that as long as I could keep up the charade of not knowing about him, I was at an advantage. In this one thing, at least, I knew more than he.

Maybe some desperate, naive kernel of me even hoped my intuition was wrong, that the man was harmless, that it was merely my own paranoia, conjuring up shadows where there were none. Yet whenever I stopped by the stalls and displays under the pretense of examining the wares, the man was still there, still trailing me from a distance.

As much as I wanted to indulge in this one, I was never one to believe in comforting lies.

Once I fully accepted my situation wouldn't change without

some intervention, I switched tactics. I turned down several streets, but the shifts surrounding the intersections never happened when I wanted them to. The man kept following. And I kept walking—spying him in mirrors and reflective ornaments, in casual glances when crossing the cobblestones where townsfolk sped by.

Unaware of my sly means of observation, my stalker dropped all pretenses. And burned the final slivers of doubt from my mind.

At least he didn't seem to be doing anything but observing me. So far. I wasn't willing to bet my life on the flimsy hope that wouldn't change in the near future. Late as it was, the town, while still very much pulsing with life, had to slumber eventually. I needed to finish this before that would happen and no buffer left remained between us.

Yet when I contemplated drawing on the pendant's power to leave the man behind, something stayed my hand.

Bitter amusement curved through me.

All the time I'd spent running in Nysa must have rubbed off on me. I refused to play the part of some ignorant prey any longer.

"Excuse me," a girl about my age called out, halting me mid-step. She quickly put down a silver bracelet with jingling charms she'd been examining at one of the stalls and bounded over. "So sorry to bother you like this. I know you must think me rude for shouting, but I'd never *seen* such a color."

Her hazel eyes were wide, admiring—even more prominent against the shimmering cosmetics that flowed like the ocean across her eyelids. It took me a moment to realize she was referring to the silver of my hair. I shaped my features into something I hoped would come across as pleasant.

My efforts must have paid off, because the girl took a step closer, cocked her head to the side, and asked, "Did you use a spell for it?"

To lie or to tell the truth? Unable to decide which would damn me worse, I chose the latter.

"It's my natural coloring." I wound a strand around my finger, showing off its glint in the soft, pearl white light streaming from the perfumery to my right.

"Beautiful," the girl murmured. Her fingers twitched by her sides. "I tried dyes, spells, but all I achieved was white. Or a mousy gray." She scrunched her heart-shaped face, a smattering of wrinkles on her nose. "I can see why you wouldn't want to change it."

In my old life, I would have given everything to rid myself of the hair that marked me as other. Now...

"Thank you." I smiled, and there was no falsehood in the warmth. "Although yours suits you perfectly."

The girl's hands flew up to her teal locks that, indeed, complemented her bronze skin and made it seem as if it were glowing. For all I knew, it might actually be, thanks to a...spell. Still, natural or not, the result was nothing short of stunning.

As were the dimples that adorned her cheeks at my words.

"May...may I touch it?"

Taken by surprise, I must have let her question hang in the intimate space between us for a fraction too long. The girl winced and retreated a step—which sent her bumping into an unsuspecting passerby. I caught her just as her full-heeled shoe wobbled dangerously on the edge of a cobblestone.

"Sorry," she called after the tall woman clad in plum-colored pants and a lacy top who merely waved a dismissive hand, then turned to me. I stopped her before she could utter another apology. It was rare circumstances that made me this comfortable, but—

"Of course you can touch my hair." I maneuvered us out of the steady stream of people. "But I'd rather avoid another collision."

The girl chuckled. "I'm Victorine, by the way. Wouldn't feel right to not at least introduce myself if I'm going to..." She wiggled her fingers towards my hair. "You know..."

Amused, I picked up a lock and brought it to her still wiggling fingers. A touch of something serious, something focused, settled upon her face as she examined the strand with only the melody of the street playing in the background. It was as if she were seeing entire worlds in the argent texture.

I regretted having to cut the moment short, but with no idea what the man trailing me wanted, I didn't want to put the girl in any danger.

"I apologize for being so curt, Victorine, but I have friends waiting for me and I'm already running late."

Not even a fabrication.

"Of course." She bobbed her head. "Thank you for taking the time." Her gaze flickered to my hair. "And that."

"Ember."

Her hazel eyes locked with my icy-blue.

"I'm Ember."

I parted from her with one last smile I meant with my entire heart, but my mind was already scanning the street. My stalker had kept his distance, busying himself with dyed scarves and glimmering headwear displayed on free-standing racks in front of a boutique, but now that I was moving once more, he didn't let the distance between us grow. I had to find an opening, something that would allow me to momentarily slip from his sight.

It was about time to turn the tables.

At the next intersection, I didn't comply with the navigational tug announcing the path to the central tavern, but took the street that harbored the thickest crowd. It was narrower than those before it, rich with a blend of bergamot, pomelo, and cinnamon that spurred my senses into an even higher drive. Cozy rustic bars and shops took up most of the cobblestones, leaving only a sliver of space to walk on. My progress was slow, but as I veered between the clusters of people, acutely aware of every innocent brush against the fragment secured to my thigh, I sensed the man losing ground.

I dared a casual look over my shoulder.

He was trying to circumvent a group of laughing men who were speaking to someone seated at a corner table. With their dresses fanning out and people streaming in the opposite direction behind them, my stalker had no choice but to wait before he could follow.

Wasting no time, I sped up and maneuvered through the crowd with renewed vigor until I spotted a teeming clothes' boutique on my left. With the racks upon racks of lively garments dominating the front part of the window-lined shop, it was the perfect place to hide—and observe.

A few people shuffled about when I entered, the shopkeeper busy explaining which fabrics would mix together well. I drifted over to the corner I'd spied earlier and pressed myself between the dresses and the mint-blue wall where thick shadows offered additional cover. There was a sliver of space right up ahead I could peer through, providing me with a clear view of the street.

Cold sweat touched the nape of my neck as I counted the seconds.

One.

A hanger clattered onto the ground.

Two.

The shopkeeper laughed away the man's apologies.

Three.

A couple slowed as they passed the display, their matching gemstone bracelets adorning their interlocked arms like droplets of water in the sun.

Four. Five.

"Can I help you with anything?" The shopkeeper, his head poking around the racks separating us.

Six.

I worked some moisture into my throat.

Seven.

"Just looking, thank you." The words tight under their false brightness.

Eight.

A fog of movement at the center of the shop I barely registered as the stalker appeared.

Nine.

My pulse feathered in my neck, my ears.

He was younger than I expected, probably no more than twenty-five, although the hard set of his face gave him an edge of someone who'd lived a long time—and experienced much, not all of it pleasant. His long, orange hair was pulled back, revealing a strong jaw, the corded muscles of his neck, and broad shoulders the skintight sunburst tunic emphasized to their full potential.

Oddly, though, he wasn't scanning the crowd. His gaze was fixed on some point up ahead I'd have to expose myself to see, and while there was determination to his step, he didn't strike me as a man who'd lost his mark. I couldn't keep the doubts creeping into my mind once more at bay.

Silver and gold rings glinted on his slender fingers as he smoothed back a rogue orange strand, the slash of his mouth softening into a smile.

Maybe I *had* been paranoid. Maybe there *was* someone else coincidentally taking the exact same route as me that he was following. Or maybe the man wasn't up to anything nefarious at all.

My instincts disagreed, but as he walked past the store without a single glance in my direction, I cursed myself for not giving him the slip before. I could have used the pendant, gotten away, and let the shifts take care of the rest while I returned to the tavern where the others must already be gathered, wondering where I was. All I achieved was wasting even more precious minutes to learn...what?

There was nothing to glean from watching him.

I sagged against the wall.

I'd chosen not to be a pawn, trapped in the current of events I'd been tossed in; a stance I was glad for and had every intention of nourishing.

But it would have been nice if this resolve had taken the reins when there was *actually* something to benefit from stalking my stalker. I rubbed my eyes and sighed as a fresh whiff of bergamot breezed through the store.

Some sleep would probably be beneficial to set my mind straight. There was only so much I could process at once. And aside from the brief reprieve at the tavern, this too-long day had been nothing but battle, loss, and confusion, mixed in with the constant sense of danger that sapped my carefully constructed inner strength.

A soft chiming rose through the air. Different from what I'd heard in the wilderness—as if tuned in another key. I tipped my head against the wall, listening to the melody growing ever louder in the abrupt silence that had swept over the store. *Silence.*

I snapped to attention, the icy lake within me a predator waiting to pounce.

The people were gone.

Behind the counter, as far away as the architecture of the space allowed it, the shopkeeper was cowering. He kept his eyes downcast, as if he didn't want to—

A flash of orange. A sunburst-streaked tunic.

No.

How—

The man was *here*, walking leisurely through the maze of clothes right to where I was standing. Although I heard no sound beyond the chiming, his lips were moving in a fast rhythm, forming words I couldn't make out.

Word magic.

Spells.

Dread pooled in the pit of my stomach as I realized that *he* was the reason behind the chiming.

Our gazes locked. Shadowfire rumbled within me under the hard weight of that grassy green, but didn't immediately surge. A last resort.

My hand flew to my pendant—

Invisible ropes dug into my skin.

I cried out, only to find the sound muffled by a phantom pressure that not only controlled my lips, but wrapped around my entire body.

Panic clawed at my neck.

Those green eyes neared. Unflinching. Unyielding. The only thing I could see as my body thrashed and screamed—just to remain immobile.

Mind whirling and tearing itself apart, I fought against the magic I couldn't see, but it made no difference. Nothing.

My body was no longer mine but a cage I'd been stuffed into. No locks, no weaknesses in sight.

Nausea ratcheted through me.

I shivered. But of course, not even that translated.

With every second I remained trapped, my breathing became more of a struggle. Awareness of the dark path I was taking only made the panic worse.

A vicious circle.

A whirlwind with no exit save for unconsciousness.

Not an option.

But I didn't know—

Shadowfire coiled and roared within the confines of my flesh, its soothing presence promising to save me if only I let go.

I wanted to. By the Sun, I did. Anything would be better than this. But...

The shopkeeper was still inside. An innocent, drawn into this just because I'd decided to veer into *his* shop.

I—I couldn't...

Couldn't risk harming him. Not when the obsidian storm inside me was raging, willing to obliterate *all* to set me free.

When the invisible ropes bound me in earnest, then hurtled me towards the man, I surrendered to his vicious grasp.

CHAPTER EIGHT

AN OMINOUS *CREAK* SLICED THROUGH THE SOMBER SPACE. BARS swinging shut, entrapping me in a cage beyond a cage.

Yet as absurd as it was, I welcomed the wretched sound of yet another incarceration.

Better than the deafening silence.

Better than the loss of all my senses, where the bounds of my captivity were not something tangible, but a nightmare wrought of an ever-voiceless scream.

Still immobile but no longer deprived of everything, I glared at my jailer. His bright orange hair fell across his temples before it curved back into a ponytail, clashing with the bleak, dimly lit setting that washed out his sharp face.

The worst kind of rot was always hidden beneath distracting casings—but when looked at from the right angle, the concealment broke. Flaked away into dust and ashes. I wondered what his was.

So I stared.

I had a lot to make up for.

It hadn't been until he'd ushered me behind these vile, repulsive bars that the world had solidified once more; became a thing of sound and sensations, all twined with my presence as I was with them. Whatever magic the man had bound me with in that shop had been thorough, leaving me utterly at his mercy.

Too restricted to attempt an escape.

Too blind to use my shadowfire when I had no idea *where* to strike.

If I even could.

The ethereal cage he'd confined me in had grown more disorienting by the minute—right up to the point where I couldn't even feel *myself* properly.

A part of me was surprised I was even still breathing.

Another crooned death could have only come at my hands.

I refused to listen to either.

It would only be another cage to torment myself with.

I had no idea how long we stared at each other. His face revealing nothing. Mine a canvas of icy hate—the kind that didn't burn but consumed slowly.

Damp, stale air adhered to my nostrils, the cool humidity prickling my skin. More—I was experiencing more than before, yet when I wanted to rub the chill away, my arms remained locked in position. At least the warm velvet of my dress kept the worst of the cold away.

The man took a step forward.

Another.

His grassy green eyes never left mine, and I refused to avert my gaze. Even when my lungs tightened, folded in on themselves, and blackness of an entirely different sort than the one blindfolding me earlier rolled over my vision.

What was he—

The oppressive ropes of power dissipated.

Air rushed into my lungs and blood flowed to my head, the many parts of me loose and rattling yet taut at the same time. Too much. Too fast.

A momentary spell of vicious dizziness sent me staggering against the dark gray, stone wall. I caught myself as fast as I could with arms about as solid as heated caramel, loathing the weakness. The shock of my shoulder colliding with the stones as one of my arms gave way was the last straw.

I peeled myself off the wall and faced my jailer who'd been observing me with concealed interest.

If he believed I was some *thing* to be studied—

He turned on his heel and marched across the dungeon, then up the stone stairs. Light spilled briefly into the gloom as he strode through the door before it bowed to darkness once more.

Snick.

I should have screamed. Should have raged.

But as the hardened composure I'd carved from the depths found no purchase, the icy hate no outlet, there was nothing inside me save for echoes not designed to withstand release.

Useless.

Even the shadowfire would do me little good against the bars that repelled my very essence as its obsidian tendrils would have no life to curl around.

The single thing I had the energy to do before I slumped against the cool rock and slid to the ground was check the fragment and pendant.

Both there. Both safe.

I hugged my knees to my chest.

Sun, I abhorred dungeons.

Cold seeped through my dress and grazed my skin. I huffed a bitter, harsh laugh. At least the Norcross cells were outfitted with hay to make prisoners more comfortable—and cover the stench of bodily fluids I'd have to face sooner rather than later.

"Ember?" a weak voice croaked from the left.

I jerked and shifted my body to the side, peering into the darkness. Inky shadows pooled beyond the scope of the faint, nearly imperceptible light that fanned from beneath the door atop the stairwell. But among them—

"Ada?" I crawled over. The seam between the two cells was just as repelling as the bars up front, but I forced myself to come as close as I could bear. "Ada!"

A glint of jade green caught the light. Labored, yet silent breaths. The longer I watched, the more details I could lift from the black canvas. A shudder rippled down my spine.

"What have they *done* to you?" I would have gripped one of the bars if I could. As it was, all I did was stare in horror, nails digging into my palms.

Ada was lying in a heap on the ground, barely moving, her face turned towards me and framed by a tangle of hair. I scanned her body for injuries, but could hardly make out anything beyond her form. Her black tunic and pants certainly didn't make matters any easier.

"Ada?" I prompted again. If they'd hurt her—

"A woman grabbed me when I entered the city. Used magic..." She swallowed, a dry sound that hinted her beaten-down state was related to thirst, not torture. My chest constricted regardless. All this time, she was here. "She locked me in here. Didn't say why."

"Someone got me, too," I spoke softly. I wasn't sure whether anyone could hear our conversation, so I strove to keep the details as vague as possible.

Maybe it would have been beneficial if I'd fed lies into the air, deceptions to weave an illusion we were here for the book fair like so many others, not travelers from another world; plant doubt if our origins *were* the reason we'd both ended up here. But Ada hadn't experienced the town. In her state, I wasn't willing to just assume her otherwise sharp, quick mind would catch on.

Another dry swallow. "What happened?"

"He followed me as I was walking through town." I traced the slightly rougher texture of a silver star on my dress." I thought I'd be able to..." I sighed and shook my head. "I couldn't escape the binds."

"And..." *The others?*

There was no need for her to utter the words. The slight tremble in her voice said it all.

I fisted my fingers in the velvet. "I don't know."

Our breaths were stark, too loud in the grim silence.

Stars, I hoped they made it. Hoped they were somewhere safe. At least Zaphine and Dantos were together; maybe that had been enough to save them from becoming easy pickings despite having no magic to counter a possible attack. Not that having it helped *me* any...

I took solace in knowing they at least weren't here already.

Possibilities, even if they came hand in hand with uncertainty, were far more agreeable than an irrevocably shattered future.

"What do you think they want with us?" I said into the dark. "We haven't done anything..."

Except arrived here from another land.

In Somraque, I'd sensed how the people, their magic, *thrummed*. Something I'd never come across in Soltzen and quickly began relating to blood magic. Maybe, from a Svitanyian's perspective, we *felt* different.

Yet try as I might, I couldn't believe the way everyone had acted around us had been a lie—a front held for long enough to leave us unsuspecting while they ran off to rat us out.

No. I hadn't imagined our integration into society. Yet it couldn't be a coincidence that Ada and I were the only ones rotting in cells. Not a single Svitanyian in sight.

Fabric scraped against stone, Ada's voice now closer. "It would have been nice if they spared at least a word before slamming the bars shut." Though faint, the edge lining her words filled me with relief. Ada might be weakened, but she was nowhere near giving up. Her jade eyes flicked towards the door atop the stairs. "No one even came here until that man brought you."

If that worked in our favor or not in the long run, I couldn't tell. All I knew was that Ada needed water. Needed food. *Now.*

The hours she'd spent here after braving the countryside would have been bad enough on their own. But if my hypothesis was correct and those with the most powerful magic suffered its loss the worst, then her body had to be struggling. Maybe searching for magic that wasn't there. Or perhaps just using any and all supplies to adjust to this new state.

My gaze skimmed the contours of her form as she tried—and failed—to get herself upright.

Even if I broke us out, there was no way I could carry her. Not when Ada had nothing left to give.

But staying here wasn't an option, either.

Voices slithered down the stairs. I tensed, then foolishly,

futilely attempted to shield Ada's weak body with mine.

A wave of horrifying revulsion ratcheted through me as the proximity of the bars separating our cells swiped and pounded at my back. I scrambled to the center of the space right as the muffled chatter crystallized into one voice—so loud and babbling it was a wonder no one had shut him up yet. The door *creaked* open to reveal the same orange-haired man, wearing the same unreadable expression. Behind him, however, clustered among three more stone-faced guards, was the rest of our missing party.

Relief and defeat clashed into rumbling thunder within me.

They were alive, visibly unharmed...

But also about to be thrown into cells.

As they descended, Eriyan kept shouting obscenities into the empty space to his left, where, I suspected, he *thought* the guard was. If the circumstances were any different, I would have laughed at how absurd the scene looked.

"Shit," Ada muttered under her breath. Whatever strength she'd lacked before must have experienced a surge, because she rolled over onto her stomach, then knelt.

It was all the incentive I needed.

I wrapped my fingers discreetly around the pendant, shadowfire already lurking under my skin, and quickly assessed the situation. There weren't enough cells for each of us to have our own. I might not have been prepared to lash out in the shop, afraid of who I might hurt, but playing it safe was becoming less and less of an option. Ivarr's tight, unseeing face confirmed as much.

Time, the one element that had always been mine, was becoming a finite resource.

The procession reached the bottom of the steps, haloed by

the light streaming through the open door. I kept my breaths steady, my stance befitting the furious but also discouraged prisoner.

Four guards. Just four.

My jailer had caught me unprepared then—I wouldn't make the same mistake twice.

And I *would* get my answers.

If we were to comb through this world in search of the fragment, we needed to know our enemies. Their motives.

Their vulnerabilities.

The orange-haired man ushered a cursing Eriyan into the last cell in the line of five, but didn't dispel the bonds pinning Eriyan's arms to his sides. As the bars swung shut, he cast a look towards the burly-looking guard dressed in formfitting lemon-green pants. Eriyan's frame relaxed.

I masked my surprise before it could show on my face.

Did the guards all possess the same kind of magic?

The smallest of the quartet thrust Zaphine into the next cell, promptly letting go of the binds. She recovered in a heartbeat and propelled herself at the bars, as if she planned to rip straight through. Her fingers curved around the iron.

A shadow of uncertainty crossed the man's face, then disappeared as Zaphine spat at his feet and kicked the barrier. I half expected she'd end up bound again—and maybe she would have, too, had she not retreated to the center of her tiny prison, spewing an endless well of curses. I hoped she would keep it up.

Any distraction was a welcomed one.

Her fire helped, too.

As a powerfully built woman with black flowers inked down the length of her exposed arms escorted Dantos into the space between Zaphine's and mine, my attention rested on Ivarr. His glower was murderous as his body moved without his permission like a puppet, muscles wound tight. He wasn't actively struggling against the hold—not in the flashy way Zaphine and Eriyan had written all over their faces and carried in their energy earlier, even when it had produced no true effect on their bodies. But the resistance was there nonetheless. Like an intrinsic response to an unnatural situation I felt on a primal, visceral level.

The burly-looking guard who had Ivarr ensnared directed him towards my cell. Zaphine's swearing blasted off the walls; Eriyan demanded to know why we were here.

So close.

So close to the bars.

Ivarr's once more seeing eyes locked on mine. He couldn't nod, but he might as well have.

Overpower the guards.

Get answers.

If the shock of my attack released Ivarr from his binds, all the better for it. I suspected he was the superior interrogator between the two of us even without his Magician strengths.

The burly guard's lips moved under the honey-colored bristles of his mustache. Seconds—there were seconds separating me from my opening.

My jailer placed a slender hand on the man's shoulder.

And shook his head.

Every muscle in my body tensed, and Ivarr's gaze tightened, reading but not understanding the shift in my expression as the quiet exchange took place behind him. Zaphine was pounding against the bars—a vicious, demanding tempo that matched my heart as I wordlessly willed mustache-man to unlock *my* prison—

The bars swung open.

Only not mine.

CHAPTER NINE

ADA HALF LIFTED HERSELF OFF THE GROUND AS THE GUARD tossed Ivarr inside with her and sealed the cell shut.

My vision blurred.

The shadowfire an earth-shattering roar inside me.

All my previous plans, fears, and reservations faded, replaced by a state that burned ice-cold and cared only for imminent results, not consequences. Or casualties. A beast meant to step into the light, not cower in musky, damp corners.

I studied the female guard who was standing the closest, her eyes on Dantos's tall, stoic figure. I wondered if I could solidify my obsidian threads into ropes and drag her to me. The rest...

I only needed *one* to release us.

One to utter those words coined through a movement of the lips that didn't carry the sound far enough for me to catch.

I could choke that damn verbal key out of her, then wring out the answers we'd been denied. But...but if she chose death, chose to join her by-then already depleted and lifeless husks of colleagues—

The inner rumble lessened.

Killing them would accomplish nothing.

Yet still, I wanted to. By the Sun, I wanted to.

My shadowfire wasn't the driving force. It harbored no desires but my own. *My. Own.*

I staggered farther back, disgusted with myself.

I'd killed before. In self-defense.

Bile splashed at the back of my throat.

This would have been murder.

A piercing flash of green to my left let me know Ada hadn't missed my reaction. Perhaps even knew what I had been thinking. But the sight of her—

"If you don't want to speak with us, that's fine," I said through gritted teeth as I battled down the nausea. "But unless this is all part of your torture, at least bring her"—I flung my arm in Ada's direction—"some water."

The burly guard looked at me and—to my surprise—nodded. All four of them exited the dungeon, but true to his silent promise, the man returned only moments later and slid a pitcher of water and a roll of bread through the bars.

Ivarr passed them silently to Ada who'd curled up against the wall.

As the soft sounds of her chewing permeated the air, I asked, "Is everyone all right?"

Affirmatives bubbled from the cells—Zaphine's carrying a touch of her former bite.

Dantos peered at me through the bars, standing far closer than I could have been able to stomach. "So what now?"

We were once again in the dark—in more ways than one—

but without fearing for the others' safety, we at least had the luxury to talk. Minding our words seemed futile under the circumstances.

"Now we're locked in a cell, in a foreign land, with no magic and absolutely no means of escape," Eriyan pointed out.

"Will you, for once, *shut up* if you don't have anything to contribute?" Ada snarled from the ground and tore off another piece of bread.

"Well, *you* certainly sound improved," Eriyan drawled on without hesitation. It wasn't hard to imagine the deadpan expression on his face. "Nice to know incarceration hasn't stripped you of your lovely spirit."

"*ENOUGH.*" Ivarr. "These people clearly know we don't belong here. I didn't escape one tyrant just to subject myself to the whims of another."

I flinched, but Zaphine's immediate response saved me from slipping too far down that precarious path.

"And what are you going to do?" She leaned against the bars, her silhouette no more than a play of shadows, but the edge in her tone rang clear. "Unless you can chew your way through stone or iron, I don't see *you* contributing any more than babblehead over here."

Sighing, I eased myself back against the wall and massaged my temples. Children—we truly were children playing a game far larger than us. But lamenting our circumstances was a foolproof way of assuring we'd never win. Tuning out the conversation, I delved into myself and went through our options—then those that were mine alone.

Each one was even less viable than its predecessor. Unless—

"I could open a portal," I whispered, keeping my voice steady, devoid of hope they couldn't stoke until they heard the entirety of my plan.

The silence in the dungeon grew absolute.

"I could open a portal to every one of you, then, once we're together, take us to Soltzen or Somraque. We could re-enter Svitanye from there, start anew."

Why not just take us out of this dungeon?" Zaphine asked. "Deposit us somewhere in the city?"

I plucked the pendant from beneath my dress, the flipped crescent moon spinning around its axis. "Svitanye isn't stable. Portals connect two geographical points, two *static* points. Our cells are locked in their respective places, but out there..." I didn't trust the intersections. The bushes and trees and meadows, all so flimsy. So small. I released the pendant and pushed off the wall, seeking familiar silhouettes in the darkness. "We could end up stuck in the in-between with no path forward *or* back. Here, we have options. There, on the other hand..."

"So we go to Soltzen." Ada rose with Ivarr's help and met my gaze through the bars. "We go there, maybe get the fragment—"

I shook my head. "Night is our starting point. The inception of my link with the relic." My fingers sought out its shape on their own. "Night. Dawn. Day. We can go to my homeland, but we must return here for this fragment before we search for that one."

"Still sounds like a damn good plan," Dantos chipped in.

A rustle of movement rose from behind him—Zaphine or Eriyan or both—but its meaning was unmistakable.

We had a viable plan. We were ready to go.

"I just need..." My gaze caught on Ada. "Do you have your dagger on you?"

The light in her eyes dimmed. "No." Her jaw clenched. "There was nothing left when I came to."

"Shit," I whispered. I needed a weapon, but the resolute silence my companions had sunk into spoke an unpleasant truth. I wouldn't find it with them.

"Zaphine," I asked nonetheless, "even you?"

Her voice was small but crackled with distaste as she admitted, "Lost all of mine during the struggle."

Concern whisked through me as her words conjured a dark image of what Zaphine must have gone through. But when she offered no more, I didn't pry. Instead, I honed my focus and scrutinized the cell, detaching myself emotionally from the memory I called to the forefront of my thoughts.

When my father had locked me up, I had been without a blade, too. And much like at the Norcross estate, the walls of my prison here were made of stone. Surely I could find one fissure, one protruding, sharp piece to use...

I walked over and lay my palms on the cool surface. Smooth, but not flawless.

I patted every inch in front of me, then moved to the side and repeated the process. Frustrated, I thrust my hand in my hair—

Hair. The braids—they were still intact, still secured with pins.

Sweat licked my palms.

I hurried to extract one when a *creak* whipped me around. The pin flew from my grip, swallowed by darkness.

My heart thundered.

The guards were back.

And they'd brought reinforcements.

CHAPTER TEN

MY PALM WARMED THE PENDANT BEFORE THE FIRST OF THE guards could reach the landing. My every nerve came alive, anticipation sizzling beneath my skin. It wasn't hard to feign the fear our jailers needed to see when my pulse became a marching drumbeat, body wound tight as another, far more elegant yet by no means simple plan burst into existence.

Just one, perfectly aligned moment to make this work.

But if I did, if *it* did...

I released a shuddering, adrenaline-ridden exhale.

My thoughts had the tendency to run fast.

My actions had to follow suit.

There was no alternative.

Guards trickled down the stairs like a languid river comprised of dyes and sharp edges. Ivarr positioned himself in front of Ada, his readiness for a fight a tangible thing that undulated through the vile, repugnant bars. A man with no magic against an army. I didn't want him to make the sacrifice.

The guards formed haphazard rows along the narrow stretch of stone between the cells and the damp wall. Their half-shadowed expressions ranged from solemn to hostile, though a few looked as if they were simply doing their jobs, nothing more. So many...

Had they learned the true extent of just who they had imprisoned?

Zaphine didn't seem to care, one hand curved around the bars and a murderous glower on her face. The light spilling down the steps and fanning across the dungeon turned her into a glacial, lethal work of art despite the rips in her dress I could now see clearly. The snarled black hair.

I dragged my gaze back to the guards, but my ears sought the whispers—the magic I wanted to catch in its inception, spring into action the second it did.

"Are you just going to stand there and ogle us?" Zaphine snapped.

To my left, Ada tensed. Ivarr and Dantos, even Eriyan, might as well have been statues.

Hushed voices twined, the pendant an anchor and a promise in the palm of my hand.

For this to work, all five cells had to be open. A slim, slim chance they would release us all at once, though given their almost ridiculous numbers, perhaps not a fool's hope either.

But one thing was clear—the instant the cells opened, the binds would be back.

My magic had to be swifter than theirs.

Ada and Ivarr seemed to have picked up on my intentions and retreated deeper into the cell where the guards couldn't reach them immediately. Ada must have shared the specifics of my temporal power with him at some point. They couldn't be touching anyone when I unleashed it if I wanted to liberate them from the magic's grasp and take them with me later on.

This part was tricky enough as it was, since I would have to unfreeze time for a split second in order to grab them, then shove the world into stasis once more. I would have to not only perform, but *excel* at it at least four times.

Failure was not an option.

Unfortunately, neither was my former—*solid*—plan to take us to Soltzen. Not with the guards present. I doubted they came all the way down here just to look.

The four of them who had been here earlier took position up front, mouths working—but not in unison.

I backed against the wall where the shadows were the deepest as my orange-haired jailer pinned me with an unrelenting stare. My reaction was one he likely anticipated, but also one that hid the predator within me wishing to rise to the surface. In the corners of my vision, the guards in the two back rows spread out, preparing to transport us who-knew-where.

With a shuddering exhale, I trained my gaze up ahead—on the mocking sunburst adorning the fabric of the man's tunic—all the while absorbing details out of the corners of my vision, mapping my paths as I counted the seconds.

The chimes peaked, something I felt in my bones, and I could have sworn the bars moved—

The hand I held splayed across my chest, atop the pendant, started to lower.

No—

Pain lanced through me as I struggled against the command, a sensation that felt like my tendons would rip if I kept at it for much longer. I refused to succumb.

A wave of nausea ravaged my insides.

The guards' lips articulated words that didn't reach me. Impossible. Impossible to tell if the dark concentration in my jailer's gaze was a reflection of his actions or a taunt.

To douse out the source, I would have to unleash my shadowfire on them all.

I wasn't willing to expose myself like that just yet.

Bile burned at the back of my throat, and the beginning of a headache had started to gather in my temples, overpowering the sinister but sonorous chiming that continued to weave through the air.

I gritted my teeth, then shoved against the invisible constraints with all I had—

My arm snapped down to my side with a soundless *pop*. The binds snaked around me, just as firm and secure as they had been the first time.

For a beat that seemed to pulse right from the heart of this wretched land, the hopelessness of our situation circled around me—then slammed into my core full force.

Eriyan and Zaphine sputtered curses from their cells, but they hardly registered over the roar that wrenched itself from my chest, but never made it past the magical gag. When the bars opened, even those curses were silenced.

Like puppets with no will of our own, the guards marched us up the stairs.

Not yet, I reminded myself.

Though its glow was gradual, washing over me like those orbs Ada had magicked into existence in her dungeon what felt like ages ago, light assaulted my senses once we were past the door. The guards swiftly switched up their formation, now flanking us from all sides. Whether they knew of the potential threat I could be or simply followed protocol, the result was the same.

Stuck in the center of this Somraquian circle rimmed with Svitanyians, I had no clear targets.

Even if I did, the repercussions, the extent of what it would mean to reveal my shadowfire wasn't worth incapacitating a guard or two.

Not yet. Not yet. Not yet.

The words became a mantra, a stopper on the vial of the one ace up my sleeve that could get us out—when the circumstances deprived us of all other pathways. Marching down a plain corridor wasn't it.

The guards had ceased their whispers, the chimes replaced by our footsteps knocking against the slate gray stone. Still, I kept waiting for my sight to vanish. For that horrifying immersion into nothingness I couldn't allow to transpire a second time to descend upon me.

Yet all there was was motion.

The guards'—free. Ours—forced.

I tried not to think too much of the latter. It was a fact that would only plunge me into depths I'd best avoid.

Before me, Dantos's broad shoulders and build blocked most of my view, though I didn't fail to notice how tense his muscles were beneath his white shirt before I directed my attention elsewhere. As much as I could with my head steered forward thanks to the binds.

To my left, Zaphine's eyes darted across the utilitarian interior while Ada, marching to my right, kept shooting daggers at the guards who ignored her without fault. I pushed against the discomfort building up in my chest.

If the guards weren't troubled by what we might see, that didn't bode well for our future.

The off-white, uninterrupted walls of the corridor changed

about forty steps in. Open archways sprouted at irregular intervals on the left side, though it wasn't until the third one that I managed to steal a glimpse of just what lay beyond.

If it weren't for the binds supporting and moving my legs, my step would have faltered.

As if part of a dreamscape after the cold, damp dungeon, a lavish hall made of white walls and gold ornaments commandeered my vision. Immaculate, glowing, with shimmering crystal chandeliers suspended from the ceiling and illuminated by what had to be magic. No light birthed from nature could shine like that. Pastel blue accents tastefully arranged throughout the space provided a link to the city's colorful style, but aside from that, the contrast to what I'd seen when roaming the streets was stark.

A palace.

This was a palace.

Resplendent in ways neither Soltzen nor Somraque had come close to—the kind of quiet yet effervescent beauty you didn't know you craved until witnessing it with your own eyes. Yet, like at home, there was something missing.

Warmth.

Life.

As my mind wanted to drift to a particular two-level study, I sealed that introspectively observant place within me and plunged into questions of a far more practical kind.

Try as I might, rummaging through the grooves of my memory, I couldn't recall seeing any structure grand enough to represent this one while I'd been scouring the city. If we even still *were* in the city...

No answer presented itself, not even that tug of the internal compass—as if the walls had blocked it off.

With nothing left to turn over in my mind, with nothing left to plan, I kept my gaze trained on our surroundings and just drank in every possible detail as the guards dragged us to Sun knew where.

AFTER WHAT FELT like ages and, I suspected, numerous detours along the back corridors of the palace so there was no hope for us to retrace our steps—not that it would have mattered with no exits in sight—we ended up in a wide semicircular room. The guards pooled around us in every direction as they lined us up, but I hardly followed the insignificant movements as I took in the room.

The dawn sky stretched beyond the nearly floor-to-ceiling windows framed by gentle, light blue drapes that added a touch of something ethereal to the already breathtaking view. The part of me that lived for beauty wondered what it would be like, seeing the canvas of stars and moonlight transform into this. How it was even possible. I forced my gaze away from the pink gradients, the intimate dance of hues, and studied the chamber over the guards' heads.

Like with many of the spaces I'd snuck glimpses of earlier, gold ornaments broke up the pearl white of the walls, the floor—what I could see of it, peering down my nose and through the small gaps between the guards' bodies—a gleaming marble that reflected the mural spread across the ceiling. I rolled my eyes up...

Had I free reign over my body, I would have lain down on the marble, eliminated every other facet of reality save for that mural. Just the part of it my vision revealed was—

I glanced through the windows, then back up. This was more than a mere depiction. The mural had life—quiet, still life, but life nonetheless.

Distantly, I was aware of movement rippling through the ring our guards formed. The twin fires burning within Ada and Zaphine. Dantos's steadfastness. Eriyan's concealed sharpness. Ivarr's equanimity.

But I was transfixed by the pastel paint shaped into the stirrings of dawn, the small corners of night seeping through and creating depths only darkness could bring.

I ached for that starry sky. For the silver glint of the moon...

But my longing was set aside as the guards before me parted, pulling my attention down—then casting it past them.

A new impression erased the mural from my mind.

Five women clad in flowing gowns held court across the stretch of spotless marble. All young, slightly older than me, perhaps, but not by much, yet they exuded confidence the majority of High Masters could never hope to achieve—though not for lack of trying. Four of them stood, spines proud and hands clasped in front of them, while one was seated in a delicate white chair that seemed to float an inch above the ground. The tips of her glitter-brushed shoes visible beneath the dress's hem rested on a gold ledge shaped to accommodate her feet.

The guards bowed in unison. Backs straight, a hand on the heart, the other behind their backs. They must have released their holds from the neck up because I was able to watch them without straining, yet I might have as well been bound, stunned into immobility by this graceful formality where not a single finger, a single angle of the head was out of line.

As the uniform stillness birthed silence, I heard the chimes, so soft they were almost inaudible.

Magic. The entire chamber was bathed in magic.

And the women were its source.

They stared at us with unreadable eyes, though the texture of their gazes varied. I was too astonished by the turn of events, the empyrean sight of them to even bother deciphering the nuances lurking in the depths.

The one in the middle, with lavender hair framing a heart-shaped face and cascading down toned, deep brown arms, dipped her chin. The guards rose and the binds loosened, but did not deliver complete liberty. I didn't doubt they would string around us the instant we attempted anything. Still, I cherished standing on my own two feet.

The skirt of the woman's opalescent silk dress rippled as she took a step closer, her demeanor cool and elegant—as if she'd spent her entire existence controlling her body to utilize as little movement as possible. She swept her gaze over our faces slowly as the chiming rose then fell in tune with the nearly imperceptible movements of her mouth. I held my ground as those near-black eyes locked onto mine.

The moment seemed to stretch endlessly—then faded in a heartbeat.

"What do you want with us?" Zaphine demanded when the stranger retook her position among the others. "Who *are* you?"

The one at the far right—a pale, statuesque woman with straight, pitch-black hair that flowed into a vivid blue, cocked her head to the side. Her expression, however, remained impassive, as if our presence here was an afterthought to the unimaginable volumes of threads running through her mind.

"We are the Council of Words," she said, the distance in her voice only further fueling my suspicion.

"And we want nothing from you," the petite redhead standing beside her added. Diamond beads adorning her hair fractured and reflected light with even the smallest of movements, making it nearly impossible to look anywhere else. "Only to rid Svitanye of the disturbance."

Maybe not *that* impossible.

Zaphine shifted uncomfortably on my right. Ada and Ivarr tensed on the other side. I didn't have to look at Dantos and Eriyan. We'd all picked up on the meaning of the woman's words. How could we not, with the look she'd bestowed upon us...

It was one my father had worn when he'd banished the seasonal workers—Magnus among them—from the estate grounds. One I'd been on the receiving end of countless times as I refused to blindly conform to his demands.

It made it more than clear just where we stood.

The icy lake within me offered its silent strength, but remained placid. Waiting.

"We don't know of any disturbance," Zaphine said, chin held high, though the slight tremors in her voice undermined the steely look she was giving the five women.

"You *are* the disturbance," the lavender-haired one replied. "Rienne..."

The petite redhead stepped forward in a sparkling halo. I had to force my attention to her face—to the full curve of her mouth bearing no signs she was enjoying this.

"The shifts experienced an uncharacteristic spike today. Maelynn"—she gestured towards the seated member of the Council with a bracelet-clad hand—"has tracked the origin of the disturbance to you." The gold and copper circlets clanked as she dropped her arm. "You do not belong in our world. And your presence here upsets it."

The way she spoke, without surprise or any sort of inflection...

They knew we weren't from Svitanye.

And they didn't seem surprised.

My gaze cut to the orange-haired guard who was staring right back at me. There was nothing—absolutely nothing there. As if dealing with people from beyond Svitanye's borders was simply part of his job.

"We arrived from the country this morning," Dantos lied. I would have told him not to bother, but the sheer shock of how nonchalant they all were about our origin kept me from uttering a single word.

"Oh?" This from the woman wearing a pastel peach dress that complemented her glossy gold hair. Her copper eyes widened, the perfect arches of her eyebrows climbing up. "What are you?" She tapped a manicured finger to her shimmering lips. "Enchanters? Spellweavers?" Her freckled nose wrinkled—as if in confusion. "No?"

"Enough, Annora." The statuesque councilor cut in, voice still distant, but the command in it unaffected. "We have expended enough time and magic on this issue already."

"Get rid of... What do they mean *get rid of?*" Eriyan muttered, the words quiet enough to make me think they hadn't been intended to see the light of day. But the Council heard him.

Their attention was a translucent force, not loud or ostentatious, but definitely *noticeable*.

Opalescent silk whispered as the woman in the middle flicked her lavender tresses over her bare shoulder and dipped her chin, head tilted to the side. "Tana is right. As much as it is remarkable to see people from beyond our land, we cannot let this go on for much longer. I'm sorry." Oddly, she sounded sincere. "The only thing that matters is the well-being of Svitanye and its denizens. All else comes second. Even travelers from Somraque."

"How—how did you know?" Ada asked.

"Your resonance." Maelynn carefully smoothed the aquamarine adorned chiffon of her dress then folded her hands in her lap.

Ada sucked in a ragged breath. "Our *resonance?*"

"Yes. It speaks of magic from within the body. Within the blood. And Sylo"—I could have sworn my jailer stood taller, prouder—"mentioned your friend was unaffected by the repellant magic placed upon the bars." Her gray eyes flicked to Zaphine. "She wouldn't have been able to touch them if words were alive inside her."

I hadn't even realized I'd been silent this entire time until the words crawled up my throat. "With all due respect, councilors, we didn't come here to disturb Svitanye or cause problems. We—"

"It doesn't matter," Rienne replied, not unkindly and yet— "Your reason or intentions are irrelevant when violent shifts are the consequence. All you are is a threat."

Just when I opened my mouth to protest, Tana's voice dominated the space, her tone as cool as her appearance. "Your foreign magic, or lack of it, now that you have crossed, is disrupting the already tentative stability. We have no choice but to eliminate the source."

"Eliminate..." Ada whispered then looked up, jaw tense and expression wrought of fortitude.

But before she could say anything more, it was Ivarr who snapped, "You mean to *kill* us?"

The lavender-haired councilor I had no name for but suspected was the leader among leaders met Ivarr's gaze—then took us all in. "You are exiled to the Waste. The land will be your executioner."

CHAPTER ELEVEN

A SILENCE DESCENDED UPON THE CHAMBER, AS DEATHLY AND as ominous as our sentence. My heartbeat dove into a daunting accelerando—

A blur of black and a *crack*.

A guard staggered backwards, blood gushing down his face where Ivarr's forehead had smashed into him. My jailer—Sylo— leaped, lips working, but not fast enough to prevent Ivarr from kneeing another guard in the groin in a swift, imaginative move my dazed mind would probably replay for years to come. As he sought out his next target, obsidian darkness rumbled within me.

But where the rumbling grew, Ivarr's movements cut off.

Sylo's magic snapped into place among the flurry of activity. Ivarr went taut, as did Dantos, but my body was still free, still—

Invisible pressure sealed my pores.

The rumbling gained volume, an elegant, lethal beast refusing to be caged.

We'd come together as Somraque crumbled. We'd traveled through a portal between *worlds* I had slashed open as the prophesized Savior I'd so reluctantly accepted to be my fate. I'd left everything behind under the night sky; we *all* did, holding on to the hope that a better, united world would be worth the steep price of loss—

"No," I snapped.

Shadowfire surged from the lake and rolled just under my skin. Seeped through it like mist. Its familiar obsidian filled me, pressing against the bonds until they started to crack. A discreet vine licked at the air, then another. They gathered where the Council of Words and the guards who'd broken formation couldn't see, ready to smother out every hostile life within these walls should I wish it.

Unlike before, there were no doubts eroding my belief that I would take out our enemies and our enemies alone. As if the invisible noose around our necks had offered up a guidebook on lethal finesse.

The answers I'd wanted—

We had them.

There was no value in their lives anymore.

And they'd made it perfectly clear what they wanted to do with ours.

"Ember." A pleading voice. "Ember, don't..."

The obsidian coated every inch of my skin beneath my dress. Darkness concealed by night.

For the first time since we'd arrived, I felt like myself. Whole. Fulfilled.

"Please, Ember. You aren't him. You're not the Crescent Prince. Don't do this."

Ada's eyes were wide, beseeching, mouth tense. I didn't have to look at her beyond a brief glance to see every fine detail of her personal horror—of concern and disquiet, too—transforming her features into a wide-open map of who Ada was. A viewing of her innermost parts.

Mordecai was the monster haunting their nightmares.

I, apparently, teetered on the verge.

She wasn't wrong. But that did not mean she comprehended the truth, either.

The Council monitored the exchange with keen gazes—like birds of prey sensing the gravity of the situation but not truly seeing the threat, believing it. A chiming sounded in the background, as if whatever magic they were calling could ever hope to counter the depths I would unleash.

There was no divide between the Ancient power and me.

"We'll find another way." Ada swallowed. Tension rode the corners of her eyes. "Please, Ember. Please."

One thought.

One thought and all that would remain around us would be corpses.

I reeled the shadowfire back in, my temper glacial. I didn't spare Ada as much as a look as I fixed my gaze on the Council of Words. I wasn't sure who I despised more.

Ada, the fearless Mage who'd never batted an eyelash at what had to be done now giving in to some foolish weakness.

Or me, heeding her pleas.

As if there were something noble in dying a better person than to live as one with scars on your soul.

But one bad choice didn't predetermine another.

I trailed my gaze across the councilwomen's unified, blocked-off expressions and bared my teeth. "Your world is *broken*. It's broken and the cracks won't stop. They won't heal, no matter how hard you try to repair them."

Bracelets jingled—Rienne, flinching before she composed herself. Neutral once more.

"If you know who we are," I went on, gaining more listeners among the guards too, "if you know where we come from, then you must also know we're not a disturbance—we're the only ones who can *save* your land."

The Council said nothing. Not that I expected them to. There was no dais, but they didn't really need it to look down upon us. Upon me—threatening to undermine and upturn their authority with lash upon lash crafted from harsh truth.

But victory was still a ways away.

"If you know who we are," I repeated, voice lower, colder, yet all the more resonant for it, "then you're well aware we can reunite Svitanye with Somraque and Soltzen, give magic back the balance it's lacking. All we need is your land's fragment of the relic"—a flicker of recognition flashed across all five faces but didn't settle—"and we'll move on. If you execute us,"—I worked a subtle edge into my tone—"the shifts that clearly concern you will remain a pestilence forever. Possibly destroy Svitanye in due time. The only chimes rising then will be the death knell."

Again, something crossed their polished, guarded expressions —an admission that I was *right*; that Svitanye *was* dying and, like Mordecai, they were fighting to keep this remnant of a world together.

"This isn't a battle you'll win if you continue to delude yourselves about the gravity of it—the consequences of *not* accepting the solution when it's standing right before you simply because, what, that would put power out of your hands?" I said coolly, exploiting the Council's weakened stance to move forward. The heavy, stifling silence seeping from my companions suggested I hit more than the Council's nerve. "Magic is the true disease here. It's what's gnawing at your precious stability. And you're using precisely that to fight it, aren't you? Magic against magic?"

When they didn't answer, I carried on. "I've seen a land worse off than yours. Witnessed the hungry, relentless crawl of destruction."

Ice-fire infused my veins.

The nothingness of the Void. The fraying tapestry of power. They were images I could never burn from my memory. Or soul.

"We can put an end to Svitanye's inevitable fall. Just take us to the fragment or bring the fragment to us, and all this"—I rotated my head, the only part of me I could move, from side to side to encompass the room, the volatile land beyond it—"will cease being a problem."

Only nearly imperceptible chimes disrupted the deathly quiet. Seconds dragged as we stared at one other—yet again two opposing forces who should stand together but stubbornly refused to bridge the gap.

I'd opened the door on my—on *our*—end.

All they had to do was cross.

"A touching sentiment," the lavender-haired woman said, long lashes touching her cheeks as she looked down and inhaled —as if carrying a burden I couldn't see. "But even if we were inclined to take the risk and let you live,"—her dark gaze speared me—"the fragment is lost."

Her words pierced me like daggers. I staggered back without truly moving, my pulse pounding in my ears.

"Lost?" That last restraint I'd kept on myself snapped. "You don't *lose* something of such importance. You *guard* it. Protect it with your damn worthless lives."

Ada was staring at me, all color gone from her face. Even Ivarr beside her appeared to be struggling not to recoil. Flee from the thundering storm I'd become. Only there was no shadowfire around me.

Just my wrath.

"How the fuck can you claim to have the good of the land at heart then throw away its one salvation?"

If they knew so much, knew it *all*, the act was inexcusable. More than mere negligence. It was treason to their own high and mighty beliefs.

"And just what is it that you propose? Storing something like that and allowing someone to claim all power?" Annora bared her teeth. There was no warmth left to coat her presence—stripped away as if it had been nothing more than cosmetics to support the impression she'd desired to project. "Our people are *peaceful*. The Council serves the land but we. Do. Not. Rule. Nor will we allow anyone else to. Our ancestors believed the fragment too dangerous. So they cast it away, fed it to the land, and fashioned a world where people could live their lives in safety."

"Safety?" I snorted, then let out a dry, humorless laugh that all but dripped venom. The guards pressed in closer behind me, but whether they were waiting for a direct order, or simply waiting, no gag came. "You dare call this *safe*? By the Sun, I was out there. I experienced the shifts. Your people are *trapped* in the city. There's nothing safe about that. Nothing free, either."

Annora opened her rosebud mouth, but remained silent as Tana raised a pale, tattooed hand. It was almost comical, the elaborate depiction of the sun sending its rays across her forearm. The tip of the moon just beyond it.

"If we allow you to return to Somraque,"—she slid her gaze, now no longer distant, across us all—"will you stay there?"

"If it's the alternative to execution," Ada said before I could answer, "yes. We—"

Chiming. A brisk movement of lips.

Ada's breath hitched, then, as if something had set her body into motion, her words flowed. "We would return the *second* you turned your backs to us. Open a portal away from your city and scour the land for the fragment you would have us believe doesn't exist until not an inch of it remained unexplored. We. Will. *Never*. Give. Up."

Her face went slack, mouth open and eyes wide. Terrified.

"And there is the truth," Tana said softly. Almost regretfully. She looked to Rienne who nodded, those diamonds shining too cruelly against her red hair for the murdered future lying at their feet. "You will be exiled to the Waste within the hour. Maintaining the focus points is becoming increasingly difficult."

That last part was not meant for us.

Maelynn nodded and with a whispered command, brought her chair forward. "I'll take them."

"The guards will suffice," lavender-hair cut in. "You're needed here."

"I know, Iesha." Maelynn pivoted her chair to the side so she could see both us and the Council. "But the shifts giving us difficulty now will be easier to manage once they're out of the city's immediate vicinity." She ran a hand down the lace sleeve then twisted the simple silver band on her finger. "I'm more needed out there than here. The anomaly they present has an epicenter—them. If there's no one to fix the local damage they will undoubtedly cause along the way, it could become irreparable. I'll keep them in check, hasten our travel."

"And you can influence the Waste to make sure there is no chance they can slip through another portal. Or emerge alive," Annora added with a touch of a smile. "You always were efficient, Maelynn."

Maelynn inclined her head, her turquoise-and-purple hair gleaming in the soft light. "Seeing as we're in agreement, I best get ready."

She glided past us, ignoring the guards, and disappeared through the open doors.

An hour.

An hour was all we had before we were to leave for our death.

Even the shadowfire stayed silent.

CHAPTER TWELVE

SNICK.

Darkness engulfed us, but the binds didn't vanish.

Our ragged breaths filled the damp space. We had no use for words. We all knew what this meant.

One hour.

No means of escape.

The pendant rested against my skin, only a trinket without my blood-kissed hand to coax the power out.

My mind reeled.

Then plummeted.

There was no fighting the exhaustion that cast me into violent sleep. The final one before we marched to our deaths.

CHIMES ASSAULTED my ears as we neared the volatile wilderness, Maelynn poised gracefully in her chair at the front, the guards trailing behind us in a semicircle now that we'd left the streets behind. Bound as tightly as we were—just as we'd been in that rotten dungeon—there wasn't much we could do anyway.

I lifted my gaze to the sky when we stopped atop a platform that could only loosely be called a square—perhaps more of a patio, granting an uninterrupted view of the land. The sky was safer to watch.

Saner.

The eternal whispers of the sun slithering across the horizon, the smattering of smoky black that crept over a silver-pink cloud... There was something inspiring in that canvas.

Whereas the land—

The land reminded too much of us.

Fleeting. Powerless. A slave to another's whims.

As if on cue, chimes blared louder from various directions—and were met by a different tune.

The melody rose from Maelynn as she took control over us from the guards. I nearly staggered when the magic left my skin, leaving nothing but my wrists shackled behind my back. It would be a mistake to take it as a gift instead of the warning it was. I'd felt the flavor of her power.

Even with six of us and one of her, she *would* overpower us in a heartbeat unless I released the obsidian shadowfire from my skin. Regardless of conceding to Ada's pleas earlier, I hadn't dismissed the option. After the binds had made it impossible to open a portal when we were left alone in the dungeon, it was starting to become more and more the single viable path to salvation we had left.

Which was why I was saving it for last.

Away from the town, from the Council, we would have a fighting chance.

Maelynn, now clad in a simple, long-sleeved, dark blue dress, turned her back to the landscape and peered past us at the guards. "I'll take it from here."

One of them stepped forward, a movement I heard, not saw, with him at my back. "But—"

"You are dismissed, Ylerian," she said in a voice that managed to be soft and intimidating all at once. Her face showed no emotion as she brought her chair level with us and tilted her head up to look him in the eyes. I chanced a look over my shoulder. "Return to your regular duties. All of you."

Our entourage hesitated, Sylo and this Ylerian more so than the others, but didn't go as far as to question her order, let alone disobey it. One by one they fell back.

Maelynn's sharp gaze didn't leave them until they disappeared out of sight, lost to the city's streets. With a tight expression, she scanned the six of us, then steered her chair forward and tugged us along. None of us struggled, unwilling to relinquish this small liberty of moving our own feet.

Her magic chimed louder the deeper we went into the wilderness and overthrew the different flavor of melodies that rose all around us. In every direction save the one we went, the landscape kept changing drastically. The shifts seemed faster, the pieces of land they brought too diverse to even belong to the same region.

A response to her magic or our presence, I couldn't tell. But I stood by what I'd said to the Council.

Now more than ever.

My one regret was not possessing the power to influence people's minds.

Though I spotted several static points brimming with wildlife, we didn't stop at any of them. A part of me wanted to inquire about the animals, their captive lives here; most of me knew better than to strike a conversation with the person leading us so calmly to our end.

So I resorted to watching Maelynn work, listened to the nuances, to the occasional gentle whisper that flowed to my ears. Although whatever words she was saying became unrecognizable by the time they reached me. I suspected she was somehow influencing which slab of land would settle in front of us. The thought, as fascinating as it was, didn't sit well with me at all.

Given where we were headed, I would have embraced the volatile shifts casting us all over Svitanye with open arms.

An inaudible, acrid laugh drifted through my mind. Such irony.

"Will we at least get one final drink before you leave us to die?" Eriyan groaned as the city winked out entirely in the background. We wouldn't be seeing it again. Not even a silhouette. "I mean, I figure one last tryst is out of the question, but a man should at least kick the can with a good taste in his mouth if not another's lips around his—"

Zaphine shot him an exasperated look that effectively silenced his words, but Maelynn didn't as much as turn around. She merely kept guiding her chair across the patch of grass, then earth, when we traversed yet another seam. There we paused for the first time in this entire journey to allow the land in front of us to change.

A shortcut—it had to have been, with the way the notes of Maelynn's magic became sharper, as if she were drawing a distant piece of Svitanye towards us.

I exchanged a glance with Ada. The grim expression on her face mirrored mine.

None of us knew how long it would take to reach the

aforementioned Waste, but if the councilor could manipulate our surroundings on a scale like this, I was angling towards sooner than we'd like.

AFTER I COUNTED SO many seconds-turned-minutes in my head that the number became too large for me to carry on, I decided the timing was as right as it would get. Even my bladder played along—though, initially, this was supposed to have been nothing more than a deception.

"I have to pee," I blurted out, then looked pointedly at a cluster of spindly bushes just off our track when Maelynn half turned her chair. "Please."

The politeness cut my very soul, but I'd grown up using pretty, empty phrases and polished manners as shields whenever I needed them. Sometimes it was hard to step out of an established mold.

Maelynn pivoted her chair the entire way around until she was able to comfortably meet my gaze. I made sure the pendant remained hidden beneath the loose strands of my hair. No one had paid it any particular attention until now, but I wasn't about to count on luck to glide me over every potential bump.

A bead of sweat wanted to roll down my temple as her piercing gray eyes remained focused on me for a too-long moment—then skimmed the rest of our group, the intensity diverted but not gone. Judging by their reactions, no one was particularly enthusiastic about being on the receiving end of Maelynn's scrutiny.

"Anyone else?" she asked. "We won't be doing this again anytime soon."

It didn't surprise me that Ivarr remained stoic. Given his presence, even restrained, was like a blade thirsting for blood, it would have been too suspicious if we both wanted out of our bonds at the same time.

What I hadn't expected, however, was for Eriyan to speak up.

Maybe it was for the best. His steps had been strained for a while now, and if Maelynn noticed, she couldn't mistake his plea to visit the bushes for the necessity it truly was.

I just prayed to the Sun he wouldn't get any ideas...

"Fine," the councilor said and motioned us to step forward.

Actually, she *yanked* us away from the group thanks to the ropes of magic keeping us bound. Shoulders. Wrists. Waist. A translucent chain between the ankles. Strategic shackles, but ones that couldn't stay on in their entirety if we were to pee.

Maelynn didn't strike me as the kind of person who would lead soiled prisoners across the land.

Then again, the twenty-something *girl* with hair that moved like the ocean and immaculate gold-painted nails didn't quite fit the image of an executioner, either.

Eriyan shifted on his feet. "I really, *really* have to go—"

Whispered words.

A chime. Two.

Then lightness—

Lightness building up inside me before it whisked through me in a way that wasn't uncomfortable, if utterly odd.

Eriyan's jaw went slack, and my own face echoed the expression once realization slammed into my addled brain.

The lightness...

I didn't have to pee any longer.

"What..." I glanced down, then back at Maelynn—as impassive as ever. "What did you do?"

"A simple enchantment to clear the urine from your bladder."

Eriyan flinched one eye. "That's...disturbing."

I couldn't help but agree.

"Where did the urine *go?*" he went on, but Maelynn had already shoved us back with the equally stunned others and spun her chair forward. I probably imagined the smile that ghosted across her lips right before her turquoise-and-purple waves spilling down her proudly held head were all I saw.

Eriyan was still muttering the same question as we waded through the following fourth, possibly fifth section of temporarily tethered land. A different silence settled onto the rest of us. In light of the unnerving *enchantment*, even I almost forgot what experiencing it cost us.

"WE'LL REST HERE UNTIL TOMORROW," Maelynn announced as a ramshackle inn with stone walls and tiny windows came into view beyond some free-growing cypress trees. "The auberge is built on a focus point, like Ausrine—our capital," she added, possibly noting our confused looks, "so we'll maintain our position relative to the Waste."

This was the most I'd heard her speak for the entire trip.

Unfortunately, I didn't have it in me to cheer her news or feel reassured that we'd pick up the next day precisely where we left off.

"Is there food?" Ada asked, a tired drawl to her voice.

She had kept to the back of our group ever since the laughable escape attempt, and I'd walked by myself, in no mood for ever-silent company. Ada had looked worn out before, but the difference now was stark. Sunken eyes. Gaunt cheeks. Her lips cracked as if she'd been biting them repeatedly.

I cut a look towards Ivarr, then Zaphine, Eriyan, Dantos. Fatigue lined all their faces, but none looked as if they were about to keel over at any given moment.

Ada did.

The corners of Maelynn's eyes tightened as she took her in, then nodded. "There will be food."

"Ohh, how *kind*. Our executioner won't let us starve," Zaphine commented flatly under her breath.

I was glad for the fire still alive inside her.

Though Maelynn heard her, she didn't react to the jab. Or paid anything more than passing attention to Zaphine's murderous stare that gave even Ivarr's a run for its money.

Maelynn guided us forward then lined us up into single-file formation when the path curved through an outcropping of rock. The already rich scent of red wine, cheese, and tomatoes intensified as we emerged on the patio beyond the cypresses and the inn's doors opened. Two men clad in demure lilac robes stepped outside, each with a long-stemmed glass in their hand. They claimed the unoccupied wrought-iron chairs on the porch beside a potted plant with sharp green leaves I didn't recognize and started to talk softly.

Merchants.

Merchants discussing how the recent, *unexpected* violent shifts had nearly cast them offtrack when the set travel time between two focus points changed, cut down by a third.

I trained my gaze on the turquoise-and-purple back of Maelynn's head. So perhaps the Council of Words truly hadn't been lying when they said our presence here was disrupting their world. But that didn't annul the fact that we wouldn't, *couldn't* give up. The fragment had to be somewhere. It was ancient. A fundamental part of everything Svitanye was.

The Council was either concealing the truth or they were ignorant. I wasn't entirely sure which was worse.

If the relic were destroyed, the world would have more than likely fallen with it. A body couldn't live without a heart, and that was precisely the fragment's role. No one could have *fed it* to the land.

It was out there—not corroded or broken down by the elements. But whole. Or as whole as a fragment could ever be.

But the piece attached to my thigh was certainly proof enough that something as trivial as time or surroundings was not enough to touch, let alone harm an object that preceded the existence of the entire world.

I let my gaze drift across the cypresses as we passed the merchants—then cast it farther out. To the rocks and fields and lone, majestic trees, here one moment, gone the next.

If I had to dig up every patch of dirt to find Svitanye's piece of the hallow, then that was fine with me.

Contrary to its exterior, the inn's atmosphere was vivacious, cozy, and enveloped us even before we crossed the threshold. Maelynn drifted inside first, followed by Dantos, Eriyan, and Ada, while Zaphine, Ivarr, and I brought up the rear. My stomach growled at the symphony of scents I always dreamed those homes I'd read about in fairytales smelled like.

It was an effort to keep going when all I wanted was to inhale and let the fragrances transport me into a reality that had been a safe haven once. Though with so many patrons milling about, we really had no choice but to move. This was no place for dreams —in more ways than one. If these were the late hours of night I suspected them to be, the people certainly showed no inclination that they were ready to settle down and embrace sleep. The wonder I glimpsed in Zaphine's eyes suggested I wasn't the only one taken by surprise.

Dishes and glass clanked, a myriad of voices entwining with the unobtrusive music weaving from the corner where four musicians had set up a makeshift stage. A couple with beards a matching shade of peach swayed as if they were the only ones in the world. My heart clenched involuntarily.

I was still watching them when Maelynn stashed us at the foot of the stone-and-iron stairs leading to the upper levels—just out of the way enough in case anyone needed to use them. Though the inn was by no means small, we made for a fairly large group in the already bustling space.

Her lips parted briefly as she examined our position, then closed. The following anchor on our binds pinning us to the spot made me wonder if she hadn't been about to *ask* us to stay here —then thought better of it.

"Any ideas?" Zaphine asked as Maelynn maneuvered along the edges of the packed floor—out of earshot.

Ada swayed, but the binds righted her almost at once. I hated not being able to reach out.

"We're not doing anything until we get food," I said.

Maelynn had reached the green-haired innkeeper—a woman with a face that had seen at least seventy summers, yet was all the lovelier for it—who smiled broadly at the councilor. I was surprised to see Maelynn return the expression. Her entire posture seemed to flow into something easier, more relaxed, but when I tested the binds, the magic was just as firm as it had been before.

The pissed-off look Ivarr shared with me revealed he'd come to the same conclusion.

"So we wait," he said.

I dipped my chin. "We wait."

Until the end if we had to. But it wouldn't be *us* dying in whatever that wretched Waste was.

A few of the patrons occupying the center of the room shifted out of the way as Maelynn floated her chair back towards us, providing her with a more direct route. As unproductive as it might have been, I mourned the end of our short reprieve. Maelynn certainly wasted no time steering us around the stairs with a gentle yank.

A corridor opened beneath them. Narrow with a tilted ceiling and slightly crumbling stone walls. No light illuminated its length, leaving the depths a dark maw—until Maelynn squeezed her chair through the frame. Dragging us behind, she progressed down the hallway and—there was no other explanation—*projected* light overhead with whispers that swept across my ear.

As I studied her, I noticed there was less than an inch of space separating the sides of her chair from the rough walls.

I glanced back.

Four bodies blocked off the exit.

The familiar uneasiness crept up the sides of my neck and sped up my heartbeat.

It made no difference that I recognized them, *knew* them. Just as it didn't matter that I wouldn't have been able to run even had the path been clear.

But dry logic, as solid as it was, rarely possessed the strength to break through the fog.

I focused on placing one foot in front of the other. Out of all the things going on, my less than pleasant relationship with confined spaces should have been the least of my worries.

My body, however, had no intention of cooperating.

I focused on the glint of Maelynn's hair, untouched as if we hadn't just crossed the same country; on the present, but not yet too horrid smell of our body odor lurking beneath the inn's fragrance. What I wouldn't give for a bath. Or just a plain bucket of water. Maybe the councilor had a nifty slice of magic for that, too.

The trivial, babbling thoughts acted as a shield against the worst of the panic, but still I sagged with relief when Maelynn magicked open a nondescript door at the end of the hallway and ushered us inside a room. Despite its small size, I noted with gratitude, it wasn't too oppressive. Textured white walls instead of stones, a small window cracked open to let in the fresh air.

Breathe.

I could breathe.

Ada cast me a concerned glance before Maelynn silently commanded us to sit on the large bed that dominated most of the space, but dropped the subject at my decisive shake of my head. I was fine now. And I didn't want my weakness out for the world to see.

When Ada's gaze slid towards Maelynn, mine followed— right in time to see her chair touch the slate tiles.

Wheels formed where there had been only smooth, curved legs before, the transition so seamless I would have missed it had I blinked. Beside me, Eriyan sucked in a breath that didn't quite fit with his jester facade.

We'd seen so much, yet this... It was different.

Maelynn secured her hair into a simple bun then rolled herself across the floor. I could have sworn I spotted a touch of relief in her eyes when she used her hands instead of those whispers—before she altered that rich gray into an impenetrable wall once more. Keeping us restrained, controlling the shifts, and maintaining her chair afloat couldn't have been an easy feat. A sliver of respect kindled within me, but quickly winked out as Maelynn looked at us, every inch the councilor who had agreed to condemn us to death.

"I won't release you,"—she motioned to the invisible binds— "so you have two choices. I can enchant your bodies until you have enough strength to forgo food, or I can feed it to you."

It wasn't much of a choice, really.

Being fed like children was an appalling thought, but I didn't trust magic to provide actual sustenance.

"Well?" Maelynn prompted. "What's it going to be?"

I glanced at Eriyan sitting beside me, half expecting he'd make one of his usual remarks, but all he did was dip his chin. "Food."

The rest of us followed his example.

Instead of heading back out, the councilor *enchanted,* as was obviously the term, a piece of paper once we told her our simple preferences for our food and drinks. We had no menu, but none of us were looking for a gourmet meal, either. Only appetizing, easy to consume dishes—and lumi. That was one thing, one *need* we all agreed to.

Maelynn flung open the door with a whisper, letting in the music and echoes of a far less morbid life, then floated our order down the hallway. How she knew where to guide it without a visual was anyone's guess, but after several awkward minutes passed, the green-haired innkeeper entered with the desired meals. The wrought-iron trolley she rolled in was filled to the brim, and for a moment, I almost regretted agreeing to this.

It was going to take forever for Maelynn to feed us.

And while she would tend to one person, the rest of us could do nothing but watch—or try to ignore just how demeaning this whole situation was.

I craved the serenity of a book perched open atop the table beside me, the uninterrupted view of the night sky beyond...

But that was no more than a dream.

Keeping my gaze firmly before me, I steeled myself as Maelynn approached Ivarr. Sitting on the far end, closest to the window, he was to be the starting point. Somehow, of all of us, it was worst seeing him relegated to such a level.

Once she started, however, bringing bite-sized morsels to his mouth, then carried on the task with the rest of us, there was nothing twisted about the act. No sadistic enjoyment. All I picked up on was a silent compassion that was completely at odds with the councilor who had had us hunted down—not to mention the executioner she was to be once we arrived at whatever, wherever, this Waste was.

I drowned those useless thoughts so they could never resurface. This lull didn't alter our course, and kindness wouldn't release the shackles.

Just because I found someone intriguing didn't mean they were good.

Like before, Maelynn took care of our bladders with her magic after the food and drinks were gone. She then shut the blinds on the narrow slit of a window, bathing the room in darkness with only two strips of light preventing it from reigning absolute. One snaking across our bodies, the other bisecting the room.

I lay squeezed on the bed between Eriyan and Zaphine, the former already snoring in his fitful sleep. The others flanked us

—Ada on Eriyan's side, while Ivarr and Dantos took up the far left. Last I saw before moving became next to impossible, Maelynn had simply propped herself a little more comfortably in her chair, a pillow cushioning the contact where her head leaned against the wall.

But unlike the others, no rest came for me.

Every second I spent with my eyes shut in the increasingly more suffocating room was torture. Too many bodies breathing. Too little space. No way to move.

I hardly even felt the outside air trickling through the window past the drawn curtains.

Just our sentence, hovering over us and gnawing on my nerves.

My hip was starting to ache from the weight—the bed wasn't large enough for us to lay in any other position except spooning. And even that was nothing short of uncomfortable, with our hands tied behind our backs. The binds on our feet also remained, allowing no more than the width of a step, but at least Maelynn had ceased controlling our *entire* bodies.

I turned my outlook around.

The shoulders, the waist—

That was all I needed. This breath of freedom. I could work around the rest.

Shutting down my thoughts as if each thread were a candle I snuffed out, I focused on nothing but sensing the six other people in the room. As my eyes adjusted fully to the darkness, I monitored their breaths, the touch of their awareness or weight of their sleep. With the distance separating me from Maelynn, her state continued to elude me, but during one of those silent moments, when even the echoes of life vibrating through the construction of the inn had faded to silence, I caught the deep breaths.

Her magic held, but the councilor—

She was asleep.

I moved.

Every shift of my body felt like thunder rolling through the room, and every time Eriyan kicked his feet or jerked, I froze, wondering if *this* was the sound that would wake Maelynn up.

None did.

So I kept wiggling my body down while pushing the pendant up, up—

Zaphine's breaths faded, fingers flexing as she readjusted her weight.

My lungs screamed for air I didn't dare accept. If she turned around, she would trample the pendant, cast it back down...

But I couldn't tell her to stop. Couldn't utter a single damn word.

Couldn't stall, either.

My butt bumped into Eriyan's knees as I forced myself to slither faster along the mattress. My dress bunched around me helplessly, the sight becoming one I wouldn't be able to write off as mere restlessness if Maelynn woke. I didn't care.

The pendant was in line with my nose now, half-covered by Zaphine's dark strands.

She hadn't stopped turning, her body almost flat against the bed. I tried to work faster, mindful of Eriyan at my back, but with the limited space—

Zaphine's eyes found mine.

Her face screamed with muted tension as she balanced precariously between Dantos and me. I swallowed a painful cry as Eriyan rammed his knees hard in the small of my back. A string of curses zinged through my mind yet became distant, irrelevant when Zaphine successfully pivoted herself on her side, facing me.

During it all, those intense green eyes had never parted from mine, and I knew—I knew even without the silent conversation weaving between us now why she had risked all of this.

With all the constrictions, I would never have been able to get the pendant over my head, let alone force it down into my hands. Not without the risk of waking Maelynn.

But *she* could.

CHAPTER THIRTEEN

S<small>UPPRESSING THE RUSH OF EXCITEMENT BEFORE IT COULD</small>
birth a mistake we couldn't afford, I gave Zaphine the barest of
nods.

I understand.

I'm ready.

Do this.

Eriyan's bony knees dug into my back again, but his snoring
was consistent, calm—as much as such a thing could be.
Zaphine's gaze flicked to him, as if reassuring herself all would be
fine, then wormed her way lower. I felt more than saw her take
the pendant gently between her teeth, the space between us so
intimate our fears and hopes seemed to breathe into each other.

But this was the easy part.

With the stone-adorned crescent moon peeking from under
her full upper lip, Zaphine's eyes fixed on mine. We held that
moment—stretched it until it offered not just a brief reprieve
from the taxing circumstances, but aligned us.

Her fire. My ice. No gap between us.

Just the sensation that we *would* succeed spreading through my—our—veins.

When the moment broke, as it was always meant to, leaving us stronger, sharper, I lifted my head off the mattress. A sliver of space separated me from the cotton sheet. The most I could do. My already sore neck protested the position, but I maintained it, watching Zaphine guide the chain over my chin, nose—

It hooked on my ear.

A thousand silent curses erupted within me. But Zaphine— she merely frowned, then set the pendant down and leaned over. Her lips brushed against my skin, her breath a gentle kiss as she picked up the chain where it lay across my cheek. Her black hair fell like a curtain around us, but still—a risky move.

If Maelynn woke, even the darkness couldn't conceal what we were doing with Zaphine on the verge of lying atop me. Maybe, if luck had it, we could write it off as a farewell between lovers before they went off to their deaths. Maybe.

The increasingly ragged breaths Zaphine fought to quell whispered a rhythm all too similar to that of my heart into my ear—then the touch of the chain as it slid higher. And higher. Over my brows, temples...

A quick locking of our gazes, and then Zaphine was tugging while I awkwardly wiggled my head and rubbed against the mattress to get the rest of my silver strands out of the way. My eyes watered when a few hairs were ripped from my scalp. Thankfully, Zaphine didn't stop.

With a final yank, she liberated the chain and lowered herself back down, still clutching the necklace between her teeth.

If I weren't already lying down, my knees would have probably given out right about now.

We remained immobile for a long while, waiting for the echoes of our movement to fade into a long gone event.

It was only when I was sure my excitement wouldn't sabotage our efforts that we continued. With Eriyan leaning into me and hogging every new inch of space I cleared, turning in the other direction and climbing higher up was a pain. I kept expecting him to wake up, to hear a startled gasp as I wrenched him from his sleep. I lifted my chin at an uncomfortable angle so I wouldn't crush his face beneath mine, then finished the maneuver.

Faintly, I marked that my muscles were shaking, wound up so tightly it was a surprise they didn't cramp.

I wanted to curse myself for even thinking about it, inviting misfortune when—

Warmth blanketed my bound hands.

Zaphine.

My fingertips connected with her jaw a second before a familiar weight fell into my palm. With a shuddering, shaky exhale, I closed my hands around the pendant and savored its familiar feel, the core of magic nestled inside, stirring in offer to be used.

Not long now.

Zaphine shifted behind me—readying herself for the last part of the plan.

The one I dreaded but knew we had to push through if we wanted to come out of this triumphant.

As Zaphine's nearly inaudible whispers swirled through the stuffy darkness, waking Ivarr and Dantos, I did the same with Ada over Eriyan's sleeping form. The latter I was still wary of startling, but after a few seconds passed and he exhibited no more jerking fits, I pressed my forehead to his. Clammy but smooth.

"Eriyan," I whispered, then, realizing there was one word that would explain everything, one word that had been a constant throughout this mess, said, "Lumi."

His eyes flashed in the somber light, a single corner of his lips upturning into a wan, but tender, hopeful smile.

One I felt with all my heart but couldn't reciprocate. Not when we still had to maneuver ourselves into a formation where everyone would end up touching me.

Just as I raked through the buzzing depths of my mind to figure out a way to get us all to our feet unnoticed, Ivarr whisper-shouted, "I'm staying behind. You move. *Now.*"

The sheer command in his voice had us all sliding towards the foot of the bed.

As the frame creaked and my brain caught up with the price he'd taken upon himself to pay, it was already too late.

Ivarr cleared the bed with efficiency that defied the binds and cast himself through the air—

Straight into Maelynn's sleeping form.

THE SCREAM DIED in my throat and we shot to our feet as several things converged at a single point in time.

Ivarr slammed into Maelynn.

Four bodies enclosed me from all sides.

Magic exploded from the pendant, halting the progress of reality.

"Is the inn under, too?" Ada asked over her shoulder, her unbound hair tickling my nose.

"It's a fixed point. It should be." The tremors in my voice didn't sound convincing. "I hope."

Her fingers dug tighter into the fabric of my dress, pinching skin on my abdomen. "Let's find out."

I released time for the split second it took to kick open the door, then drew on the power again. The clamor from behind had been so brief, a spike in the silence, that it was impossible to make anything of it. I didn't dare look back, though I could have sworn that slight ripple transferring from Dantos's form pressed snugly against my back indicated he'd done precisely that.

But whatever he saw in the dark, he didn't comment.

With the slowness and uncertainty of someone barely learning how to walk, we pushed across the threshold then hobbled down the corridor. Zaphine and Eriyan cursed whenever their bodies, turned outward to maintain the most stable contact possible, scraped against the too-narrow walls, but the sound was a welcomed change. Anything to keep my mind off Ivarr—off what would happen to him once time reverted to its true pace and he would be left alone at Maelynn's mercy. If only he'd moved *away* after tackling her, I would have been able to go back for him once the others were safe. But tangled as they'd been...

Foolish. Brave. Unnecessary.

Dantos leaned into me harder, as if he'd been on the verge of stumbling. "How long do you think the magic will hold?"

Not mine. *Hers.*

"All magic has a range," Ada snapped, though her anger wasn't directed at him. The exact same culprit stirred annoyance in me as well.

Our ignorance of this world, of how it worked, put us at a dangerous disadvantage. For all we knew, the first shift might undo Maelynn's bonds—or we would have to traverse the veil between worlds to break free.

"We'll cross that bridge when we come to it," Zaphine huffed as she leaned back to keep a protruding stone from snagging her in the face.

We heaved a collective breath of relief when we emerged from under the staircase. Then another when the sight revealed the inn and those few patrons who had lingered, drinks in hands, were frozen by the pendant's magic. A quick exchange of glances to confirm we were all still all right was the only reprieve we allowed ourselves.

Hands tightened on me. And I tightened my grip on the elegantly curved silver.

Just a little longer.

We shuffle-walked along the edge of the floor where there were the least obstacles to hinder our progress, then out the door a willow woman held wide open. Her face was turned away —as if she'd called out something to the trio sitting alone on the patio, half-empty glasses of red wine on the table before them.

Feeling hollower and more drained by the moment, I was acutely aware that the power's hold neared its end. The stone path we had taken with Maelynn on our way in wasn't an option with all of us clustered as we were. And even if circumstances were different, it would have taken too long—

"Go left," I commanded. "Hurry."

We pushed ourselves as fast as we could towards the first patch of what, judging by the mismatched flora, was shifting ground just as the chiming rose.

The pendant's power snuffed out.

The land changed.

This time, I didn't bother using the slowing of time to get us across the puzzle pieces of Svitanye. It didn't matter where we ended up, as long as it was *away*.

We held on to one another as if we didn't want to cede a single second that could be spent moving. It didn't even matter that the changes were taking us to new geographical locations all on their own. The act of physically crossing the terrain became synonymous with freedom.

By the third shift, Maelynn's magic dissipated. I stumbled over Ada as she did a head-dive to the ground, Dantos landing on top of me.

But the groan that spilled from my lips as his weight crushed me and Ada's elbow dug into my ribs morphed into a laugh.

Four others joined in.

We lay there just for a moment longer, a tangle of limbs and sweaty bodies—bodies that were finally, completely free. Sun, I hadn't realized just how much I cherished something so simple as *moving*.

As the laughter ebbed, silence crept upon us like mist rising from a lake. I didn't doubt we were all thinking at what price our liberty came.

I'd be damned if we squandered it.

Eriyan seemed to have followed a similar line of thought. He got to his feet and offered a hand to no one in particular. "What now?"

Ada flashed him a tight smile and wrapped her fingers around his. "Now we walk."

WITH NO DESTINATION IN MIND, we traversed Svitanye in hopes of finding a suitable place to hide in, rest for a while.

Eventually find food and water. The meal we'd had earlier wouldn't hold us indefinitely.

There *was* one location where we could get that last in abundance, but—

Returning to the city was out of the question.

What those merchants, the book fair implied... There were other towns to explore, other venues to pursue. We just needed to gather our bearings and figure out where to start, how to get there.

Just the mere thought that there *was* somewhere else to go was enough to drive us forward, regardless of how uninhabited Svitanye seemed at first glance. Regardless of the overwhelming number of unknowns we were facing, too.

"Ada," I said once the newest burst of chimes quieted, "when you spoke of those records your family kept..."

I treaded carefully—not wanting to scrape open wounds the unity that bound us through our escape had closed. The time for that would come. Later.

She peeled away from Eriyan's side and stepped over the raised roots crisscrossing the ground. "What about them?"

"Was there anything else about Svitanye in them? Anything that might—"

"Narrow down our gargantuan search?" Eriyan supplied helpfully while popping open his jacket's buttons.

Zaphine rolled her eyes and rushed up to Ada's side, leaving Dantos to walk with his cousin behind us—though not *too* far. The last thing we'd need right now was to end up separated again.

We walked beneath the massive chestnut boasting a lush green canopy that didn't fit the season.

"You truly think the hallow is somewhere out there?"

Zaphine peered around Ada, then dragged her gaze across the wilderness.

The Council of Words had claimed the fragment was lost, but while I allowed the possibility that they were telling the truth, that somehow their ancestors *had* cast the relic into such oblivion there was no hope of recovering it, it wasn't the version I accepted.

They might preside over Svitanye, have an overview of what went on in this land, but they hadn't even attempted to conceal the fact that they had their own agenda.

Somewhere, there had to be someone who knew of the fragment. Of the past.

We just needed to keep going until we found them.

I glanced at Zaphine, then Dantos and Eriyan over my shoulder, before my gaze landed on Ada's. She needed to hear this more than anyone.

"Yes. Yes, I do."

THE TERRAIN KEPT SHIFTING MERCILESSLY as we progressed, as if the land were trying to expel us, and the chimes sounded so often I hardly paid attention to them anymore.

I'd reached the point where silence would have felt unnatural.

We crossed another patch, this one a vast lavender field that ensnared the senses, three old but healthy chestnut trees standing sentry in what I presumed was the middle. Their bright green leaves swayed in the breeze, as did the lilac flowers, blanketing the ground. A seemingly endless ocean—or at least as endless as the distance to the next shifting strip we were rapidly approaching. Reddish earth and rocks shaped the barren terrain, a lone olive tree with a gnarled, twisted trunk defying the odds by its lonesome.

An image that imprinted into my very soul.

Perhaps more than just mine.

Our steps halted as our feet touched this harsh slice of Svitanye. A smile drifted across my lips.

Circumstances could only define you in conjunction with your desires.

With what you were willing to let in. And what you wished to repel.

I drank in the sight. The ages the olive had preserved here; the blunt, proud defiance; the splash of purple and turquoise—

Someone yelped, but my body was pinned in place, my mind unable to comprehend the information my eyes were feeding it.

Maelynn.

Maelynn was *here*, her chair hovering above the ground and arms crossed in front of her chest.

Annoyance riddled her heart-shaped face as she glared at us. "I'm an Enchanter. A core member of the Council of Words. Did you honestly believe your magic could overpower mine in *my* world?"

Shaking off the stupor, I reached for the pendant, but the blend of exasperation and command in Maelynn's voice cut me off like a sobering slap before I could draw on the power.

"Will you stop that?" She sighed when my fingers curled tighter around the silver, the temporal magic pooling just beneath the surface. "I'm not taking you to the Waste, for Dawn's sake."

I had no idea why, but I obeyed. Let my grip loosen—though I didn't let go entirely.

"Enough games. And you"—*me*—"don't even *think* about trying anything." Maelynn brought her chair closer and leveled her gaze on mine. I might as well have been a child in for a scolding. "That is unless you *don't* want me to help you locate the fragment..."

CHAPTER FOURTEEN

"Isn't the fragment *lost*?" I threw back the Council's own words, not entirely sure why I wasn't pulling the temporal magic from the amulet and getting us away as fast as I could.

We were already in formation.

And we weren't bound yet.

Beside me, Zaphine seethed through her teeth, "If you think pretending to be on our side is going to work—"

"I don't need to convince you to stand down," Maelynn snapped. She dealt us an uncompromising, hard look, and although she was seated, it felt as if she were staring down at all of us.

I recoiled a step—right into Dantos who steadied me with broad hands.

"I have no need for ordinary words to craft honeyed lies when I can shackle all of you with a single whisper." Her gray eyes blazed as vividly as the halo of orange around the rising sun. But when she spoke next, her words were quiet. Deadly so.

"Though maybe I *should* utilize the latter since your recklessness just might make all of my efforts worth shit."

I blinked. The others seemed to have succumbed to the same surprise that swept through me. I doubted I even breathed.

Maelynn's anger pulsed through the dry air, the fact that she was fed up with us plain for everyone to see.

Chimes broke across the silence, rearranging the land.

Maelynn continued staring at me—then down at my fingers hovering over the pendant. Still the binds didn't come.

None of it made any sense, but I managed to recover and, following Maelynn's lead, dropped the volume of my voice. "What are you talking about? What *efforts?*"

The councilor soundlessly crossed the remaining distance between us. Red dust rose with that first push, then settled. Only the barest of movement of her lips revealed the magic she was wielding to make her elegant gliding possible.

Not that working the power took the edge off that sharp, penetrating gaze—but this time, I held my ground against the weight of it.

I wasn't the only one.

"First you want to execute us, now you're claiming you want to *help* us?" Zaphine's tone dripped with incredulity. She came forward so we were standing shoulder to shoulder—a wall Ada filled on my right, with Dantos and Eriyan fortifying the edges. I regretted not being able to give in to the beauty of the moment; how right it felt after all this time.

"The ladies asked you something," Dantos said rather pointedly. Despite it all, I had to fight to keep the corner of my lips from quirking up.

Maelynn looked from him to me, then Zaphine. She briefly

closed her eyes, her nostrils flaring. If she intended to use other means of persuasion—

"Magic can record conversations," she said, her expression softening as she opened her eyes, though echoes of the previous severity remained. She twisted the simple silver band on her middle finger. "We're a long way from Ausrine, but the auberge is a popular focus point. Even now, we're still within its sector. I can't be sure who's listening."

She glanced at the landscape as if the endless shifts were about to deposit us straight on the inn's doorstep.

Which, now that I thought about it, was more than likely the truth given how easily Maelynn manipulated the environment.

I tensed as she let out a quick series of words, the chimes intensifying, and my fingers skimmed the three black stones on the pendant. But instead of connecting with its power, I merely arched my eyebrows and said, "And that matters because..."

I didn't think I imagined the annoyance flash across her heart-shaped face. Good.

Emotions made weaker façades.

Weaker control.

"I can't hold us isolated for long without raising the wrong kind of attention," she explained, perfectly composed. But I saw it for the front it was. She swept her gaze across our faces, our bodies—still poised to react the instant this conversation took a turn we didn't like. "Look, I never intended to take you to the Waste or fulfill the Council's decision."

Ada snorted and muttered, "Decision."

"If what you're saying is true, you're a fucking fine pretender," Zaphine drawled with venom to her voice.

Perhaps it was only the play of shadows from the drifting

clouds overhead, but something shifted on the councilor's face, came to light—a regret, maybe. Or resignation.

"I'm sorry for binding you,"—she thrust a hand in her hair, tangling the purple-and-turquoise strands—"but I *had* to keep up appearances so that no one would question my intensions. But most of all, I couldn't have you running away. Not before you heard me out."

Dantos muttered something under his breath that sounded suspiciously like "You could have written a note."

He had a point.

A single damn note would have solved a lot.

"The fragment..." Maelynn finger-combed the tangle, more a fidgeting gesture than necessity. "I don't believe it's lost. Hidden away somewhere, yes, but not lost."

My fingers fell from the pendant, now brushing the side of my skirt—the fragment there.

"I want to help you find it. Help Svitanye by offering you any aid I can. The fact that you're here—"

"Wait." Eriyan's voice cut through her words.

I peered at him, the sharp, hardened face that was his but so rarely broke through the easy demeanor he wore like second skin.

"How could you know?" he asked. His boots kicked up red dust as he took a demanding step forward. There was something fierce in the way he held himself. Played his height. All those sharp angles. "You weren't surprised when Ember told you she can reunite the worlds, but the prophecy of the Savior"—his gaze briefly flickered to Ada—"came after the break. Came from Somraque."

Impatience flirted with Maelynn's face, but the brunt of my attention was on Eriyan.

I hadn't even considered that. Not when I'd spoken up at our hearing. Not when Maelynn had revealed hidden motivations.

"How *did* you know?" I echoed his question.

"I didn't." A purple strand drifted across her cheek and nose. She shoved it away, gaze alternating between all of us. "I knew it was someone from the group, but not who."

I arched an incredulous eyebrow. For someone claiming every word shared between us could be a potential threat, she certainly didn't mind beating around the bush.

Eriyan raised his chin, arms crossed. "That's not an answer."

I thought that would be the end of the discussion as Maelynn pressed her lips together and stared into the distance stretching behind our backs. I stifled the impulse to follow her gaze. Whatever she was seeing, it wasn't part of this visual reality.

But just as Ada restlessly shifted her feet, the councilor turned to Eriyan. "We don't call her Savior here,"—a lengthy breath comprised of annoyance or exhaustion or a blend of both —"but we do have our own version." She fisted her hands in her lap. "I'll explain it all to you later, I promise. Every moment we've spent talking out in the open is a chance for our conversation to carry back to Ausrine, and that would not end well for any of us. I want to help my home, more than anything. If you can pretend to be my prisoners for just a few more hours, we'll leave the auberge then make it for the river. Once we're across, we can speak freely. Whatever questions you have, I'll answer."

Nothing in her words sounded insincere, nothing to indicate some hidden agenda. If anything, the way her features had closed off when she mentioned helping Svitanye...

Maelynn knew her slice of the world was dying.

In the distance, chimes thrashed.

"What about our presence here?" I couldn't help asking, then added softly, "I can feel it, you know. The impact we have."

Not just her fists, something in her entire posture loosened. "Don't worry about that. I'll fix things along the way, stabilize the worst of it. Once we reach the Cognizance Repository, the protections around it should provide a sufficient buffer."

"Cognizance Repository?" Dantos asked. "What's that?"

"You'll see soon enough." The way her eyes darted behind us made me think her curt answer wasn't because she was fed up with our questions. Not truly. The following quirk of her mouth only supported my theory. "It's safe. And if there's anything, any scrap of paper that points in the direction of the fragment, it will be there." Behind her, the lavender field we'd crossed earlier rose. "We need to go."

Ada who had been uncharacteristically silent so far planted her feet wide and crossed her arms. "No more shackles."

"As soon as we're in the clear tomorrow, I promise. The risk is too great if anybody saw you and reported back." Her gold-painted nails set a series of clicks against the smooth armrests. "Right now, we can return the same way you left"—she shot me a look that was more of a question than a statement, as if she couldn't be certain *how* I got us out—"but it would be too suspicious if we just disappeared in the morning. At least the innkeeper has to witness our departure."

As much as I hated to admit it, the logic behind her plan was solid. I looked at the others—wary, but acceptant. Besides, it wasn't as if we had much of a choice. If Maelynn remained true to her word, our odds of finding the fragment seemed a whole lot better with her on our side.

"All right." Ada relented, then, after locking gazes with all of us, added, "We'll play along."

As Maelynn guided her chair past us, away from the olive tree and the lavender field on the verge of changing, I couldn't help the amusement drifting through my mind. Amusement that only grew when Ada fell in step with the councilor. Still a touch reluctant. Definitely questioning. But also accepting.

A week ago, that had been the two of us.

The thought stayed with me as we cut a path back towards the inn, Maelynn's magic influencing the land and piecing together the shortest route. When the shifts became more volatile, she herded us together, as if the proximity somehow helped lessen the effect. I didn't know the extent of the damage or the intensity of the repairs she bestowed upon our surroundings, but I sensed her intent clearly—a note of warmth and kindness in her whispers, in the answering chimes, too. Even if it weren't for her warning about our words carrying, I doubted we would have walked in anything but silence as Maelynn became concentration personified.

After a few more shifts and a staggering calming of the terrain, the multicolored stones of the inn came into view. The familiar small windows bore gentle illumination, but no more patrons occupied the patio.

Though the building's exterior struck me just as ramshackle as it had the first time, there was something charming about it. A serenity—

"What happened to Ivarr?" I blurted, mortified.

None of us had actually inquired after him.

I hadn't even thought about—

Maelynn looked up at me with unreadable gray eyes and said in a perfectly neutral tone, "Knocked out."

But I could have sworn that had been a smile curving up her lips before she claimed her position at the front of our peculiar parade and led us back to the place we'd fought so hard to escape.

IVARR REVEALED nothing about how the councilor had magic-smacked him into unconsciousness. Nobody probed.

We didn't linger at the inn for long, just enough to let Ivarr in on the plan with as few words as possible and for Maelynn to enchant our bodies with strength to brave the travel. Breakfast was too far off for us to wait.

My sleep-deprived mind didn't even register being suddenly full despite not eating a single bite, though the councilor took care of the former, too, shortly afterwards.

"It's just a balm," she'd said as she enchanted endurance into our bodies, fixed us like she did the land. "You'll almost certainly crash when we reach our...destination."

Needless to say, none of us complained.

When the inn grew perfectly quiet at last and even the innkeeper—Cara, as Maelynn had called her—retreated to her quarters by the kitchen, Maelynn snuck us into the communal bathing chamber. Modesty had no space to rear its head as we stripped and bathed in some kind of hot spring-bathtub combination. If the touch of water hadn't felt so good on my skin, I might have worried about all the filth we were leaving behind.

But the bliss coursing through my veins overpowered all.

TRUE TO HER WORD, Maelynn only bound us once we set foot outside the room when the time for our departure came. The invisible ropes were just as uncomfortable as I'd remembered them, although reminding myself that this was only temporary helped. Just a security measure that would be gone the instant we crossed the river.

Regardless, I counted every step under the dawn sky.

Six hundred fifty-three.

Six hundred and fifty-three steps before the same magic that made it possible for Maelynn's chair to traverse the rough landscape swept under our feet. The river extended below us, its crystal water revealing a bed of endless stone inscriptions. Not a single chime caressed my senses, as if whatever magic the currents sang created a wall that sealed us in from both sides. Only Maelynn's invisible touch remained, the melody nothing more than a whisper maintaining us in the air.

The very instant we crossed the seam between water and land, the chimes erupted anew. Maelynn lowered us to the bright grassy ground, releasing the bonds along the way. I rubbed my aching wrists and stretched the kinks from my back, then met the councilor's gaze.

"Are we in the clear?" I asked.

When she nodded, some of the temper I'd kept under the surface but had fed on all the silent conversations I'd had with myself broke through.

Maelynn's revelation, the bath... Our time at the inn had provided a much-needed reprieve from the endless turbulence, but it hadn't erased the underlying issues. Or my feelings towards them.

Alone with my thoughts, the subjects I'd stashed aside, temporarily glazed over, even detached and isolated themselves

—then evolved into observations and questions and contradictions I couldn't turn a blind eye to. Perhaps it hadn't been the wisest thing, turning them over and taking them apart as I'd counted those steps, but the glaring holes they revealed and the warning bells they rang...

A gust of wind matching the storm within me mussed my hair and tangled with the velvet of my dress.

"There's one thing I can't figure out, councilor." Warmth leeched from Maelynn's face at my tone. "Why did you send the guards to hunt us down if you planned to help us all along? If you knew who we are? What we're capable of? What if the rest of your cronies wouldn't have let you take us away on your own?" I pressed. "Present it any way you want, but it won't change the fact that you. Gambled. With. Our. Lives."

Ivarr cocked an eyebrow as if he agreed, but the others only observed me in silence—as if any moment now, my shadowfire might erupt.

They were wrong.

This was nothing but anger. The remnants of fear I had yet to shed from my system.

It was always after the fact that wounds burned the worst.

"You owe us answers, Maelynn," I concluded, the softness of my voice matching that of my father whenever getting what he wanted wasn't a question of *if* but *when*.

Maelynn looked at each of us in turn. "I do." She spun the silver band resting around her finger. Again. And again. "I'll answer any questions you have"—she forcefully pried her hands apart—"but we should at least keep moving. The Cuer River protects us from the city, but it's the Cognizance Repository that will truly keep us safe. Keep *me* from draining myself."

A chime sounded and three more joined in.

Maelynn threw a hand in their general direction. "You're making a fucking mess of the land."

We glared at each other, two immovable pieces on an ever-changing chessboard.

A hoarse laugh wrung itself free from my throat.

I felt, more than saw, Ada frown. But Maelynn—

Her lips quirked.

"Fine, fine. You made your point." I gestured ahead. "Lead the way, Maelynn."

She inclined her head, nothing concealed or subtle about her smile now. "Please, call me Mae."

ONCE AGAIN ON the move and with the tension dissipated, we went through a round of introductions we hadn't dared make back at the inn, then gradually eased into the subject we all needed to discuss. Our presence here. Her actions. The future we all could share.

Although the imprisonment and subsequent events had brought our world-crossing group closer together, offered a taste of unity, friendship, I couldn't shake the feeling that Ivarr and I continued to stand on the opposite bank of the river as the rest of them. The shady one, where malevolence lurked.

Maelynn, not burdened with the shadows of our past, treated us all equally. But what—*who*—surprised me the most was Ada, attempting to mend the gap and gradually becoming more at ease in my company. Rekindling what we had shared before I had chosen Mordecai.

Before I'd revealed the shadowfire.

More lavender fields rose with new shifts, these somehow

wilder, even less tamed than those in the vicinity of the city. The sky boasted gradients of violet and blue, the emerging sun nothing more than a splash of pale orange in the east.

"I had no other choice," Mae said, drawing my attention from the land as she, at long last, approached the precipice of the largest chasm gaping between us. "I had to act fast." She knitted her eyebrows together and traced a gold nail along the curve of her armrest. "The entire Council of Words was aware something—*someone*—was disrupting the balance. If I hadn't traced the signal back to you, another one of them would have soon enough. I thought..."

She craned her neck to glance at all of us, the apology clear on her face.

"I thought that with you being, in a sense, *my* prisoners, it would be easier to convince the rest of the Council to let me accompany you." A soft chime. A shift. "At least I was right about that. Though I *am* sorry I couldn't say anything sooner. Even sending an enchanted note was too much of a risk in the capital."

"And outside it?" I asked, then, remembering Dantos's comment, added, "How about a regular one?"

We might not have had any ink and paper on the road, but the inn certainly had supplies.

Mae's cheeks burned.

"You forgot that was an option." I laughed quietly—surprised I even *could* when a note would have saved us so much trouble. But there was something about the powerful councilor forgetting such a fundamental thing that made it impossible for annoyance to kindle.

She twirled the ring on her finger and shot me a grateful look when I refrained from commenting. "Yes, even outside Ausrine, it would be too big of a risk with the way information can travel. Just speaking with you as candidly as I did..."

"You fear your own council?" Ada asked.

Maelynn opened her mouth, but Zaphine was faster, "What do you even *do*? The Council, I mean."

"The five of us are the gatekeepers separating Svitanye from utter chaos." Her voice was small, words harboring roots I suspected reached deeper than merely the land. "To answer your question,"—she turned to Ada—"no, I don't fear the Council. I fear their beliefs."

CHAPTER FIFTEEN

WHEN NONE OF US REACTED, STILL BUSY DRINKING IN THE unspoken implications, Mae continued with a bitter smile. "As you might have noticed, the land is volatile. Dangerous. Your presence might have made it more unstable, but it wasn't you who broke it. Ever since our worlds cleaved, it's been like this, slowly but progressively getting worse."

A hint of raspberries drifted through the air, but not even the sweetness of the scent could cover the bitterness saturating her tone. Let alone the quiet sorrow.

"The Council of Words, our magic... It created and continues to maintain every single one of the eight thousand six hundred and nine focus points, save for the Cuer River and the Cognizance Repository. Those Svitanye wrung into existence itself. The rest, however, fall on us to preserve.

"And just like we provide stepping-stones across our world, we hold together the cities, smooth the flow of magic our people generate so that it doesn't create more damage to the already fractured land."

"Odd choice of words," I commented.

Mae's smile revealed she knew precisely what I was referring to. What it meant. *Fractured.*

"I have read extensively of how the world once was." The matter-of-factness with which she said the statement delivered a punch. Not unpleasant, exactly. More of a heavy awareness of the differences between us.

Soltzen knew no past. In Somraque, it belonged to select individuals who'd searched for it and kept it alive; here…

I didn't think it was Mae's position on the Council, holding those gates open.

"I know we're merely an imperfect third," she continued after she brought another bit of land to us—an overgrown vineyard, long abandoned to the elements. "Just as I'm aware that it's because of the fracture"—her gaze met mine—"that Svitanye suffers. But the other councilors… Change terrifies them." The words were spoken almost without inflection, but Mae's face was drawn, the fingers of one hand curved tightly around the armrest of her chair while she tucked her hair behind her ear with the other. "They believe it would only make matters worse."

Ada opened a button on her tunic and frowned. "Even reuniting the worlds?"

"Even that."

"But why?" Ada powered on. "When you could benefit so much from it?"

"Uncharted territory," a voice said from behind.

I looked over my shoulder, surprised that Ivarr had broken

his silence. Of all of us, he'd been the only one who hadn't participated in our conversation except for the bare necessities.

The eyebrow-raised expression on Eriyan's face made me believe I was far from the only one he'd caught by surprise.

Mae held his gaze for a long second before she nodded. "We —the Council, I mean—worked hard to establish this system. Mostly, it works."

"Unless people barge in from Somraque," Eriyan muttered under his breath, but just loud enough for everyone to hear.

A melancholic smile whisked across Mae's lips. "Doing what we do... It takes everything from a person." She pushed on, and we seamlessly fell in step—clustered closely together to make things easier for her. "But the process is familiar and the results expected, guaranteed. To reunite the worlds would mean unraveling this elaborate net,"—she hesitated, as if sampling what she wanted to say next—"*winging it*. The Council is all about structure. You're harbingers of chaos."

There was more to discuss, so much more, but we sailed forward, needing the moments of silence as much as Mae needed to devote her attention fully to the land. She whispered her magic to pave our way, the pieces she brought in front of us breathtaking in their wild, untamed nature. But as beautiful as the view was, the air remained polluted with the poisonous fumes her words, our questions had released into the atmosphere.

Rather than dwell on the subject I could never hope to set straight on my own, I turned yet again to observing how Mae worked. Her brand of magic struck me as delicate, maybe even fragile as it manifested, yet held undeniable strength within.

To say that I was fascinated would be a serious understatement.

And to claim I hadn't been from the very start a lie.

Ada's gaze kept drifting to the councilor as well, her expression holding interest and impatience alike. Surprisingly, she didn't press—and neither did Zaphine, walking by Dantos's side just behind her, green eyes sharp and clear.

When we crossed onto another patch of land, this one enclosed with narrow cypress trees that brushed against the sky, Mae slowed. She glanced back at us, body partially turned. "My fellow councilors refuse to see that the lives we lead here aren't lives at all."

"Because of the shifts?" Dantos pushed to the front of the group and rolled up his sleeves. Where his jacket was, I had no idea. I didn't think I even saw it since we'd left the tavern in Ausrine. I shoved the images of just how he might have lost it out of my head.

While logical, the tactics Mae had employed to get us where we were now would always carry a dark stain.

"For the people, yes. The changes, while manageable, are disruptive. Occasionally even dangerous." Mae whirled her chair around, halting our procession. "But for us... I'm sure you noticed no one on the Council of Words is older than twenty-eight."

I had, although at the time, I hadn't thought much about how young they all looked, with only lavender-hair appearing as if she had a few more years under her belt. But I had good reason for it. A death threat didn't leave much room for...well, anything else, really.

The others appeared as if they were in agreement.

Mae left it at that for now, this new load of implications yet another weight to lug around. But as vague as it was—though not *too* difficult to presume the context—I was glad for the insight.

Mae's chair glided across the terrain with a swiftness that made me think she was trying to get away from her own thoughts, leave them where she'd given them voice. We caught up with her then settled into a steady pace—Ada on Maelynn's right, with Eriyan, Dantos, and Zaphine trailing behind them in a semicircle. Ivarr and I kept to the left.

As the chimes twirled around us and crafted yet another patchwork masterpiece, Mae whispered something intelligible, then said, "The amount of magic we have to expend to stabilize the world is enormous. Without us, their land would be a death trap." She gestured ahead, precisely to where another chime rang out. Grass shot through with gray rocks. "These seams... We have them all under a permanent, complex multi-layered spell fortified with enchantments to prevent them from ripping people apart if one would find themself with one foot on one segment and the other on the next."

To my right, Eriyan sucked in a breath. Our gazes met, and he shook his head, the color drained entirely from his cheeks. Beside him, Zaphine and Dantos seemed just as pale. Ivarr cursed.

None of us had even *considered* that when the land cleaved, our bodies could have, too.

We had been lucky—so damn lucky these enchantments and spells were in place. The bisecting realities I'd seen when I'd slowed the shift crashed into my mind. To be caught in the middle of that—

"You do all of that through your magic? Just the five of you?" Ivarr asked, rubbing his fingers across the slight stubble coating his chin, as if he couldn't quite comprehend how such a feat was even possible.

He wasn't the only one.

Mae inclined her head, no pride—nothing but a distant sadness turning the gray of her eyes more vibrant, if darker. "The focus points, the seams, the shifts... Every second of every minute of every day for as long as we serve."

"Why wouldn't you accept more into the Council?" Ivarr waved an elegant hand. "Spread out the work?"

A half-smile touched her lips. "The system, at the very beginning, was created for five powerful individuals. Two Spellweavers, two Enchanters, and a slot that can be filled by either." She twisted the silver ring. "The reins of our control wouldn't be as tight with more people joining. And to change the entire net of magic, tweak it..."

She didn't have to say it. Her earlier words on the Council's inflexibility were still very much alive among us.

"We have established rotations so that we can sleep, cover for someone in case we're needed elsewhere, but those few hours of repose aren't nearly enough to replenish what we pour into Svitanye. Becoming one of the Council—it means wedding death."

The soft cadence of her voice was almost too much to bear. I couldn't tell what was worse—the defeated acceptance or the suppressed glimmer of hope.

If we succeeded...

"No one but the strongest Enchanters and Spellcasters work on the Council," she went on, gaze trained on the landscape. "But even so, in all our history, there have been only two who lived over thirty. At twenty-eight, Iesha has already had a...a longer life than most." She shrugged dismissively, but there was no mistaking the sheen in her eyes. "I know it's just a foolish dream, but I would very much like to see nine more years, if nothing more."

"It's not a foolish dream," someone said. It took me a moment to realize that person was *me*. The words spilled into the air as if they'd had a mind of their own. "I've spent all my life entertaining thoughts no one believed would accumulate to anything but a waste of time."

No one save for Magnus. Then, once I found myself under that starry sky—

The part of me I'd locked away after Mordecai had cast me from his side cracked, the contents seeping out, reassessing themselves in my core. They wouldn't leave again.

"I imagined there was more to our existence than a sun-kissed land and rigid, wretched rules no one questions because that simply *isn't done*. I imagined there was more to life than following a role I was assigned to whether I wished it or not." The icy lake woke, every coil of it a caressing murmur. "I imagined the beauty of the night, the calm touch of darkness beneath endless stars where who you are doesn't matter. For eighteen years, nothing changed. Until it did."

Without conscious thought, I approached Mae and entwined my fingers with hers. She tightened the grip. "Dreams have power. Don't give up on yours just because others would have you believe they do not."

Mae swept the moisture from her eyes with a blink of her long lashes, but the dip of her chin she offered was laced with strength. I retreated, joining Ivarr to escape the unguarded looks that were far from negative yet too much for me to handle after laying myself bare like that, when Mae's voice drew me back.

"Your presence here—" She shook her head, then, after a

sobering sniff, started anew. "Trust me when I say I'm willing to do *everything* I can to help Svitanye. And that means helping you. I'll get you the fragment, Ember, protect you until you can set off onto the next plane. The Council is merely masking the illness. I want to cure it."

WE CARRIED ON IN SILENCE. There were still so many facets of Svitanye, of their society, that we were unaware of but might help us in the long run—not to mention *how* Mae knew of the prophecy when the Savior was a concept belonging to Somraquians—but for now, we were content with sharing a common goal. And the passion to reach it.

The rest would ensue once we settled at the Repository.

With my gaze trained on the flush of colors drifting across the horizon, the odd puffy cloud that looked as if its edges were alight with fire, I forgot about the shifting land, about everything, really, and let my mind run free.

Our group was still cleaved in two, with Maelynn a bridge between us, seconded by Ada's attempts, but the atmosphere was less strained now, the gap a leaping distance instead of a ravine. I suspected the absence of shadowfire had a lot to do with it.

Without the obsidian strands coiling from my skin, it was easier for them to pretend I wasn't a killer. Easier for me, too.

Yet whenever I tried to attune myself to the person I had been before Mordecai, I failed.

That girl was gone.

If she had ever even been anything more than a front, shielding what lay beneath until the time to emerge was right.

The land shifted before I could delve down that particular rabbit hole, and Maelynn's relieved laugh scattered the remnants of my thoughts. She gazed at Ada who was walking half a step behind her, then pivoted around to face me, a smile bright on her lips.

"Welcome to the Cognizance Repository."

She'd made it seem as if we were headed to some far-off library. But what I couldn't stop staring at wasn't the image my mind had supplied. Not a library—

The Cognizance Repository was a sprawling estate filled with lush greenery, trees that ensconced the impressive castle resting at its heart. Larger than Mordecai's palace, larger than any structure I'd ever seen. And, as we strode through the majestic iron gates then across the luscious garden, my feet almost stumbling on the gray stone path, I realized that every inch of the building was composed of carved words, some visible from afar, some merely blurs of scripture readable only from up close. Some even beyond that.

I'd seen this—on leaves and bark, on stones at the bottom of the river, and on dainty petals... But never on buildings. Never where wilderness didn't reign.

"What *is* this?" I whispered, the palm of my hand warm against my chest.

The paths, the plants, the trellises—written magic was *everywhere.*

Mae's lips quirked up, her eyes the softest I had ever seen. "It's home."

CHAPTER SIXTEEN

I HADN'T FELT THE TEARS STREAM DOWN MY CHEEKS UNTIL Ada's fingers curled around my forearm. Her gaze seared my skin, and I opened my mouth, waiting for words to spill out— but in a courtyard dominated by them, I had none inside me.

The soft rustling of scriptured leaves washed over the distant chimes, their brilliant colors drawing the eye as completely as their serene presence drew the heart.

Ada's warmth seeped through the velvet. No longer a question but—companionship.

For the first time since we had arrived in Svitanye, a sense of calm settled inside me. Not the wholeness of releasing my obsidian, or the wonder that had gripped me when I watched people shop for books in town as if they were the grandest delight. This serenity rose from the depths of my soul, maybe from a place beyond it, and filled me to the point where all I wanted to do was kneel on the word-patterned light gray stones, place my palms flat upon their ancient surface, and weep. As if the Cognizance Repository, with its magic untouched by the volatile nature of the world, was a force too vast, too venerable for a single person to contain. To even carry a sliver of it within our stained hearts.

"Ember, what's wrong?" Ada asked, voice more attentive than I'd heard in a while. It wrapped me in silken ribbons and lured me back to the surface.

The jade of her eyes concealed nothing. She might not have been touched by the Repository's presence the same way but—

This moment between us was pure.

Unable to form a reply that would encompass the truth—I refused to settle for a lacking "I'm fine"—I touched my fingers to the hand she still had wrapped around my arm, then looked past her to Mae.

The girl, less and less the cold councilor we'd met in that semicircular chamber, was observing me as if she knew precisely the impact this place could have on a person.

On me.

A gentle smile curved up her lips. She nodded, our silent conversation weaving through the honeydew-and-lavender-tinted air.

She did.

Mae knew the effect, had *lived* it. Even now, the tendrils of tranquility softened her features. On the backdrop of magic and rosebushes and fig trees, she was luminous. I returned my attention to Ada and gently squeezed her hand.

When she snapped her head back around, she looked as if she, too, had been enchanted by Mae's transformation. I offered her a nod—all she needed to know that I was all right. The corners of her lips quirked up, and she stepped away as Maelynn guided her chair over. But didn't go far.

"This is your home?" I croaked, then winced. My voice seemed too loud, too rough for this magnificence that was somehow peaceful and fragile and vibrant and eternal all at once.

"I grew up here." She trailed her gaze over the rippling blades of grass, the lavender-rimmed stone wall, the red and pink roses climbing up the sides of the Repository. "The librarians took me in after I was orphaned during a spike in the shifts just a little over eighteen years ago."

Eighteen years.

The pool of serenity froze over, cracks spreading across the merciless ice.

Deep within, the icy obsidian lake stilled, too, as if my entire existence hung—

"The Winter Solstice?" Ada rasped. She looked to me, then back at Mae, voice louder now. "Was it during the Winter Solstice?"

"How did you—oh." Maelynn's wide gray eyes met mine. "Oh. Was that—was that when you were born?"

Bile splashed at the back of my throat, my body a stiff, crawling prison. "How many died?"

Zaphine's and Eriyan's laugh twined through the scented air from the bench by the entrance they were currently occupying, Ivarr a slash of darkness halfway between here and there. As if he sensed—

Wind wrapped around me from behind, tossing and tousling my silver hair, but I felt nothing of its touch on my exposed neck.

All my mind allowed through its bent, unraveling gate was the sight of Maelynn.

Her downcast eyes.

The dark blue sleeves of her dress she tugged on before she pushed her hair behind her ears and lifted her gaze once more.

She looked as if she were about to twist the truth. Or refuse to answer. But whatever desperate plea she saw etched in my face overpowered the notion to spare me.

"Hundreds," she whispered. Her eyelids fluttered shut. A heartbeat. Two. "What the Council does, preventing two planes from cleaving a person apart when they shift..." She twisted her ring—a keepsake from her parents? "The spell failed. They died instantly."

That last was a lie. I could taste it in the air, the falseness. Unless they were ripped clean in half, unless something vital had been claimed by both segments of the land, they had felt every agonizing moment of it.

I whirled on Ada who instinctively took a step back. "You said Somraque felt my birth. Was that just a nice way of saying my existence slaughtered your people, too?"

A pained expression pulled on her features. Her gaze darted between Mae and the others, now deathly silent. But when no one as much as breathed, she pressed her lips into a tense line and faced me like the natural-born leader she was.

"I didn't know. I didn't know, Ember." She kept her voice steady, as if something like that could prevent the accumulating scream within me from tearing my sanity apart. Tearing the world apart. As was, apparently, my destiny. "Everybody assumed the Crescent Prince lashed out after Telaria protected you."

Not even the moniker, the image wrought of night and moonlight it conjured could slash through the adamant caging me in.

Though knowing the mark he'd been given should have stained *my* soul did sting.

"What." I bunched my fingers into fists. "Happened."

"An influx in madness."

I flashed back to Nysa, to the woman in the alley when Zaphine and I had slipped through the back door of the tavern in the brothel-dominated district.

Blood and darkness. Salvation not hurt.

She hadn't been wrong about the former. My lethal gift to them was nothing but blood and darkness.

But salvation—

"I pushed them over the edge," I said flatly, distantly, from the one place that didn't rage when all around it thrashed and thundered. "Those who were already struggling with their magic... I broke their minds."

Not a Savior. I was *poison*.

Maelynn reached out and took my hand in hers. I ripped it from her grip.

"I don't blame you, Ember." She glanced down at her hands, shook her head, then fixed me with a stare carved from stark sincerity. "*No one* could blame you for something you had no control over."

She glanced at Ada who nodded and said, "It's not your fault."

But the others were pale, pale shadows—frozen canvases among too much life. I didn't want to think about who they'd lost—who I had taken from them.

The final bubble still left untouched within me disintegrated.

I craved for the dark torrent to claim me. To end this.

A strong arm wrapped around my shoulders and held me above the surface.

"Give us some time." Ivarr.

He drew me away without waiting for a reply.

How my legs could work when I felt nothing yet splintered under the churning weight of everything, I didn't know. But Ivarr's arm—as much a comfort as it was support—kept me close to him; kept the putrefying pieces of me from scattering on the wind. He led me into a grove of birch trees, far enough off the path that no one could see us. And that I saw no one.

After he eased me down against the striped trunk, he leaned back on one hand beside me, the scripture-ridden grass a soft carpet beneath us. I didn't even have it in me to run a finger across its blades.

But as time passed with Ivarr gazing into the distance yet somehow being *here*, I found my lungs had cleared. The now faint honeydew scent free of the sour taste.

"I don't—" I tried, then cleared my throat, tracing the silver stars embroidered on the velvet dress with a trembling finger. "I don't know what to do."

Ivarr brought one leg up, arm resting casually over a bent knee. "You don't surrender. Even when your nails chip and bleed from clawing at the dirt that wants to put you under, you don't give up."

I shook my head, but his voice stole away my denial. "You're marked by your past, but it doesn't govern you. Don't give it that strength. Don't let it suffocate your potential."

What potential? I wanted to say. *Of a Savior whose very existence is death?*

But all I did was stare at the tip of a wisteria-bedecked trellis, the swaying purple a near-perfect match to the sky beyond.

No warmth or wonder stirred inside me but...

I didn't feel *nothing* either.

"Killing is easy," Ivarr said after a fashion—a quality to his tone that disabused me of any notion to question the statement, counter it. "Or it becomes easy, at least—as brutal as it sounds." He shrugged. "It's the lives we never meant to take that spread like fucking parasites through our conscience. I wish I could burn the damn thing from me sometimes. But I don't think I'd like who I'd become."

"A monster?"

"Ember." He placed a finger under my chin, and with gentle pressure turned my head until I had no choice but to look at him. "We're all monsters. The world won't let us survive otherwise. But we're not dispassionate. However damaged, we still have hearts."

CHAPTER SEVENTEEN

A SLENDER MAN IN FLOWING TURQUOISE ROBES LINGERED AT the edge of the surprisingly airy stone enclosure I sought refuge in after Ivarr had left to check on the others—which was a perfectly reasonable excuse to leave me alone. We both knew I needed it.

I kept my gaze on the tree, on the leaves with scripture extending from end to end. To see what the young man would do, yes, but also to let my mind tackle a puzzle that had nothing to do with my existence or the path still ahead. I cocked my head to the side and narrowed my eyes.

Unlike in the wilderness or the grass I'd sat on earlier, the bark of the birch I'd rested against, the words weren't blurred or too small to read. Whereas the former had given me an impression the writing was not intended for our eyes, these leaves of a peculiar shade of green shot through with blue suggested otherwise.

It was certainly new that the sentences, although in a

language I didn't know, flowed through my mind with ease. I wondered if it would be the same for others—or if it was just the latest in the long line of Savior things.

I ran my hands down my arms, wishing to rub away the chill that had infested my flesh earlier.

Despite Ivarr's words and comfort, despite deciding to not surrender, a kernel of ice remained. I doubted even the heat of sowhl could make as much as a dent in that glacial core. Doubted anything ever would.

I flattened my palms against my sides—the left brushing the fragment—to rein in the temptation of curling into a ball on the floor and just wishing the world away.

I was past that.

Ivarr had highlighted the way forward, and I meant that first decisive step that took me along it—just as I did the following ones. But I was also tired, a bone-deep weariness weighted on my limbs and made even standing here an effort.

A single green-blue leaf detached itself from a low-hanging branch. I tracked its descent as the fresh, clean-smelling wind curving around the Repository's corner sent it on a spiraling path towards the ground. Its slightly jagged tip caught on the edge of a chiseled word as it landed on the white stones. Curious, I leaned over and picked it up.

Although it felt just like any regular, healthy leaf to the touch, there was something about it—something besides the markings—that made it impossible to mistake this piece of nature for what it was. Magic.

Turquoise shimmered to my left.

I'd forgotten about my observer.

He approached with the gentle caution of someone who didn't want to startle a distracted mind. The swish of his robes blended with the rustling foliage, then quieted as he stood beside me, facing the same direction, our bodies a small yet respectable distance apart. I ran my thumb along the leaf's soothing texture, then partially turned and offered it to the young man.

"No, no..." He shook his head, his narrow, kohl-lined blue eyes piercing under thick, dark lashes. "The spell—it belongs to you."

It chose you, was what his smile was saying.

The thought was almost too much to comprehend in my still tentative state, so I asked, "This is an actual spell?"

Then nearly rolled my eyes at the question.

At least knowing I could feel like a complete ass for asking something I already knew meant the ice was thawing—I hoped.

But the man didn't seem annoyed. He waved his hand towards the tree, the light opal on his ring finger catching my eye with its demure beauty. It fitted, somehow, with the tranquility of this enclosure with its sole tree and white, scriptured stones.

"This is a spell-tree." He gestured towards the small leaf I now clutched with both hands. "And *that* is a spell-leaf. I admit, for a people who are so fundamentally tied to words, the lack of imagination our ancestors used while naming this is jarring."

Mirth touched his eyes and pronounced his curved cheeks. Another layer of ice within me receded.

"At least it's accurate, right?"

"Stripped of embellishments, things usually are." His gaze dropped back to the leaf, the smile still lingering on his lips. "Keep it safe. The tree doesn't shed these things often."

I opened my mouth to offer the spell-leaf back to him again. I supposed a part of me *was* from this world, and the affinity I felt for the lovely blue-green thing in my hands backed up the claim. But taking something they considered precious still made me feel like a thief.

The stranger, however, stopped me before I could as much as utter the first syllable. "You're Maelynn's friend—and a daughter of three worlds with the essence of balance-keepers. Please do not decline this small token of ours."

Speechless, I could only stare after him as he made for the single path leading away from the enclosure, the midnight blue waves of his hair mirroring the languid movement of the sea that felt as if it belonged to an entirely different lifetime.

I WAS STILL OBSERVING the spell-tree, still feeling the presence of the small leaf that I'd stuck in my bra for safekeeping, and sifting through the tangled layers of myself, when Ada called out my name.

As if the enclosure were sacred ground, she didn't enter, merely waved me over when I turned—a question, not a demand. But I'd spent enough time with nothing but the breeze keeping me company. I joined her on the path curving among the bushes, and we continued down the stones towards the Repository's main entrance together.

Our steps tapped a steady rhythm against the stones—then gravel, as we crossed beneath an iron trellis to meander past topiaries shaped in abstract forms pleasing to the eye. A tabby cat darted in front of our feet and, just as fast as it appeared, vanished into the shrub lining this small section of the garden. I smiled at the jostling bushes, and when I glanced at Ada, her expression mirrored mine. Not carefree but—a beginning.

"The librarians agreed to let us stay here," she said softly, ignoring my previous meltdown entirely—something for which I was more grateful than I could ever convey. "Mae explained that they tend to keep their distance from the Council, as the Council does from them."

I recalled how the people had steered clear of Mae and the Council's guards when they'd led us through the city. They might have trusted the Council to run their land, to keep them safe. But they weren't at ease around them.

We exited the topiary garden and circled back to the path.

"Any particular reason?" I asked.

"Something about a collision between those who catalog the past and those who're creating a future through nourishing the present."

I stopped in my tracks. "Catalog the past?"

"Yes." With Ada's gentle prompt, we continued our languid stroll. Glimpses of the others came into view up ahead. I instinctively sought out the dark glint of Ivarr's hair. "Apparently, the Repository has chronicles my ancestors would salivate over."

Though she said that with humor, I didn't miss the tremble in her voice.

I had no sympathy for Telaria after what she had done, what her recklessness had inadvertently caused—but I knew Ada cared.

Cared more than Telaria deserved.

"The Cognizance Repository harbors every spell and enchantment known to us, as well as a grand collection of various literature," a voice said from behind. Both Ada and I jerked. "But they also keep records of all that has happened."

I hadn't seen Maelynn, but now that my heartbeat calmed and I peered behind her, there was a small rest area cocooned in blooming roses that must have kept her out of sight. A low laugh escaped my lips.

"Did you plan to ambush us?" I arched an eyebrow.

Mae's sly smile was answer enough. "Maybe. Though, really, I wanted to catch you up on what I already told the rest before we head inside." She set the cat that had been curled up in her lap on the ground with a parting kiss, then glanced at Ada. "I'm not sure how much attention this one was paying."

Ada bristled, but couldn't keep the corners of her lips from quirking up.

"Besides, the enchantment I used to keep you all going won't last forever."

She said it as if she knew *precisely* when it would unravel. Maybe even at her own command.

Ada must have picked up on the nuance in Mae's tone, too, because she narrowed her eyes at her and asked, "You mean to drop us?"

Mae snickered—actually snickered. "I think you all will be just fine on your own. But maybe just a *little* push..."

Though I hated to interject, curtail the banter that breathed normalcy into the air, the desire for answers was a burning need within me that refused to be ignored. "So the records of the past... That's how you hope to uncover the fragment's location?"

Mae nodded and guided her chair forward. Ada and I walked with her, each on one side. "I've read accounts about the time after the break. How Svitanye adapted, how they even came to realize what had happened—which had been through the fractured third of the hallow. But I never got farther in my studies than that; focused more on the shifts and the land itself than a relic which, at that point, wasn't...a viable way of healing our world."

A lump formed in my throat. Of course she'd focused on the land when, though not entirely by itself, it had claimed her parents' lives. Claimed hundreds.

"What happened to the fragment has to be noted somewhere," she went on. "These books—some are written by hand, others through magic that is entwined with Svitanye's essence, marking down most of what happens. Here and there, things slip through the net, but for the most part, the power is accurate. It will all come down to figuring out which chronicles to peruse."

Meaning we might be here for a while.

It struck me as odd that references to the fragment wouldn't be bound separately and stored in some easy-to-find, if perhaps secure, place, but even before I could open my mouth, I realized that it might *not* be that unusual after all. If Svitanye never sought the Savior like certain bloodlines in Somraque, then why pay so much attention to a fragment when you had the entirety of history to store within your walls? After all, the latter was a concept my worn out mind still struggled to process.

"And the Council will leave us alone here?" My elbow brushed against a rose as I stepped around a wall lizard that showed no inclination of moving from its spot directly in my way.

Mae slid her attention from the lizard and glanced up at the impressive castle walls. "At least for a while. The natural protections will block your signal, so unless you venture beyond the river—the Repository's walled perimeter, if we want to play it perfectly safe—you should be fine."

It didn't escape me that she'd said nothing of herself.

"What Ada said is true," she continued. "The Repository and the Council don't see eye to eye. The librarians believe that if the leading five would pay more attention to the past, they might learn something they should—or shouldn't—do in the present. Mistakes. Patterns. Ideas." She exhaled and peered at me. "I agree with their views and theories, but since being appointed to the Council..." She shook her head and spun her silver ring. "It's a good notion, but one that's impossible to execute. Keeping the world together takes *everything* from us. I'm just grateful for the childhood I had, sifting through tomes and gathering as much knowledge as I could. Most of my fellow councilors weren't as lucky."

We were nearly by the others now—Eriyan gesticulating something and sending Dantos and Zaphine into soft bouts of laughter while Ivarr's gaze was on me, scanning to see if I was all right. I inclined my head in answer, then turned back to Mae.

"Did you know?" I asked. "That you would be on the Council?"

A sadness swept across her lovely features. "No. No one does." Her smile was bittersweet. "There's no school or training or some apprenticeship program to take us into the fold. The magic simply points to the strongest replacement when one of us dies."

A chill crawled down my spine. "You have no say?"

"Our lives are chosen for us," she said with a shrug. Her lips briefly twisted to the side, then those gray eyes found mine. "Although I suppose you know well enough how that is."

The quiet in her words stopped me in my tracks. "You never said—"

"How I knew you were..." Her gaze cut towards Ada who spun around to face us—just a little ways ahead. "Savior, you call her?"

More than likely overhearing the turn our conversation had

taken, the rest of the group pooled around Ada and spilled onto the wide mouth of the path. I inched a little closer to them, but kept a buffer of air between us.

Company, I could handle.

A crowd at my back...not so much.

As Ada nodded, Mae folded her hands in her lap. A whisper of a smile softened the corners of her eyes as she tilted her head lightly to the side. "If I recall correctly,"—her gaze swept across us all—"you mentioned a...prophecy?"

"Of the One who will reunite the worlds, yes," Zaphine pitched in.

I pursed my lips as a thought wormed its way to the forefront. "You don't have a prophecy, do you?"

"No."

"Then what?" Ada crossed her arms. A hint of impatience had crept into her tone, but Mae didn't seem to be offended.

A cunning, smug smile curved up her lips. "Theory."

CHAPTER EIGHTEEN

"Theory," Zaphine repeated, enunciating the word in a way that made her disbelief perfectly clear.

But if Mae was in any way bothered by it, she didn't show it. She simply picked up the ginger cat that had padded back to her side and stroked it behind its ears.

"When the break happened, people wondered how any of it was even possible. The fragment you seek provided a more than solid basis, a miniature version of the state of our world—or at least an approximation of it. The inscriptions pulsed with power while the other two magics... They weren't gone, but they *were* muted." She petted the cat absentmindedly, a furrow between her brows. "I can't recall all the details as it's been a while, but their study of the fragment led them to craft theories." The cat purred, and a wan smile touched Mae's lips as she glanced down at the cuddly creature. "The people back then—they weren't inclined to leave Svitanye as it was and worked hard to return it to its original state. But the more their theories developed, the clearer it became that it would take a very special, *very* specific person to achieve what they wanted.

"With only our native magic capable of existing in this ripped-out version of Svitanye, they suspected the same held true for Soltzen and Somraque. And if magic was needed to restore order, then so was a person who wouldn't lose it depending on the land." She met my gaze. "Do certain facets of your power feel stronger on native soil?"

I opened my mouth, ready to say that I hadn't exactly had the opportunity to test it out—or the means, with my power all but locked until I arrived in Somraque and no true blood magic running through my veins, not like what my companions had, to even experience how *that* felt. But I realized that was a lie. There *was* something I'd tried out—in all three worlds, actually.

My pendant.

I skimmed its delicate shape with my fingertips.

Although the artifact belonged to the Ancients, its temporal and geo-power was Soltzenian in nature. I recalled the almost sluggish way it responded, the lack of depth to its capabilities here and in Somraque...

I nodded and dropped my arm. "My object-based magic was strongest in Soltzen."

Mae's eyes gleamed. "But because you're a child of *all* worlds, it didn't wink out entirely on non-native land."

"And that was the theory," I concluded, the parallels between their rational explanation and the prophecy unmistakable. "The only way someone can bring the lands together is if they cannot only travel, but *function* in said lands."

The ability to use magic across the fractured world wasn't just some trait that marked me for who I was, a way to identify the Savior. It was a necessity.

"Unbelievable," Eriyan muttered, exaggeratedly crestfallen. "This is just like when you learn it's not the stars dropping from the sky to leave you birthday gifts when you sleep."

Someone let out a sound that was a blend of a snort and a chuckle. Ivarr, I suspected, by the amusement in his green-brown eyes when I glanced at the group.

Maelynn's lips quirked. She arched an eyebrow, meeting my gaze before she turned to Eriyan—to all of them. "Wouldn't you rather know the truth than believe a pretty lie?"

I held my breath, but the only answer that came was the cat's drawn-out *meow*.

A FOCUS POINT potent with magic *beyond* the one holding the point together was a conundrum my mind couldn't explain with the pitiful amount of knowledge I had of this world. That my body somehow *felt* the stability wrought of powers that should have caused the Repository to fracture and alter made matters worse.

Though after the conversation we'd had earlier, I was grateful for the distraction.

Soft chimes ebbed and flowed in lovely currents as we crossed the grand hall, open to reveal the many levels rising above us beneath a vaulted ceiling. Wide, spacious corridors, illuminated with the same gentle yet bright light I'd seen Maelynn use, spread out on the sides, large double doors resting up ahead. Barely a glimpse of the Repository, yet my appreciation was a living, breathing thing that filled depths and crevices within me I'd believed the emptiness would never release from its talons.

I couldn't imagine what it would be like once we actually set foot in one of the chambers where the Repository stored its many tomes.

Our little group with Mae up front climbed up the winding ramp I suspected was made to accommodate chairs like Maelynn's on the occasion the person in it wouldn't or couldn't use magic to keep it afloat. Actually, as I observed the distances the hallways uncovered and spied open chambers within them, the entirety of the interior seemed to be without stairs or raised thresholds, the castle built for easy access despite its many floors and wings. I hadn't seen anything quite like it in Svitanye *or* Somraque.

"The librarians have given us free use of the rooms in the east wing on the third floor," Mae explained right on that last bend before the aforementioned floor. "Everyone has a chamber of their own with a small en suite, but we'll have to take our meals downstairs in the common hall. Only the head and senior librarians have full apartments."

"We didn't even expect to remain breathing for more than a couple of days," Dantos commented. "I think we can live without a personal kitchen."

Mae smiled, though there was an apology in her eyes. While we *had* cleared the air between us for the ordeal she'd put us through in Ausrine, it was nice to know she hadn't just brushed the incident aside.

"The keys are in the locks if you want to use them, though everyone here respects privacy, so just pick whichever room suits you best and it's yours." She paused, amusement framing her features. "Except for the one at the end of the corridor. That one is mine."

"Your old space?" I asked as the ramp smoothened into a

landing and we made for the eastern hallways. I trailed my fingers along the ornate stone walls, the inscriptions pleasant grooves against my skin.

"My old space." Her teeth sank into her lower lip. "Not so much for sentimentality's sake than to keep you from seeing the collection of smutty books I kept under my bed."

"What, the librarians didn't clear it out?" Zaphine arched an eyebrow, and Mae scoffed.

"I asked a Spellcaster to set a ward around the books. The librarians would probably fight to the death over the collection if I'd left it there for the taking." She chuckled. "We all appreciate a good romance."

"The hotter the better," Zaphine agreed under her breath.

Eriyan groaned while Dantos—and even Ivarr—chuckled.

The first of the paneled light blue doors with a key in the lock appeared on the right, an identical one a little bit ahead on the left. The pattern continued to the very end of the corridor where a single door faced us head-on. Mae's room, I presumed. We all looked at each other, but when no one wanted to go first, I snagged the white iron key and palmed it.

Ada flashed me a grin, one of those she used to back before everything went to shit, but even though she eyed the door diagonally from mine, she didn't claim it. I didn't think it was because she didn't want to be near me.

But she clearly *did* want to be near someone else.

I glanced at Mae who was pretending not to watch Ada— pretending she wasn't relieved when the Mage kept walking on, deeper down the corridor. I wondered when that had happened. If it hadn't been there all along but simply lacked the light to grow.

Unsurprisingly, Ivarr took the room beside mine, but when

the others kept shuffling about, deciding where they wished to sleep as if having choices became an unfamiliar concept after only losing them for so long, I slipped through my door instead. Mae would come get us to eat in a short while anyway, and stretching my legs for a few moments was a far more appealing scenario than lingering outside.

I strode across the room—larger than I imagined it would be with a corner armoire and inviting bed bedecked with rose-patterned white sheets pressed up against the wall on the side where another blue-painted door led into the bathing chamber. A wrought-iron nightstand with a clean glass resting atop it was positioned at the end of the bed before the space transformed into a study. I strode past the square desk, its two chairs tucked in close, and advanced to the window overlooking the gardens.

Without the threat of death or concern for missing people looming over me, I could appreciate the sight at last.

I braced my palms against the stone ledge—and my breath escaped my lungs at the sudden influx of life.

Where before the grounds had been perfectly empty, now numerous librarians in turquoise robes glided among the trees and bushes, walking along the cultivated paths or simply enjoying a moment for themselves under the widespread, spell-leafed branches of a young copse. There was even a small lake I hadn't spotted earlier to the far left, with several librarians reading on multi-hued blankets they had spread across the grassy bank. I touched my head to the cool stone.

If it weren't for the serenity of the sight that seeped into my very bones, I would have probably wondered if they had cleared the grounds just for our arrival. To protect this purity—or maybe to shield us, too. As it was, it was all I could do to drag my weary body to the comfortable, yet not too soft mattress.

Sleep took over the instant I lay down; this time, without dreams.

Or nightmares.

A KNOCK on my door yanked me awake—with an embarrassing half snore.

I peeled my head off the pillow and tossed myself onto my back, trying to make sense of it all.

No, I hadn't dreamt up the late lunch we'd shared down in the main hall, which meant I must have dozed off a second time. For quite a while, judging from the stiffness in my neck.

Mae had already boasted a smug expression when she came to rouse us the first time around. As if she knew damn well we'd all underestimated just how hard we'd crash once her magic let go. I was fairly certain this would only amuse her harder with the way we'd all thought we'd replenished our strength during the shared meal.

The knock sounded again, less sure but persistent.

"Coming!" I yelled, though I really didn't want to.

The bed. The solitude.

The sense of just *being* with nothing but a free current of thoughts running through my mind...

I forced myself out of the bed and padded over to open the door. Not Mae—*Ada* waited on the other side, her jade eyes taking me in, undoubtedly noticing my disgruntled and not too cheerful state.

"I'm *so* sorry, Ember." Her gaze darted past me to the bed, then skimmed my hair before falling on my face again. I smoothened out a wild tangle. "I didn't think you were asleep yet."

"More like *still*." I stifled a yawn, then I mustered a smile that was all sincerity despite the effort it took me to regain some control over my still slumbering facial muscles. "But really, don't worry about it."

Ada shuffled from foot to foot. Either she didn't believe me or...something else was going on.

"Is—is everything all right?" I frowned.

Her booted feet stopped as if something had adhered them to the ground. She winced. "Yes, yes, everything's fine. Sorry if I gave the wrong impression. I just came here to see if you wanted to join us upstairs."

The quick cadence of her voice, the torrent of words—

Warmth whisked through me at the echoes of the Ada I'd met...before.

"Eriyan managed to score some lumi," she elaborated, "and given this is the first time we can actually take a breath, we figured we might as well let a few things out, too."

Right as I'd loosened, tension slithered down my spine and poisoned my muscles once more. The last time we *let a few things out* was not something I'd care to repeat. The memory of their faces as I released my shadowfire, showed them the true me, raked its vicious claws down my insides. But from the way Ada was looking at me now...

Refusing her would probably set us back worse than whatever our words might unearth.

I inclined my head. "I just need to use the lavatory, and I'm good to go."

I could have sworn that was relief that ghosted over her face the second before she turned around and walked to the opposite wall to lean against it while she waited. I made a beeline for the en suite, and once my bladder was empty, quickly splashed my face with cool water to chase away the final remnants of sleep.

Though I really could do with a change of clothes, seeing that Ada was still in the same attire, I figured I wouldn't be out of place in my less than fresh dress. Besides, if we were to talk about the past...

Might as well do so while wearing it, too.

For better or for worse, there was...strength in the star-sprinkled fabric and phases of the moon arcing along the neckline. A reminder.

The final thing I did before I left was check the spell-leaf in my bra and the fragment still tucked in my stocking. I'd need to find a place to store them later—the hallow, especially—but for now, I welcomed the gentle press of their weight.

When I walked out of my chamber and gently shut the door behind me, Ada jerked as if I'd snapped her out of deep thought.

"Sorry, didn't mean to startle you."

This time, it was she who waved the apology away. "I just have a lot on my mind."

I didn't ask what. If she decided to open up, I'd find out soon enough. If not—the thoughts were hers and hers alone. Sun knew I'd dread voicing a fair part of my own.

Swishes of turquoise broke up the Repository's light stones as we climbed higher and higher, but it was the pleasant, softly chiming silence that reigned within its walls. A content sound, full of quiet life that blanketed me with serenity and calmed those final doubt-ridden tremors that had plagued my body.

"Where are you taking me?" We were nearly to the topmost level, the winding ramp offering a stunning view all the way to the ground floor where a trio of librarians walked, books in hand, towards the main doors.

Mirth lit the jade of Ada's eyes when I turned to her. "You'll see."

After we reached the final landing and there was nowhere higher for us to go, Ada took the large hallway extending to our left. Like what I had seen of the Repository so far, no artwork adorned the walls. Then again, the castle had no need for it.

With its clear and stained glass windows, the elegant scriptures running across every inch of it, and intricate embellishments carved from stone, the Repository was a work of art in itself.

We followed a series of smaller corridors once we crossed some kind of communal area strewn with pillows and books, then pushed through a wrought-iron door that opened up onto a wide, fenced terrace.

From up here, the sight of the colorful sky was nearly overwhelming.

I lingered on the threshold even as Ada walked across the smooth stones to where the rest of the group lounged in padded iron armchairs and loveseats around a matching iron-and-glass table. Including Ivarr. But as much as this inclusiveness surprised me, I couldn't dwell on it. Or on the ripple of warmth it uncurled in my chest—the ever-growing hope that maybe we could overcome our differences.

Try as I might, I couldn't resist the magnetism luring my gaze up.

The sky called to me.

Whereas the star-brushed night had touched something deep within my soul, dawn ensnared my senses.

I skimmed the outlines of the drifting clouds, the way the

colors seeped into one another, tainting the sky in so many shades that I wanted to kneel before its greatness.

I must have been more tired than I even realized to have such ridiculous notions flying around my head. But that didn't erase the truth.

Dawn was nothing less than majestic.

An ever-changing masterpiece I could never grow tired of watching.

It wasn't until the delicious scent of lumi wafted over on the gentle breeze that I snapped from the daze. I didn't attempt to make out the pleasant chatter dominating the terrace as I walked over to the group, but simply let the normalcy, however brief, wash over me instead. I snagged the empty spot on the loveseat beside Ivarr who greeted me with a dip of his chin, and the instant I made myself comfortable, Eriyan slid a full glass of lumi my way.

I wrapped my fingers around it with a smile, then eagerly took a sip of the delicious ruby-red drink.

"So is this some sort of therapy session?" Zaphine asked, though despite the humor she tried to infuse into her words, a touch of strain remained.

Her hair was pulled up in a casual bun which drew attention to her prominent cheekbones, full mouth, and slender neck. A clever way to also *divert* it. The bags under her eyes weren't the kind mere sleep could cure.

Ada drew her legs up onto the chair and sat cross-legged, balancing her drink precariously on the slender iron armrest. "Maybe it wouldn't be bad to share a little."

I could almost hear Zaphine's snort in the look she shot Ada. The latter wasn't exactly renowned for her sharing tendencies. Not to mention—I glanced at Ivarr—that her withholding information had been the very topic of our argument back in Saros, right before everything changed.

What surprised me, however, was that Zaphine didn't give in to the impulse to take a jab at Ada. Instead, she tipped her head in silent acknowledgment. "All right, then, we might as well give it a try. Who wants to go first?"

Silence swept through the group, but was quickly replaced by low, awkward laughter. Even I joined in, despite the lingering sensation of being out of place that I just couldn't shake.

"He called the meeting." Dantos thrust his hand in Eriyan's direction who flinched almost imperceptibly. "Maybe my little cousin should kick this off as well."

"I'm not the one who lost the most here," Eriyan confessed in a voice that was so raw I couldn't help but clutch my glass tighter.

Beside me, Ivarr went still. I wasn't sure if he wanted to bolt or was just assessing how wretchedly wrong this conversation could go.

Ada reached over and entwined her fingers with Eriyan's. "It doesn't matter how much we lost, because we *all* did." She sighed. "It's killing me that we left like that. That I don't know what happened. To Nysa. To my mother. To..."

Her downcast eyes gave shape to the unvoiced name.

Lyra.

She hadn't been with us when I opened the portal to Svitanye, but given how clever the dog had proven to be over and over again, I also had high hopes that if anybody could have escaped the unraveling of magic unscathed, it was her.

I cleared my throat. "I know that...that the Crescent Prince did everything in his power to keep Somraque from falling apart."

The words came out slowly, painfully, as if there was a tug-of-war going on inside me, undecided just how much to reveal. The extent of what I could say without making matters worse.

There was so much they had to hear, but sharing those things would mean nothing if their gut reactions prevented them from truly *listening*.

I polished off the rest of my lumi, and Eriyan—Stars bless his soul—handed me a fresh one straight away.

"Everything I told you in the Whispers is true," I went on—softly, tentatively. "I'm not saying that I condone the manner, or that I'm trying to excuse all the suffering you've lived through, but everything, *everything* Mor—"—I pressed my lips into a tight line, then exhaled—"the Crescent Prince did, he did it to help maintain Somraque's precarious balance. When the palace was attacked"—I let my gaze briefly drift across the shifting land in the distance—"I learned how to open a portal through the veil between worlds. He—he had the fragment." *He had me*, I added silently. "There was nothing standing in his way…"

My own beseeching words, forever chained in the vaults of memory, rang over the gentle chiming.

If we go to Svitanye, if we leave this place, they won't have a reason to fight any longer.

Please, Mordecai, don't make me go without you.

The crudely stitched wounds threatened to rip.

I opened my mouth, willing my voice to remain calm despite the depths churning beneath. "The reason he sent us here alone was because he wanted to stay behind and repair the damage the Void's hunger left behind. He stayed and let the Savior go because he couldn't bear to let Somraque fall."

Ada shifted in her seat, but didn't fire back at me right away. Progress.

"And you think... You think the people caused the Void to surge?" Eriyan's blue-green eyes, now leaning towards the latter rather than former, dug into mine. His knuckles were bone-white on the armrest. "My parents were at the celebrations when the march on the palace started. I don't know if they got out in time,"—his gaze flickered to Ada—"but I *do* know that they wouldn't have joined the rebels."

I nibbled on my lower lip. He'd asked a question. But it wasn't *that* part he truly wanted an answer to.

"When I..." I set my lumi on the table, glass clinking against glass, but thankfully not breaking under the uncontrolled force. I ran my hands down my face, then let loose a long breath. Ivarr observed me keenly, but it was Eriyan's gaze I sought out. "Before we all ended up outside Nysa—it was bad. Worst in the immediate vicinity of the palace where the concentration of magic was the highest..."

"But not limited to just there." His voice trembled.

"No." Instinctively, I rubbed my thumb against an embroidered star. "I'm not sure how Nysa fared. If Mordecai"—I couldn't call him the Crescent Prince, not when saying this —"had been able to contain the damage immediately or not. All I can say with certainty is that there isn't a sacrifice he wouldn't make to protect the town and its people."

Lie.

He hadn't wanted to sacrifice me.

But that was one secret, one vulnerability that wasn't mine to share. Nor would I want to.

Zaphine crossed her legs, strands of dark hair coming loose from her bun in the wind that whipped across the terrace. "How can you be so certain of his intentions?"

My heartbeat, the blood in my veins, everything inside me thrummed—

"Because I know what he is."

The collective silence spoke volumes. Five pairs of eyes bored into me—as if they felt this was something larger, far beyond anything they had considered could be the truth of their...tyrant.

As if they knew I was on the verge of ripping out their hooks and letting them clutch on to the unforgiving stone with nothing but their fingertips.

It was Ivarr who first shifted, gently pushing me to go on with a slow nod. I swallowed a mouthful of lumi and traced my fingers along the smooth glass.

I wasn't entirely sure if Mordecai had chosen to hide this fact, or if the absence of his explanations had been purely a product of not having an ear willing to listen. But this story... It was mine, too.

And for better or for worse, they *had* to hear it in order to move forward.

"Remember when you told me about the origin of magic?" I asked Ada far more calmly than I felt with the wariness so alive in her eyes.

Once she nodded—once the rest of them confirmed that they were all familiar with it—I ventured on. "There was a fourth race. People who came into existence purely to watch over and balance the different branches of magic and maintain their balance. Ancients, as they called them back when the world was whole. The keepers of magic." I straightened my spine. "Mordecai belongs to them. And so... And so do I."

CHAPTER NINETEEN

A SOFT MELODY COAXED ME FROM SLEEP. NOT CHIMING, BUT notes and harmonies and textures beyond any music I had ever heard.

I cracked open my eyes and stared at the gentle light filtering through the curtains I hadn't closed entirely before going to bed. Faint pressure throbbed in my temples from the lumi I'd drunk yesterday—or was brought on by the staggering relief that everything was out in the open now.

But as that melody wove through the morning serenity, it wasn't our late-night discussion that occupied my mind.

Magic.

I'd never been woken up by magic before.

Smiling, I drew the duvet up to my chin and turned on my side, reveling in the comfort of my bed and the beauty of the composition. A Spellweaver had visited all of our rooms the previous day to weave the magic into an alarm that would wake us all up at the same time the following morning. And every one after that.

Remarkable. Not just the ability, but the difference in their powers. Mae had explained that over lunch, when we had all bravely claimed we'd already recovered. Thankfully, despite my body giving out shortly after, my mind had been sharp and absorbed information greedily, like a sponge left dry for too long.

People like her, Enchanters, possessed magic that was activated when spoken, irrevocably tied to their voices and will. The latter took over when they ceased whispering the words, a kind of extension, though no less powerful.

Once they let the magic go in their minds, it dispelled—much like the bonds Mae had used on us or the hold she had over the land. I could hardly imagine how many threads she had to keep alive day after day, working for the Council. How exhausting it must be to know that a single negligence had the power to unravel an entire enchantment.

Spellweavers, on the other hand, had no such restrictions or harsh demands. They could shape their magic into something as permanent or as temporary as they liked. But that also meant the resulting creation didn't necessarily remain theirs alone.

Like the spell placed upon the entirety of Svitanye—the same one my birth had so cruelly disrupted—that kept the shifts from ripping people apart, they existed as a separate entity from the person who created them. Although occasionally, the spells did require to be "topped off," as Mae had explained.

Something as simple as the alarm, however, didn't demand any additional attention.

I rolled onto my stomach, sprawled diagonally across the bed, and stretched my legs. Lingering aches plagued my muscles, but nothing as bad as I'd expected with the staggering amount of walking I'd done over the past two days. The linen smelled faintly of lavender, and the urge to bury my head deeper in the pillow almost won.

If we weren't supposed to plan our next step over breakfast, there would have been no struggle, really. As it was, I flipped on my back and cast the duvet off my body.

Fresh but not cold air licked my skin the camisole that had ridden up my abdomen exposed and gave me just the kick I required to spur into motion.

Possibly sensing that I rose, the melody softened, then quieted, though echoes of it continued to drift through my mind.

After a quick visit to the bathing chamber, I stalked over to the armoire and sifted through the outfits the librarians had prepared for us. No robes, as those were earned through their dedication and devotion to the written word, but undergarments and dresses, even the occasional pants and matching tunics if we were inclined to wear something less ornate.

I ran my fingers along the assortment of colors.

When I'd inquired about the garments over lunch, Mae told us it had been the librarians' pleasure, tailoring clothes with spells and bare hands to fit our size. No one had measured me as far as I was aware, but with magic everywhere, I wouldn't have been surprised if someone had done it on the sly. Maybe Mae herself, long before she even set foot in the Repository that first time, if she'd planned all this from the very start.

I chose a beautiful dusty pink off-the-shoulder dress, its layered flowing skirts gradually transforming into a light blue. With the top of my silver hair pinned up and the strands flowing down my back, I looked almost regal, but the demure coloring had an oddly soothing effect—quite the opposite of cold. I slipped my feet into a pair of flat, elegant shoes, then checked on the fragment where I'd hid it in the bottom drawer of the armoire the previous night. Not the best of places, but even if someone sifted through the shawls and undergarments filling it nearly to the brim, they would have to search well before they found it, all bundled up in silk and lace.

My instincts claimed no such thing would happen, but I didn't want to take the chance. Recalling the Council—

I shook my head and glanced at the midnight dress draped over a chair. Then the spell-leaf on the nightstand.

For a moment, wonder filled me at what my life had become, and I held on to the sensation with both hands, wishing I could somehow capture and preserve it as I turned my back to the room. Voices drifted in from the corridor—Eriyan's bubbling, howling laugh drowning out the words I was fairly certain belonged to Zaphine. I opened the door a crack and peered through.

Ivarr lingered by his room, silent though not solemn, an elegant sight in a black shirt with the sleeves rolled up and close-fitting black trousers tucked into knee-high boots. He didn't see me, his gaze fixed on the trio just a short distance away. My eyebrows rose, and a smile tugged on my lips.

If I hadn't known better, I would have believed them to be Svitanye natives.

Eriyan had gone all out and donned a cropped pink brocade jacket over a simple black dress with blue highlights that hit him mid-calf, showing off the lacquered black boots similar in design to those Ivarr wore. Dantos, who had one arm around his cousin's shoulders and was listening to Zaphine with an unmistakable spark in his blue-green eyes, had opted for something demurer—but definitely Svitanyian. A classic white shirt with the sleeves rolled up, coupled with trousers the same shade of pink as Eriyan's jacket. Casual but elegant shoes in mint completed his outfit.

They both seemed in excellent spirits—and the garments truly did suit them—but it was Zaphine who shone. I stepped outside and quietly closed the door behind me, not wanting to interrupt the conversation. Not that I could make out a single word, busy as I was appreciating Zaphine's attire.

Flowing, high-waisted white pants paired off with a shimmering gold blouse and high heels. With her dark hair softly curled and falling past her shoulders, the kohl lining her eyes, and a touch of rouge on her lips, Zaphine looked more than just recovered.

She struck me as reborn.

Perhaps, even cut off from her magic, she found her place here, in a world ruled by colors and textures.

Ivarr pushed off the wall when he noticed me, but just as I wanted to meet him halfway, a door closed, luring my attention elsewhere.

Ada and Maelynn approached the group from the far end of the corridor. They didn't speak, but the look that passed between them spoke volumes on its own, even if the finer nuances of the message were more than likely lost to anyone but them. After a quick bout of "good mornings," Ada walked up to my side.

"Stars, I'm hungry," she grumbled.

My stomach answered her before I could.

I pressed a hand to it, laughing as I *shushed* the damn thing, then offered her my elbow without any real thought. Hesitation swept across her features, along with something fragile I couldn't quite place—but was gone the instant she looped her arm through mine. Even the faintest echoes of whatever had gone through her mind were replaced by a familiar kinship.

"Food?" I asked.

Ada grinned. "You read my mind. That lumi *really* did a number on me."

I wanted to ask if it was because of the lack of magic since, unlike me, Ada was no lightweight, but I bit my lip before I could utter a word. The state of their bodies had been the single subject they had all avoided touching last night. If they didn't want to share, I wouldn't push them. Though it didn't escape me that the new form-hugging tunic she'd put on had three-quarter sleeves...

By the time we reached the spacious hall, our stomachs were growling as if they were having a conversation of their own. Several clusters of librarians in turquoise occupied the long tables dominating the bright space, but there was enough room for our entire group to sit together without feeling crowded or encroaching on anyone's personal space. Ada picked out a spot at the second table from the right just as the others started trickling through the wide-open double-winged doors.

Much like last night, the librarians paid us no particular attention aside from kind greetings, the atmosphere easy— though I had no doubt that even a single person within these walls was ignorant of our origin.

After exchanging a few words with an older librarian with intricate floral tattoos spreading up her temples, Mae's whispers brushed against my senses. She floated an assortment of food and drink over from the massive counter set up against the far wall, tucked between the two doorways leading to the kitchens beyond. A stab of guilt struck my gut.

If this was also her reprieve from the Council, expending her energy on something we could have fetched for ourselves rubbed me the wrong way. Though seeing how ours wasn't the only meal drifting through the air, maybe this was such a common, everyday occurrence she didn't even think twice before doing.

I tried to catch which string of words she used, but with the cadence of her voice so soft, it was impossible to make anything out despite sitting right next to her. Actually, my attempts hit the same wall every single time.

A part of me burned to ask about their magic in detail, but I wasn't sure if the whispering was simply a way to use power unobtrusively or if it was a testimony to how private they considered the act.

In Somraque, while Ada had never hidden her blood, Eriyan had been far more reserved when it came to displaying the workings behind his illusions.

I grabbed a bread roll from the sky-blue platter that landed near me, mentally dropping the subject. We weren't going anywhere at least for a little while yet. The right time for questions would come.

As I munched on a piece of the still-warm roll that crunched and melted in my mouth all at once, I scanned the available drinks. Water, juices that struck me as freshly squeezed, a vast assortment of teas and—

A dark brew that smelled absolutely *delicious*.

Mae caught my ogling and smiled. "It's coffee," she explained, then poured herself a steaming cup. "Ground beans mixed with hot water that will give your mind *and* body a mean boost."

Beside me, Ivarr tuned in to the conversation, one elbow braced on the edge of the table. I shot him a questioning look. He nodded.

I poured us both half a cup, then inhaled the rich fragrance before trying a sip.

Stars above.

This was *divine.*

A groan slipped from my lips before I could control myself, and, as Mae chuckled, everyone else seemed to lurch for the clear decanter. They passed it around, filling their cups until *everything* smelled of the mouthwatering brew. Eriyan grimaced, the only one of us who clearly wasn't enamored with the taste, but when Mae sent some milk and sugar over to him, then used her magic to add a measure of each to the drink, he didn't set it aside again.

"You don't have coffee in your world?" Mae asked after a fashion—more than likely sensing we were once more capable of holding a conversation that extended beyond grunts of delight.

"No." Zaphine shook her head, holding the cup up with both hands.

"Not in my world, either," I added and reached for a second bread roll, this time with poppy seeds on top. "Maybe the High Masters are hiding it in vaults along with their prized objects of power."

Ada snorted. "After all that you told me, it sounds like exactly the kind of thing they would do."

SOME PEOPLE EXUDED POWER. Not magic, but the silent strength that came from within and demanded respect.

Chloenna, a stunning, statuesque woman in her fifties, was all that—and more.

Intelligence shone in her amber-speckled eyes, her posture

proud as she formally greeted our group gathered in front of the massive mahogany desk positioned two-thirds into her spacious study. And yet there was nothing cold about the head librarian's demeanor. As if she knew she had no need for such tactics.

The High Masters could definitely learn a thing or two from her.

Not that they ever *would*, given they would more than likely stab themselves in the eye than listen to a woman, but it was a good thought to entertain.

Chloenna picked up a bouquet of parchments off the edge of the black leather inset top with slender, manicured nails and handed them to Mae who waited just to the side. "I assigned several rooms to you where you won't be disturbed, as well as all the librarians the Repository can currently spare."

Mae only stared at her for long seconds before she blinked and lowered the scrolls into her lap. "Thank you."

She unrolled the parchments one by one and quickly read through the contents, her face locked somewhere between complete focus and wonder. When she looked back up, however, the gratitude was plain to see.

Chloenna smiled and went on, addressing all of us once more. "My people have already prepared tomes we believe could include references to the relic. There are..."—a corner of her lips quirked in mischief but no malice—"a lot of possibilities. However, if you require or think of anything else, don't hesitate to ask the librarians on your team." She clasped her hands in front of her body, graceful gold bracelets jingling. "I wish I could do more. Sadly, with everything the Repository is keeping track of, it's impossible to lay out chronicles devoted to single objects —even those as important as the one you seek."

With what I had gleaned about the Repository from Mae

when I'd questioned her over breakfast, I wasn't surprised. Covering every facet of history, writing down the present as it unfolded... My mind struggled to wrap around the idea that they had a working organizational system at all.

Eras. Towns. Bloodlines.

With how entwined the various aspects of the world were, keeping them clear without neglecting connections was no small achievement.

"Thank you. This is already more than we could have hoped for," I admitted.

Chloenna graced my comment with a smile.

"It is our pleasure." A strand of short, pastel blue hair fell across her forehead as she looked at her clasped hands, then told me softly, "Give us our world back."

Though I knew she had been speaking to me specifically, I said, "We will."

An arched eyebrow was all the reaction Ivarr gave once a blue-and-white haired librarian by the name of Briar showed us our section within one of the many library halls. Books lined the shelves from floor to ceiling, what must have been hundreds— no, *thousands*—of spines staring at us, though Ivarr only had eyes for the ones already prepared atop a large white desk in the smaller chamber just beyond the open double doors.

The first batch of many.

"This is impossible," I muttered, even as something inside me rejoiced at the sheer volume of tomes.

Ivarr's gaze slid sideways. "You don't like books?"

"No—no, no, I do. I adore books."

But for how impressive the collection was, I dreaded even thinking about how we would find any kind of reference to the fragment among all these pages. We had the team of librarians working with us, currently poring over their own assigned stacks Chloenna had already narrowed down, but a very good possibility existed we would have to comb through most, if not *all* the Repository to get the answers we sought.

I had a suspicion we would need our numbers at least quadrupled if we wanted to make even a dent.

"I guess I just didn't imagine there would be...so much," I confessed. "What about you?"

His mouth twitched. "I'm not *that* kind of reader"—he jerked his chin towards the white desk—"but I enjoy a good novel with a glass of wine when times are quiet."

Just because something unlocked in the atmosphere, I asked, "Not sowhl?"

"That"—his smile turned wolfish—"is reserved for a different kind of party."

I snickered, then swept my hand towards the wide-open double doors. "Shall we?"

Ivarr sketched a bow and obediently strode ahead, a slash of darkness against the bright setting. We sat opposite one another, a downright mountain range of books spread across the surface between us, and locked gazes over the embossed leather covers. The delicate scent of old paper playfully teased my nose.

I caught myself before I could sniff my soul out.

"How about you start from your left," I suggested, "and I'll start from mine?"

With a look that was such a clear *we've got this* he might as well had said it aloud, Ivarr dug in. I grabbed the first book and, minding the spine, spread it open. The pages were adorned with midnight blue ink so vibrant it was hard to imagine the neat lines had been written centuries ago.

Rationally, I knew they were protected with subtle magic, but it did nothing to lessen the effect. I traced my finger along the elegant cursive, sensing the gentle texture beneath my fingertips—

And fell into the page.

CHAPTER TWENTY

Colors and faces and voices and scents assaulted me.

A glass breaking.

Its shards scattering across the stone—

My palms hit the edge of the desk the instant before the chair toppled backwards and took me right along with it. Pain sliced through my back, then my elbow as it collided with the hard floor.

"What the fuck?" Ivarr was beside me before my surroundings could snap back into focus, but all I could do was squeeze out a hiss through gritted teeth. His solid grip was a comfort on my shoulder. "Ember, are you all right?"

I placed my hand in his when he offered and allowed him to pull me up. The flowing skirts of my dress swished down my legs. "I'm all right. I think..."

My back was alight with agony, but at least I managed to stay upright. Which, I supposed, had to count for something. Still clutching Ivarr's hand, I glanced at the book with its midnight blue ink—the images that had overlaid reality ensconced within it.

What the fuck was right.

I looked up at Ivarr and let go after a grateful squeeze. "I need to speak with Mae."

He didn't prompt me for more. He simply made for the second, smaller door leading out of the room in a light jog that sent a flurry of amusement through me. His steps ricocheted down the hallway all the way to the chamber where Mae and Ada were holed up by the entrance to the wing.

I hadn't expected *him* to go when I'd uttered the words, but quickly realized I could use a few moments to catch my breath. Giving the tome wide berth, I pressed my hand against a clear part of the desk just to have something solid beneath my fingertips and closed my eyes. I tipped my head back as I inhaled deeply, then let the air flow from my lungs.

My body was still feeling every small consequence of the fall, but at least my thoughts gained some structure. The bruises I'd just have to live with.

As I took another measured breath and mentally shoved the rest of the clutter away, I searched for the proper words to explain what I'd experienced. How this...manifestation felt.

Just a glimpse—that's what it had been.

Yet I found no plain description could do it justice.

Another inhale.

So real. It had seemed so real.

Exhale.

"You witnessed a remembrance?"

My eyes flew open.

"Remembrance?" Ivarr crossed his arms, gaze shifting

between an almost chipper Mae who glided into the chamber and me.

I slumped against the table. "I saw...a memory?"

Mae nodded, the enthusiasm now plain on her features. "I know you come from all worlds, Ember, but I didn't think the books would—"

A breathless laugh bubbled from her, and that just might have been the glint of tears in her eyes before she buried her head in her hands and shook it. It was actually kind of endearing, seeing her like this—so passionate and excited. Mae never struck me as austere—aside from the very first impression —but there had been a constant air of control around her. One broken up by spontaneous spikes of emotion and flowing, placid kindness, but nothing quite like this.

Ivarr looked at her as if he couldn't believe what he was seeing either. But found it delightful.

Mae wiped what was indeed tears from beneath her eyes, somehow not smearing any of the kohl. "I apologize." She flung the ends of her seafoam-white cardigan over her knees. "This is simply...too remarkable."

I had a feeling there was a whole line of different adjectives she'd wanted to use.

Ivarr leaned casually against the doorframe as Mae said to me, "Some parts of the chronicles are spelled, made from memories of people who wrote these tomes, or those who agreed to have their recollections and impressions extracted for a detailed account. Fresh memories are nearly infallible, and if compiled from multiple sources, accurate. We pride ourselves on truth, and magic cannot be tricked."

"A little warning would have been nice," I said softly.

I hadn't considered my abilities could lead to something like this as I had no idea the tomes were comprised of more than just paper and ink, but Mae operated with more knowledge than I had at my disposal. Yet regardless of how unsettling the experience of falling into a book—into a *remembrance*—had been, my curiosity overtook my annoyance at the lack of preparation on Mae's end.

I ran the flat of my palm over my half updo to check if everything was still in place then looked down, chasing the proper description of what I'd gone through. A frown pulled on my forehead.

A remembrance clearly fell in the sphere of Svitanye's magic.

But had my connection with it been normal—or some kind of Savior anomaly?

In the corner of my vision, I spotted Mae containing her excitement, giving me the time and space to sort my thoughts out. Ivarr still lingered by the doorframe, stoic yet attentive.

A laugh shimmied up in my chest.

Of all the things going on, I couldn't shut off the voice wondering how all of this must be like for him. Assassin Magician, yanked crudely from his life into another world where he ended up stuck on research duty while his partner, the prophesized Savior, fell into books.

No, absurd didn't even begin to cover it.

I stifled my laugh as Ivarr quirked an eyebrow and looked at Mae instead, the words I was searching for suddenly there for the taking.

"When the remembrance happened, I lost contact with this world. But I could still...*feel* it somewhere behind the moving images. Is that normal?"

Mae gestured to the chair I'd overthrown. Ivarr glided over in smooth strides and picked it up before I could. I sat down, eyeing Mae warily as she settled beside me. Her silence wasn't exactly the answer I'd been hoping for.

"I really do apologize for not warning you, but...there's a reason for it." She flicked a piece of lint off her cardigan and glanced towards Ivarr who positioned himself directly behind my chair, fingertips touching the backrest. "How did you activate it? The remembrance?"

Oddly, I didn't find Ivarr's proximity intrusive. If anything, his presence at my back had a reassuring effect.

If anything went wrong, he'd be there to catch me.

I sent him a grateful look over my shoulder then turned back to Mae. "I touched the ink. That's all."

"Interesting," she muttered, studying me with a gentle furrow on her forehead. No telltale chimes sounded. Just observing, not spelling, then.

I fidgeted in my seat nonetheless. "You have a different way of accessing remembrances?"

"Usually, we have to pour our magic into a command. *Recount.*"

"Of course I can't do anything the normal way," I half-joked. Might as well go along with it.

Mae pursed her lips, but her gray eyes twinkled. "You could try it, you know."

From behind, Ivarr's interest sharpened. Not from some malice or ill intent, but the curiosity I, too, felt rushing through my veins. I hadn't performed blood magic, hadn't woven a single illusion the entire time I was in Somraque. But if the power of my ancestors was nestled inside me, then maybe—

"How do I do it?"

Mae's first response was a brilliant smile. Then her gaze

dropped down to the upturned crescent moon nestled atop my chest.

"Do you channel yourself when you use that pendant?" When I nodded, she continued. "I think it's safe to say the process is similar. Only instead of pouring yourself into an object and entwining your will with its power, you do so with a word."

That seemed...pretty straightforward.

The shadowfire within me stayed perfectly silent, too. Actually, now that I considered it, its obsidian surface hadn't stirred even the first time around—despite my heartbeat going wild and the less than pleasant fall.

Safe.

This was safe.

I exhaled, then turned in my seat until I faced the open book. I almost placed my hands on the perfectly preserved pages when I remembered this was something I should be able to do *without* touch.

"Go on," Mae prompted gently, her warm tones infusing me with strength. "Neither Ivarr nor I will let anything happen."

I didn't answer. Couldn't. All my thoughts, everything I was, what I harbored beneath my flesh and skin, focused on a single word that fluttered through my mind—an almost tangible thing that I grasped with ethereal hands and irradiated with my presence, my will...

"Recount."

The word was no more than a whisper, as if something inside me knew there was no need to shout—that this magic preferred a softer touch, one that coaxed and caressed, not demanded.

A courtyard of burnt orange flagstone painted itself over the Repository's walls, men and women in colorful attire and even more vibrant hair gathered around a dazzling two-tiered fountain that looked as if it were made of celestite. Above, the sky was nearly devoid of clouds, presenting a stark gradient of colors spanning between light and dark. My own reality hovered just beneath the images, close enough to touch yet sufficiently distant as to not distort the remembrance.

The voices, the scents, the touch of a breeze that slithered through the heat of merriment... Everything felt utterly alive, as if I were a true part of this sequence derived from a time born centuries ago. My feet moved across the roughened surface of the flat stones.

Unlike before, when my stillness had highlighted only the outer sensory input of the two parallel realities, motion made me keenly aware of my stoic body back at the Repository—even as the act of walking through the crowd seemed real. Like I had a separate self here; one that was fully functional and transferred nothing of its actions back to the original while at the same time existed only because of the latter's will.

A faint throbbing began in my temples as my thoughts chased one another, crafting a maelstrom of sensations and theories.

I forced myself to focus on the remembrance and what it was revealing. The rest could wait.

Right as I turned to bypass the broken glass shattered on the floor no one appeared to be bothered to clear away, a woman with glittering gemstones for a dress rushed at me. I twisted, but with the ornate low pillar serving as a table blocking my left, I couldn't get out of her path entirely.

I braced myself for the cut of her jewels—

Only to have her pass *through* me.

Of course.

Embarrassed by my spontaneous, impulsive reaction, I

watched her rush up to a pale, thin woman with coiffed green hair. They kissed—just as they had *ages* ago.

I snorted and shook my head.

Though my presence here *felt* physical, it most definitely wasn't.

I embraced it.

People passed through me whenever our paths crossed, distorting what would, in Somraque, be a perfect display of a Mage's powers. But even as the figures moved through my flesh, the resemblance this scene bore to reality was uncanny.

I walked around the fountain, then found a moderately clear spot just to the right of a glass door. With my back against the wall, I observed the casual revelry. The longer I looked, however, the more I noticed the details. Or the lack of them.

A face obscured beyond recognition, with only a few markers visible. A drink of undeterminable fragrance. Then—a seam.

A thin, white gap, there one moment then gone the next.

This wasn't a memory of one person. It was the conjuncture of *many*.

I pushed off the wall and traveled around the bubbling fountain, seeking out more signs I'd missed initially, overwhelmed by the sheer marvel of the experience. As I'd suspected, this remembrance was a compilation.

If I stood in one spot, the seams brought together, in chronological order, the events one would have seen from that specific vantage point—an uninterrupted flow if my location was strategic, less so if I chose one I suspected the many memories sewn together couldn't cover all that well.

But if I moved...

The seams became even more frequent.

Like Svitanye's landscape fitting its pieces together, the

magic fueling the remembrance joined accounts to let me stride across the memoryscape at will. Only where the true land of Svitanye joined the pieces with no rhyme or reason, the remembrance was crafted so that I would lose no information, regardless of how I traveled across it or where I looked.

Intrigued, I attempted to venture beyond the courtyard but found the wide-open gates barred. Whatever lay beyond had nothing to do with this past sequence. Paragraphs beyond the boundaries of a page.

A pull tugged me back—similar to the one I had experienced in the city. I followed it to a tan man in a glittering pink vest.

He raised his goblet and, using the rim of the fountain as a platform, addressed the gathered crowd. "To the successful merger of our families!"

Dizziness swept over me. It drowned out the celebratory cheers, my senses overwhelmed by an oppressive white fog. Instinctively, I reached past the gossamer layer to the reality beyond, grabbed onto it, and yanked myself through.

My stomach lurched.

Mae's arm was a warm comfort on mine, Ivarr's steady on my shoulder—balancing me lest I topple off the chair. With a shaky hand, I pushed the old book away. I rested my forehead on the table and sucked in large gulps of air, doing my best to not lose my breakfast.

It wasn't until the worst of the tremors had passed and the nausea dulled to a mild annoyance that I straightened.

I peered at Mae who was grinning at me wildly.

"Congratulations, Ember," she beamed, "you're an Enchanter."

CHAPTER TWENTY-ONE

AN ENCHANTER. A FLEDGLING ONE, AS MY STRUGGLES TO command my voice into anything beyond three basic words —*recount, illuminate, elevate*—proved. But Mae's spirits or her faith in me never faltered.

She made herself comfortable on her bed, her chair cleared to the side, but within reach of a whisper. Content—that was how she appeared in her pastel sea-green dress against the surprisingly demure sandy sheets, hair tousled around her, and an unyielding curve to her lips.

I readjusted my position on the quatrefoil floor pillow Mae had sent for when it became clear the ground, with the window and the richly hued sky beyond resting straight ahead, was to be my study spot. It might have been no more than my imagination, but gazing at the spill of colors somehow brought me closer to the land and its magic. A pulse in my veins I could become one with.

"Try *illuminate* again to ground yourself," Mae said from

above, once more toying with her silver ring. The difference was that this time, the gesture held no edge. No fidgeting. Only the placidity of connecting with something that has been with you through the beauty and the hardships alike.

I didn't even try to hide that I knew *precisely* what she was up to as I stared at her. Give the frustrated novice an easy task to boost their gradually decaying confidence.

Mae, for her part, didn't sugarcoat it either.

She shrugged, then wound a strand of turquoise hair around one finger. "Go on."

Still shaking my head, I reached within me and poured myself into the word.

"*Illuminate.*"

The room exploded in golden light.

As the whisper faded, the gentle command remained rooted in my mind, my will holding the magic where it was. Although easier with every subsequent attempt, I struggled to let the thought *float*, as Mae had put it.

Having iron control while at the same time *not* being preoccupied with it was a concept I was a long way from mastering.

"Good." Mae let go of the strand and used both hands to push herself higher against the stacked pillows. "Now instead of releasing the command from your mind, you'll adjust it. Have the light rise towards the ceiling by using *elevate*."

Frowning, I firmly held the magic already wanting to slip away and chanced a look at Mae. "But light isn't...tangible."

"True. Light is not matter. But our magic *can* influence energy. What else do you think the *illuminate* command does?"

Her words slammed into me, and my hold faltered. The room reverted to its normal state with only Mae's enchantment chasing shadows from the corners. I blinked to adjust my eyes to the dimmer light—and process the information. Scientific terms weren't something my tutors or the books I'd read back at home covered in any great extent, but Mae had given me a rundown of the basics tied to their magic before we began our lesson.

"Huh." I leaned back, bracing myself on my palms, and dragged my teeth over my bottom lip. "I guess I thought I was affecting the room, like an illusion, not light itself."

Mae just looked at me, suppressing a smile.

"I...I influenced *light.*"

"Yes, you did." Her smile bloomed. "And, Ember, you'll be able to do *so* much more if we keep this up."

I lowered myself to the ground and stared at the ceiling, not caring how cold the stone was against my back. There was so much still wrong, still missing—yet a smile stretched across my face.

Sometimes, a mere moment of feeling like yourself, however new and frightening, emanated the brightest light.

WHEN DINNER FINALLY CAME AROUND, I all but collapsed in what had become my standard seat at the long table, drained worse than when I'd stolen minutes with objects of power back in Soltzen my *female hands* should never have touched.

I couldn't help the hint of smugness that rose at the thought of where I was now. How far I'd come from that girl.

For once I...truly looked forward to braving the far from easy path ahead.

After the brief repose when I'd failed to guide light, Mae and

I had worked hard on expanding my skills. Calling forth the magic came naturally to me, but the various commands...

There were definitely levels to them.

And I, for one, was exhausted from attempting to push beyond the utter neophyte steps. Or maybe that was just my starving stomach talking...

After winking at me, Mae floated an assortment of food and drinks over, all comfortably within arm's reach, which was something I was immensely grateful for. I'd half expected she'd make *me* do it—a little demonstration to follow up her announcement to the group that they had another Enchanter in their midst; a fact that reaped a round of *whoop-whoops* and applause—but since I hadn't been able to infuse a sense of direction into my enchantments all that well, the meal would have probably ended up smacking someone in the face.

If past experience was any indicator, that someone would have been me.

With my mind sluggish from exertion, I caught only snippets of conversation that flowed through the space. I ate in silence, locked away in a bubble nothing could truly disturb. It wasn't until I devoured more than two-thirds of the roasted venison that I latched on to the relaxed exchanges.

"I think my eyes are about ready to fall out," Eriyan grumbled and dragged a hand down his face.

Mae tore off a piece of bread stuffed with candied fruit, her hand hovering midway to her mouth. "I can enchant your vision as long as we're in the same space."

"Can you enchant his snoring, too?" Zaphine asked dryly. "I can hear him through the damn walls."

Ada arched an eyebrow. "At night or during work hours?"

Eriyan shot her a warning glare and Dantos laughed. He

slapped his cousin hard on the back and said to Ada, "What do you think?"

"Work hours," she replied solemnly, then grinned and reached over to ruffle Eriyan's already wild hair.

By the looks of it, he'd spent the day running his fingers through it—when he wasn't dozing off, of course. Slight annoyance I would have missed if I hadn't been paying as much attention as I was crested his face. But in the span of a heartbeat, it was gone, and Eriyan gave in to Ada's affections.

He said to her, "As if you're Miss Perfect." A gleam entered his eyes. "I *distinctly* remember you slobbering—"

"That was *ONE* time, Eri."

"—all over my pillow. Had to burn the damn thing when you finally stopped hogging the bed."

"I. Was. Drunk." She buried her head in her hands and groaned.

Mae chuckled, then floated a glass of lumi right in front of Ada.

The entire table erupted in laughter that buried the jagged edges of exhaustion far more effectively than anything else could.

"Any luck today?" I asked no one in particular when the moment passed.

They all shook their heads, but it was Zaphine who said, "Some of the text I read covered the period right after the break. It was...chaotic." Her voice dropped, and she glanced at Ada before looking back at me. "There was a mention that families who'd held a respected position before the break had stepped up and created the first Council of Words from their strongest members. I jotted down the names. The first councilors, as well as the other...well, almost royalty. If the fragment wasn't hidden during the time immediately after the world fractured, I'm willing to bet it was someone from those eleven bloodlines who secured it."

"Do you have it with you now?" Mae asked.

"It should be..." She stood and patted the pockets of her high-waisted pants. "Ah, here." She extended the neatly folded paper to Mae. "I know you probably know all this, being on the Council—"

"No." Mae's fingers tightened around the list, the paper crumpling. "I know of the initial members and the five families they came from, yes, but not the others."

Zaphine sat back down and chewed on her cheek, her hands tucked between her knees. "I hope I transcribed the names correctly. Some were a bit...unusual."

Dantos shot her a look so affectionate I almost gaped, but it was Mae who stole my attention.

The focus creasing her brow.

The pursed lips.

She guided her chair away from the table and offered us all an apologetic look. "I'll take this to Chloenna now. She'll make sure the proper volumes will be waiting for us tomorrow."

"Don't you think it's odd that no one thought of that approach sooner?" Ivarr asked.

Even with what Mae had spoken of the librarians' workload, his question was solid. Losing track of the fragment made sense in the grander scheme of things. Not thinking about the prominent families, however...

Mae waited as five librarians from the neighboring table strode past. We all returned the kind nods and smiles and words that, I noted with no small amount of surprise, weren't fake or forced. And stirred no irritation.

Though Mae *did* look as if every second spent here was one she'd rather dedicate to talking with Chloenna. Understandable but—

"From what I know of the world before," she said when we were once again alone, "the people—even those who could be considered royalty, as Zaphine said—had no access to the heart of magic." She flicked the upper corner of the note. "Anyone could have snatched the fragment after the break when it was no longer protected."

"But you don't believe that, do you?" I ventured, meeting her gaze—the truth there.

"No, I don't." Her index finger flicked the paper one more time before she stuffed it in her dress pocket. "I'll speak with Chloenna straight away."

As she left and the too-potent silence we'd fallen into gradually dissipated, Ada leaned towards me across the space Mae had vacated. "Do you have any plans tomorrow evening?"

"Aside from passing out after Mae puts me through the enchantment drills again as she enjoys her sizzling romances?"

She grinned. "Aside from that, yes."

"No, I don't."

"Would you—" A sudden, boisterous laugh from Eriyan visibly crushed Ada's focus. She jerked back, shook her head, then looked at me anew. "Would you maybe go for a walk with me around the grounds? Just the two of us?"

"Well," I drawled, the ever-present tightness inside me thawing, "if I don't fall headfirst into my dinner, I'd love to."

WITH MY BODY trapped in that odd state between exhaustion

and excitement, I decided to wander around the Repository before going to bed. I had only seen a small fraction of it, and this bastion of knowledge, it—it spoke to me in some way that reached beyond logic. So much of what I had always craved but had been denied resided within these walls.

Somraque had given me magic. The Repository a means to quell my hunger for knowledge.

I peered into chamber after chamber, took in the seemingly endless rows of spines, and basked in that unique scent books wore so lovingly that, to me, was richer and far more entrancing than any perfume. A few librarians I'd crossed paths with along the way kindly offered their assistance but quickly caught on that I was wandering the halls for an entirely different reason— had probably realized it even before I had.

Despite the drive that had led me through the halls, I hadn't pulled a single tome off its shelf. Hadn't perused any of the chronicles or delved among the pages covered with magic theory. Botanics. Architecture. The art forms of Svitanye's couture.

The mere sight of so many books, so many immortal imprints of people filled me with a deep kind of beauty that was heavy and light all at once. It made me feel as if I resonated with the Repository—made me feel myself while at the same time painted a canvas of how grand, how vast the world's existence was.

The past, present, and future the tomes destined to outlive generations embodied—they intersected within these walls, made eternal through the lives the authors had offered to the pages.

Remembrances. Chapters. Careful accounts of times past or

the facets of life and living crafted from matter that transcended
ink.

Some derived from fact, others wrought from imagination.

Paper portals to other worlds.

Or a loupe held above ours.

I touched a finger to one of the spines, then stepped back
and spun on my heels, drinking in the circular chamber with its
domed windows on one side, an intricate coffered ceiling
spreading above.

Regardless of the circumstances that had brought us here and
the reasons behind our stay, being in the Repository was nothing
short of a dream come true. I was among people whose life's
devotion and passion was to maintain the stories, the histories,
the details in every shape and size the world had put into words.

No amount of ugliness could touch such purity.

As I ventured back through the wing to return to my room, a
melodic, familiar voice caressed my ears. I followed the sound
along the generously lit hallway, past a reading room with a small
balcony overlooking the garden, all the way to the chamber that
had been closed when I'd started my tour.

Cautiously as to not disturb the lovely cadence of his voice
rising and falling in flawless rhythm, I positioned myself by the
door and peered inside.

Beyond the small ocean of children seated on soft cushions
and tiny chairs, reclined in a gold-and-pale-blue armchair, was
the librarian I'd met by the spell-tree. Midnight blue waves
framed his sculpted face as he read from the large clothbound
book he held open in his lap. The gold-lined pages shone under
the magic-birthed light.

I wanted to slip into the chamber, but as his words sank in, as my own memory rose in tune, my step halted on the threshold.

"With his fur of perfect black, the little wolf hid in the embrace of night. Stars watched over him and the moon revealed her gentle face as she looked upon her child—though he did not see her, with his nose trained low to the ground and eyes hunting for the very shadows that hunted him. In the distance, across the woods, footsteps rustled.

"The little wolf's keen nose caught the men's scent, the malice that marked them. He couldn't understand why they wanted to hurt him; why it was wrong for him to be who he was. His little heart clenched as he hurried in the other direction as fast as his paws could carry him. Alone. Completely alone in the night he tried to become one with. All the other animals had shied away from him. None had come to his aid when he'd run, losing sight of his home, of his parents the hunters had already taken. As they would take him now.

"Shivering and frightened, the little black wolf hid in the foliage. He glanced up, again and again, as the hunters neared. The sound seemed to come from every wisp of the inky darkness coating the woods. Every whisper of the wind. He wondered if the moon would tell him when to run, *where* to run, or if she would merely gaze down upon him, silent and cold. Just as he wanted to flee, escape the endless roll of vicious footfalls though he had no direction, no path to safety, the moon shone brighter. A second. Only for a second, her light seeped brilliantly into the charcoal night. Then the glow faded. The little black wolf didn't know if he had imagined it, but he continued to look up, ignoring the thunderous pursuit that matched his heart beat for beat. He searched for another sign—

"There, to the left. A star winked. Though he didn't

understand why, the little wolf trusted her. The footsteps grew closer and closer, and he ran towards the star. He had just covered the length between five looming spruces when he saw a flicker of torchlight precisely where he would have gone had the moon not interfered. Without slowing, the little wolf lifted his little muzzle to the sky and looked for another sign.

"Farther to the left, another star winked. He followed the blinking lights, over and over, zigzagging across the woods for what felt like hours, yet he never tired. His paws didn't hurt; his lungs were never short for air. As if under the watchful eye of the moon and her beloved stars, he was invincible.

"More than that.

"As if he was loved.

"Farther and farther he went, and the steps faded and faded and faded into silence. Still, the little wolf didn't stop. The stars continued to show him the way, guiding him on his path to a great unknown. And when at last, every star in the sky blinked to darkness then back to life, he saw them—

"Eyes. Numerous, numerous eyes were staring back at him. Not bright with fear, but with guarded affection. Kinship. One by one, the animals emerged. A bat swooped down from the branch. A bear nuzzled its way from its cave. More and more stepped forward. Some animals the little wolf had been taught to fear. Some he had been taught to hate. But he didn't. He couldn't. They had never done anything to him, just as he had never done anything to the people who hunted him. So the little wolf walked closer and dipped his head towards the ground, showing he meant them no harm.

"An eagle landed on his back, and the bear stepped aside to reveal a lovely cavern. A home. The little wolf, however, didn't enter and succumb to the sleep he hadn't had in a long, long time. No, he went to greet each and every one of the animals, embracing them as he would the closest of family.

"Because in that moment, he knew—he knew that he could choose his own path. Just as he could choose those who would travel upon it beside him."

After a stunned silence, the twelve children who had been drinking in every single word that had left the librarian's mouth erupted in applause. Their clapping was soon exchanged for excited chatter as they immediately spun their own tales about the little black wolf.

Over the ocean of their bobbing heads, the librarian's gaze fell on mine. A smile curved up his lips.

He closed the thick tome he held in his hands, set it aside, and with one last look at the children, marched over to greet me.

Only it wasn't a word that passed between us—but a handkerchief.

I hadn't even felt the tears marring my cheeks.

"Thank you." I accepted the small piece of cloth and dabbed under my eyes. "I'll get this back to you as soon as I clean it."

Amusement danced in the corners of his broad mouth. "No need. Plenty more where that came from."

Those narrow, vibrant blue eyes seemed to pierce straight through the many layers of me. And didn't balk at what they saw there.

He stepped into the corridor. "Walk with me?"

I nodded, then, as we moved away from the room, said, "I remember the story."

We turned right at the end of the hallway and looped back towards the spiraling ramp.

"Of the little wolf?" A smile I could have sworn was wistful brushed across his lips. "A beautiful one, isn't it?"

"The version I found at home was a little different, but not the message. It was..." I hugged myself as if I could physically contain the rush of memories and emotions surging through my body. As if I could prevent the painstakingly crafted seams holding me together from coming undone. "It was one of the tales that made me fall in love with the night."

That vibrant gaze swept across me. "I didn't think your land would have allowed such stories to live on."

My bitter laugh entwined with our footfalls. How he knew what Soltzen was like, I didn't know. But if it had always been such, always under a gilded rule of men who wanted nothing but to be revered during the time of their lives and shaped others to suit their liking, I suspected the tomes about the world before the break were more than revealing.

"No," I said as my laughter ceased ricocheting off the towering walls. We ascended the spiral. "They didn't—don't. I was lucky enough to have found them in a crate of discarded, unwanted books and claimed them for myself."

"A Savior right from the very start. I like that." He smiled broadly now, and I couldn't keep my own lips from quirking up. I wasn't sure when, exactly, the title had stopped bothering me, but hearing it used like this... It seemed fitting. Right.

"It isn't always me who runs the story hour," he went on, tracing one hand along the smooth railing, "but we do carry it out for the little ones every evening. If you want to revisit your own childhood, you're more than welcome to come join us. I can even set up one of the miniature chairs, so you won't have to lurk out in the hallway."

I laughed and rolled my eyes, though the answer was a definite yes.

But it was not a simple one.

"I have to confess—" I bit my lower lip and let my gaze trail beyond the librarian to the stained glass adorning one of the word-chiseled walls. "I'm hoping we'll be able to unearth the fragment's location and move on quickly—if with a heavy heart. But a part of me..." I huffed a laugh, meeting his gaze again. "A part of me wants nothing more than to come listen every night."

"Tempting the Savior?" He quirked a midnight blue eyebrow.

"*Definitely* tempting the Savior. Though that sounds like a title belonging to one of Mae's romance books."

He stopped in his tracks and narrowed his eyes at me. "She loaned you the legendary collection?"

"No." I chuckled. "But I *might* have snuck a peek or two while working with her on my enchantments."

"All right, then. No treason committed." He offered me his elbow, and I looped my arm through, letting him escort me the rest of the way to my wing.

As we walked in comfortable silence, I couldn't help but think that when I had read the little wolf's story as a nosy child, it wasn't just the night I had fallen in love with.

It was the idea of choosing the family who would escort you through life that had made me survive all those years.

THE MIDNIGHT GOWN *flows with movement as I swirl across the floor, the melody of magic and revelry all around me. Pulsing. Thrumming.*

A perfect representation of life that unspools within me with every rapid beat of my heart.

A strong hand rests on my waist, the sapphire drinking me in as I bathe in the heat of his body, in the strength of his presence, for the first time in my life feeling as if I truly belong.

My arms curve around Mordecai's neck right as his find the small of my back. I burn for him to obliterate what little distance remains between us.

Pulse racing, I gaze at his handsome face, the innocence and hunger he fights to keep hidden but the argent shadowfire rippling out behind him exposes with no restraints.

His fingers sink into my skin—to keep me there or bring me close, I can't tell. But I know what I want. What I crave with every atom of my body.

My lips part—Mordecai's reactions mirroring mine.

"I miss you," I whisper and trail a finger along the sensual curve of his lower lip.

Reality flickers. An interference I don't understand—and ignore.

Mordecai draws my finger into his mouth. His teeth graze my skin before he lets go. I never want him to. But the sense of loss can't settle as he cups my cheek in his palm, the sapphire of his gaze alight with longing. Pain.

So much more than mere loss.

"Don't leave me again." I choke out the words. A tear breaks free and rolls down my cheek. "The silver of the moon to my everlasting night."

The declaration comes from a place in me that had existed long before I was born.

Mordecai's lips close over mine, and our tongues meet. He deepens the kiss as I hold on to him, cherish him. His arms encase me completely. They bring me to him until there is nothing but the fabric of our clothes between our heated bodies. The groan that escapes him reverberates through my chest, and my moan echoes it.

I can't control the tears streaming down my cheeks as we continue to dance across the floor, through the magic I couldn't care less for with him in my arms. This...

This is everything.

My back collides with a pillar, and Mordecai's body traps me from the front. Desire stirs low in my core and courses through my veins, my every nerve coming alive under his touch. A gentle gasp escapes me.

Slowly, as if he has all the time in the world—even when the way his mouth claims mine speaks otherwise—he lifts up my dress. I shiver as he slides the fabric higher, then higher still, until his hand curves around my bare thigh. His thumb creates lazy circles, and Mordecai parts from my lips, turning his gaze on me as if he wishes to memorize every last detail of my flushed face.

His hand travels up.

I writhe under his touch, back arching involuntarily, but I don't break our locked gazes even when it takes all I have not to throw my head back and beg him to reach just a little higher.

"Ember..." His voice fills me, commands me.

I shift my position until his thumb brushes against my core, and a ripple passes through Mordecai's body. The sapphire darkens, lids heavy. He presses his forehead to mine.

"I love you," I whisper as I unravel.

Words I might have said in haste once before but had meant with all my heart. Ancient's. Savior's. Mine.

I cup his face with my hand.

These threads weaving between us reach beyond infatuation. Beyond desire.

An inexplicable draw, yet one that comes from the very soul.

Reality flickers again, and the glint of Mordecai's eyes opens up the hidden depths between us before everything fades to black.

LONG, slender wisps of shadowfire danced above me, licking the walls of the chamber, the ceiling and casting the room in a darkness that soothed my soul as it threatened to fracture.

The pillow beneath me was wet from the tears that still seared my cheeks. I wrapped my fingers around the pendant and, curled up on my side, watched the shadowfire through blurred eyes as it descended, cocooning me until there was not a sliver of my surroundings left.

Only the beautiful obsidian, mourning the loss of its light.

CHAPTER TWENTY-TWO

"Fuck," Ivarr muttered.

I took one look at his pained face and broke out laughing—though I knew I'd probably regret it soon enough. Our fate was, after all, irrevocably tied.

I slapped a hand against my mouth in a futile attempt to stop laughing before my eyes watered and ruined the kohl, but Ivarr was decidedly *not* making things easy.

Devastation and anguish pulsed from him in waves, a wavy black strand tossed over his forehead and brushing against his cheek as if someone had physically punched him and turned his previously polished appearance disheveled. My laughter turned into mortifying snorts as I peeled my gaze away from my companion and looked at the space ahead instead.

The slender-legged table, with the books we had left from the first batch stacked neatly on one side in four, not piles, but *pillars*, were now joined by what looked about five dozen additional volumes. Ivarr swore again while I made a mental note to pay attention to any creaking. The white iron slab making up the top of the table seemed to have curved a little under the weight. Undiluted amusement coursed through me and scattered the final remnants of last night's dream.

Hurt born of something I had no influence over couldn't stain my present.

Its roots, however, I left.

They were as much a part of me as was my magic.

As the pleasant calmness nestled in my core, I dared look at Ivarr once more—finding him just as crestfallen as he'd been. I reached out and dragged him deeper into the room by his hand.

"Come on. Don't tell me a few books is all it takes to threaten the big bad Magician?"

The scowl he'd carved on his face remained there by will alone. And when *that* wasn't sufficient any longer, a smile broke across his features—open and tentative at the same time.

He tugged on our still entwined hands, but when I moved to let go, he stopped me with gentle force I could have easily countered, had I wanted to. A silent confirmation and assurance that the impulse I'd acted on was all right—that this gradually budding relationship between us wasn't a one-sided figment of imagination. Nor was it something he wanted to ignore.

Our exclusive outcast club might have brought us together, but we didn't intend for the label to be the only thing we shared.

A dark-wrought friendship.

I liked the sound of that.

Once he read from my face that I'd understood his message, he let go—if only to wave an overly dramatic hand towards the book-filled table. I snorted and went over to my chair, a small dent on its side the only evidence of yesterday's tumble. I bit the inside of my cheek.

The pile was undeniably...impressive.

After the two chronicles I'd read through the previous day before Mae had hauled me away to practice enchantments, I *really* hoped the ones I'd get today weren't filled end to end with parties.

A *screech* speared through my mind.

I jolted in my seat and frowned when I saw Ivarr drag—

Oh.

He positioned his chair so we sat side by side, close but not encroaching on my personal space, then bumped his shoulder against mine. The gesture was more casual than anything I'd ever seen him do—but alongside the warmth it stirred inside me rose tendrils of something colder, too.

One truth this companionship between us couldn't overcome.

Wasn't...

Wasn't built to.

Ivarr might have been the first to catch on *why* Mordecai wanted my power, but he'd also deeply despised the figure of the Crescent Prince. If—*when*—he learned of the place Mordecai held in my heart... How could he not hate me?

Something so deeply rooted...

I snuffed out the unproductive thoughts and flashed Ivarr a smile. Perhaps I was naive, but I couldn't bring myself to *not* embrace the friendship weaving between us. Even if, in the end, it would crush me when I would have no choice but to let go.

"Do you have any preferences?" He jerked his chin towards the books as he finished rolling up the sleeves of his black shirt —silk, I noticed, with a faint dark gray pattern.

I barely swallowed a snort.

Skulls. The pattern was skulls.

"I'll take the"—I leaned closer to peer at the spines and make out the shiny text that had caught my eye—"Dasolann family, and you can start with the Blamores." I traced a finger along the black tome adorned with gold foiling, then snatched it off the pile and shoved it in Ivarr's arms. "Nice and dark to match your style."

He glowered, but failed spectacularly as an amused chuckle escaped his lips. "Yeah, yeah... You just wanted the baby blue books for yourself."

I grinned. The Dasolann chronicles *were* divine, protected in colored cloth of light blue with bright silver letters that were almost white glistening across the front and spine. Matching ornaments framed the edges, creating delicate tree branches in bloom that reached towards the title.

Holding the—perhaps a bit heavy—book up, I swept my other hand down the teal gown with silver-white accents. "Accessorizing is everything. *One* true thing I'd learned from my lessons on being a proper High Master's daughter."

Something flashed in Ivarr's green-brown eyes in that second before he shook his head and set the book on the table with an *oomph*.

"What?"

"Nothing."

I wasn't buying it, but let it be.

I placed my baby blue tome in front of me, flipped it open, and propped my head on my hand.

"Best Magician in Somraque turned book dweller," Ivarr muttered.

The lines of the opening paragraph I'd started to read blurred as my frame shook with chuckling I couldn't quite contain.

AFTER SIX HOURS—AND despite the generous amount of coffee and food Ivarr had fetched for us, claiming he wanted to stretch his legs—the words my eyes skimmed across were blurring from something other than humor. I yawned and turned another page. From the adjacent chamber drifted a soft echo of footsteps—a librarian, no doubt—but no one entered our increasingly stuffier space to deliver some good news. I squinted at the window.

Maybe some fresh air would clear out the dust bunnies clogging my mind, but my butt refused to move from the chair.

I settled for a prolonged stare at the dawn sky.

Ivarr flipped his *third* page when I hadn't even moved past a single paragraph, the crisp sound of thick paper and gilded edges a fleeting burst of music with no comparison. I trained my gaze on the immaculate letters and continued reading of the meetings held at the renowned Dasolann estate—the central building built on and around a focus point, the outer regions held firmly together by magic. There had been at least fifty pages dedicated to how the family employed a whole assortment of powerful people to keep their sprawling house and luxurious gardens from scattering all over Svitanye.

While the entire home presented an incredibly impressive window into history—especially the sections containing their employees' freely given recollections filled with their desire to work at an estate that brimmed with joy and parties—my focus was starting to drift to places I wasn't certain I could resurrect it from.

The Dasolanns were an artistic force, their bloodline including many prized architects, painters, and fabric designers. That last part was one of the few I could see through the *recount* command, and the blends of rippling colors, as if the many hues were shifting liquid, not dyed threads, had stolen my breath away.

Unfortunately, the awe had died down about four hours in when, after the introductory chapter and the details of the magic, the writing became a time-stamped string of the many lavish feasts and concerts and expositions held at the estate. If it weren't for the camaraderie and easy atmosphere noticeable even from the ink-on-paper paragraphs, I would have said there weren't all that many differences to what I was used to from home.

I reached for my cup of coffee, only to find there was barely a mouthful of the now cold liquid left. Still, I downed every last drop, then strained my eyes across the next section.

Lovely. A wedding party. Hadn't had one of those for at least nine pages. I sighed.

Why, with all the word magic Svitanye had to offer, no one had thought of a command that would highlight a reference to the fragment in the books was beyond me.

I turned to ask Ivarr if he'd worked out some sort of system that allowed him to cruise through the chronicles at that envious pace, but where he'd been mere moments ago, there was nothing but his empty chair tucked neatly against the desk.

My gaze skimmed my depleted cup. I hoped he went for more coffee.

Stifling another yawn, I began reading the details of the lavish ceremony when a tingling at the back of my neck snapped me to attention.

Only far too late.

I barely glanced up as Ivarr's honed body slammed into mine, knocking me straight onto the hard floor.

CHAPTER TWENTY-THREE

Twisting sideways, I evaded my fallen chair—and Ivarr's subsequent blow.

The skirts of my teal gown tangled wretchedly around my feet, but I managed to use the table's slender leg to drag myself around the corner and out of his way. Mercifully, the mountain of books kept it pinned firmly to the ground—and the precariously stacked tomes didn't topple over.

Briefly, I entertained the idea of using them as weapons, but not only were they too high, the part of me that thought them sacred protested wildly at the thought.

Murdered because she refused to bend a spine.

My breath came out in harsh, quick rasps and my pulse slammed against my ribs even as *severely* misplaced amusement almost coaxed a laugh out of me. I propelled myself to my feet and faced Ivarr's imposing figure carved from nothing but silent lethality, the shadowfire liquid dark under my skin.

I lashed out with a fist.

He blocked it, those brown-speckled green eyes twinkling.

"You bastard," I hissed and swung at him again. Ivarr laughed, sidestepping the blow with enviable grace, then returned the favor.

I careened to the side, cursing the impracticality of my dress —and missed that his attack was a feint while the real danger came in the shape of a fist barreling straight for my stomach. His hand connected with my flesh, but the pain I was expecting never blossomed.

"The *fuck?*" I panted.

Ivarr let his hand swing down by his side, though his stance remained alert. "Thought you might need a little something to get your blood flowing." A smile curved on his lips. "You looked half dead, Savior."

My glare lasted no more than a second.

"Ass." I punched him in the shoulder, then leaned against the table, unable to deny that while unconventional, his method *had* been effective. There were no lingering traces of drowsiness left. Something dawned on me. "*That's* what the look was about!"

"What look?" he asked with mock innocence.

I slugged him in the shoulder again. In the exact same spot.

The only thing I regretted was not having any rings on my fingers to *really* drive the point in.

"When I mentioned accessorizing. You planned this." I jabbed a nail in his chest. "You wanted to tackle me while I was at a disadvantage!"

Ivarr lifted his hands in a casual shrug. "The thought might have crossed my mind."

"Don't appreciate women in dresses?"

"Don't appreciate an attire making you helpless. Doesn't matter what you wear as long as you can fight in it."

I stared at him. The fire roaring in my veins now a cold, foreboding entity. "You think I have fighting ahead of me?"

A head surrounded by curly, cherry-colored hair popped through the doors connecting our room to the book-filled chamber beyond.

"Everything all right in here?"

No admonishment in the woman's voice, just genuine concern for our well-being.

"We're fine." Ivarr leveled a look at me, and I nodded.

We *were* fine, even if his previous statement had...unsettled me.

I ran a self-conscious hand through my partially braided hair. "I apologize if we disturbed you."

The warmth of the librarian's smile reached all the way to her gold-brown eyes. "Is your research going well?"

I let Ivarr take that one, only half listening as I strode over to the two long-backed armchairs set by the window. I threw my legs over the armrest and nestled my head against the brocade cushion. A moment later, Ivarr joined me.

He sprawled his long legs in front of him, interlaced hands resting in his lap. "Ember, do you think everybody will be happy when you unite the worlds?"

The graveness in his tone, but even more so, the conviction, stunned me. Though I'd braced myself for what our conversation might entail, I needed a moment to deal with the fact that I hadn't given much thought about what would happen *after* I fulfilled the prophecy. Granted, I had a reason. With all the obstacles, it had seemed fruitless to occupy myself with things that may not ever come to pass if we—if *I*—failed.

But my own doubts and fears didn't excuse such an oversight.

"You already know the Council is against you," he went on, my silence answer enough. "They won't change their tune."

"But if they come after me, they'll do it with magic. And I have—"

"Your shadowfire, yes." He inclined his head, watching me not as a friend, but someone with experience. Someone who'd led a dangerous life and came out on top time and time again. Someone I should consider myself lucky to have on my side. "That kind of unparalleled power does work to your advantage. But you'd be a fool if you let it become a crutch."

I scrunched my nose at him, although I couldn't deny he had a point. I might not face the same issues as the rest of them with my magic working across all three worlds, but the incident at the clothier's, when the orange-haired Sylo had trapped me, was proof enough that shadowfire alone was not a sufficient defense.

Of course, back then, no tactic or skill that came to mind would have saved me. Except, maybe, getting as far away as I could.

I picked at a loose thread on my dress.

My pendant. The Ancient obsidian. Even the enchantments I was learning with Mae...

They were a part of my arsenal. But they couldn't be the entirety of it.

I swept my gaze along Ivarr's fit form, remembering how he moved, the calluses gracing his hands—

Somraque's deadliest Magician, dangerous even in a land that had stripped him of the very power responsible for the title.

"So what do you propose?" I asked.

"Run with me every morning before breakfast."

My eyebrows rose.

"And"—he smiled, one of those brilliant, earnest smiles that carried just a hint of mischief—"whenever you feel like falling asleep, we spar. Dresses and all."

WHEN I'D ASKED a librarian if a Spellweaver could come to my room during the brief break from perusing the books Ivarr and I took in the afternoon, I hadn't imagined it would be him. Hadn't even considered it was a possibility.

Though why I'd never know.

His turquoise robes flowed around him on phantom wind, his face kind and eyes crinkled into a smile, as if he, too, was glad for the outcome. Maybe even volunteered to assure it.

"Nice to see you again." He hesitated, a touch awkward.

Sun, we hadn't even introduced ourselves yesterday, despite baring slivers of our souls as we walked through the Repository.

Mortified, I quickly closed the distance and offered him my hand. "Ember."

"Nyon." His long fingers were warm against mine, the handshake firm, but not aggressive. "Pleasure to properly make your acquaintance. What can I do for you, Ember?"

I motioned to the small square table and two wrought-iron chairs set in the corner by the window. I sat in one, while Nyon folded his lean body into the other. When I noticed his gaze drift towards the bottle of lumi Eriyan had suggested was an excellent means to unwind right before bed, I grabbed the clean glass and poured him a generous measure.

He accepted it with a bow of his head. Midnight blue hair grazed his cheekbones. "Much appreciated."

"You're the one who's doing me a favor," I said as I stalked to the nightstand where my plain glass, still half-filled with water, waited beside the spell-leaf. I drank the water, then poured the lumi to roughly the same level.

"Which is?" Nyon looked at me over his glass.

"Oh, right... I was wondering if you could set the alarm for an hour and a half sooner than it is now. In my room, and my friend Ivarr's, too. He's just next door."

"Of course." The smile in his eyes spread to his lips. "Want an early start?"

An unguarded chuckle preceded my words. "Something like that." I crossed my legs and leaned against the desk. "It's—it's okay to use the grounds for recreation, right?"

"Not many do, though they *were* created with such intentions." Nyon's gaze slid to the dawn sky expanding beyond the clear glass. He swirled his lumi, sending its fruity aroma coursing through the room before he took a sip. "There is also a recreational chamber on the ground floor. A bit dusty, perhaps,"—his mouth twitched—"but if you're looking into weapons training, it's well equipped."

"Thank you," I said, more than a little surprised he would offer such a thing to strangers. Then again, the librarians had been on our side from the very start, knowing what we were after. What we planned.

Allies. The word slithered through my mind.

We were allies.

"I'll ask Ivarr if that kind of drill is part of what he has in mind for me," I added a touch dryly, and Nyon laughed.

"I had someone like that, too. Instead of training my body, he trained my magic, but the principle was the same. I never could be sure just what kind of devious torture he had planned until I was in the thick of it. But as much as I cursed him, he was right. Theory and practice are one thing. Thinking *beyond* the confines of what's safe and applying yourself in situations where disorder reigns above the expected—that's where true mastery lies."

The opening was one I didn't dare miss. I rubbed my thumb along the rim of the glass. "I hope you don't mind me asking— beyond the effect, how does your power differ from that of Enchanters?"

"Thinking about trying it?"

Every atom of air in my lungs froze—before it clicked that Nyon knew who I was. *A daughter of three worlds with the essence of balance-keepers.* Had known from the very first time we spoke under the spell-tree and had more than likely heard of what Mae had been teaching me.

We hadn't kept my magic a secret, didn't even consider it, actually, when we started honing my Enchanter affinity. I needed to remind myself that within the Repository, I wouldn't be treated differently for the sum of my abilities. Or feared, it seemed, for any of them.

"Yes," I admitted and relaxed into the chair. "I understand there's no one in Svitanye who can wield both powers,"—I cradled my lumi with both hands while Nyon sipped his—"and while it would be pretentious to assume I could pull off something no one else can—"

Nyon shook his head, stilling my words. "Don't apologize for what your instincts are telling you, Ember. The only foolish thing would be not to attempt the impossible."

With his words settling into my very core, I nodded. "Thank you for that."

Those words, while sincere, would never be enough to convey the depths of my gratitude. This went beyond messages I needed to hear, beyond mere acceptance of a girl sewn together from not three, but four worlds. Nyon was...a kindred spirit.

Perhaps even a twin soul. Something that did not find form in words or gestures but passed between us, silent yet at the same time almost tangible.

It wasn't always necessary to cross great distances together to get to know a person.

Sometimes, all it took was the right moment in time.

With one last sip of his lumi, Nyon placed the glass on the table, then motioned to the ceiling just above the bed. I followed his gaze, but even more so, *listened*.

A soft chime preceded his words.

Words that were in no language I knew, yet somehow intuitively understood.

Shimmering tendrils shone against the slightly darker backdrop of the ceiling; a net of interwoven threads that seemed alive somehow, full of bright lights reminiscent of shooting stars I'd read about traveling along the length of individual vines.

"Enchanters use the common tongue," Nyon explained as he leaned back in his chair, one arm over the backrest, and observed the marvelous hovering form, "but ours is older. Books cannot contain it, nor can it be taught to anyone who is not a Spellweaver. The syllables simply..." His brow furrowed, as if he were searching for a word that lay just beyond his grasp. "They disintegrate before another person could process them."

I waved a hand towards the spell. "You asked the magic comprising the alarm to reveal itself."

Nyon looked at me, disbelief and wonder shaping his features into something even lovelier.

"Before," I clarified, although a bit unnecessarily. Nyon knew I wasn't drawing conclusions based on what I saw, but— "I heard you command it."

"You understood the Spellweavers' language."

The entire chamber seemed to pulse with something tender. Not shock or stentorian excitement, but fragile amazement on the verge of bloom.

"It...translated." I wrung my fingers together—now free of the glass I'd all but dropped when I set it on the desk. "I don't think I could repeat the actual words you voiced, but I heard the meaning behind them."

Nyon leaned across the corner and placed a gentle hand above my heart. Oddly, the contact didn't make me flinch. It wasn't even uncomfortable, not truly. Like Nyon wasn't touching my body, but whatever dormant thing I had yet to meet that lay beneath my skin. He lifted his gaze to mine.

"The language is inside us," he said. "We're born with it. While weaving spells requires study, the bones of what we need for their creation are already ours."

"Did you know?" I asked. "The spell-leaf—did you know I would be able to use it?"

"The tree did."

Cryptic, but it would do. When we eased apart, I went to the nightstand and picked up the leaf, then twirled it in my hand. Nyon's gaze never left me.

"Is this Enchanter or Spellcaster magic?" I ran my fingers along the blue words all the way to its jagged tip.

"Nature provides for all." He motioned to the spell-leaf with an elegant hand. "The contents are the base, but the effect, how you will use it... It depends on the bearer."

CHAPTER TWENTY-FOUR

I WAS GAZING AT ONE OF THE SPELL-TREES ON THE WESTERN side of the garden, turning over Nyon's words and the training I'd gone through with Mae earlier this evening, when footsteps echoed from behind—though I'd sensed her approach long ago.

Even without her magic, Ada's presence was a force that couldn't be ignored. I smiled at the thought.

"Stars, I'm glad you're here," she said, coming to stand beside me. She turned her gaze to the softly rustling tree with its russet-and-red leaves—as if she wanted to conceal the dissipating concern shaping her features. Her thick lashes kissed her cheeks. "When you didn't show up for dinner, I thought that maybe..."

I reached out and entwined my fingers with hers. "I wouldn't miss this for the world."

Her grip tightened on mine, the blunt relief so clear on her face my chest contracted. In the distance, voices traveled on the light breeze, barely louder than the Repository's eternal chiming heartbeat. We unlaced our hands and spun northwards, tracking the origin of the sound. Ada chuckled.

Zaphine and Dantos had apparently decided to go on an evening walk of their own.

"Are those two together?" I asked as their forms flickered in and out of sight, meandering between the many blossoming trees and tall bushes lining the labyrinth of walkways on this end of the estate.

Mirth touched Ada's eyes. "I honestly can't tell."

We crossed the grass surrounding the spell-trees until gravel crunched under our feet.

"Even back in Somraque, they were practically glued to each other's side, but nothing more than that as far as I'm aware of." She scratched the back of her neck—the diagonal scar shooting across her skin there. "I *can* see they both want it, though."

"Are you all right with that?"

A bush to our right rustled. Our heads simultaneously snapped in that direction—then a low laugh escaped my lips.

Just a cat.

A *kitten*, actually.

Ada crouched, her long braid falling over one shoulder, and called the small beast over. She ran her fingers along the glistening striped fur. The kitten rubbed up against her, purring softly.

"I'm fine with Zaphine dating Dantos, if that's what she wants." She scratched the kitten beneath its chin then looked at me as I sank to the ground beside her. "I'll always care for her. I can't imagine *not* caring for her. Zaphine was the first person I… loved, I think. But I'm not interested in rekindling an old flame. And Zaphine—" Her expression shuttered a little. "She deserves better. I wasn't exactly a good girlfriend to her."

I bit back the questions poised at the tip of my tongue. It would be all too easy to give in to the moment, ask her in detail about her past—as well as the present I suspected leaned towards Mae. But that was something friends did.

"Maybe they're just waiting for this whole reuniting the world thing to settle before figuring things out." I tipped my head towards Zaphine and Dantos. Or at least the tops of their heads visible above the lush greenery.

"Maybe." Ada petted the kitten one last time before rising and offered me a small smile when I did the same. "I'm thankful *we're* not."

Her words were so fragile the light, fresh breeze might have easily whisked them away. But I heard.

I heard and I agreed.

A silent pact weaving between us, we headed southeast—away from the section Zaphine and Dantos were enjoying. The grounds were vast enough to offer privacy, and we needed it as much as they did. My thoughts churned and rolled as we explored the gardens, skirting around small ponds rich with fish and benches tucked in green alcoves where one could observe the chirping birds flitting about.

Though I missed nothing of the scenery, nothing of Ada's presence beside me, calmer than I had seen her in a long while, it was my search for the proper words that hugged the forefront of my mind. But unlike magic, the correct syllables to mend a friendship weren't quite so forthcoming.

So I said the one thing Ada not only should know, but wouldn't fail to miss what my confiding in her signified.

"Turns out I'm a Spellweaver, too."

She whirled around, holding on to me with both arms. "That's—"

"Impossible?"

"*Amazing.*"

I chuckled, and the chimes seemed to echo the sound. "I didn't actually *cast* anything just yet, but Nyon agrees I have all the predispositions for it. He'll train me."

"The librarian I saw leaving your rooms this afternoon?" Her eyebrows rose. "He's kind on the eyes."

A surprised laugh bubbled from my lips. "He is."

But only that.

Likely noticing the momentary stillness my muscles locked into, Ada linked her elbow through mine and guided me farther down the light gray path comprised of scripture-adorned stones. I didn't fight the contact.

The unease with its coiling tongues flicking up my insides had nothing to do with our physical proximity.

Though I wondered—if she knew of the lightning flashes of night-wrought images that shot through my mind, would the contact repel *her*?

I hoped the time for that verdict was still a ways away, when these threads between us wouldn't be quite so...tenuous.

We passed under the arched trellis rich with wisterias I had to gently push aside with a hand lest my hair tangled in them. Ada, just a touch shorter, merely chuckled and sent me an amused look.

One that faded as her gaze caught on the pendant that had slipped free from the sweetheart neckline.

"We never tried if you could do blood magic," she said quietly, her tone edged with remorse. Maybe even guilt.

I veered down a path that was barely more than packed earth, so narrow we partially treaded on grass to remain side by side.

"Given how little time we've had together, I think we accomplished quite a lot, don't you?" I asked, one eyebrow arched high.

The grin she graced my words with coaxed a mirror one to spread across my face.

"Besides," I continued, "you and Eriyan were plying me with sowhl. I'd hate to rival *your* legendary drunken performance."

Ada scoffed, then broke out laughing.

"Fine, fine." She swatted the air with a hand. "You made your point. An uncontrollable fire illusion wouldn't have been exactly inconspicuous."

Though it had been *my* words that had steered us here, I stilled within. Too close—we'd come too close to the cleaving point. There had been one reason, one man fueling the need to keep our heads down in Somraque. I'd already touched the subject that first night on the terrace when I spoke of the Ancients and their—our—role as guardians of magic. But that had been it.

My allegiance, my decision to trust and work with Mordecai who had only ever been their nightmare—

Even if, rationally, they were aware his actions had been fueled by the threat of the voracious, lethal Void that was drawn to magic like High Masters to power and prestige, unable to refuse what was there for the taking...

His reasons could never cast the past in a light where no darkness lurked.

And that I had *chosen* him...

It was a subject best left untouched until those gaping wounds closed.

Ada traced the curve of a bird's flight, her expression distant, shadowed. Yet when the bird settled in a cherry tree and she returned her attention to me, that heavy veil dispelled. I loosened a breath.

I was tired of fighting.

Thankfully, so was she.

"I'd be honored to teach you," she said, voice soft. "When I get my magic back. Of course, if you even want—"

"I do, Ada. Thank you."

We meandered around widespread rosebushes, then entered the striking, tall lavender that reached to our waists. Ada's fingers skimmed across the tips and sent gentle ripples skating through the aromatic ocean.

"I think..." She halted, then dropped her arm and turned to me fully. "I think now that we're here and everything kind of... hit me...I understand what it must have been like for you, coming to Somraque."

She let her eyes roam the versatile grounds, then the Repository at the heart of them, before looking up at the cotton streaks of color. I didn't have to follow her gaze to know precisely what she was seeing—every nuance of what passed through her reflected on her face.

"Thank you for bringing me here, Ember."

It had been Mordecai, not me, who'd made that possible, but I only offered Ada a smile and said the words I meant with my entire heart, "I'm glad you're here."

We both pretended the sting in our reddened eyes had nothing to do with the rawness we'd exposed ourselves to and carried on towards the Repository's front gate. The stone wall came into sight, then the elaborate wrought-iron gates—

We stopped dead in our tracks.

"Shit," Ada muttered, but I hardly heard her over the roar in my ears.

Mae levitated in her chair by the partially open gate, blocking the orange-haired figure looming over her from entering. Everything about his posture conveyed a threat, but what sent chills down my spine was the shock of recognition.

Sylo.

The Council's guard and my jailer.

My lips pulled back in a sneer even as Ada yanked me behind the thick rosebush, her face drawn into a tight mask. The teal fabric of my skirt snagged on a thorn, but all that mattered was staying out of sight.

Beyond the figs, Mae seemed to be holding her own. She looked fierce with her hair neatly coiffed in an updo that was playful and regal all at once, her dress shimmering with small stones set against the gray fabric. Sylo, on the other hand, was far from content with whatever she was saying. I glanced around the grass and bush-filled stretch of land.

Too open.

Impossible to cross to the fig trees or the stone wall to hear the exchange. Act, if we had to.

Ada's hard breaths hinted she was ready to lash out the second Sylo threatened Mae. But if we were to reveal ourselves, we needed to be sure of the situation—that we wouldn't act recklessly. If we could somehow get closer...

A word Mae had taught me—a word I'd failed to put into action—flew into my mind. I laced my voice with power, hoping for a miracle, and commanded, "*Resonate.*"

Chiming, then—

"They've been taken care of, Sylo. The Waste consumed the threat as it does everything. I've made sure of it." Her tone was that of a royal, leaving no room for argument.

Not that the guard cared.

"You're needed back in the city."

"And the city needs a fortifying spell," Mae fired back.

I pushed the sound towards Ada who kept glancing between me and the scene unfolding by the gates. Her eyes widened as Mae's words hit her, but she remained composed—as composed as either of us could be, crouching behind thorny roses.

"Leaving Ausrine and the Council is not something I take lightly. But as I was already away, *not* visiting the Repository would have been a waste of resources. I know you're merely following orders, Sylo, but do not think even for one second that you have authority over me. So take this message back to the only ones who do. We *need* what's inside these walls, and if the Council doesn't like it, they should check their priorities."

The fierceness in her voice released a wave of goose bumps down my skin.

"I understand the strain my absence has put them under, but if we were to lay new protections across the town, perhaps even beyond it, everyone would benefit in the long term. We serve the land. We serve the people. They're all that matters." She sighed, but the sound was sharp, laced with annoyance. "Now, the sooner you let me get back to work, the faster I can return to Ausrine. Or do you honestly believe I *enjoy* being away from my duties?"

"This was your home."

"Precisely, Sylo. *Was*," Mae snapped, voice ice-cold. "I'm sworn to the Council. I am not only willing, but I am *giving* my life, day after day, to uphold my vow. As I am now. This spell will aid Svitanye. Tell that to the Council. We're done here."

She turned her chair around.

A heartbeat. Two—

"Wait."

I held my breath and Ada's grip tightened to the point of discomfort, though it was nothing compared to the dreadful anticipation of the worst coiling within me. Mae pivoted back towards Sylo.

The tension in her shoulders was evident even from all the way over here. "What?"

"There was a second notice. From Annora. The focus point in Nebla is nearing destabilization." Mae swore as he said, "You can reach it easily from here."

Mae dipped her chin, what I could see of her expression past the roses solemn, though she managed to hold on to that sharp edge she'd dealt Sylo earlier. "Consider it done. And do give the Council my message. I will *not* take kindly to having my integrity doubted a second time."

She turned around, and this time, Sylo didn't stop her.

Nor could he any longer as the iron gates swung shut.

I wasn't even sure if it had been Mae or the Repository itself that had shut them, but I was glad to see Sylo on the other side. His grassy green eyes stared after Mae as she drifted down the path, every inch a person with purpose, then scanned the Repository gardens—as if he hadn't taken her at her word about our execution. Or her sentiments about this place.

Ada and I ducked right as his palpable scrutiny veered in our direction. The rosebush seemed so poor a cover, with Sylo still visible past the petals and leaves and thorns. What I wouldn't give for an illusion...

The way Ada's fingers curled and uncurled, as if yearning to wrap around a dagger, made me think I wasn't the only one.

Just as I brought my hand to the pendant to get us out of here, Sylo swept his gaze up the Repository, studying every gently illuminated window within his line of sight. Zaphine and

Dantos were probably safe on the other side of the building, but Ivarr and Eriyan—

Sylo muttered something under his breath. A spell or just a plain curse, I couldn't be sure.

But it didn't matter. Not as he spun on his heels and stalked into the volatile land, his long orange hair a lash of a whip with every step.

Ada's hard breaths matched mine and twined with the melodic chiming and cheery bird songs that struck me as that much purer in light of the intrusion of the harsh world Sylo represented.

A fierce protectiveness rose in my chest—but stayed there. I had neither the time to pry it apart nor *could* I have done anything as my cramping muscles remained locked in utter stillness.

Even after the first shift whisked Sylo away.

Even after what must have been a full minute passed with nothing but the changing landscape visible beyond the iron gates.

Right as we relaxed, a shimmering blur rushed at us.

I caught Ada as she tipped back into me, then felt her entire body relax in my arm when she saw just who was making a beeline for us.

Whether Mae had picked up on my magic or simply *knew* we were stashed behind a rosebush like two children not wanting to get into trouble, she showed no surprise at our being here. No annoyance, either, despite the fact that we *had* intruded on her privacy, regardless of how good our intentions had been.

Still holding on to each other, we rose, then stepped apart when Mae reached us. The stone-cold lines of her face that she'd crafted for Sylo dissolved entirely, and all that was left was weariness—though a dry undercurrent of humor ran in her voice as she confided, "I'd hoped it would take them longer."

"You knew they would come after you," I said with zero accusation in my tone.

Mae nodded, twirling the silver ring, then looked up. "It's only a matter of time before the Council grows suspicious. Sylo... Sylo was just the beginning." A mirthless laugh. "A *mild* one." She folded her hands in her lap, as if she had to physically restrain herself from fidgeting. "My tie to the Repository isn't a secret, nor is my belief that the two forces should work together. But a prolonged visit..." She let loose a long breath. "Without me, the Council *will* become weaker. The responsibility is designed to be shared among five. For a while, we can redistribute the burden so that the absence has no true impact on the land or the Council. But that frays eventually. It always does. And if that happens before we finish here, before I can return, there's only one course of action left for the Council to take."

"They'll send the guards to retrieve you," Ada finished for her, green eyes flashing.

If she had her magic, whatever force the Council would have sent after Mae wouldn't have stood a chance. As it was...

"I'm guessing there are no deserters among your ranks?" I asked.

A sad smile curved a single corner of Mae's lips. "Only the dead."

CHAPTER TWENTY-FIVE

"Ember, can I talk to you for a moment?" Mae called out as I came out of the kitchens with some extras to hold me through the night and early morning, when Ivarr and I had our first training session planned.

Studying the books alone had thrown my appetite in overdrive. I suspected adding physical exercise to that would only ramp up my hunger.

Better to be prepared than left with a growling stomach—even if it *did* currently make me feel as if I intended to eat my way through the Repository's stores.

I repositioned the fruit and neatly wrapped pastries, courtesy of the cook, then walked up to Mae. "Of course."

Ignoring the heap of food, she motioned to a discreet set of doors leading out of the main hall. I'd never checked to see what lurked on the other side, and my breath nearly got knocked out of my lungs when the sight revealed itself after a whispered command. A patio, shielded from all sides by a low stone fence and widespread cherry trees, their white petals blanketing the ground.

"How come I didn't see this before?" I whispered as I set my food on one of the many wrought-iron tables. One of the pastries rolled precariously close to the edge. I caught it with a distracted hand.

When my focus circled around to Mae, she was smiling at me, though the expression faltered a little around the edges. "You couldn't. Not unless you came here through the hall. It's the Repository's little hidden nook." She lifted her chin, motioning to the cherry trees. "They're planted in a pattern designed specifically to keep those who wander the paths from peeking inside. And likewise from here. Librarians love companionship, but they also value privacy."

From all that I'd seen so far, that made perfect sense. I pulled out a wrought-iron chair with a curved, ornate backrest and sat on a pillow that matched the white of the cherry blossoms perfectly. "What was it you wanted to talk to me about?"

"Nebla."

"The town Sylo mentioned?" I tore off a piece of the pastry and chewed on it, meeting her gaze. "You're going?"

It would mean one less person working the books, but if it kept the Council at bay for a while longer, then the sacrifice was well worth it.

Mae nodded, and I could have sworn that same glimmer of a tutor's pride shone in her eyes as it had when we'd discussed my use of *resonate*. "I was hoping you would come along."

I almost choked on a rogue chocolate bit.

"Why? Don't get me wrong," I hurried to add, "I would love to see more of Svitanye,"—the absolute truth—"but don't you think I'm needed here? And, more than that, won't it be too risky taking me beyond the Repository's walls?"

"May I?" She motioned to the spiral-shaped pastry.

I nodded and slid it closer to her, the paper wrapping crunching softly. She tore off a piece then nibbled on it, her face drawn and gaze fixed on some point in the distance. Whatever currents she was battling, I suspected they ran deep. She'd refused to place any particular weight on Sylo's visit beyond the warning that it was—had almost brushed the entire encounter off by the time we'd made it back into the Repository—but I didn't doubt for a second her mind had never ceased sifting through the possibilities, the dangers that would come hurtling our way if we didn't find the fragment in time.

As I watched her in this intimate pocket beneath the dawn sky, with no interruptions, no veils surrounding what might otherwise escape the eye, the gravity of what she had done, what she was *still* doing, slammed into me.

I would have called it playing a dangerous game, but the sheer magnitude of her actions and the way they were affixed into the wider setting went beyond something so...trivial.

My fingers jerked with the need to reach for her, but I knew that, at times like this, I cherished proximity more than touch. Perhaps Mae was different, but the tumultuous intensity rolling behind those gray eyes lessened nonetheless.

Eventually, she sighed, tore off another chocolate-rich piece —but kept it in her hand.

"Don't worry about anyone finding out you're with me. We'll stay on the right side of the river, and I'll enchant your appearance and suppress your magic signature. The Council will never know. But"—her gaze flicked down—"they're also the reason why I want you by my side." She broke the piece into two smaller ones. "If it's a trap, you're... Well, you're my best shot of getting out of it."

The tension and uncertainty that had built up within me deflated as understanding spread its warmth through my veins.

I thought back to the shop—to Sylo caging me in my own body and the roar of shadowfire I refused to release from fear of harming innocents. It had been a one-time occurrence, that loss of control. And while that didn't mean it would never repeat, I was fairly certain I wouldn't panic like I did back then. Even if my body somehow ended up bound.

It had been the inky terror clawing up my neck at the unexpected, suffocating prison I'd found myself in that had torn the reins from my hands. Now that I'd experienced it once, I could just breathe through the worst. The unnerving sensation would remain, yes, but I wouldn't lose myself to it. Not like that.

I leaned back in the chair and waited until Mae met my eyes before I said, "You want me because I can use the shadowfire to keep them at bay. Act as your shield."

Mae, apparently, hadn't read my reaction the way I'd hoped. "I wouldn't have asked this of you if it wasn't—"

"Mae, it's fine." I laughed. "Really, it is."

Her relief hit me like the sweet scent of honeydew mixed with the headier fragrance of raspberries that had blown in from somewhere beyond.

"When do we leave?"

"Early tomorrow morning." She ate the two smooshed pieces of pastry at long last. "We'll take Nyon with us, since he's an excellent Spellweaver—and you already have a connection with him. I figured we might as well use the time together to expand on your spells and enchantments. If you'd like, of course."

I nodded with shameless enthusiasm and treated myself to another bite as well. "How long will we be gone?"

"If everything goes according to plan, we should be back in the evening. A little after dinner, probably."

"I better get some rest, then." I rose and started piling the embarrassingly large amount of snacks back in my arms. Mae brushed the crumbs off her fingers, then her bejeweled gray dress. When she peered up at me right as I secured everything, I added, "Thank you. For putting your faith in me."

Mae didn't say anything. But the stunned, grateful silence spoke volumes on its own.

I KNELT ON THE BANK, watching the girl staring back at me from the river's surface.

Unlike Zaphine's illusion that had transformed and aged my every feature, Mae had only modified my eyes and hair. No one from the Council, not even Sylo or the rest of the guards, had been around me long enough for the finer nuances to settle in their minds. And the mane of pastel pink hair with glittering gold streaks tumbling over my shoulders had altered my appearance more than I thought possible. Combined with sea-green eyes, skintight black pants adorned with a series of round gold buttons, a lace cropped top, and a long, light gray cardigan perfect for the mild weather, I doubted even my own parents would have recognized me.

I knew I'd spend a good long while gaping at the mirror as Mae and the blue-and-white-haired librarian Briar observed their handiwork.

I sat on my haunches and twirled a strand between my

fingers, observing the versatile pink nuances coloring the individual hairs. A smile cupped my lips. Remarkable. After all the years of attempting to change my natural color—with absolutely zero success—I'd finally experienced a change. Though if I'd picked this shade out in Soltzen, I would have been just as much the odd one out as my silver marked me to be. We were supposedly people of bright, stark colors, of light and intensity, but being in Svitanye had taught me we were, if anything, tame.

"This really is a good look on you," Nyon commented as he wiped the droplets of water from his face. He still appeared a bit sleepy, but the cool river had certainly helped us all wake up a bit. "A spell could make it as permanent as you want."

Mae chuckled from farther up on the bank. "An enchantment is fine for now, Nyon. Conserve your energy. Ember is a voracious learner." Heat seeped into my cheeks as she winked, then said to Nyon, "Wait till you get her in swearing mode. That's when you know she won't give up until she cracks the magic."

"You mean literally?" I asked dryly, which only resulted in a wide grin as we both recalled my...somewhat more disastrous attempts.

"Plus," Mae went on, readjusting the tailored lightweight mint jacket that complemented her dress, the pink so light it came across as white unless you truly looked, "I just might need you in Nebla once we assess the damage."

"You'll assist?" I asked him. As far as I was aware, librarians and the Council did not get along. And they certainly didn't mix magic.

When Mae said she intended to bring Nyon along, I

presumed his role, like mine, would fall under the umbrella of security, not Council-work.

"Mae will cover my interference with the focus point." He rose and offered me a hand. I let him pull me up, then quickly brushed a few specks of dirt off my pants. "She's a strong Enchanter, the best, actually, but magic like the one she has to realign usually requires both an Enchanter and a Spellweaver."

I frowned and turned to Mae. "Why did they send you alone, then? Is that why you think this could be a trap?"

"Sadly, no." Her bitter laugh mixed with the gentle rumble of running water. "It's standard protocol. The point is nearing destabilization but isn't there yet. Unless there's an absolute emergency, only one councilor at a time can leave Ausrine. Normally, they would have sent a Spellweaver, yes, as they're more suited for this kind of work, though Nyon is right." She slid her gaze to the librarian. "Still not the same as if they would have assigned a pair, but definitely a better choice than an Enchanter. As it is, my proximity and absence, as well as the fact that I had done this several times before, mark me as the best candidate."

I couldn't even imagine the life she led in Ausrine, with all these limitations and responsibilities bundled up tight. I always thought I had no freedom at the Norcross estate, but compared to the shackles Mae wore day after day, I felt I was more a cloistered, spoiled child than a true prisoner of my so-called duties. I pursed my lips, then stopped the thoughts trying to run in a thousand directions.

Measuring grief wasn't some kind of competition. There were nuances, yes, and layers—but just because someone had it harder than you didn't negate your own struggles.

I knew what kind of punishment marrying someone I didn't

love would be, what existing as no more than a pretty decoration on their hand and their personal breeding mare would do to me.

Casting one last look at my reflection in the brilliant water, I joined Mae and Nyon—then breezed across the shifting land with ease and comfort I hadn't felt before.

As if the part of me that originated from Svitanye had truly unlocked.

CHAPTER TWENTY-SIX

THE SWEET SCENT OF POMEGRANATE ENSNARED MY SENSES AS we passed beyond the uniform stone wall that embraced the town with protective affection.

My mind had comprised a roughly sketched image of what to expect when we'd approached Nebla and I'd glimpsed the multicolored buildings rising behind the wall with their shuttered windows and long balconies facing the countryside. But while not entirely inaccurate, the image had nothing on the sight before me.

I was forced to pause—unable to take as much as another step forward as I drank in the curve of the narrow street, the buildings pressed closely together yet still possessing a spacious quality that spread across the entire setting.

It should have been impossible, for something so small to feel so grand, and yet Nebla was precisely that.

My gaze caught on a facade four buildings down, arch

moldings adorning its large windows and delicately crafted aprons protruding beneath. A style so different from its neighbors that hardly had sills, yet despite the variation that should have disrupted the flow, it only increased it. Made it playful.

Nyon and Mae had stopped a few steps ahead and were smiling, far from unkindly, at the wonder that must have shown on my face. I hurried to catch up, though the impressions kept filling me, awakening that place that responded to this quiet beauty.

A few people walked down the street, baskets filled with fruit and delicacies from the market I could smell all the way from here, washing over the pomegranate and lavender fragrance the very air seemed to be made of. Judging by the voices drifting up the slight slope, the market must rest just around the corner.

"Impressive, is it not?" Nyon swept his gaze along the buildings as we advanced, and I couldn't help thinking he *became* like the town—his expression serene with multitudes of undertones that gently unveiled depths and facets of who the librarian truly was. His voice was tender as he said, "I've always loved the small towns. Nebla was one of the first I'd fallen for."

We hastened our steps to trail behind Mae who led us in the opposite direction of the market, her magic carrying her swiftly up the incline.

"Why then choose the Repository?"

As soon as I said it, it struck me that my question might have been too forward, too personal to simply blurt out, but Nyon didn't seem troubled by it. His gaze lingered on a display of white wooden baskets filled with lavender stalks, then turned to me.

"It's my calling, tending to history. To the books." He motioned to a tiny bookshop farther down the street. A woman with vibrant lime hair shaved closely on one side sifted through the tomes set on a rotating stand. "Some librarians do leave the Repository once they finish their apprenticeship. Or later on in life, if they find themselves in need of change—or simply uncover new aspirations."

It sounded lovely, this freedom of choice. I said as much to Nyon.

Up ahead, Mae slowed as she maneuvered past a group of children playing some sort of game with marbles and figurines on the cobblestones—though by the looks of it, just catching the marbles before they rolled too far away was half the fun.

"What do the librarians do if they choose to leave?" I glanced at Nyon, noting the hint of wistfulness lining his features. "I can't imagine simply...stepping away from all that knowledge."

"They don't—not necessarily." He grabbed the hem of his billowing robe as another group of children came running down the street. "Only rarely do they abandon the life entirely. More often than not, they open their own shops with specialized titles or carry on as teachers in the many schools across Svitanye." His gaze slid past me to the bookshop on my right. "But while those are noble professions—and I'm certain fulfilling for those who follow such paths—my heart is with the Repository."

I glanced into the shop as we came in line with its window. Indeed, there was a man wearing turquoise clothing standing behind the counter. Not the rippling robes Nyon wore, but an altered version of them. Meant for everyday life beyond the Repository's walls.

"Are there many librarians out here?" I tore my gaze away from the shop.

Nyon nodded, but it was Mae who answered, peering over her shoulder. "More than there are at the Repository."

My eyebrows shot up. I'd seen far from everything and everyone, but the sheer number of librarians I'd passed in the halls or shared a meal with in the broader sense wasn't exactly modest.

"The Repository is either one of two things," Nyon picked up as Mae turned left, then guided us through a narrow passageway that barely fit the width of her chair. "It's home, or it's the best possible school, even for someone who wants to return to this life. It wasn't constructed as such"—he shrugged and smiled—"but sometimes things have a mind of their own." We emerged on a similar street to the first one, lined with small shops and what appeared to be residential spaces on the floors above. "The heads of the Repository have long since stopped fighting the current and gone with it instead. So while we don't advertise the educational aspect, it *is* there—and free for anyone to take advantage of."

Intrigued by how it all worked, I wanted to ask more, but when Nyon's attention roamed across our surroundings and mine followed, the questions faded from my mind.

Wrought-iron decorations spanned across the width of the street, strung from rooftop to rooftop. Some shaped like books, some like birds, flowers, then the sun, moon, and stars, as if it were normal, so utterly normal to bear symbols of a world long gone.

The Council, perhaps even Svitanye as a whole, might not strive to reunite the lands, but they treated their past with affection.

I commanded my body to move, though neither Mae nor Nyon pressured me, but I couldn't resist one last look at the constellation of symbols representing precisely what we were fighting for. The wind chimes attached to them sang as softly as the magic in the background.

"Is it the same as in Ausrine?" I asked, tuning in to those chimes. "The magic? With streets shifting but intersections remaining the same?"

Mae paused as we neared one, halting us firmly within the confines of the street. "Take a look."

No more than five seconds ticked by before the chimes sounded. In a blur of movement, the alleys to the left and right switched—exchanging places with absolute precision. The one up ahead remained the same.

Definitely different, then, from Ausrine.

"Nebla is one of the more stable towns," she explained. "The shift you saw right now is a flux. That's what I came here to fix. As one of our oldest settlements, we strive to keep it as pristine as possible."

Pristine... Of course. "Svitanye was stable before the break."

"It was," Mae said solemnly. She glanced around the intersection as the alleys changed again, then led us forward, down the slope and deeper into Nebla's core where the predominantly empty streets became livelier, but not crammed. "The knowledge the Council passes on to every new member, one of the few areas that actually touch our history, not just our present, says the shifts didn't happen all at once. Svitanye fractured gradually."

She stopped by a shop and purchased a single rose, then took us into a slumbering passageway where we wouldn't interrupt the pedestrians' flow.

Mae ripped a petal. Then another.

"Large land masses broke apart first." Another petal drifted down into her lap. "Vast bits of landscape. Regions, really. Then"—she picked up the petal and tore it in half—"those pieces developed their own cracks and seams. And what remained"—she shredded the smaller bits until what remained of the rose's petals was no more than a sprinkling of red-pink scattered across her dress—"continued to fracture, over and over, until the Council managed to throw its net across the entirety of Svitanye, prevent the changes they—we—could control from destroying the land further, but not stop entirely on such a scale."

I hadn't even realized I'd stepped closer to Nyon until his warmth batted the chill Mae's words—the alternate world they painted had it not been for the Council—had planted within me.

Mae dusted the rose off her lap. "The original Council started tending to the settlements immediately, but we still lost several towns to the change before they had even come together, before they could come up with the proper spells and enchantments. When they did, the focus points came into being. Ones that are complex and encompass entire towns." A half-smile, albeit carrying a twinge of sadness, played upon her lips. "We're aware of what Svitanye would be like without these points."

Unlivable, was what she didn't have to say.

"Which is why we maintain them so vigilantly."

We reentered the gentle stream of pedestrians, then skirted around the right-hand side of a charming market brimming with jewelry and knickknacks before we progressed down a somewhat wider street lined with cafes and small restaurants. It was an effort not to succumb to the magnetic scent of coffee that seemed adamant to lure me into one of the establishments. The amused look Mae sent my way hinted she knew precisely the struggle I was going through.

Few of the townsfolk paid us any attention at all—unlike the three of us who kept our eyes open for anything amiss. Mae would recognize anyone from the Council or their guard, but Nyon and I, in silent agreement, refused to leave all the work to her, even if we were operating more on instinct than anything else.

A tiered fountain of light pink and blue hues that were almost kaleidoscopic rose in the square up ahead, every last inch of its translucent structure covered in markings. We approached it from the far side, where the current of passersby cutting across town wouldn't bother us. I sat on the ledge above the three scriptured steps and swept my fingertips across the dainty grooves. Nyon scooted up beside me, his robes brushing the edge of my cardigan, while Mae faced the sculpture, her gaze scanning the magic I had yet to see.

Or maybe—

Her attention fell on me, and before I could even finish the thought, Mae dipped her chin, an encouraging smile on her lips. I glanced at Nyon who did the same.

They couldn't be serious.

But, apparently, they truly were.

"I don't know how..." I shook my head, sliding farther down the ledge—away from the determination and mischief all but pulsing from them.

Nyon took my hand between his before I managed to scoot too far. "You heard me command the magic to reveal itself, Ember."

"Yes, I did—but that doesn't mean I can just *replicate* it. I don't even know the words—"

He rested his free hand over my heart. "Feel them, Ember. They're inside you." His warmth was a lifeline. "A revealing spell is one of the few you don't have to be taught. It's... It's like opening your eyes. Or breathing. You already know everything you have to do."

I exhaled and started to rise from my perch, but Nyon tugged me back down.

"No ceremony." He chuckled. "You don't need that. Just relax, Spellweaver."

I let out something between a snort and a laugh, then did as told despite the blood still racing through my veins. Remaining seated, I merely looked at the stunning fountain.

No ceremony.

All right, then. No ceremony.

Like opening my eyes.

Breathing.

Right.

Nyon's voice swept through my mind as I repeated his words so many times I doubted there was anything natural about them *or* my state any longer, but on its wings came something else. Something that rose from the depths of who I was—an undetermined substance that then took shape and flew from my lips in a gentle, gentle whisper before the rational side of me could ever hope to analyze it.

My heart hammered against my ribs.

Did I—

The fountain transformed before my eyes.

The translucent stone was still there, still crafting a kaleidoscopic tiered masterpiece, but much like in Somraque, with the tapestry of power, the magic overlaid reality here, too.

As the latter became more and more transparent, the former bloomed into existence.

Beautiful.

The amazement that swelled in my chest when I'd seen Nyon reveal the alarm spell had nothing on the insurmountable wonder that overcame me now.

Complex—the spell was so complex, an inexplicable part of me wanted nothing more than to gaze at it for days, try to unravel the finer details of how such a structure could keep an entire city not only together but fixed on a particular geographic point. Small lights flickered and traveled along the curved, deeply interwoven threads wrought of pure power—its own pulse. My lips parted, then pulled into a broad smile.

"I did it," I whispered. "I actually did it."

Nyon looked at me with kind, bright eyes, as if I had been silly to entertain any other idea, while Mae grinned, broadly enough to flash all her teeth.

She appeased the design my *spell* had unveiled, then met my gaze. "That was excellent, Ember. Next time we do this, we'll try an enchantment."

I understood full well why we'd gone the spell route now. Given how awed I'd been—still was—the enchantment more than likely would have escaped my too-happy mind within a few seconds of its creation.

"Now," she drawled and quirked a turquoise eyebrow, "for a taste of what you'll be able to do once you master the full scope of your abilities."

I got up from my perch and descended the three ornamental steps, then moved away from the fountain. There was no way I was missing even a second of this.

Nyon curled one leg beneath him, his turquoise robes spilling over the edge of the fountain, and peered up. "Ready when you are, Maelynn."

Lights continued to flicker across the design. Silence swept our side of the square as Mae and Nyon both focused on the power, the contrast between the breathtaking concentration and the bubbling life of Nebla so vivid I suspected magic was involved. Maybe I could have seen the spell, sensed the enchantment, but tearing my eyes off the speeding light and intertwined threads proved impossible. I tried to see what Mae and Nyon were seeing—the error that caused the instability. But the construction of the spell was far more complicated for my inherent understanding of such things to comprehend.

To think that I once would be able to...

My mind quieted as I spied a discrepancy—a short line of thread that never illuminated.

I narrowed my eyes at it, marked its position, then traveled across the wider composition to make sure I missed nothing else. Mae began whispering, as did Nyon.

The words were too silent for me to make out anything beyond the basics I had already become acquainted with, yet I felt their weight. The silent force of them as they seeped into the spell. I returned to that darkened thread. At first there was nothing. Then—

A flood of colors.

Like the nuances of the dawn sky, the magic became alive, shifting, the hues blending into one another and morphing into something entirely new. As if adding layer after layer, the thread thickened.

As Nyon's and Mae's voices died down, the colors disappeared, and the rope of magic returned to its normal state.

Every muscle tense, I didn't dare look at them. Had they failed—

A light shot down the strand.

Then another.

I blinked and took in the grander design, my breaths coming out loud—perhaps even halfway morphed into a cough.

Where the spell had been vibrant with the traveling lights even before, the movement seemed to pick up now. Faster. Smoother. As seamless and as beautiful as that fountain of starlight in Nysa's center, yet wholly different. Wholly its own.

"You fixed it," I said, voice barely louder than their earlier whispers.

Mae flashed me a smile over her shoulder. "Not quite yet. There are still some minor tweaks we need to do—fortifications to keep it from unraveling again."

Eyebrows drawn, I looked up at the bones of the focus point. "Is it—is it my presence here that's making it worse?"

"Not any longer," she said softly. "The focus points are far sturdier than the natural magic fueling the shifts. Those of cities and towns more so than any others. Even if I brought your entire group here, the effect on it should be negligible."

I remembered the conversation between the two merchants I'd overheard back at the inn where it had all changed between Mae and us—how they had barely managed to get through a tried crossing with the times and distances all wrong. "But the focus points in nature—we *had* influenced those, hadn't we?"

Nyon followed our conversation, a thousand thoughts seeming to churn behind his piercing gaze.

"A chain reaction." Mae leaned on one armrest. Her fingers twitched as if she wanted to spin her silver ring but thought better of it. "The shifts turning temperamental and violent inadvertently affected those points."

"I'm not sure I follow," I admitted.

I glanced at Nyon, but there was still that air of distance to his gaze—as if the conversation happening out loud was merely the backdrop for whichever one he held with himself in his mind.

"Why would we affect those points, but not this one?"

Though Mae remained serious, a corner of her lips twitched. "Sometimes it truly is about size."

Nyon coughed a strangled laugh, but quickly returned to the faraway places of his mind.

I pulled the cardigan around myself like a wrap. "A single tree doesn't possess the volume of a city."

"Precisely." Mae nodded. "When the pieces of land deviated from their usual routine, they created...abrasions. Shaved off parts of the spells holding the focus points. We"—the Council, she meant, a different quality in the way she said *we*—"reacted, but we definitely were *not* prepared. Some of those points are old, very precise spells with roots anchored deep in our land. The enchantments accompanying them are always fresh, infusing the spells with additional lifeblood, but their base is a permanent fixture. We rarely interfere with them aside from scheduled checkups since there had never been a need until now. It's possible some of them were already fragile, but still in good working condition, which is why we hadn't paid attention to them sooner."

Although her words were frank, she tried to sound reassuring. But all I could think of was the damage we'd caused. The scars we would continue to leave if we failed to move on soon. That dark part of me I'd locked away after Ivarr had brought me back from the brink threatened to rise but—

It would be unfair. Not a single one of us was a stranger to sacrifice. To loss. My existence might have caused more of it than I could bear, but nothing I could do would change that. I could only work on securing the future where there would be no place for such things left.

Somraquians, Svitanyians, and, yes, my own people, as wretched and convoluted as our society was, deserved better than these shattered pieces of lives.

I squared my shoulders and burned away the rogue, unwanted thoughts as if I'd unleashed my shadowfire upon them.

More than likely seeing the change, Mae dipped her chin—a simple gesture that conveyed volumes of her understanding—then returned her attention to the fountain. She said to Nyon, "Are you ready for another round? I'll fortify the threads while you lay the spells."

But Nyon looked at me, curiosity alive in his eyes. "I wonder... If you develop your abilities further, would the world accept you more as one of us?"

With that, he nodded at Mae and started working. Stunned as the question left me, I only partially followed how they fueled their magic into the threads, repairing what was damaged and strengthening the structure so that it would withstand whatever changes were still coming Svitanye's way.

If Nyon was right, then developing my magic was more important than ever.

Yet at the same time, I couldn't just forget that not merely its imbalance, but magic itself was what was causing Svitanye to deteriorate. Maybe they were divided between Spellweavers and

Enchanters because a combination of the two would be too much for this world to handle.

Flashes of Somraque overtook my mind. How the tapestry of power had frayed from magic overuse, allowing the Void to slither into the cracks.

Svitanye could never hope to survive an occurrence like that.

Lost in my thoughts, I hadn't heard anyone approach until a female voice said, "The Council working with a librarian? Now *that's* something you don't see every day."

CHAPTER TWENTY-SEVEN

THE SPELL'S THREADS FLARED AS MAE AND NYON'S WHISPERS fumbled.

They caught themselves between one heartbeat and the next, stabilizing the design, but didn't carry on with their work as all three of us stared at the tall, unfamiliar woman with sharp cheekbones and tightly coiled curls that shone like pure gold spilling down her bronze shoulders.

Behind her, the townsfolk carried on with their lives like before, oblivious to the tension crackling on our side of the square. I glanced at Mae, unsure what she wanted me to do.

The brief look she gave me wasn't an answer—just more of the same question. At least the woman wasn't from the Council or their guard. I doubted Mae would hesitate attacking if that were the case.

Still, I held my shadowfire close beneath the surface of my skin; if not to incapacitate, then at least to create a barrier and hold it long enough for us to get away. But revealing my obsidian, as we'd agreed beforehand, was a last resort. While Nebla stood on the same side of the Cuer River as the Repository, where it was supposedly safe—or *safer*—from anything getting back to the Council, we'd risked enough talking out in the open as we did. A report of coiling black magic would certainly waste no time getting to the proper ears.

"You can relax." The woman waved a debonair hand. The stone beads of her layered bracelets *clicked* together in a waterfall of sound. "I won't tell anyone, though I think it's about damn time the Council changed their stuck-up ways."

A surprised laugh escaped Nyon. Both Mae and I glanced his way, then back at this stranger who truly didn't look as if she meant us ill—and seemed content to give us however much time we needed to shake off the wariness.

In the silence that ensued, with only the fountain's serene bubbling connecting us to the world that existed beyond our encounter, I blatantly studied the woman as she, in turn, casually looked at all of us. Small lines creased the corners of her eyes and mouth—more laughing than frowning, though a vine of intuition niggling at the back of my mind suggested the latter had taken over at some point and had only recently begun to recede once more.

A swish of Nyon's robe filtered through to my thoughts, but when I slid my attention to him, he hadn't moved from his perch —maybe only came across as a bit uncomfortable with this standoff.

And he was right.

If our goal was to draw the least notice as was possible, then what we were doing here had to come to an end. I inclined my head at Mae.

Recognition flashed in her eyes, and she eased, allowing me

to maintain control of the situation in the background. The shadowfire coiled gently beneath my skin—at my command, should I need it.

"You know who we are," Mae said in her authoritative councilor voice. "It's only proper that you extend an introduction."

Cordial words, but the demand in them was clear. As was the insinuation entwined in the way she pointedly swept her gaze across the rest of the square, as if searching for whatever ambush we'd just stumbled into. She returned the full force of her focus to the golden-haired woman.

A hint of something that might have been sadness passed across the stranger's face, but was gone faster than I could read it. "Do you know who Ines was?"

"Yes." Mae frowned. "She was the councilor before me."

The one she replaced, I realized, after the strain had robbed the girl of her life.

The sadness seeped back into the woman's expression—a heavy, glissading thing I could taste in the air. She didn't bother to hide it. Not as she said, "Ines was my daughter."

VIVAELLE, as the woman had introduced herself, had retreated with me to the potted fig trees standing sentry in front of the nearest narrow house that made up the walls of the square. By the fountain, Nyon and Mae continued tending to the focus point, creating bursts of color that signified their repairs, though even without them, I could now tell which parts they were treating. Could see the results, too.

Vivaelle and I exchanged no words this entire time, simply

observed the councilor and librarian work side by side—
something, as had become clear, few people had ever had the
opportunity to witness.

What it meant to her, that she had the privilege to see it
now, was probably more than I could imagine or comprehend,
because the contained, silent storm of emotions I spied
whenever I glanced at her...

If experiencing the night had been a fulfillment of my soul's
desires, then this was hers. Her dream people had perhaps
wanted to disabuse her of, shatter it just because it wasn't
conventional.

I could have sworn we stood closer in those moments.

Nyon and Mae shook hands once they were done, both flush
with life and boasting matching smiles—until they remembered
the newest addition to our party.

To give them some more time, I turned to Vivaelle and asked
softly, "May I ask what drove you to seek us out? You must have
known you wouldn't get a kind reaction given the situation—"

"—is one you would prefer to keep concealed?" She huffed,
but the sound was good-natured. As if learning we were all doing
this on the sly had only acted in our favor. Endeared us to her.
"In all honesty, I was curious. Curious to know if I was even
right. What you would do..." She shook her head, the gold
reflecting the fountain's kaleidoscopic light, then looked around
to encompass us all. "Maybe I saw something of myself in all of
you."

"What do you mean?" Mae furrowed her brow.

Vivaelle shrugged. "I'm not one for following the rules
blindly, either."

No one seemed to know how to reply to that. We were all
breaking rules, to a far larger extent than just a librarian and a

councilor working together, but that was something Vivaelle couldn't know. Though I wondered what *my* role in all of this was through her eyes.

"Come," she said, "let me make you a meal. I presume you traveled here directly and must be starving. I know I am."

My stomach growled in response, and the quick, silent exchange between Mae and Nyon revealed they weren't any better off than I was. Still—

"Why?" I stepped closer to Mae and tugged the cardigan tighter around me.

Vivaelle leveled us with a no-nonsense stare. "I want to support change. In whichever way possible."

While there was a chance she could be leading us on, trying to win us over for who knew what reason, the weight in her voice told me that wasn't the case. She'd lost her daughter to the Council. To their harsh ways that maybe truly could have been ameliorated were they open for assistance.

"All right," Mae said. "But we can't stay long."

Satisfied, Vivaelle turned on her heel and motioned us to follow. She led us farther south down the street we'd used to approach the fountain until the numerous boutiques spaced out, then unlocked a heavy set of daffodil-colored doors leading to a pale stone-fronted building with a whisper.

The faintest of *creaks*, then a spacious, though small courtyard opened up beyond the short corridor. Three patios, one before each wall, harbored a wrought-iron table each and some chairs, along with an assortment of potted plants and small knickknacks that marked them as residential, though all currently vacant. Vivaelle took us to the one on the right and gestured to the empty seats.

"I'll be right back." She opened the glass-paneled door

leading inside and paused on the threshold, one hand braced against the frame. "Do you want some lumi, too?"

We all nodded, then watched her disappear into an orange-painted kitchen filled with rustic white cabinets, green plants with sharp leaves like the ones I'd seen at the inn, and a whole assortment of artwork-adorned tins I presumed were storage. A citrus rich fragrance flowed to us, then unobtrusive music—as if Vivaelle had wrought it from an enchantment. I traced my gaze up, to the airy curtains hugging the partially open windows, then along the globes of light in peach and pink strewn across the trellis cordoning off one corner of the patio—a spell, I noted, to keep the glowing twined at their hearts like a ball of yarn.

The clink of dishes drifted above the cheerful yet languid melody, followed by the sound of running water.

Nyon propped one elbow on the table and said to Mae, "What do you think?"

She didn't take her eyes off the sliver of kitchen visible from the outside. "I don't know." As if it had taken tremendous effort, she directed her gaze to him. "But I also don't think there's anything malicious about her invitation..."

"You *are* the councilor who replaced her daughter though," I pointed out, voice low, and sat down at long last. "Maybe she needs...closure. Maybe to extend help to you when she can't anymore for Ines?"

Though we all knew that a meal, as kind as it was, wouldn't be enough to save Mae from her fate.

Mae dropped her gaze to the table and traced her finger along the iron embellishments. "We should hear her out at least."

"I'll stay vigilant," I said, then asked, "Nyon, what's your take on this?"

He stayed quiet for a long while, brow furrowed and midnight blue hair sweeping against his cheeks in the almost imperceptible draft meandering through the courtyard. "If Vivaelle dislikes the ways of the Council,"—his blue eyes anchored on Mae—"maybe she could offer safe harbor if they come for you again."

"But that would require us telling her what we're doing." She twisted her ring and looked not at me, but the Savior. "I'm not sure we can risk it."

I placed both palms on the table, body pitched forward. "So we don't tell her everything. Just enough for her to understand that these changes you're working on put you on the Council's shit list. And that things might get worse before they get better. It might not be the entire truth, but it isn't a lie, either."

A soft thud from the kitchen sent us all skittering back until we looked as if we were only lounging instead of plotting. Vivaelle joined us on the patio and set four large glasses of lumi and bundles of cutlery down before she hurried back inside.

We didn't broach the subject again as we waited for her next appearance. True enough, it didn't take her long to bring out mouthwatering plates of roasted venison and seasoned sweet potatoes, with a little bit of salad on the side.

"Bon appétit." Vivaelle smiled, then wasted no time digging into the food right alongside us.

The meal passed in companionable silence, all of us too ravenous to carry a conversation beyond small talk which I normally abhorred yet, with Vivaelle, was oddly pleasant. Maybe because her words weren't empty, but sprinkled with facts of herself that formed a charming mosaic of insight.

The man, the *friend*, who had had offered himself to her when she spoke of her desire to have a child, had been a librarian turned teacher. He helped her raise Ines when she still traveled a lot as a musician before she chose to settle and teach others how to play an envious variety of instruments, keeping her own music for her friends, herself, and her daughter. A daughter with an artistic soul who had enjoyed sculpting as much as Vivaelle—and, indeed, I spotted figurines embedded in the wider setting, locked in such harmony my gaze had actually skipped over them earlier.

By the time there was no more food left, it wasn't just my stomach that was full, but my heart, too.

Vivaelle had even written down Mae's romance recommendation to pick up during her next visit to the bookstore. The woman...

The woman was a world of her own.

She retreated inside with the note and our plates—firmly refusing our assistance and magic.

"I like her," Nyon confessed in a tender tone, cradling his lumi.

His gaze rested on the open glass-paneled door. The kitchen beyond.

I glanced at Mae and knew I was speaking for the both of us as I said, "You're not the only one."

The sentiment lingered in the air long after the words had dissipated.

Even Vivaelle, when she returned with a fresh bottle of lumi and something I couldn't quite make out in her other hand, seemed to pick up on it, the contours of her face gaining an even warmer curve. She set the lumi down, then reclaimed her seat, covering whatever she'd brought out with her with both hands.

There was a fragile sheen in her eyes as she set her gaze on Mae.

"I wanted to give you this." She placed an elegant bracelet on the table, the gold glinting in the shafts of morning light and the diffused soft glow of the colorful bulbs.

"What is it?" Mae reached out just as Nyon said, "It's a spell." She turned to him. "Why can't I see it?"

I frowned and focused on the bracelet, willing the magic to reveal itself with soft words. Gradually, with the shyness of a blooming flower, the shimmering threads overlaid the metal, only the design was too small to make out—like the words written on blades of glass, almost obscured.

"I see it," I said, "but I can't distinguish the details."

Nyon leaned back in his seat, head cocked to the side and an expression that was partway between shock and admiration adorning his face. "This is exceptional work." He looked up at Vivaelle. "To have such a powerful, stable spell embedded in something so small... Who made this?"

"You know what it is?" Mae asked Nyon before Vivaelle could answer, then shot an apologetic look at the woman. But Vivaelle brushed it aside with a smile and silently gave them the space.

"I think"—his gaze flickered to Vivaelle, as if seeking confirmation—"it's three spells merged into one. The first for augmenting the Enchanter's abilities, the second for protecting the body from magical overuse. And the third..." He sucked in a sharp breath. "It can't be—"

"A portable focus point." Vivaelle gave him a close-lipped smile as Mae's jaw went slack. "It is."

I stared at the closely entwined magic, now recognizing a part of the design. Similar to the fountain, yet different.

If the fountain was a masterpiece, this reached into realms beyond it.

"But that's impossible," Mae muttered, her fingers clenched so tightly in a fist the knuckles whitened.

Vivaelle stroked a finger over the gleaming metal then pushed the bracelet closer to Mae. "By all accounts, it should be. But you have to know this only stabilizes the wearer and the land they're on, as long as the piece is not too vast. This—this was meant for my daughter but..." She cleared her throat, and a single tear caught on her lashes. "She died before Altas finished it for her."

The way she said the name, with so many nuances and undercurrents encompassed in a single word... This Altas must have loved Ines. And shared Vivaelle's pain in the years without her.

We were all too wrapped up in the significance and the undercurrent of sorrow to do much beyond breathe, so it was no surprise that Vivaelle's voice was the first to carry across the patio after she drank a third of her lumi—her eyes on the bracelet that entire time.

"Atlas believed there was a way to prolong Ines's life. She was often sent across Svitanye on repairs, and that drained her more than her tasks in Ausrine. They were together—before she was forced to join the Council. Just sweet, innocent love that hadn't yet had the room to grow. But they met again, during one of her travels." A tear rolled down her cheek. Then another, somehow bringing out the striking beauty of her emotions. Of her. "Altas always was an inventor who liked exploring the boundaries of magic. He wasn't exactly loved by the Council for it, so he mostly worked in secret, trying out different ways to make people's lives easier. And for Ines—he just wanted her to *have* a life.

"He worked for three years. Three years during which he had

to watch my daughter diminish under the strain. He gave her small trinkets when he could, spells to help her, however momentarily. But this"—she leveled her gaze on the bracelet now in Maelynn's hand—"was his crowning achievement. Something that would last almost perpetually, grant Ines at least another decade..."

Her voice broke, and she rubbed away her tears, as if the mere physical presence of them was a weight dragging her down.

"The Council sent Ines on another repair mission. She and Altas were supposed to meet in Noiterre." She sniffed and wiped her nose on the back of her hand. "Ines collapsed three shifts outside town. Altas went searching for her when she failed to show. Found her. But he was too late."

My chest was heavy with the weight of her story, threatening to cave in on itself as the waves of Vivaelle's love and sorrow crashed into me over and over. Nyon swiped the tears from his cheeks and met my gaze over the table as he reached for his lumi with a trembling hand. But Mae—Mae clutched the bracelet with bone-white knuckles, the color entirely drained from her face.

Then, as if gradually resurfacing from inky waters, she unclenched her fingers and stared at the gold band. She looked at Vivaelle, her voice raw as she said, "You—you're giving me...life."

The woman smiled, and a fresh tear revived the path down her cheek. "I want you to have what my daughter couldn't."

CHAPTER TWENTY-EIGHT

ICE-FIRE CONSUMED MY GRADUALLY COLLAPSING LUNGS.

I didn't even have the strength in me to glower at Ivarr as he pushed into another lap—*past* the point where we were supposed to stop.

Only a thin sheen of sweat glistened on his forehead when he flipped around to wink at me, now jogging backwards. Bastard.

He pivoted, showing off his honed back and firm thighs that could probably carry him for ages.

I snorted, but even that came out as nothing but a weak, choked sound.

For Sun's sake...

I should have known he would dangle false promises in front of me like a pitcher of water to a man dying of thirst. The fact that he'd insisted we start training today despite my late return from Nebla the previous evening had, after all, spoken volumes. Ivarr had *zero* intention of taking it easy on me.

"Come on, Savior, you can do one more," he tossed over his shoulder.

Not without vomiting, I couldn't.

His long, athletic legs carried him forward while I slowed my pitiful jog into a dragging walk. Briefly, I considered smacking him over the head with a strand of shadowfire, but the obsidian was lying low, apparently harboring the exact same aversion to exercise that was the key component of my salty mood. Though the annoyance at least kept me from turning into a puddle of flesh. Hard to be angry when you were unconscious.

Once I was sure I wouldn't toss what little was in my stomach onto the grass, I stopped by the almost nauseatingly fragrant rosebushes. I bent over and braced my palms against shaky knees, sucking in measured breaths that I wasn't entirely certain made matters better or worse. Ivarr was nowhere in sight, but it didn't take him long to finish his extra lap and run—far too cheerfully—to my side.

I straightened and glared at his smug face. "Don't you dare—"

"You look like shit." He laughed, paused, then broke out in barking laughter once more when I glared harder. I could have sworn those were tears, not sweat, lingering in the corners of his eyes. "Good thing we didn't have to carry you all the way out here, Your Majesty."

This time, I *did* smack his head. The tiny wisp of shadowfire whipped at him, then retreated close to my body, coiled and tense like a baby snake ready to strike again.

Ivarr looked at the obsidian, wide-eyed—

Then nearly choked on the avalanche of laughter.

I drew the shadowfire back inside. So much for *that*.

Arms crossed, I watched him suffocate on his uncontrollable

amusement. The longer we both kept it up, however, the harder it became to maintain a straight face. Eventually, one corner of my mouth flicked up. Then the other.

I snorted and rolled my eyes, but my composure had already frayed beyond saving. A husky, still more than a little breathless, laugh spilled from my lips at long last. I slung a slightly limp and *definitely* sweaty arm across Ivarr's shoulders. The stink he'd just have to brave.

"You're a complete asshole," I crooned, "and damn lucky I like you. *But* you get to go through two more books than me today. Fair is fair."

"Yeah?" Mischief shone in his gaze and irradiated his ruggedly handsome features. "Who are you to decide that?"

I smirked. "The Savior who can still throw up all over your shoes if you don't obey."

AFTER NEARLY FALLING asleep in the bath, I slipped into a pair of wide-legged emerald green pants. The shimmering top I chose clung to my form, accentuating the lovely fall of the trousers. I braided my wet hair since I had no enchantment to dry it yet, the moisture cooling my spine where it lay heavy between my shoulder blades. Thankfully, it was warm enough in the Repository that I didn't have to worry about getting a cold.

I caught my reflection in the mirror, my focus drifting to the silver. The pink enchantment had faded when we'd returned, and although a part of me missed the gorgeous pastel, I realized I'd grown...fond of the silver.

To what extent the reason behind my change of heart rested

in Somraque, I didn't want to know. Didn't want to even think about. Simply accepted the fact for what it was.

Ivarr was waiting for me in the hallway, his black hair slicked back and a thoroughly content expression resting on his face, as if he'd finally found a piece of himself he'd been missing.

"Since I'm not as petty as some," I drawled, then gestured to his appearance, my tone warmer now, honest, "you look good, Ivarr."

He bowed his head. "As do you, Ember."

We smiled at each other, the moment pulsing between us, then linked elbows and walked down the winding ramp. Several librarians bid us good morning as we crossed paths; most, however, were doing precisely what we were—following the scent of delicious food straight to the large hall.

My gaze immediately caught on the patio doors now that I knew where they led, but the wet state of my hair—and the damp of Ivarr's—decided I'd have to take him there another day. I wasn't entirely sure why, but something told me he'd enjoy the setting.

"Stars, I love that smell," he muttered as we stepped fully into the hall and the fragrance of freshly brewed coffee hit us full-on.

I inhaled so deeply one would think I could actually ingest it that way.

From Ivarr's chuckle, it wasn't a stretch to assume that was precisely what I'd appeared to be doing.

"What?" I shot him a daring look. "Don't deny your senses aren't having a tiny coffee orgasm right now..."

A librarian—no, not just *a* librarian, but Briar—burst into a wholehearted laugh behind us right as Ivarr succumbed to a coughing fit laced with snorting chuckles.

He barely got himself under control when we reached our table, the others already gathered and almost halfway through their meals. Eriyan's mouth was crammed with enough food that he looked like an overstuffed squirrel. I snorted softly. Where all of it went, I had no idea. I wondered if the Repository had enough sustenance to satisfy him if he ever decided to train with us.

Sun, even *I* was ravished, now that the nausea had finally subsided.

Ivarr held out a chair for me.

"Chivalry won't save you from the extra books, my friend," I teased, then laughed at his answering scowl.

He plopped down in the seat beside mine and started piling food onto his plate without another word, though I didn't miss the smile tugging on his lips.

I touched my knee briefly to his—a gesture he returned—then leaned to my left and quietly asked Mae, "How are you?"

We hadn't seen each other since late yesterday evening when I retired to bed, leaving her and Nyon to fill the others in on what had happened during our trip. They both seemed to understand that after an entire day spent in company, however pleasant, I required some solitude to reenergize.

Light briefly illuminated her eyes, but the gnawed marks of guilt lurking beneath hinted she was preoccupied with a more pressing matter than what she had gained through Vivaelle's gift. Something her words, as if summoned by the thought, confirmed.

"The visit to Nebla will keep the Council off my back, but not for long." She set down the bread roll and sighed. "If I return to them, I won't be able to come back for you. Help you cross the land to wherever the fragment is."

I paused, mulling the question over before setting it free, no judgment attached. "Is that what you want to do? Return to them?"

Mae opened her mouth, then closed it, shaking her head. A tremor rushed down her limbs, fingers tightening around the steaming cup of coffee. I caught the glint of the bracelet beneath her long, white sleeves.

"A part of me does," she admitted just as the conversation around us cranked up a notch, offering protection for her words. "We might not see eye to eye in everything, but we're in this together. I hate the thought of turning my back on them. Hate that I even put them in the position that weakens them even if part of it is of their own making. But my heart—it's with you."

Her gaze was lowered as she said it. Coffee threatened to slosh over the edge as she gripped the gold-rimmed mug so hard her fingers started to tremble. I placed a hand on her forearm and drew her attention to me.

"Breathe, Mae," I said, then, once I felt her muscles unclench under my touch, went on. "I'm not a stranger to difficult choices." *Everyone's* attention was on me now despite their pretending otherwise. "But I've also experienced what it's like to have it stolen from you. The only thing worse than making a bad decision, is not having the ability to choose at all. And sometimes, when you face a fork in the road and both paths feel right and wrong at the same time, decide which one will persevere. Which one you'll have the chance to return to after you explore the other—or if picking one will, in the end, lead to the other. Not in the most straightforward way, maybe, but after endless drops and sharp turns, they just might join when the terrain isn't quite as treacherous any longer."

"And if they don't meet? If you can only have one?"

"I think things are rarely that finite." I drew back. "But if they are, then you'll at least know you tried. Perhaps mourn the loss, but not regret it."

Mae nodded and a shuddering exhale unburdened her chest. Still, her voice was barely more than a whisper as she asked, "Which path is the Council?"

My lips drew into a sympathetic line, but where our skin touched as I lay my palm atop her hand, I fed nothing but reassurance. Nothing but my belief in her, even if the message might not be one she wanted to hear.

"The Council is the path you will make it to be."

AFTER SPARRING with Ivarr for a good forty minutes in the moderately spacious chamber adjacent to one we were working in, thankfully devoid of librarians this time of the day, I was panting softly, feeling the burn in my muscles from learning how to throw a mean punch—but still in a no more enthusiastic mindset to return to the Dasolann family chronicles.

My instincts continued to nag me that there would be no mention of the fragment there. Reason, on the other hand, insisted that just because someone *looked* like they wanted to do nothing more than create and throw parties all the time, that didn't mean they should be written off. Sometimes an easy, carefree demeanor served as an excellent shell for storing secrets.

To a point, it was how I'd kept mine in Soltzen, though I'd always carried the impression I was a mere neophyte at the game whenever surrounded by the oh-so-esteemed men of Soltzen's high society.

No, the Dasolanns couldn't be written off purely for the image they projected.

Still, when Ivarr claimed his seat by the table, looking refreshed after our training, I found myself wandering along the high shelves next door, gaze skimming the many volumes placed on display before I begrudgingly entered our study room—and stopped short of the desk.

"Need to go another round?" Ivarr asked, holding his place in the book with a finger. Asked not to mock me—but a sincere offer.

I gazed at the dawn sky, then back at him, and shook my head. "I need another subject to read."

Ivarr didn't press for more.

Once I did an entire circle around the adjacent room and found nothing that caught my interest in the way I felt it should, I ventured out into the corridor. Beyond the study where Ada and Mae worked, in another branch of the wing, I pushed through the set of doors that brought me into a long, rectangular chamber that was actually more of a hall with its tall ceiling and incredible collection that spanned down the sides like twin rows of portals. A few librarians were sitting behind the many desks set in a straight line down the center, with additional tables tucked between the windows and bookcases. I took a few steps to the left, confirming it had the same layout, then took in the entirety of the sight once more.

A softly chiming spell bathed the room in a glow that was kind to the eyes, bright, but not so much that the light would reflect sharply off the paper. How I had overlooked this part of the Repository before, I didn't know. But I was glad to have found it.

Of their own volition, my feet carried me past the librarians to the volumes at the far end of the room. They appeared ancient, robust in their leather bindings—far sturdier than even the chronicles Ivarr and I had been going through. Curiosity piqued, I silently slid the ladder kept off on one side to the center of the stack, then climbed its wooden steps.

The low-grade ache in my muscles was oddly...pleasing, if a reminder that I was a long way from getting in shape yet.

But any thoughts of what I might accomplish in time with Ivarr sank into the background as I examined the books up close. The letters on the spines had lost their color over the ages, some barely readable, although some, I noticed, were marked with nothing more than a symbol.

No, not a symbol. A crest.

I tilted my head to the side, easily balancing on the ladder, and studied one after the other.

Crossed daggers entwined with thorny vines.

A raven carrying a scroll.

A crown ensconced in glorious wings.

Three stacked tomes, with a sharp quill perched atop.

A sword slicing down a blazing sun.

My breath hitched, and I nearly lost my footing. The ladder groaned as I jerked to right myself, and yet throughout it all, I couldn't tear my gaze off the symbol.

I worked some moisture into my too-dry mouth, then, once I was fairly positive I wouldn't splatter onto the ground, drew the volume from its shelf with a trembling hand.

With my shaky knees and airy head, I took extra caution climbing down while clutching the book to my chest, though there was no relief to bask in even when I had both feet firmly on the bright stones.

The librarians paid me no heed as I half ran to a small desk tucked beneath the window on the other side of the stacks—set the farthest away from them all. I placed the book down and wiped my sweaty hands against my pants before I sat.

Sat and just stared at the embossed sword-sliced sun.

I traced a finger across the crest as if the mere texture of it could convey volumes. But there was only one thing that truly would.

I opened the tome.

The same symbol was painted on the yellowed page, and beneath it, a single name penned in ornate letters.

Norcross.

CHAPTER TWENTY-NINE

LIFE BEFORE THE BREAK. MY FAMILY'S HISTORY, THEIR *history*, when the world had still been whole.

My heartbeat pulsed in my ears and distorted the quiet sounds of pages turning, robes swishing, and whispered commands. I tried to read past the first paragraph, but couldn't focus beyond the roar of my thoughts.

Soltzenians lived for the present. The past existed as nothing more than a dusty pedigree that perhaps added some flavor to the prestige, but could never hold a candle to current actions— the status in society a High Master had at the precise moment of the present.

Another's achievements, even if they were your ancestors, meant nothing.

Established High Masters could open doors for their beloved sons—or use their daughters to form alliances that were more for show than anything else—but even those sons had to create a name for themselves, every second of every day of their lives.

The rest was left to fade among the rubble of memories the years would eventually clear away until not even a speck remained.

I *had* glimpsed some of those specks, and through them, gleaned that my bloodline was old; that my ancestors were among the first High Masters. But everything I'd pieced together from the disconnected snippets sprinkled throughout my life was limited to the time when Soltzen existed as a separate entity.

Of course I hadn't known any better at the time—but even when Mordecai had spoken of my people as a whole, when Ada had revealed we had all once lived together, Svitanyians, Soltzenians, and Somraquians alike, my mind had never considered that the Norcrosses, too, had been among them. Not in the manner this book suggested.

An entire chronicle.

Perhaps it had simply been too much to take in. Or maybe my upbringing *had* blinded me, just as it was always meant to.

My fingers danced along the side of the tome, feeling the hundreds of pages bound together that presented a part of history I would never have been aware of. My own family wasn't aware of.

Then again, when all that mattered was the role you played in the present, *why* would anyone ask themselves where their true lineage started? Why bother when it would gain them nothing in society, only cost them hours they could be basking in or improving their standing?

Although I wondered...

Those books I'd read, the stories of night, dawn, and all the beautiful things that were not part of our sun-kissed existence— maybe some resilient shavings of our history *had* survived the churning of time, regardless of the oblivion or negligence the people were set on.

This, however...

I lay my palm flat atop the smooth paper, letting its ages-old essence permeate me.

This was a window into knowledge I never even knew I craved with every bone in my body.

I closed my eyes, inhaled deeply, then folded my hands in my lap as I pitched a little forward and focused on the page. The first paragraph outlined where in the *region* known as Soltzen my family originated from. Not High Masters, not yet—but the following paragraphs marked the first mentions of a small, yet well-off estate, where villagers congregated to pass through portals a man named Vichelory Norcross created day after day to ease their travel.

The book portrayed him as someone with ambition, but not without compassion. He did not charge the villagers use of his portal. The only thing he asked in exchange was their loyalty.

"Ember."

I jerked up and glanced over my shoulder. The tall bookcases creating a corridor towards my table were empty. Beyond them, a glimpse of turquoise, just as before. I grabbed the edge of the desk as I twisted in the other direction to see who—

"Ember, meet us in the blue room. Now."

Again, the voice came out of nowhere. Only now, there were no doubts who it belonged to.

Mae.

She must have spelled it, projected it over to me much as I had augmented her words to monitor her conversation with Sylo. A useful enchantment. I needed to ask her about it later, but even more so, I burned to know the reason behind the summons.

Just as I carefully slid back the chair to make as little noise as possible, Mae's voice—a single, simple statement—sent it grazing against the floor.

"Zaphine... She found a reference to the fragment."

THE ROOM WAS, like its name suggested, bedecked with ornaments, chaises, and tables, all in various shades of blue. Soothing yet elegant, the color offset the many volumes stored on the floor-to-ceiling shelves dominating the walls and comprised a breathtaking image with the nuanced sky visible above the splash of green through the window.

With my mind still drifting on another plane, the sight would have easily been one I could lose myself in, replay the many images the first chapter of the Norcross chronicle had painted.

I directed my gaze at the group clustered around a large desk set in the very center of the space—precisely where my focus, too, should be.

Undivided.

Ada stepped aside when I approached, though her fingers briefly skimmed my elbow. Her outwardly contained excitement leaped at the touch, and I flashed her a quick smile before taking in the thick book laid open on the light blue surface. Zaphine's pearl-colored fingernail pointed to a densely written passage, blurred a little from this distance. Ivarr breezed inside and squeezed beside me, bringing with him a breath of fresh air the room seemed desperately in need of.

Half leaning against me, he looked at Zaphine. "What did you find?"

"One more time for the latecomers?" Eriyan grinned and not so subtly tipped his head in our direction.

I glared at him—not without noting Dantos caught somewhere between a chuckle and an eye roll—but my attention was whisked away the instant Zaphine's voice swept through the room. "The Hazeldyne family were collectors even before the fracture. They established and ran several galleries, devoted their lives to exhibiting the various art forms of magic, as well as objects either shaped through it, or forged by it. Being for the majority Spellweavers, they could preserve illusions, separate them somehow from the blood so that they existed in a sort of cocoon, a—"

"A time loop?" I offered.

Zaphine blinked, cheeks tinted pink with the same excitement that had pitched her voice a note higher. "Y—yes, precisely."

"So they either had mixed blood in the family," I mused, leaning into Ivarr who supported me with a firm hand, "or they found a way to recreate the effect of our powers. Soltzen's powers," I amended, not entirely sure if I could truly count myself among them any longer.

Zaphine nodded, but didn't provide a definite answer. She brushed her fingers along the page almost absentmindedly. "I was fascinated by this prospect, then thought who better to take care of a relic than a group of individuals who had devoted their lives to preserving artifacts? So I checked the lists of every artwork in their possession, every heirloom, or unique piece of magic that had found its way into their hands. It took a while to track down mentions of those stored in their personal vaults since so few people knew about them, but one of the Hazeldynes had a gift for the written word. Stories, poetry, but also a diary."

She turned the book around, and although the others had probably already seen the passage, the entire group tilted forward, closing around the table like petals of a blooming tulip wound in reverse.

I read the sentence from where Zaphine marked it with her finger. "...a piece of a flat metal disk bearing inscriptions." I whipped my head up. "That's the fragment." A huffing, disbelieving laugh left my lips. "They had the fragment."

Perhaps even still did.

"Where are the Hazeldynes now?" Ivarr asked, his grip on me so tight I wasn't sure he was even aware of what he was doing.

The light in Zaphine's eyes dimmed. "The last died just under a century ago."

WE ALL PROMPTLY EXCHANGED OUR current reading materials for volumes on the Hazeldyne family. While better than endless passages about parties, with every new page and no mention of the fragment, poring over the books made me more and more restless. Even the shadowfire sensed my mood, sending its icy vines through me in an attempt to douse the searing heat.

But this was one battle it couldn't assist me in.

Ivarr propped his head on his knuckles and peered at me. "A quick round?"

"Honestly, I think I'm too wound up for that." I blew out a frustrated breath. "Might knock you out."

"Come now, Savior." Ivarr rose and strode far away enough

from the table and shelves so that nothing was at risk of breaking. He planted his feet wide, then ran a hand through his dark waves to push them away from his face. "Get some of that tension out."

I rolled my eyes, although that was a smile I felt tugging at my lips. "Fine. What do you have in mind?"

His gaze took in the attire I'd changed into once I realized finding the Norcross chronicle had made me sweat as badly as one of Ivarr's sessions.

The dress was a beauty of flowing dark purple-blue, adorned with silver hems; glittering dust of the same shade spread from the bottom up. Lavish to the eye, but its cut was practical, not nearly as restricting as the garments I would have chosen before we started our exercises.

While Ivarr made a point I should be able to fight no matter what I wore—and I agreed—it was still early days. I wasn't about to let even the smallest advantage slip by.

"I want *you* to attack first," he said at last, done with his appraisal.

"What?" This wasn't how we worked. "I thought you were teaching me how to defend myself?"

"And sometimes,"—he leveled a pointed look at me—"the only way to do that is to lash out first."

L*ASH OUT FIRST.*

While in the context of our fight, that had turned out to be a complete disaster since my body, apparently, gave away my intention long before I executed a move *and* I had "fucking zero tactic" as Ivarr had so kindly put it—then groaned when I slugged him in the shoulder—it also made me realize all of us had been on the defensive this entire time.

But most of all me.

Friends, allies, the relationships between us didn't matter. I was lagging behind. Behind their knowledge. Behind the Sun-damned *world*.

Once I swallowed as much dinner as I could muster with my stomach twisted in a knot, I left the bleary-eyed group behind and marched out into the gardens. Though there was no good reason for keeping the others in the dark, I felt like this was something that was mine alone. Something to be viewed and observed in isolation.

In the pocket of greenery suffused with fragrances that flowed through me in a velvet blend, the foundations of my resolve anchored within me.

I slipped back into the Repository through the back door, then curved my way to the rectangular chamber with its high ceiling and twin, neatly spaced rows of bookcases, past the librarians who remained engrossed in their work—right to the small nook where I'd stashed the Norcross chronicle after I'd heard Mae's call. As if a part of my subconscious knew what would happen. What I would do only hours later.

Tucking the book under my arm, I marched up to my room.

Voices brushed against my ear. Dantos's. Ada's. Without second thought, I curled my fingers around the pendant and slowed down time. The corridor was empty, but the volume I'd picked up on earlier suggested they were conversing just on the other side of the threshold to his room.

I didn't release the power until I stood directly in front of my door, and even then, I hardly breathed as time sprang back into motion and I shouldered my way in, grateful I hadn't locked the chamber.

I did now, though.

The book sat heavy in my arms, heavier than it had been, now that I was ensconced within the familiar walls, alone. But I also wanted to keep it that way.

Had I known how to craft a spell that prevented outside disturbances, I would have wrapped the entire space in it.

I tipped my head against the door in an attempt to curb the thundering roll of anticipation shooting faint tremors down my limbs, but the sensation refused to yield. A somewhat bittersweet laugh rose in my chest.

Reaching and accepting a resolve was one thing.

Actually upholding it—

I pushed off the door and cut across to the bed before my mind traveled to places where focus was next to impossible. The duvet seemed to curve around the tome as I set it down, cocooning it in its painted flowers. I observed the Norcross crest embossed on the front cover a little longer, then climbed onto the bed—but didn't touch the chronicle just yet. Instead, my fingers sought out the blue-green spell-leaf.

I held it towards the light.

Having this, being who I was—

I glanced at the book.

Part of it came from the word-preserved times in there. Ages of threads aligning and connecting to form this present.

Form...me.

I caressed the scripture adorning the leaf, then tucked it in my brassiere—right next to my heart. The chronicle's presence by my feet tugged at me. I curled up on the mattress, my back to the wall, then propped the tome on my legs and bared its pages.

Any strain that had ailed my eyes earlier disappeared the instant I began sifting through the chapters.

My gaze cut sideways across the paragraphs, skipping harmless annotations, records, and recollections, driven by a force I had attempted to mute, but couldn't any longer. It was about halfway through that I found it.

A remembrance.

"Recount."

The whispered command spilled from my lips almost of its own volition. The plans of a different reality erected around me, obfuscating my surroundings and plunging me into the lively echo of times long gone.

My family's history.

My heartbeat pounded in my ears.

But Mordecai's too.

CHAPTER THIRTY

A TALL MAN HELD COURT AT THE HEAD OF AN OVAL TABLE SET at the heart of a chamber bearing all marks of Soltzen's architecture—save for what reigned beyond the window with its wrought-iron grill.

Darkness.

Though I had known, known on a rational, logical level that the night had once graced my homeland, too, seeing it for the first time—

I would have probably spent the entire remembrance marveling at the textures of the past, the different hues it painted upon that which was familiar. But there was a far more prominent aspect of the scene that demanded my attention.

Clad in a rich green-and-gold tunic, his fingers bedecked with heavy, gemstone encrusted rings, everything about the man, from his immaculate, slightly curled golden hair to the clothes, the posture, screamed of power. Of wealth. Yet all of it paled in comparison to the sigil embroidered across the wide expanse of his chest.

The sword. The sun.

Norcross.

"Have you received confirmation from Saelen yet?" He lay his palm flat against maps strewn across the oak surface and peered at the new arrival, a man with hair a warm shade of brown who pushed past the two guards flanking him on each side.

He filled the vacant spot by the table and inclined his head.

"The Ancient in the northernmost territory has been taken care off," he said, then lowered his voice—almost conspiratorial, if it weren't for the blunt satisfaction coloring his tone. "A wise decision to risk sending Saelen in with a small force. Some of the villagers beneath the mountain noticed their approach, but they were easy to eliminate while the rest advanced on the keep. Once the Ancient's guards on the perimeter fell, there was only the bastard and his whore to take out."

The smile that spread across the golden-haired man's—my *ancestor's*—face chilled me to my bones.

"Excellent." He drank deeply from the crystal goblet then set it on the only clear part of the table close to the edge. "We move tomorrow, cut a portal to the groove of oaks just beyond the temple,"—he tapped a location on the gorgeous, detailed map unlike any I'd ever seen—"another by the river,"—his finger swept up—"then we press in from both sides."

"What if the families expect us, Ekelyon?" The auburn-haired man to his left, another High Master, judging by his refined, almost extravagant clothes, asked. "If someone had evaded Saelen's men and is loyal to the Ancients, they might warn—"

"You doubt me, Virel?" The amusement in Ekelyon's eyes was

lethal. "You can always stay, hide behind your walls—though I cannot guarantee which slab of land you will end up on once we're done. Perhaps bisected, if fate will lay the break across your path."

The man—Virel—paled and didn't answer. His silence seemed to satisfy Ekelyon, because my ancestor turned to the two men on his right—one with a crown inlaid not with jewels but portals embroidered on his tunic, the other boasting a dagger cutting through the heart of a rose across his shoulder.

Nausea climbed up my throat. I recognized the crests. The families. The first was of Azarius Bryne's bloodline—a suitor who would have been Father's first choice before my affair with Magnus had "sullied me." The second...

It belonged to Aegan Rosegrave's line—the heir whose life my shadowfire had snuffed out when he had tried to force himself on me, refusing to take no for an answer. A memory I doubted would ever cease staining my soul, but held no true power over me as every piece fell into place and rendered an image laced with icy horror that twisted my stomach.

Three families to create a portal. One entry point, Mordecai had said, three different exits to fracture the relic, the lifeblood of the world.

But what he hadn't told me was that it had been *my* ancestor who was a key player, perhaps even leader, in the rebellion.

The very cause behind the disease.

"Conserve your strength tonight," Ekelyon said to his Rosegrave and Bryne coconspirators then turned to address the entire chamber, the gathered men all boasting the same zealous glint in their eyes. "The hallow will not give with ease. But neither will we."

As a series of nods swept around the oval table, Ekelyon

marched towards the heavy doors the guards immediately drew open. I swore, torn between staying in this memory drawn together from the recollection of others or entering the one belonging to Ekelyon alone.

The war within me waged for what had probably been no more than a second even if the roll of arguments seemed to take forever to settle.

Just as a discussion started behind my back, I closed the distance to my ancestor. The instant we were beyond the threshold and the guards dutifully shut the doors behind us, the perception shifted, thrusting me *inside* the man.

An inaudible gasp left my lips as I flailed and scrambled to adjust.

My already weak stomach stirred at the momentary disorientation, but thankfully *both* unpleasant reactions subsided before we even passed the first of the torches illuminating a hallway far darker than they could be in my sun-dominated times.

By the next torch, I had gotten a grip on myself—and regained the capacity to note details as...as disturbing as they were.

I couldn't feel Ekelyon's emotions or read his thoughts, but there was nothing standing between me and the reactions of his body, the way he walked, where his gaze lingered... That alone made a terrifyingly complete picture.

One I wanted nothing more than to leave behind.

Only I did no such thing.

Resting within Ekelyon, I observed as he climbed a wide stairwell to the upper level, then entered the first of the many chambers branching off the semicircular landing. Twins no older than a year rested in matching cribs, their chubby faces heavy with sleep while a young girl watched over them. She stood with a speed that hinted at fear, not respect—something her downcast eyes and the way she attempted to make her entire body smaller only further proved.

"Any changes?" Ekelyon asked, standing taller and not bothering to keep his voice down.

Unlike the girl. "No, sir. The light illusion yesterday was the only manifestation of your daughter's power. Your son revealed nothing at all."

"I suppose it won't matter soon," Ekelyon said dryly. "She'll be parted from her mother's people, from her magic." A low laugh rolled off his lips. The girl recoiled slightly. "It was a good safety net, but I suppose she'll be able to serve the family in another matter." Ekelyon closed the gap between them, and with a crooked finger under the girl's chin, forced her gaze up. "As will you."

"Of course, sir."

"Good." He brushed his thumb along her jaw, then let the touch fade away. "Make sure you keep guards around you tomorrow at all times. And do *not* leave the manor. For anything."

Another nod from the girl, then a shimmering distortion undulated across the remembrance, as if whatever had happened after Ekelyon retreated from the chamber had not left a lasting imprint on his memory. As I closed my eyes against the past that flowed like rippling water, I wondered *how* this memory even existed. If the world had fractured the following day, there wouldn't have been time to extract these fragments from Ekelyon's mind. Unless...

Unless he wanted to be written in history as a victor.

I couldn't see into his mind, but this small glimpse of him

along with everything I knew about my family was enough. They craved power above all else.

In Soltzen, once broken, Ekelyon would have it. For the duration of his life, he would reign within society—the meeting with the other High Lords had certainly placed him at the very top.

If Soltzenians had always been as they were now, then whatever happened after his death wouldn't matter. Prestige meant nothing when you weren't there to reap its benefits. And I had a suspicion the High Masters as a whole wanted the memory of others they deemed...more powerful, maybe even a threat, to fade through the generations. The only true legacy, as wretched as it was, they'd left.

But Ekelyon...

What if that wasn't enough? What if he went beyond what Soltzenians craved?

A different statement—he would have had to leave a different kind of statement to those who would not be there to see him reign.

My stomach twisted, bile splashing at the back of my throat in my distant, yet connected, body.

He *wanted* people to know.

Ekelyon had had his memory preserved so that at least through one avenue, he would not only gain immortality, but the sadistic satisfaction of reminding people who had carved their lives.

A change in the atmosphere rocked through me, and I opened my eyes, once again a separate entity in a shared remembrance.

The sun, far lower in the sky than I had ever seen it, blazed across the green land as men moved towards a beautiful temple carved of smooth white stone. The power of the memory swept me right along with them, as if an invisible barrier pressed against my back. The edge of the remembrance, I realized.

My phantom body started running along with them just to get rid of the peculiar sensation of not moving on my own—but also to gain a better view.

Bryne and Rosegrave were both among the fray, flanked by several other High Masters whose crests I couldn't make out. Much to my surprise, Ekelyon didn't cower among guards, but led the charge himself, the sword I recognized as one of my father's—the same sword I had held in my arms, sister to the one in Mordecai's vault—now cutting through those who would protect the Ancients residing within.

Everything within me recoiled.

Ekelyon was using an object of power for slaughter.

Forcing myself forward as nothing but slashed corpses remained, blood staining the green, took every inch of my will. But I didn't dare stay behind with the men who brought up the rear as Ekelyon barged into the temple, casting its doors wide open, and in the very next moment bathed the stone in crimson.

He sliced the familiar blade across throats, chests, stomachs, severing limbs and heads of those who would stand between him and his grand prize.

"Take the right," he bellowed at Rosegrave and Bryne, who immediately took their forces up the winding stairwell while he barreled on, only three heavily armed men at his back.

My point of view narrowed, but mercifully remained shared. I didn't think I could withstand a firsthand experience—feel the calmness and assertiveness of Ekelyon's body as he stole lives like they were nothing.

He pushed through an elegant archway, then through a set of

white, double-winged doors. A trail of crimson remained in his wake. He stopped on the threshold, and the three men positioned themselves behind him, constraining the remembrance further with their focus. Not that losing details curtailed the sickening impact of the memory.

A rolling wave of nausea rushed through me, and I was almost certain my body shuddered in another realm.

Ekelyon...

He wanted this for himself.

Blood dripped from the tip of his sword, my *father's* sword, as he planted his feet apart and stared at the two figures standing with their fingers entwined. Shadowfire blazed behind them, concealing the shrine where the relic must have been kept.

A weak cry wrung itself from my lips as I truly took them in.

The woman's soft mouth. The man's sapphire gaze.

Her cheekbones. His brow.

These weren't just Ancients.

They were Mordecai's parents.

CHAPTER THIRTY-ONE

HE—HE NEVER TOLD ME. NEVER SAID IT HAD BEEN *HIS* FAMILY who had protected the hallow.

The three children who died... Mordecai had grown up with them. Perhaps not siblings in blood, yet family in everything that mattered.

I dry heaved, but without a body, I couldn't even throw up.

So all I did was stare at the hauntingly beautiful couple, the icy-blue and stark silver shadowfire unfurling from their forms— at Ekelyon's blade, the steel coated in crimson and glinting in its ravenous desire for more.

Attack, I begged. *Please, please, do something.*

But Mordecai's parents weren't killers.

They were guardians.

The silent yet unmistakable bond weaving between them nearly brought me to my knees. They faced my ancestor, a unified front of pure power that should have been presented with bowed heads, not snarling, bloodthirsty faces.

Ekelyon took a step forward. Then another.

The echo of his leather boots against the stone was a demand in itself.

"Leave," the woman, Mordecai's *mother*, warned him, her tone gentle yet firm. She looked from Ekelyon to the guards who had fanned out wider, her gaze brushing over, but not seeing me as I stood beside them. "Your lives do not have to end like this."

"End? You misunderstand." Ekelyon smirked. "There will be no end to our lives. We're merely stepping into a new one."

He lashed out.

But so did she.

It all happened almost too fast for me to comprehend. One moment, her icy shadowfire speared towards Ekelyon; the next, it was sucked into the chain of portals he'd erected around himself—every wisp drawn into the controlled rips in reality as if they were a vortex. Ekelyon advanced seemingly without caution, without any kind of fear of an entity so much greater than him.

Mordecai's father released a wave of his argent, his sapphire gaze searing and so familiar my chest clenched and air became an impossibility.

Even more so as Ekelyon, ensconced in his halo of portals, marched right through the blue and silver embers.

My insides turned glacial yet burned all at once.

The shadowfire was supposed to be a barrier. A pure, impenetrable force through which, if anything, only death crossed. But whatever magic was embedded in that sword, in our heirloom, Ekelyon had found a way to elude and overpower the embers—and enervate their bearers in the process.

With every new strand that passed through the portal and

fell beyond the here and now, their lovely faces grew gaunt. Stark shadows fell upon their features as they realized a man, a single man with a slab of magic-laced steel and a thirst for power had prevailed over Ancient balance. Over the very lifeblood of the world.

Like the Void, Ekelyon's portals hungered for magic.

He would steal away every last ember.

The strongest force, a magic above all magics, deflected and scattered beyond reach. No, more than that.

The shadowfire was *ripped* from them.

A vile transgression there was no coming back from.

My own darkness roiled with fury, but was helpless against the chilling pocket of a time long gone.

Mordecai's mother unsheathed a dagger. She moved to protect herself, and my gaze caught on the glint of silver around her throat—on the pendant that had slipped free from beneath her ivory dress, its familiar crescent shape and three obsidian stones ravaging my insides.

My hand shot up to touch it, the future version of the necklace that rested around *my* neck, and I wondered—I wondered if my body, locked away in my chamber, was holding the silver. Holding it like Mordecai's mother should have. To allow them to escape. To take the relic, her consort, her son, and flee.

But the hard set of her features, the same ones Mordecai's father's face mirrored, was one I recognized.

The final stand of someone who knew they'd lost, but harbored a kernel of hope that a ray of light would survive.

If Mordecai was in this chamber, I couldn't sense him.

Couldn't see him when none of the men had.

So I watched, unleashing my voiceless screams into the remembrance as Ekelyon slashed the man's throat, then, before she could as much as tilt her dagger, drove the sword straight through the woman's heart.

CHAPTER THIRTY-TWO

I FELL FROM THE MEMORY, CLUTCHING THE BOOK WITH BONE-white knuckles, my body drenched in cold sweat.

Your people, Mordecai had said. It was *my* people who were responsible for everything that had happened.

The shattering.

The genocide of the Ancients...

I had assumed he had meant men native to Soltzen, not my... my family.

A wave of nausea rolled through me, so violent I jerked and brought a hand to my mouth. A thin, slicing pain ripped across my fingers where I'd snagged them on the paper. The copper scent invaded my nostrils but, thankfully, easing my stomach instead of agitating it. The sharp gash on my skin parted. I focused on the smell, on that thread of sweetness within the copper, of *power* embedded in it...

A drop splattered onto the page below.

Then another.

"Shit," I said softly and placed the book aside as my hand continued to bleed. I started to climb off the bed to find a bandage when movement that should not have been possible drew my gaze.

The crimson trail of my blood mixed with the ink, tainting yet not smearing; simply seeping through the paper onto the page beyond, where the chronicle had cut off when the world had fractured. I turned the inconceivably unmarred paper.

A swirl appeared first, then a letter, a word—a sentence.

My lungs refused to accept air as I watched the chronicle continue in red ink—no, not ink. Blood. *My* blood. The writing filled the page. Then the next. It sprawled across the previously untouched surface, spilling out the history of my bloodline.

After the break.

Vivid chiming swept through the room and calmed the rush of panic. It liberated me from the thorns of horror that had sunk deep into my skin, and allowed another sensation to prevail.

A tug.

The force ripped me from the stupor, and I flipped the pages, my wound now healed, following its call almost to the very end of the tome. There was magic here. A kindred pulse that matched my heartbeat.

With a shaky whisper, I commanded, *"Recount."*

CHAPTER THIRTY-THREE

THE MAN'S BACK WAS TO ME, HIS PARTIAL PROFILE FRAMED BY the sunlight that spilled through the lightweight drapes. His golden hair brushed against his shoulders, no sign of the gray strands I'd come to know as a fundamental part of him.

Younger, yet I would have recognized him anywhere.

Vandor Norcross.

My father.

The straight line of his nose, the classical high arch of his brow set in perfect balance with his full lips. In his youth, we were even more alike. But it was something else that claimed my attention.

My father seemed taller, more imposing from my vantage point as usual, as if... As if I were resting in—

A cradle.

A glimpse of white-painted wood just before me, the soft-edged carvings etched into its surface. This wasn't just any cradle.

My heart sped up.

I was in my own memory.

One my mind must have recorded, but my consciousness had released into the vaults of years I was too young to remember. Not without aid, at least.

"High Master Norcross." A female voice sounded from behind me. "Your daughter."

Father turned around fully, dispersing the bright stream of sunlight, but didn't look at me. No, he looked at the blanket-wrapped child who cried softly, breathlessly, as if she had already screamed herself into exhaustion and these whimpers were all the fuel she had left to rage at the world. My father approached the wet-nurse, a battle waging on the stark planes of his face.

Adoration, but also anticipation—and something darker. A cool steel that lay beneath it all, holding him together.

He pushed the edges of the lilac blanket farther down, revealing a round face. My...my sister's face.

Carefully, he took her in his arms, then dismissed the nurse with a rough dip of his chin. She didn't linger.

"Hello, Eira," he said once the door clicked shut. His voice was gentle, yet cautious. So very cautious.

My sister, *Eira*—a sob lodged in my throat—hiccoughed, then calmed. She reached for my father with tiny, chubby fingers. But before they could wrap around the smooth fabric of his tunic, the memory-me shifted in the cradle, drawing Eira's attention.

Our gazes locked, Eira's blue-green on my icy-blue, and I *felt* the echo of the emotion that had run through me in that moment. Felt that joy spark up, a bond growing taut between us. Sisters. My happiness was almost tangible, but in my true body, a foreboding chill crept down my spine.

I had always been an only child.

Still, the memory didn't feel like a lie, and soon I was drawn back into it fully, back into that overwhelming joy the child-me experienced. I reached towards Eira with small fingers. My skin snagged on a splinter in the lacquered white wood.

I didn't cry out. Not when Eira was still gazing at me, as if afraid of the vastness she had suddenly found herself in, which must have appeared even larger, grander in the blazing sunlight.

Blood welled atop my finger, but the pain fell second to an unbearable, uncontrollable need to look after my sister that raged through my small body. It stirred something inside me until the sheer pressure of it broke through the confines of my skin and—

I darkened the room.

Painted it a soothing purple-black, with stars sprinkled across the canvas.

Eira laughed as she gazed at the illusion I had gifted her, her bubbling voice almost drowning out my father's quiet, "No."

He set Eira on a padded table with appallingly little care and marched out of the chamber as if a phantom whip snapped at his heels. My sister's wailing cut through the room, so I created more stars, a silver circlet resembling the moon to shine upon her, to calm the discomfort I didn't want her to feel.

Just as she fell silent, mesmerized by the night sky I must have plucked from some collective memory, my father returned —carrying my mother in his arms. A harsh gasp escaped her when she saw what the chamber had turned into. She looked at Eira, her lovely, lovely features twisting into a grimace lined with primal fear.

She averted her gaze.

"We'll tell them—we'll tell them she passed immediately

after birth." Her voice was low, trembling. "That she passed before the healer could arrive."

My father placed my mother on the small sofa beneath the window. He grabbed a decorative pillow from beside her and walked over to the cushioned table where Eira still lay on her back. There was no compassion in his face, no remorse.

The very same chilling look I had seen on him numerous times when he faced an inconvenience he had to overcome.

"We shouldn't have tempted fate after we had Ember," he muttered, then positioned the pillow across Eira's face.

He pressed.

My illusion died along with my sister's breaths.

CHAPTER THIRTY-FOUR

AIR. I NEEDED AIR.

I staggered out of my room into violent silence. I didn't know how much time I'd lost to the remembrance, but our wing, with its overpowering quiet, painted a stark contrast to the whispers of life still weaving from the heart of the Repository.

A stark contrast to my rasping breaths, too.

Everything inside me crawled as if I wanted to come apart at the seams, but the unbearable pressure coating my skin and clogging my pores wouldn't allow me even that mercy.

Undone and constrained.

Constrained and undone.

And the silence oozing from the walls—

I pulled hard on the pendant's magic and cast time in stasis.

Better. This was better.

But only in the way one flavor of mind-shattering pain was better than another.

The aggressive proximity of the walls, the weight of the ceiling above me—

I fled.

Past the librarians roaming the lower level.

Past the threshold of the Repository.

I ran until I found a secluded spot at the far end of the gardens, cordoned off by a wall of strawberry trees.

The power faded.

I sank to my knees and buried my fingers in the soil.

Vicious tremors gripped me, my entire body convulsing as if poisoned. But the truth was a toxin I couldn't expel, only accept.

So I let it surge.

My father had murdered Eira while my mother watched— urged him on.

He had murdered my newborn sister because he believed the illusion, *my* illusion, had been *hers*.

My stomach recoiled, and I barely had time to shove my hands aside before I vomited all over the ground.

Innocent. Eira had been innocent. *Normal.*

The love I'd felt for her, my care for her, had somehow ripped through the spell Telaria had placed on me.

And had signed Eira's execution.

I heaved again, bile scorching the back of my throat as tears streamed down my cheeks. Agony ravaged my insides, and I choked—choked on all the vile, cruel brutality that wasn't mine yet stained my essence.

It should have been *my* breath that had died. *My* life that tainted my father's hands.

In a violent surge, I heaved again.

And again.

Cleaving. Crumbling. Shattering.

Telaria might have saved me from the world, but she'd failed to save me from myself.

The harbinger of death.

Shivering and shaking, I crawled away onto an undisturbed grassy patch. I knelt on all fours, gagging and dry heaving as my mind threatened to fracture so completely no spell could bind the wasted shards. Too much. All of this was too much.

Yet among the chaos, a thread crystallized.

And the more I focused on it, the lesser the churning of all else became.

I wiped my mouth on the back of my hand, my breaths steadier now. But no calmer.

The way they had spoken, had *waited* to see what would happen—my parents had known. They had been aware of the possibility their child might possess powers beyond those belonging to the people of Soltzen. As if they had been *prepared* for it.

Telaria's words returned to me. How quickly the presence of newborns with mixed bloodlines had faded; how fast she had worked to cast a protection spell to keep me from Somraque until I was ready—a spell that had also suppressed my powers. Conserved them.

Telaria had believed I would slip from her reach.

If she hadn't acted when she had, I would have. Only it wasn't the veil between the worlds that had snuffed out all previous signals.

Sun...

I swallowed bile.

How many times had that happened? How many offspring had the prominent bloodlines—my *own* bloodline—killed when their magic had revealed itself?

The past had never been forgotten. It was a closely guarded secret that guided their cowardly hands to build their dreamland of endless sun on the blood of the powerful, the innocent, the different.

I dragged myself over to a strawberry tree and sat down, hugging my knees against my chest. The bark was a comforting whisper of cool against my heated skin, the gentle chiming cocooning me even as the dreadful list turned over and over in my head.

Ancients. Mordecai's parents. Eira.

Ancients. Mordecai's parents. Eira.

Ancients. Mordecai's parents. Eira.

If we were all monsters, then the Norcross line was an entirely new breed of nightmare.

I choked on a sob.

Was I any different?

My existence alone was a death sentence, trapping those I loved in the crossfire of a battle I had never wanted—

No.

I pushed off the ground then placed one foot in front of the other as I marched across the empty garden towards the stone well. A ghostly apparition of me stared back, but underneath was a silent darkness that slowly spread through my withered veins and fortified my every cell with unyielding obsidian. With utter, perhaps terrifying, calmness, I washed the soil off my fingers, then rinsed out my mouth, drawing more and more water until the rank taste was gone entirely. After I swallowed a few handfuls that remained in my stomach, I splashed the cool liquid across my face and dissolved the salty traces of tears.

The only reason I strode into that chamber of the Repository was because I was done lagging behind. I might not have expected to find my family's past among the pages, but what was that if not another step forward?

I knew now, what they had done. That they weren't naive or ignorant of the world as it once had been. Of what my heritage, the power nestled in my core could bring about.

It was you, was what my father had said when I'd collapsed next to Aegan's corpse. The words my then unraveling mind had shrouded, kept just beyond my reach, but now lay bare before me. *It was you.*

They only reaffirmed my resolve.

Once we obtained the fragment and entered Soltzen, I would come prepared. For the treacherous, cold-hearted filth that was my family. For whatever resistance the founding bloodlines would throw our way.

There would be no mercy for their crimes, the pain they had inflicted upon the world and its people.

I was the Savior.

Not the Forgiver.

I drew the dagger I had taken to carrying at Ivarr's suggestion from its sheath under my skirt—precisely where the fragment had once been. Its sting kissed my palm, releasing the magic within my blood as I wrapped my fingers around the pendant—

And cut open a portal to Somraque.

CHAPTER THIRTY-FIVE

DEADLANDS.

Somraque had always struck me as quiet with its desaturated trees, shadowed, sharp mountain range, and streets of stone, all of it blanketed by the endless expanse of the night. But as I stood on the outskirts, the rocky desert behind me and one of the many diagonal avenues stretched out front, the silence was deafening. The dark absolute.

No light breathing life through the windows. No sapphire glow casting its ray across the roofs.

Not even the dome of silver, as terrifying as it had been beautiful, to mark the battle for Somraque's very existence.

There had been a pulse in that radiance of shadowfire.

Now, there was nothing.

Even the cold that pressed against my skin and seeped through my purple-blue gown made for a climate kinder than this failed to deliver that frigid bite I'd expected. Or perhaps it was purely the numbness of my own body, mirroring that of the town, that dulled sensations.

Tentatively, I took a step forward. The sound sliced through the still like a slender arrow.

I paused, waiting for something, anything...

Nysa's utter hollowness was the only reply.

Another step.

I'd always craved quiet, solitude. It had been a comfort, not a burden. But this—this was unlike any silence I had ever heard.

Sinister wisps of it enclosed around my throat.

My breaths came out in whispered rasps as I progressed across the cobblestones between the lifeless buildings, yet my spine remained straight despite the chilling fear that seemed to have replaced my very blood. I didn't have to venture far before I saw it.

Gradually, like vines creeping across the facades, the echoes of destruction manifested.

A cracked stone.

A shattered window.

Then more.

Deep grooves that cleaved houses and threatened to ensnare my feet as I walked over their outstretched talons.

Rubble spilling onto the street in neglected streaks, eerily reminiscent of the blood Ekelyon Norcross had shed.

The absence of magic.

The omnipresent touch of death embedded in the very scent of desolation.

Hollowness.

Such hollowness my heartbeat was an impostor disrupting this tomb where stillness reigned. I curled my fingers into fists to prevent myself from reaching out to a decimated facade.

The Void might not have consumed Nysa, but the town carried the scars like gaping maws of voiceless memories.

My feet moved of their own volition as my gaze roamed the once vibrant jewel turned saturnine mausoleum. What little remnants of the solstice celebrations not wrought of power that had escaped the ripping forces of magic were visible beyond the half-crumpled arch, its moon phases lost beyond the waxing crescent. I dropped my gaze from the symbol. And dropped the memory of seeing it for the first time, too.

All it would do was rot within me.

I skirted around the debris and entered the square where there had once been an entire new world contained amidst the proud buildings. No trees of ice crossed my gaze, the stalls in splinters and shards. I searched for bodies that weren't there.

But had been.

Streaks of dried blood tainted the chipped stones, the power it had once carried gone along with the person. I knelt and pressed my fingertips to the stain. How many, if any, had survived? Had they fled for the rocky desert, for Saros and the small towns beyond in time?

There, at least, the threads of the tapestry hadn't been tangled when I had last brought the superimposed reality to mind. Although then, the unraveling stability had not yet finished its voracious crawl.

I didn't dare examine the lifelines of magic to see what remained.

Not yet.

The deeper I went through the heart of town then towards the one place where my heart burned to be, the worse the destruction became. All that remained of the second archway were blocks ravaged beyond recognition.

The smaller debris fled from under my feet and caught on the hem of my dress as if beseeching my attention as I climbed over. I strode forward. Entered the deathscape of broken existence.

The darkness seemed to coalesce here, where the illusion of a blue sky had been at its richest. But I knew now that sunlight concealed the worst atrocities.

Here, at least, there was honesty.

And I carried its weight with every step.

Several times, I had to pause as I followed what had once been the main avenue, backtrack when entire buildings, once even an entire street, when I'd ventured farther, littered the silent battlefield. I didn't allow the kernel of ice within me to spread, regardless of how the deathly quiet suffused and tainted my bones.

Only a tear streaked down my cheek, falling onto the dust and blood of memories.

A flash of eyes in the distance disturbed the abandoned cityscape.

I stilled, the shadowfire coming alive beneath my skin in response to my uncertainty, but not piercing its surface. The eyes peered at me from the pool of darkness caught between a mountain of rubble and the still-standing wall of the shop with its door thrown off the hinges, as if a too-large mass of people had pushed past the threshold, not caring about the injuries they sustained as long as they got out.

The eyes shifted, lowered, entering the starlight's reach.

Claws scraped against the stone.

A touch of black, then a spill of white—

I fell to my knees. By the Stars...

I spread my arms open with a hitch in my breath as Lyra ran

towards my awaiting embrace. Her lithe, slender body sent a pulse of warmth against my stomach and chest. I held her as she licked my face, tail swishing low, as if fighting the joy that had no place on this somber plane of loss.

"Clever dog," I whispered.

Lyra's ears bobbed in agreement when she shimmied back. I trailed my fingers through the brilliant white strands, just as silken and bright as I remembered them. She looked...well. Taken care of. As if what had befallen Nysa hadn't touched her at all.

A humorless laugh fluttered through my mind. It wouldn't come as a surprise at all if Telaria had survived the very chaos she had inadvertently unleashed.

Only Lyra didn't start towards the outskirts where Ada and Telaria's house stood sentry.

Instead, as I rose to follow her, she trotted down the path I wanted—yet feared—to take.

My mind went as silent as the town, body moving of its own accord as we turned our backs on the shattered avenue and its surrounding streets. Nysa's once vibrant core hadn't been the very epicenter of ruin.

Rationally, I'd prepared myself for this—the truth, the *fact* I had known long before my gaze had swept across the evidence. And yet no amount of obsidian I wrapped around my spine and heart like armor possessed the capability to soften the brutal, devastating impact of the sight.

Even the air tasted different here, marred by the lingering traces of a future that had almost come to pass—and the present that had barely remained.

Eyes set firmly before me, I trailed behind Lyra who passed through the bent gates—open, with the courtyard extending beyond no more than a canvas of abandoned shadows. I didn't have the courage or the strength in me to lift my gaze to the manor looming above as I crossed the open space, dreading the marks I would see there.

Mute walls rose around me.

Lyra's claws on stone spurred to life a rhythm that drew me forward, up the stairwell my fingers brushed in a fleeting caress of remembrance before falling away. A vine of shadowfire unfurled from my back. Then another.

The burgeoning veil of obsidian trailed in undulating ripples behind me as I strode in Lyra's wake down the corridor, through the double doors, its every elegant swish releasing the pressure threatening to crack open my rib cage and spill into the atmosphere.

I hesitated on the threshold, just for a moment, as Lyra padded to the solitary figure carved of eternal darkness and alabaster standing by the window. His black strands brushed against the sharp jawline as he looked down at her, then stilled.

Slowly—as if a sudden move might ignite the volatile charge saturating the space between us and set the night ablaze— Mordecai lifted his gaze.

CHAPTER THIRTY-SIX

Sapphire blazed with turmoil his heartbreakingly unyielding features revealed nothing of.

I crossed the gaping vastness of the chamber, Mordecai's attention never leaving me. Never wavering.

The stark white of his knuckles was the only change wrought upon his stoic body as I came to stand beside him, shoulder to shoulder, and gazed at the deadlands under the beauty of the night. Mordecai drank me in—the somber lines of my face, the regal posture, the obsidian shadows rising behind me.

I kept my gaze on the field of ruin even as shards of ice cracked open my heart.

"Norcross," I said into the still. Destruction befitting the devastation. "I know, Mordecai. I saw the ambition. The hunger. The bloodlust." I pressed my fingers against the cool glass. "The death." My hand dropped to my side, my voice quiet but not weak. "Your parents in the temple."

Mordecai remained silent, the sapphire scalding where it fell on my skin. I remembered all the times he'd closed off whenever a kernel of light had grown between us, cast once more into the throes of a struggle that had been his, yet touched me in echoes I hadn't understood, couldn't hope to comprehend—until now.

I hailed from the people who slaughtered an entire race to carve their throne.

More than that, I was the direct descendant of the man who had murdered his family.

And I was the Ancient he had fallen in love with.

Two forces fated to forever war.

A tear broke free from my lashes even as my voice rang clear. "You must hate me. For who I am."

Somewhere, in a forgotten crevice of my mind, I knew I wasn't my family. Never had been. But I *was* the spawn of cutthroat, depraved killers. How could such a stain not taint?

A barely imperceptible slice of Mordecai's head to the side. Then—

"You must hate me, for who I've become."

Somraque's monster.

But not mine.

Never mine.

"It's not me who lived through those nightmares, Mordecai." I met the sapphire at last. "Even this..."

I didn't have to gesture to the ruin spreading beneath us to know he understood my words. The desolation, the blood crusted on crumbling stones—yes, there was loss. And destruction. Existence built on death.

But there *was* existence.

His jaw tightened, but underneath the hardened planes of his face lurked a vulnerability so stark it threatened to rip me apart. I took his hand in mine.

"Mordecai, you know I saw you. You know I *chose* you. And I always will."

"How—" He lowered his head, gaze slipping to our entwined hands, then back to me—to my eyes that concealed nothing even when we treaded so, so carefully. "How can you still say that?"

I released his hand and brushed my fingers up his arm, tracing a gentle path all the way to his neck, his jaw. The way he gazed at me, a blend of caution and sorrow and raw desire, the nuances altering his features nearly imperceptible, yet I felt each and every one as if they were my own.

With a soft caress of my thumb, I cupped his cheek.

"I can't absolve you of your darkness. But I can exist with you in it. If you'll have me."

CHAPTER THIRTY-SEVEN

A SHUDDER ROLLED THROUGH HIS BODY.

"I don't deserve you." His breath fell upon my wrist.

"Then it's a good thing I'm not something that can be deserved." I brought my other hand to his face, turning him towards me and drinking in every line of this beautiful Ancient —even those that went far beyond the visible.

My shadowfire fanned wider, transformed into a billowing manifestation of all I felt in my Ancient heart that had only now liberated itself from the shackles of who ignorance would have made me to be. The thunder within my rib cage overpowered the sweeping quiet.

"I love you, Mordecai. You're the silver illuminating my night." That Ancient pulse beat harder, louder, punctuating the raw honesty. The unrestrained truth. "Let me in. Let my dark fuel your shine."

Wings of silver unfolded behind him as he broke from my touch.

Not away, but *past* it.

The ice still holding my insides captive barely had time to shatter into a thousand pieces before Mordecai's lips claimed mine.

His hands wrapped around my neck, my back, the length of his body an inferno against me. I moaned, and Mordecai deepened the kiss. His flavor stole away my breath as our tongues met, igniting the desire pooling in my core and sending it coursing through my veins like a river of bright-hot stars.

I couldn't hold him tightly enough. Couldn't feel him close enough.

My shadowfire sought out his, and as they touched, with no room left for teasing or play, everything inside me blazed. Those final restraints snapped, dissolved.

I kissed Mordecai past my tears, past my raging, thrashing heart, our passion reigning in the darkness where we belonged.

Yet even as his touch became possessive, demanding, as my body responded to his, burning for more, the tenderness never fled from his caresses. Nor did the love, written in every stroke of his tongue, in the press of his fingers against my spine. Lower.

I shivered and drew him to me. Mordecai's hands slid down to my thighs, digging into the sensitive skin as he lifted me up onto the windowsill—without breaking the kiss, the relief-entwined craving that pulsed between us until neither of us could take any more. Still, the absence of him as he drew away was staggering.

With half-parted lips, Mordecai took his time drinking in my swollen mouth, my flushed cheeks, the way my throat bobbed under the weight of his gaze that bared me entirely. His breaths deepened as he stood there, observing me as if I were an apparition he chased in his dreams but never expected to see again.

A sob lodged in my throat, but before I could tell him that there wasn't a force in existence that had the power to keep me from him, Mordecai's eyes locked on mine, whisking the words away.

"I love you, Ember," he whispered. Gently, a single corner of his sensual mouth curled up. "My soothing dark of the night." The sapphire seemed to pierce right to my very soul. "My home."

"My eternity," I answered into his lips, sealing the promise.

THE RAW EMOTION gradually faded from Mordecai's features as he led me by the hand across the scarred chamber to the sofa by the unlit fireplace. We sat, thighs touching—for as long as it took Lyra to rush towards us and shimmy onto our laps.

A raspy laugh unlike any I'd ever heard escaped Mordecai when she propped her butt in my lap and nestled her head in his. Clearly, she had a new favorite, the traitor. I stroked the delicate curve of her spine, then peered up at Mordecai.

"When did you two become so close?" I asked, the casual question leaving the depths beneath it open for Mordecai to delve into. If he so wished.

His throat bobbed, but his gaze was hard, as was the set of his jaw. "She found me in Nysa. After."

In Nysa.

The reel of impressions unspooled within me. "You—you took care of the..."

Corpses was what I couldn't bring myself to say.

Not that I needed to.

Mordecai nodded, fingers brushing through Lyra's long white strands. "I burned them. So that they could return to the stars."

I'd thought I was done crying, but the tears came regardless of my beliefs. Regardless of the steel that fortified my body or the command of my mind to learn of the events I was still missing to compose an uninterrupted trail of the past like one of the Repository's books.

I forced myself to ask, "How many?"

Mordecai's fingers halted, earning him a *harrumph* from Lyra. She nuzzled his hand, and I wondered how much of her adorable demand was for her benefit. How much for his.

"My shadowfire took everyone in the palace. And its vicinity." A long exhale. A distant shadow in his eyes.

Different from the earlier times when we had spoken of what he had done to preserve Somraque—who he had fashioned himself into to protect the people from themselves. Heavier, somehow.

Perhaps even laced with resentment.

"It didn't make a difference. Even with the cause of the disruption gone, the rip in the balance was too grave to readjust itself. Too grave for me to find its equilibrium in time."

"Mordecai..."

"You saw the destruction upon your arrival?" He turned to me sharply. "Saw where the cracks began?"

I dipped my chin. I had only seen a part of Nysa, but it wasn't hard to imagine where the path of ruin ran elsewhere. The gradual deterioration had been a sight I doubted even the ages spanning ahead could make me forget.

"Consider the farthest, faintest crack a demarcation line." His voice was tight, the edge of a blade in the vast silence

Somraque had succumbed to. "Life on the outskirts. Death within."

"Everybody?" I asked, even when I felt the answer in my bones.

Mordecai replied with a long, slow blink before the sapphire burned my skin again—as if some reckless, hurt part of him challenged me to see him as a monster.

But the images his confirmation had spun into existence—

All those people at the celebrations. Every rebel. Every vendor, shop owner. Everyone who had come to celebrate the solstice. Merayin, my sweet maid. Gone.

I swallowed. "And the rest?"

If there even were any...

"They fled to Saros. No one tried to return since. Not even to claim their dead." His face shuttered. "I killed hundreds in the palace, in its vicinity, and still I couldn't save the town."

Lyra scooted off our laps and padded to the corner with a water bowl and lovingly arranged nest of blankets, giving me the freedom to take Mordecai's hands in mine. He kept staring after Lyra, though I had a suspicion he wasn't truly seeing her. Just the life she presented in this forlorn monument of a town.

Hope, I'd like to think.

A reminder of loss, I suspected.

I swished my thumbs across Mordecai's skin.

There was so much I wanted to tell him. So much he needed to know. But in the vortex of it all, one thought, one sentiment reigned supreme.

I stared at Mordecai until he met my gaze, then said, "Come with me to Svitanye."

When he didn't answer, his silver-rimmed eyes unyielding on mine but not challenging any longer, I gripped his hands tighter.

I shifted my legs beneath me so that I was kneeling on the couch, the touch between us an open conduit.

"You might not have saved Nysa the way you wanted to, Mordecai. But there's still hope for the worlds." I leaned closer. "For the rest of Somraque to have a future that won't end on this abject note. Come with me. Just come with me."

His lips found mine, but the kiss tasted like a goodbye.

"It's taking everything to hold the Void at bay," he rasped, voice rough and tender at the same time. Aching. "If I leave, the magic will finish what it started, and the Void *will* spread."

I had suspected, but didn't know just how bad it was under the surface. The very reason behind my reluctance to brave a look at the tapestry. I sank to my heels, the pendant resting heavy atop my breasts. If I could—

"Ember?"

Releasing Mordecai's hands, I reached beneath the neckline of my dress and drew out the spell-leaf I'd tucked there before my harrowing dive into the Norcross chronicle. The words, not in my language, but the ancient melody written in my very essence, stared back at me. So simple yet...

"You don't have to stay here, Mordecai." I lifted my gaze to his chiseled face—seeking the sapphire that churned like the ocean when the rest of him gave nothing away. "Not if we submerge Somraque in stasis."

CHAPTER THIRTY-EIGHT

MORDECAI'S UTTER STILLNESS BROKE AS WONDER PIERCED through it like rays of sunlight, the hazy glow softening the edges reminiscent of uncensorable faith.

In my words.

In the reverie they painted.

In me.

Stunning. He was utterly stunning, and it took every ounce of my will to resist seeking out his lips, to chase away the weight and the sorrow dominating the vast landscape of his soul until there was nothing but that undiluted beauty left—nothing but us, without the chains of past.

Instead, I slipped my legs from beneath me and held the spell-leaf in both hands.

"I have magic, Mordecai. All of it." A faint, faint smile played across my mouth. "Even combinations that shouldn't be possible."

He cocked his head to the side, not saying anything, merely

staring, watching. And holding on to my every word. My fingers burned to brush aside the dark strands that swept across his forehead and now rested against the prominent line of his cheek.

"This spell"—I raised the spell-leaf a little higher—"found me before I knew any of that. Before I knew I could use it, let alone that I *would*. I tried to give it to Nyon when he approached me in that enclosure, but he said—"

A dry but sincere laugh—*my* laugh—drowned out the rest as my mind finally caught up with how all of this must sound to Mordecai. I shook my head, then planted a loving caress across the spell-leaf's blue-veined surface. I met Mordecai's silently amused—perhaps, perhaps even a touch enamored—gaze.

Fire spread through my veins, and my chest lightened at seeing him like this, but I didn't surrender to the moment.

As tempting as it was.

"Sun, Mordecai, there's so much I have to tell you."

We had been in Svitanye a little less than a week, yet our stay there had proven to be a flurry of events none of us had expected. Including some I was certain we would rather have avoided altogether. And Mordecai—he knew nothing of what had transpired.

Where was I supposed to even begin when everything seemed so intertwined?

I pursed my lips, turning the spell-leaf over in my hands. "We found safe haven at this glorious library." This—this was the foundation. "Found like-minded individuals to aid us in our search for the fragment. We don't have it yet," I quickly added as something shifted in his posture. "But we will. I *feel* it."

"And your magic?" Mordecai asked softly, as if understanding I couldn't possibly convey everything I wanted to. Releasing me from the burden of fitting magnitudes into inadequate paragraphs.

"I don't know how well acquainted you are with Svitanye"— our discussions had never touched the fragmented lands in such a way—"but the people are either Enchanter or Spellweavers."

A long, affirmative blink. A fleeting breeze of a smile whisked across my lips.

"I—I'm both. But this"—I held the spell-leaf higher and angled it until it caught the gentle light—"happened before I learned of my capabilities. Nyon, a fellow Spellweaver and one of the librarians working with us, revealed that the spell belongs to me, that it...it chose me."

It had been his expression, his smile, that had revealed that last part, not words, but Nyon might as well have said it out loud for how evident it had been.

I arched an eyebrow, the memories of the encounter unfurling warmth throughout me. "Apparently, the spell-tree rarely releases its leaves. And, *apparently*, it also possesses a knack for foreseeing the future."

The mirth in my words was met with a curl in the corner of Mordecai's mouth I would have missed if I weren't so fixed on him. As if he didn't want to allow the relief to fill him until we were certain this would work. A part of me agreed, but the other... It *knew* it would. Just as it had known Mordecai would be waiting here when all else was gone.

This time, I didn't stop myself from reaching out and tracing my fingers down his jaw.

"And the spell will last?" he asked quietly, breath warm against my wrist. "Even when you cross into another world?"

"Yes," I said with conviction that came from some primal,

intuitive core where my Svitanyian power lay. "It will last until I lift it."

Lyra jumped in Mordecai's lap, wedging herself between us, and his fingers immediately glided down her spine. I leaned back, my fingertips still carrying imprints of his heat. I formed a fist just to retain the sensation, but my attention never truly left Mordecai's face.

His features turned contemplative, then closed off, remote in a way that made my icy darkness ache to wrap around him.

"*She* might not be bothered by my presence," he said into the silence with another caring stroke down Lyra's back. An understatement if there was any, given the low sounds of content she let out when he moved his hand up and scratched her behind the ear. "But I suspect"—he lifted his gaze to mine—"the others will be less than willing to work with the Crescent Prince."

There was no self-pity in his voice. Just hard fact. One I might not have put much thought into, but considered nonetheless when I'd walked down Nysa's abandoned streets.

It hadn't changed my mind then—it didn't have the power to do so now.

"I'll keep you hidden until the time is right. Everyone understands the importance of bringing the worlds together. Animosity comes second to that."

A whisper of surprise brightened the sapphire. "You have that much faith in them?"

"Oh, no." The laugh that fled from my lips lacked true amusement.

I shifted closer and leaned my body against his, savoring his intoxicating presence.

My palm settled on his chest. "They would fight you given the chance."

His pulse *thumped* against my skin.

"But I *do* have faith in their determination."

LYRA TRAILED behind me around the lifeless husk the once-beautiful palace had become while Mordecai gathered his most vital belongings. Clothes, weapons, objects he believed could help us with our cause, though he didn't say much on that front. He had, however, mentioned packing some food for Lyra to ease the transition, although I knew I would have to figure out a way to steal things from the kitchens soon enough. Or fake a peculiar change of diet.

But whatever it took, I would do it.

To have him by my side and stand by his.

To see things through to the end.

Together.

Using the momentary solitude, I prowled the halls that had been my prison but had somewhere along the road become my home. The *click* of Lyra's claws accompanied my soft footsteps as I opened up not only to the endless threads of sensations running through me like unspooled ribbons, but the essence of Somraque.

Its flavor might have changed in the wake of recent events, but the core, the heart that made Somraque what it was remained pristine.

I let it fill me. Bond with my own. As if we had been created for this, my perception of it became vivid, bearing a different texture—one wrought of so many nuances it made even the dawn sky seem flat. Dim.

I scraped my fingernails up the iron-and-silver railing.

Born of three worlds. Belonging to them.

As they did to me.

A fierce protectiveness rolled and crackled beneath my skin as I took in the deep gouges slashing across the walls as if the Void had become a beast of fangs and claws. I gripped the railing and closed my eyes, but all that did was unlock a series of flashing images that turned the crackling into thunder.

The amassing thrumming of magic as I found the dinner abandoned.

Mordecai's uniformed guards standing like a dam before the masses.

The hallway strewn with black-veined bodies.

The wrongness of feeling Somraque come apart at the seams.

Then—

The study.

The escape I hadn't wanted to make—and now knew I hadn't.

Not an escape, no.

Mordecai might cast me out of the palace for more than just the role I had yet to fulfill, but in its bare bones, that was precisely what the act had been. On both our sides.

We had enacted the part Somraque had required at the time.

And in my heart, I knew I would never hesitate to make the same choice again. Nor would Mordecai.

Whether it was this Ancient presence within me or the affinity for all three worlds, when I reached the topmost floor, I embraced being more than just a Savior.

I was a protector, too.

I glanced around the familiar, soothing space. It had been instinct that had guided me to the one room in the palace that had survived the destruction and could withstand another burst of magic. Although I suspected a spell wouldn't have the same impact on the balance as power derived from blood, Mordecai and I nonetheless decided we would have to be careful. He'd hold the world to the very last second, then release his magic when I unleashed mine. Neither of us knew if the stasis would trap his power, too, if it was still entwined with the world when the spell settled, and that was a risk I didn't dare take.

But as my fingers grazed the full moon handles, as the vast chamber with its glass walls spread before me, all my thoughts quieted—yet roared.

I whisked my gaze along the empty space, the serene backdrop of the night just as glorious as it had been the first time I'd seen it. No violence, loss, or wreckage touched the deep violet and blue hues breaking up the dark. I let my eyes wander to the silver glow of the moon as my feet carried me forward, then brought the tapestry of power to the forefront at long last.

The staggering absence of threads hit me like a blow to the stomach.

Magic was still here, but it was Mordecai's blend, fending off the hungry crawl of the Void.

I stretched the superimposed reality farther—to Saros, to the villages and small towns resting beyond, each a beautiful, complicated pattern of threads pertaining to the lives we were saving. Hoped to, at least. I held on to that image, willed it to write itself in my heart, then released the tapestry.

Lyra touched her paws to my thigh. I lowered myself to her level and stroked her silken strands. "You'll get to see a new world, girl."

She cocked her head to the side then pressed her cold, pitch-black nose to mine.

Content calmness radiated from her, and the languid swishes

of her tail were an encouragement I hadn't known I needed until I felt it settle inside me.

With a parting caress, I rose. Lyra remained nearby, offering her pure, silent support as I went through the process of not only quieting, but *clearing* my mind. I connected myself to that core deep within until it wasn't a separate entity living inside my body, but a presence entwined with everything I was.

Even Lyra had gone still, something I sensed more than saw as I gazed into the star-bedecked distance through the all-encompassing glass, now completely grounded, the spell-leaf a familiar weight in my hands.

One with the world.

One with the magic.

My obsidian leaked from me in gentle wisps.

Wholly, fully myself.

I sensed Mordecai enter the chamber before I saw him. With a small smile on my lips, I turned.

He had always been devastatingly handsome.

The ink-black hair framing features no sculptor could ever dream to recreate. The piercing sapphire and full lips—ones that parted ever so slightly as he beheld me. Observed me watching him.

His moon phase tattoos dipped beneath the collar of his black jacket, the cut emphasizing his honed build and lovely height. I let my gaze drift down his dark trousers to the jet-black boots, then back up again—finally noting the leather bag he carried in his left hand, fingers curved so tightly around the handle I was positive his palm would bear grooves for hours to come. My obsidian tendrils curved, as if beckoning him closer—conveying my wishes before even I became aware of them.

Mordecai obliged.

His steps were slow and steady across the marble floor, as if he didn't want to disrupt this higher state I had not only entered with my mind, but honed myself into. He needn't have worried. Lyra's gaze slipped from me to him, then back again. Without me uttering a single command, she pressed herself against my leg.

I offered my left hand to Mordecai.

"Ready?" I asked.

Mordecai slid his palm into mine.

A single tremor spread down my fingers as I directed my attention to the writing adorning the leaf. But what little trepidation rippled the calm surface of my being vanished as soon as the foreign language left my tongue, its seamless translation an echo in my thoughts—reassuring me, *shaping* me, somehow.

Out of the corner of my eye, I noticed Mordecai's brow furrow in concentration, his body utterly unmoving as he focused on the magic. Mine and his alike.

We were conduits. Beacons.

Twin epicenters.

And so much more.

My whispering voice carried on as my conscience enveloped the entirety of Somraque, all the way to the edge of the Void—then beyond it.

Only two sentences left spread across three blue veins. Seventeen more words. And the magic would settle on the land, refusing a single thing to change.

Mordecai's jaw clenched, our matched heartbeats counting down the time...

His power rushed inside him as mine snapped in place.

We stared at each other, wide-eyed and panting. My heart

thrashed against my ribs as I *felt* the stasis surround us—the sky, the land, the people. Only the three of us remained, a foreign, too lively presence in the land of perpetual still.

"Will you be able to break it?" Mordecai asked, voice hoarse.

I didn't have to retreat inside me to sense the spell. It was there, cocooned in my core of power, a lock I only needed to snap with a single thought when I wanted to, and the elaborate design would unravel.

I let the now blank spell-leaf flutter to the ground—not discarding, but releasing it. "Yes."

Mordecai's fingers tightened around mine.

It wasn't just relief that we had shielded Somraque, I realized. After ages—after *ages* spent trapped here, Mordecai would get to see another facet of the world he'd once lived in, then lost.

I leaned over and brushed my lips over his. "Ready to face the dawn?"

CHAPTER THIRTY-NINE

I RIPPED THE PORTAL OPEN STRAIGHT TO MY CHAMBER.

I walked through first, just to make sure everything was all right, then motioned Mordecai to follow. For a fluttering heartbeat, he hesitated, then scooped Lyra up with one arm and entered the room.

In the glow of morning light, he was even lovelier. Another quality seemed to permeate his features, and the sapphire—

It had been a jewel in the night, but here, it radiated.

He dropped the bag on the floor to cradle Lyra in both arms and kept on walking—past me, past the table with its two chairs, all the way to the window where the blue, purple, and pink of dawn tainted the sky. Framed his silhouette, the perky triangles of Lyra's long-coated ears as she stared straight ahead.

They were both utterly silent. Utterly still.

Breaking the moment would be a treachery.

So I stood beside the bed, barely breathing, while they took in the sight. One seeing a long-lost friend, the other experiencing the wonder for the first time.

Slowly, Lyra's white-tipped tail began to swish. Then faster. And faster. She craned her neck until those dark eyes met mine, then she shimmied higher up Mordecai's chest, sticking her tongue out and reaching for Mordecai until her sloppy wet kisses snapped him out of the stupor. He chuckled—the sound rich, resonant, if a touch breathless—then set the dog down.

Lyra didn't hesitate to jump on my bed and nestle herself between the pillow and rumpled duvet. She let out a low, content sigh.

The book was still there, right on the edge of the mattress, harboring the bloody Norcross history. But I didn't have it in me to hate. Not right now. That sensation had sunk into my bones, lingering like a coiled viper that would strike when needed.

But that wasn't in this room.

In his presence.

Mordecai stretched out his hand in invitation. With one last look at Lyra who seemed fast asleep, I joined him by the window. His arm wrapped around me just as I curved mine around his waist, the gash on my palm already healed. The heat of his body caressed my skin, and I'd never felt such vulnerability and strength coexist within me. Two forces that should have opposed one another, but fed each other instead.

With Mordecai, there were no contradictions.

Only the beauty of existing in this time, in this place, precisely as I was.

I traced the moon tattoos climbing up his neck with a finger then leaned my head on his shoulder and observed the incandescent dawn with him.

"Thank you." A caress of his lips against my hair. "Thank you, Ember."

ONLY THE DRIFTING multicolored clouds marked the passing of time as Mordecai and I stood before the window. I hadn't noticed the silent tears slipping down my cheeks until Mordecai stole them away with lingering kisses, the air between us heavy with everything we wanted to say, but couldn't fit into words. Him even more so than me, I suspected.

"We should sleep," I said to save us both and braced one hand against the wide windowsill. It didn't create much of a distance, but enough to clear my mind. "Make yourself comfortable. I'll slip into the kitchens, fake the need for a late-night snack if there's anyone down there, and scavenge some food for breakfast."

"It can wait until tomorrow."

I bit my lip, then shook my head. "I have an early start. Actually, I *always* have an early start." Mordecai's eyebrows rose. "I've been...training."

Mirth touched the sapphire.

"Don't you dare laugh." I shoved him lightly in the chest. "A wheezing, gasping for breath Savior is something no one needs."

"You run?" Again, that hint of mirth. But the question was sincere.

"Run, fight hand-to-hand... I suspect weapons will be included soon, since Ivarr and I have access to the training grounds."

The dagger strapped to my thigh had been a mere

355

introduction—a way to familiarize myself with handling a blade. But I'd never used it in combat before.

"Ivarr Revere? *He's* training you?" The too-familiar shutters claimed his face, erasing the amusement. "Does he know—?"

"About the shadowfire? Yes," I said softly, then wrapped my hands around his neck.

That his first response hadn't been outrage over me working with his sworn enemy, but concern for my safety... It warmed something within me.

Mordecai might have chosen to include Ivarr when he'd cast us all beyond Nysa's limits, but for all his wisdom and skill to see the grander picture, I suspected this was one he hadn't truly thought through.

I brushed my fingers up the back of his neck, through the silken black strands. He hadn't known Ivarr had already witnessed my shadowfire in the Whispers. And I didn't doubt the thought that someone who hated everything Mordecai was could be fine with my icy obsidian sounded impossible.

But sometimes...

Sometimes impossibilities crafted the sturdiest truths.

"Ivarr's a friend, Mordecai. I've tried patching things up with the others, too, and we're making progress." Progress I was certain would crumble to dust the instant I revealed I'd brought their Crescent Prince into the midst. "But Ivarr—he understands. Doesn't judge." I shrugged, leaning back a little with my palms braced on Mordecai's shoulders. "Like calls to like after all, and regardless of everything, Ivarr and I are not like the rest of the group."

Killers was what I didn't have to say.

That we were of a different brand didn't matter in this context.

Only the blood coating our hands did.

Mordecai inclined his head, his muscles relaxing even as a twinge of compassion shot through his sapphire gaze. He pulled me closer. "Then I hope Ivarr will train you well."

I snorted. "Wait until you see me spewing curses after tomorrow's run."

A low laugh against my lips before Mordecai drew away—not without effort.

"I'll be right back," I promised, then slipped out the door and down the curving ramp before the temptation to return to his arms spun me right back around.

Aside from the gentle, ever-present chiming, the Cognizance Repository was dormant. Even the kitchens, much to my surprise, were devoid of people, save for a petite librarian who had taken to raiding the shelves for something sweet. It must have been even later than I thought. The librarian shot me a guilty smile, pocketed a paper-wrapped pastry, then swiped a thick slice of cake off the counter before hurrying off.

Relieved I wasn't truly breaking any rules since it had always been one of the cooks on duty providing me with additional treats, I got to work—but did so fast regardless. An empty bowl for Lyra to fill with water. Some bread. A few pastries I wrapped in the same thick paper as the librarian had before me, joined by a small assortment of fruit I temporarily stashed in the bowl.

A part of me wanted to search a little longer, find something appropriate for Lyra aside from the strawberries Ada had once told me she enjoyed, but I vowed to return tomorrow instead. The food Mordecai brought with us would last Lyra for a few days, and I really didn't want to push my luck.

Writing off my late-night rummaging to hunger would work

only if I didn't have enough items in my hands to get through an entire week.

I clamped down on an unexpected laugh and left the kitchens.

Mercifully, I didn't encounter anyone on the way back, and the wing where our rooms were situated offered no sounds—save for the occasional snore coming from a little farther down. I paused. Mordecai and I would have to be careful speaking until I managed to put a spell up to keep any sound from escaping the chamber. *If* I could even do it on my own.

My teeth worried on my lower lip, and I shifted the food in my hands. Maybe I could hide Mordecai and Lyra in the bathroom while Nyon worked. Maybe. At least Eriyan's snoring offered up a good reason for the magic, though I'd still have to figure out how to explain why I didn't just want to prevent sound from getting *into* the room, but from allowing it *out*, too. I grunted.

I wasn't about to come to any conclusions standing out here in the open, my arms overflowing with goods. No, this was a matter better tackled after I got some rest.

With that decided, I eased myself into the room and somewhat clumsily locked the door behind me. I winced and spun around, but the sight rooted me to the ground before I could take another step.

Mordecai lay on the bed, his dark hair falling across his forehead and cheek. He still wore the same clothes as before—as if he'd only meant to close his eyes for a moment. Lyra was pressed snugly against him, curled up just beneath his chin with her nose buried under her bent legs. Yet as endearing as the sight of the two of them together was, I could hardly look anywhere but at the serene expression on Mordecai's face. As if this was the first time he'd truly gotten to rest in a long while.

Perhaps ever.

I forced my feet to move as my chest still bore the weight of that thought. Carefully, I transferred the food from my hands onto the table, then strode into the en suite—forgoing the bath but taking care of other necessities. Just for a heartbeat, I hesitated when I slipped off the purple-blue dress and took the thin, flowing garments I usually wore to bed in my hands. Not sheer exactly, but definitely revealing in contrast to Mordecai's buttoned-up dark attire.

I rolled my eyes at myself and put on the camisole and short culottes.

Mordecai and I were done playing power games.

I padded out of the bathing chamber, grabbed a blanket out of the closet along the way, then climbed onto the bed behind Mordecai and covered our bodies. Lyra let out a satisfied sound, but otherwise didn't move.

As I lay my head on the pillow, observing the silken spill of his black hair, Mordecai fitted his back against my front—not waking, as I initially feared, merely seeking out my warmth. Offering his.

The last thing I remembered before sleep took me into its realm of oblivion was my arm, snaking around him and resting against his chest as if it was the most natural thing in the world, to hold him close.

CHAPTER FORTY

COMING CLOSE TO DYING ON THE FIFTH LAP AROUND THE Repository grounds was progress.

Even Ivarr's teasing dropped down a notch when I doubled over by the rosebushes that marked the finish line, sucking air into lungs that refused to accept any considerable amount of oxygen. But at least my head wasn't spinning too much, which, with the turbulent evening and too-few hours of sleep behind me, I supposed was an achievement all on its own.

Letting the cool, but not chilly, air caress my heated skin, I straightened on somewhat wobbly knees—finding Ivarr still looking at me. He gave me what could only be called an acknowledging, almost proud look before he broke away to complete his own exercise. I huffed a laugh, though I wasn't entirely sure just what I found amusing.

All I knew was that it belonged to the good kind.

A stitch dug into the side of my abdomen. My cue to go.

With one hand pressed against the unpleasant ache, I

trudged to my room. The librarians I passed on my way up the winding ramp wore nothing but kind, good-natured expressions, though I knew that with my tunic and pants soaked in sweat and my face resembling one of those ripe tomatoes they were growing outside, the image I projected was far from seemly. True enough, when I slipped into the chamber, Mordecai needed no more than a look at my state before he broke out laughing.

The sound, so free of burden, startled me so that for long, long seconds, I only stared at him, one hand still on the handle, and marveled at this side of Mordecai that was without a doubt his, yet so, so different.

I didn't even care that it was my unfortunate look fueling this unguarded mirth. Maybe, if anything, felt glad for it—though some distant, useless part of me cringed at not being at my best in front of this gorgeous man.

Luckily, that part found no foothold.

I did, however, cross my arms and arched an incredulous eyebrow. Mordecai tried, and failed, to school his features into something more serious, clutching his stomach where he lounged on the bed with Lyra beside him.

I rolled my eyes and, fighting to keep my voice leveled, muttered, "Ass."

Which only made him laugh harder.

I winced at the sheer volume of it, but let out a chuckle of my own as I strode into the en suite. The Repository had come alive while Ivarr had put me through his rounds of torture, and the vigorous chatter drifting through halls and down corridors would help mask whatever sounds were coming from my room. We would be fine even if the Crescent Prince *was* intent on laughing his ass off.

A smile still teased his lips when I strode back out, devoid of sweat and clad in billowing turquoise pants and a dusty light blue, draped blouse, pinched at the waist. Heat flooded my cheeks as Mordecai's gaze devoured me, any traces of mirth gone.

He pushed off the bed and prowled towards me, his every step giving wings to the boundless desire I could never hope to fully contain. Didn't want to. But letting go would mean losing myself in a way that had no room to exist in these circumstances.

We stood close enough to touch, everything about him magnetic and peeling off those protective layers as if they were scraps of flimsy clothing, made for him to strip off me.

Right when I was positive I couldn't take any more, Mordecai drew me into his arms. For several heartbeats we remained like that, my hand splayed across his honed chest, warm through the fabric of his shirt, while his rested against my spine. Our lips met.

The kiss was gentle at first, then possessive.

I'd felt wanted before, but this—

It was as if he yearned for me with every sliver of his soul.

A groan escaped me before I could stuff it down.

Mordecai didn't miss the invitation.

He backed me up against the clear stretch of wall by the door and pinned me against it with his body. With the hand he'd had on my spine now braced beside my head, he used the other to tease the curve between my ribs and my hips. The light blouse was an almost nonexistent barrier against the searing heat of his touch.

He smelled like the night, the pleasurable dark that augmented the senses, and his taste carried the silver-lined essence of something eternal, yet carnal. I burned for it to consume me.

All those things I hadn't allowed myself to feel poured out of me, written in the grazes of our tongues, the pressure of teeth on lips, and in the press of our bodies.

Maybe some kernel of me would always dispute this reality—unwilling to believe that something like this could exist beyond the realm of dreams. But here, in this moment, I was powerless.

I gasped as he tore away from my lips, then moaned once his mouth traveled along my jaw before dipping down to my neck to caress the wild pulse beating against my skin.

Stars...

Just when I had half the mind to thrust him back and push him onto the bed, breakfast be damned, Mordecai slipped away.

He observed me, smug satisfaction shaping the upswept line of his mouth as I stood there—undone and ravenous. "Enjoy your meal, Ember."

"Bastard," I rasped, earning myself a chuckle. And a lingering, heated gaze.

I ran out of the room while I still could.

FOR BETTER OR FOR WORSE, the inner, wicked turmoil—*and* the flush in my cheeks—subsided before I entered the large hall. Composed once more, I took my usual seat between Mae and Ivarr, who had decided to show up in all his sweaty glory as if he'd run straight here, then quickly piled the food onto my plate. I poured myself a generous amount of coffee, and only once I inhaled its delicious scent, eyed the spreads. The cherry marmalade caught my attention, and I dragged it closer, a piece of neatly cut bread already in my other hand. I slathered on a layer of butter then a thick one of the aromatic marmalade.

I had to swallow a satisfied groan as the taste exploded in my mouth. Ivarr's chuckle grazed my ear.

"Whatever torture that one," Eriyan drawled from across the table, his gaze flicking briefly to Ivarr, "is putting you through is having a nice effect."

He saluted me with his coffee, then treated himself to a slurping sip all the while keeping his eyes on me.

Before I could come up with a retort, Ada leaned around Mae who was studying me with a cryptic expression. Ada raked her gaze across my face. "I never thought I would utter the words, but Eriyan's right."

I chewed down the food and chased it with a generous swallow of coffee. "Maybe *Eriyan* could try running under Ivarr's mentorship," I said slowly, dangerously—a threat wrapped in silk. "See if that grin will still be there after he feels like throwing up his guts."

Ivarr matched my predator with his. He perused Eriyan as if he were a map spread open for anyone to read. Out of the corner of my eye, I noticed Ada slap a hand to her mouth to contain the snickering while Mae pressed her lips together, body shaking silently.

Ivarr said to me, "I bet one lap." He flung another look Eriyan's way. "Tops."

"Make that half a lap," Dantos bellowed from the entrance.

We all whipped our heads towards him—and I nearly spilled my coffee, the mock chill gone, when I saw Zaphine was with him. *Truly* with him. Holding hands and looking as if a weight had rolled off her shoulders. Her cheeks flushed as the five of us shamelessly gawked, but she recovered quickly.

With envious grace, she planted a kiss on Dantos's cheek, then marched over, chin held high. "Yes, yes, I had sex with a man. Everybody can move on with their lives now."

She delivered the sentence with an arched eyebrow as if daring us to say something. Needless to say, there was just one person who couldn't keep his mouth shut.

We all looked at Eriyan right as he grumbled, "I *knew* we should have betted on those two."

Though the effect was ruined by the mirth lingering in the corners of his eyes.

Dantos slapped him on the shoulder, hard enough that Eriyan's thin body pitched forward. "And we would've made sure you lost, cousin."

He sat next to Zaphine, that adoration he had kept a leash on before now fully on display. Images flashed through my mind, of a similar kind of wonder—one that had cupped Mordecai's face when he woke to find me beside him. All those regal, sharp lines of his features had seemed sharper yet somehow more pronounced, more *him*. A layer, I suspected, few had the honor of seeing.

As fast as I could, I put a lid on the memory, grateful everyone was still preoccupied with the grand news of the morning. Only Ivarr glanced at me, as if he saw right through everything—but didn't comment.

I cleared my throat, then, before I even knew what I was about to do, just felt in my bones it was right, said to them all, "I feel terrible for putting a damper on the fun..." My gaze locked with Zaphine's but the only reaction she gave me was an understanding nod, though she couldn't possibly predict the depths I was about to take them too. "But there's something I learned yesterday that you should know. Need to know, I think."

Unsurprisingly, the atmosphere took a plunge. Around us, the soft chatter of librarians continued, painting an even starker contrast to the tension-ridden silence. To the food forgotten on our plates and the steaming coffees cooling as seconds skidded by. I wished there was another way to do this, but I was already keeping one secret. The last thing I wanted to do was add more to that list.

Perhaps the girl who'd stumbled into Somraque would have. But I hadn't been her for a while now.

"Is it...is it about the fragment?" Zaphine asked and blindly reached for her cup, her gaze on me. Dantos slid it closer and made sure she was holding it securely before letting go.

"Yes and no."

Ivarr twisted in his seat so he faced me, but there was comfort in his gaze alongside guarded curiosity. I wrapped myself in it.

"I found a book on my family's history while browsing the shelves." The bitterness returned. Along with guilt I rationally knew I shouldn't carry but did nonetheless. "The rebellion that caused the world to fracture was a joined effort, but led by one man. Ekelyon Norcross. My ancestor." The blanket of silence that had fallen over our end of the table became even heavier. "It had been *his* agenda to cleave apart the lands. His desire to create a place where those with no magic within their bodies could rule."

"Are you—are you sure?" Ada asked, but the quietness of her voice revealed her lack of conviction in another explanation.

I nodded. "I saw him lead the others into the temple where the relic was kept and slaughter the Ancients protecting it." I blew out a breath, only faintly noting my hands were shaking when I picked up my cup. The heat of it barely registered "I just thought you should know. I mean...I *am* of his blood."

Mae touched me lightly on the shoulder. I jerked, but quieted as I noticed the realization in her gray eyes. Even more so, the lack of condemnation. "Of course. You're a Norcross."

She'd known—how could she not? As a child brought up in the Cognizance Repository, someone must have taught her the bare bones of history.

Yet the one reply that came to my mind had nothing to do with her withholding information none of us had inquired after.

"I never knew until now just how much I wish I wasn't."

"Maybe the Savior was supposed to come from the line that ruined it all," a voice said to my right.

I turned towards Ivarr, taking in the hard lines of his face— but also accepting the conviction in his statement.

He went on. "Consequences aside, it took balls to do what they did. And it will take balls to reverse the damage. Maybe it's because of who your family is that you have the steel needed to see things through to the end."

No one spoke as Ivarr's words rang out. But when we finished our breakfast and strode off to our respective reading rooms, the fire we all shared burned brighter.

COMBING through the books helped keep my thoughts at bay, though dark kernels of them managed to slip through my defenses whenever I thought I was on the right path. Cut-out sequences of the remembrances. Followed by the abandoned ruin Nysa had been reduced to.

All because Ekelyon Norcross had felt threatened by those different than him.

Scouring the tomes for any further mention of the fragment was the only way forward. The only productive one. But for the life of me, I couldn't just erase the churning that disturbed my depths.

How could one man, one selfish, wretched, swine of a man unleash an avalanche of horrors that continued even when he had long turned to dust?

I groaned inwardly, more and more frustrated with myself. As if giving Ekelyon even more power by letting him commandeer my thoughts would end up in anything but a waste of time and nerves. I raised the chronicle and tackled a new segment.

"Do you have volumes eighteen through twenty?" Zaphine asked way too energetically as she popped her head into the room and successfully startled me into dropping my book.

Ivarr laughed as I swore, but missed my answering glare as he went to inspect the spines of the considerable number of tomes we still needed to comb through. The Hazeldyne family had a *lot* of branches, all of them involved in the business of gathering and displaying artifacts. Even with all of us, including the librarians, sifting through their history, we had enough reading material to last us at least a week. Or four, if my grumpy, less optimistic side was to be believed.

"No," Ivarr answered. "Why?"

He glanced up at Zaphine who shrugged. "Didn't think so but it was worth a shot." She clicked her nails against the doorframe. "I'll check with Ada and Mae. Maybe they grabbed them off my desk by mistake."

"Wait," I called right as she was about to turn around, "you already gave them a second round of books?"

Ivarr and I hadn't even reached a third of our pile. We exchanged a quick, but very telling look before I focused my attention back on Zaphine. She braced one shoulder against the frame, her lush dark hair spilling to one side as she cocked her head and crossed her arms.

"Don't get me wrong, we're all pulling our weight, but... You two train. Eriyan is a lazy butthead who can't resist chatting up cute librarians. And Dantos and I..."

"You're otherwise occupied?" I arched an eyebrow.

Her smile was brilliant—and a touch smug. "Precisely. Ada and Mae, on the other hand..." She laughed. "I swear they're courting each other through a battle of brains and discipline."

I opened my mouth. Then closed it.

That was surprisingly accurate.

"You know"—she glanced at her painted nails—"when I snuck into Dantos's room last night, I caught a glimpse of Ada going into Maelynn's."

"Gossip, Zaphine?" Ivarr asked, leaning against the tallest stack of books with a wolfish smile that really suited him stretched across his face and the humor in his tone evident.

Zaphine flashed him a guilty look that, combined with the mischievous twitch of her lips, made it absolutely clear she didn't feel guilty at all. She lifted then dropped an elegant shoulder. "Happens to the best of us."

"Or maybe that's just Dantos rubbing off on you," he fired back.

"He's definitely rubbing onto something," I muttered, sending Ivarr into a fit of laughter.

Zaphine sighed and clasped her hands in front of her body. "I'd act insulted, but what would be the point when you're so deliciously right?"

With that, she spun on her heels and disappeared down the hallway, giving me no choice but to let my laugh join Ivarr's.

Once we were done chortling, however, and Ivarr reclaimed his spot beside me, Zaphine's words—the ones *before* the gossip —pushed through to the surface. Along with an idea that just might cure us of this painful slowness.

"Zaphine has a point," I said into the newly established silence, punctuated only by the turning of pages as Ivarr skimmed through the illustrations adorning a section of his book. "We work, but we also *do* get sidetracked a lot."

Our "casual" sparring matches had multiplied from the intended one to three. And that was *before* noon. Knowing we were closer to finding the fragment's location helped, fueled the drive, but it was only a matter of time before procrastination, often masked as an unbearable need to get coffee that very instant, got the better of us. So we sparred instead. Truthfully, I'd come to love our little matches. Looked forward to them even when my mind should have been focused elsewhere—and so, I suspected, did Ivarr.

"You want to quit training?"

I could have sworn there was something akin to remorse lurking beneath his otherwise leveled voice.

I shook my head as he turned another page without really looking at it. "No way. I'm not giving it up for anything." I drew one leg up and tucked it beneath me. "But maybe we should set a schedule and stick to it. Use that training room below for a set time." I tapped my fingers against the open page. "It could be our motivational system. If we work for three hours straight, we get half an hour of sparring. Or something like that. You're in charge, so you get to decide the actual amounts."

Ivarr leaned back, long legs stretched out under the table and fingers interlaced at the nape of his neck as he considered my offer. He nodded. "Since we already run in the mornings, we could do a short weapons training between ten-thirty and eleven, then a hand-to-hand, hour-long session in the afternoon at four. Sound good?"

"Sounds great." My gaze dipped down to my allocated column of chronicles. "Would you mind if I worked in my room in the meantime? It should keep me from resisting the temptation to tackle you during one of the boring paragraphs."

Which wasn't a lie. But it didn't mean it was the entire truth, either.

Ivarr smirked. We both knew how me tackling him would end. But he sat straighter in his chair and gave me a smile— though not an entirely innocent one. "See you downstairs at four. Bring a towel. You're going to need it."

I snorted. "You know this wasn't an invitation for you to go harder on me..."

"It wasn't. But I'm going to anyway."

We grinned at each other, then Ivarr made a shooing gesture, his attention already back on the book laid flat before him.

I stuffed several thick volumes under my arm and marched out of the room, perhaps a touch more entertained than I should have been at the prospect of dumping at least half of them in Mordecai's lap.

CHAPTER FORTY-ONE

SPRAWLED ON THE FLOOR, I OBSERVED THE THREADS OF A spell dance above me. Nyon's work.

After seeing different structures from different Spellweavers, asking magic to reveal itself whenever I had a moment to spare while walking around the Repository, I'd begun to note the slight tells marking the spell as his—like handwriting, the twists and turns, while universal, bore a personal touch.

But for all my observational skills, I was no closer to crafting one myself unless Nyon prepared the base for me and I simply tweaked the design with a few simple commands until it was finished.

I propped myself on one elbow after yet another failed attempt and looked at the Spellweaver in question. "What am I doing wrong here?"

"You're not doing anything wrong, Ember, except maybe overthinking," Nyon said, sitting cross-legged with his back against his bed. He tossed me a strawberry from the plate propped on his nightstand.

I snatched the fruit a little awkwardly from the air, then rolled onto my back. "Can you help me *not* think?" I sighed. "I'm starting to believe my mind isn't made to be quiet."

A rustle of fabric, then Nyon was sitting beside me, a slight furrow resting between his brows. He tucked his midnight blue waves behind his ears. "What makes you forget about everything else?"

I turned the strawberry over in my hands, inspecting the perfect fruit as I dug for an answer. Even when Ivarr pushed me to the brink of exhaustion, there were always errant thoughts running through my head. Reading offered up more of the same.

"I'm not sure," I confessed. "It's like I can bring something to the forefront, but there's always an entire ocean of threads still alive and wriggling beneath it."

A knock sounded at the door, and Mae entered before Nyon could reach the threshold. He stepped aside to let her pass. I didn't move from my spot, but waved—maybe a bit halfheartedly, with the numerous thoughts churning in my cursed brain.

I snorted mentally.

Hopeless. I was damn hopeless.

"Sorry I'm late," Mae said in way of greeting. Her gray eyes looked about as tired as mine felt from reading so many pages, but her expression was bright. "What did I miss?"

Nyon, once again at his post by the bed, threw her a strawberry. "We're trying to find out what can quiet Ember's mind."

"Oh." She popped the fruit into her mouth. "Overthinking?"

I bit out a grunt.

Mae chuckled. "That will actually serve you well while doing enchantments." She motioned to Nyon who promptly pitched another strawberry her way. "But I can see how it can be a hindrance when crafting spells."

"Any suggestions?" I asked and pushed into a sitting position. I tucked my legs beneath me, nibbling on the fruit at last. Even the slightly sour situation couldn't diminish how delicious it tasted.

Mae glanced at Nyon who said, "I like to meditate, but that's just my personal preference. A lot of Spellweavers have other means of entering the proper state to cast spells. A few lucky ones are born with the right mindset."

"That's *really* not helping," I ground out, though amusement lined my voice.

"Sometimes," Mae said, "it's a person."

I brushed my hands down my pastel pink trousers. "What do you mean?"

"Well"—she gestured to Nyon for another strawberry—"if being by yourself means your thoughts run wild, then maybe *you* aren't the cure for that particular ailment. But if there's someone who makes you forget everything but the present, the actual reality unfolding at that moment, then that's the state you want to be in. And as long as you're familiar with it, you will, with time, learn how to replicate it at will."

I kept my face as neutral as I could as her words seemed to expose me with zero effort. She couldn't possibly know, but—

There *was* someone who quieted everything.

Someone who whisked away all noise and allowed me to simply *be*.

"Is that what it's like with you?" I asked, not wanting to

linger on the subject of my own issues—let alone the suspected solution to them.

Mae flashed me a wide grin. "Enchanter here. Overthinking is kind of my thing." I snorted, but Mae went on. "But it helps to know how to shut down when I need rest. Sometimes, tuning out everything was the only way I survived being on the Council."

Fabric swished as Nyon eased himself next to me, a worn, well-loved book I hadn't even seen him pick from the color-coded shelves beside his bed resting in his hands. He offered it to me.

"This might help."

I skimmed the title, then peered at the table of contents. "Spellweavers' diary excerpts?"

A smile graced his lips. "You'd be surprised how often all it takes is merely knowing someone had walked this path before you."

I RETURNED FROM THE LESSON, book in hand and an idea brewing at the back of my overthinking mind. Mordecai lounged on the bed like sin incarnate with the top buttons on his shirt undone and reading one of the tomes I'd brought up to my room yesterday, and it took more will than I cared to admit not to climb up next to him.

On him, an utterly helpless part of me corrected.

Lyra, unsurprisingly, lay on her back within arm's reach, head tossed back and vying for Mordecai's attention. He stroked her chest absentmindedly.

When she saw me watching her, her tail started to swish against the bed. I strode closer.

Mordecai slowly lifted his gaze from the page, presumably finishing the ridiculously long paragraph I spied spilling across the paper. "How did it go?"

"I have some more material to study." I waved Nyon's book through the air, then sat on the edge of the mattress where it was safe. *Safer.*

Lyra wasted no time rolling onto her feet and padding over to bop her head against my elbow. I set the Spellweavers' diary on my lap and ran my fingers through her soft white hair. Once she deemed she'd received sufficient affection, she jumped off the bed and trotted over to her bowl of water. I stared after her, marveling at how small, everyday gestures could be so beautiful —but deep down I knew that, while the sentiment was sincere, there was a whole other breed of musings dominating my mind.

"What is it, Ember?" Mordecai's voice rolled across my skin and, with the sudden transition I doubted he was even aware of triggering, more than proved my theory right.

I slid closer to him. "I think I need your help."

Mordecai arched a haughty eyebrow, but that was amusement dancing in his eyes. He glanced down at the book in my lap. "Need some incentive to work magic?"

Unbidden, the memory of his teasing as he'd pushed me to open portals surged, and I struggled to keep my face straight. The shadowfire from purring. I wasn't giving him the satisfaction *that* fast.

"I don't need a peek into your bedroom, if that's what you mean," I said dryly.

"No, you already have me in yours."

When a new, far more powerful rush of heat coursed through

every inch of me, I didn't fight it any longer. Not just for my sake, but Mordecai's too.

I let my fingers find their way to his hand. Then closed them around it. There was so much I wanted to do. So much I wanted to share with him.

The teasing, this harmless, yet charged playfulness between us that defied all odds was lovely and meant more than I could ever put into words. It was also something we both desperately needed, but—

Much like my thoughts kept returning to the remembrances I'd carry within me always, so was Mordecai burdened by his own recent past.

He might not have cared about taking on the role of a monster and doing what was necessary to ensure Somraque's survival, but before the attack on the palace, he had never truly failed, either.

It didn't matter that without him, Somraque would have long been lost to the Void. The skeletal husk of Nysa haunted him.

The banter might help chase away the shadows, but neither of us pretended it would erase them entirely. I—I didn't think either of us would want that.

We were who we were.

And together, we could carry the scars without losing our beauty.

Without letting just one side of us reign.

I traced my fingers up to his wrist, then higher, caressing the contours of his corded forearm. Mordecai's gaze branded me, but I didn't lift mine from the smoothness of his skin, writing upon it the multitudes of what I felt for him—what he stirred and nourished within me.

Right as the moment teetered on the verge of becoming

something more, Lyra jumped up on the chair by the table and lay down with a loud harrumph, eyeing us as if we'd claimed her rightful space.

"Don't look at me like that," I muttered, barely holding back a laugh. "I'm doing this for you."

Another grumpy harrumph was her answer.

"What, exactly, *do* you plan on doing, Ember?" Mordecai asked, not bothering to mask the innuendo in his voice.

I smirked. "Reclaiming my teacher."

I scooted off the bed and yanked Mordecai with me. He quickly set his book aside—and so did I. I'd connect with the Spellweavers' experiences later. With what Nyon showed me still fresh in my mind, I wanted to try this out first.

Mordecai's eyebrows shot up as I dragged him into the en suite, then instructed him to sit against the bathtub—directly opposite the patch of grass and soil I'd pilfered from the Repository grounds and set into a square-shaped gardening tray. Lyra's makeshift toilet during the day, when I couldn't safely sneak her outside.

"Spread your legs," I said once Mordecai was on the ground.

Mirth and something else swept across his features— something that reminded me of just who I was ordering around. Thankfully, the excitement stirring within me made it next to impossible to care.

I fitted my back against him, drinking in his warmth, the breath that played across my ear as Mordecai leaned forward. I closed my eyes.

"Anytime you want to fill me in on your plan, Savior..."

"You make my mind quiet," I whispered and wrapped my fingers around the arm Mordecai had placed over my chest. "With you, I'm calm."

"You need me to ground you." His lips caressed my neck.

I smiled. "I need you just to be."

As I said the words, I felt something change. Slowly, I opened my eyes and saw a new world. One wrought of magic, crafted and raw alike.

So many wisps, waiting to be woven.

Whispers flowed out of me, the spell Nyon had showed when I'd asked him how they preserved the fruit regardless of the climate. The strands entwined and floated down upon the grass, spelling it to last indoors. I wove another layer atop it to prevent any odor from escaping beyond the green blades.

Throughout, Mordecai's presence cocooned me, his heartbeat steady against my back even as adoration seemed to seep from every pore of his body.

I released the spell.

And watched it stay.

THE MOMENT I released Lyra from my hands, I released time, too. Sneaking around the Repository and scavenging food had become second nature over the past two days. Easy, even. It was when I strode outside whenever I hoped everybody was asleep, but could never be certain, that set me on edge.

I detested the thought of Lyra cooped up in the room when the grounds were so beautiful, but being out here with her—the solitude reminded me of my lies.

It didn't feel right, concealing so much right as we relearned to trust one another. Yet I couldn't bring myself to reveal my trip to Somraque to anyone. Or who I'd brought back.

I didn't doubt there were no lengths they wouldn't go

through to find all three fragments and heal the shattered worlds.

I only questioned their capacity to understand just what having Mordecai by my side meant to me.

Sometimes, I wondered if even I truly did.

My footsteps crunched softly on the gravel as I took the shortcut between two stone paths, following Lyra's flicked-up tail as she sniffed around. I rubbed my hands down my arms, but the chill had nothing to do with the lacy sleeves of my dress.

Every moment spent in Ada's company during the days deepened my regret about keeping her and Lyra separated. Those encounters always left me with a foul sensation crawling under my skin—though I had to admit it had at least been manageable until that one time, when Lyra had caught Ada's scent, tail wagging and black eyes bright, but didn't act on the impulse I could see written in her slender body. As if she understood why we had to wait.

For how long, I wasn't sure.

Maybe I was hoping we would uncover the fragment's location before I sprang the news on everyone. A breakthrough like that would make it easier for them to swallow my confession. Or so I kept telling myself.

I crouched and snatched a pink-and-white pebble off the ground by the small pond Lyra had thankfully ignored. Flipping the stone over in my hands and feeling out its ineligible scripture, I stopped on a crossroads between two paths. I scanned the gently illuminated gardens for someone out on a stroll while Lyra explored another section and enjoyed her slice of freedom. When I lost sight of her behind the field of lavender, I ventured after her.

Without the tall bushes and fruit trees shielding me from the

Repository's direct line of sight, I rushed to the somewhat less exposed spot between a gazebo overgrown with roses and the plane tree by its side. I didn't see more than the tips of Lyra's ears from this vantage point, but it was good enough.

A few strands of lavender swayed here and there when she brushed against them, but luckily, they weren't the only ones with the wind slithering around the Repository's edges.

"Ember?" a voice called out.

My spine locked up, and the pebble slipped from my fingers.

Shit. Shit, shit, shit.

"What are you doing up so late?"

That wasn't *a* voice.

It was *Ada's*.

CHAPTER FORTY-TWO

I CURSED MY THOUGHTS. MY FEARS.

Useless superstition, but how could I not feel as if I'd *willed* this mess into existence?

And with it being no secret that I usually crashed in the evenings—or at least had before...everything—*of course* my presence here drew attention.

Sun damn me...

Feigning a causal demeanor even as my mind worked in overdrive, I turned around until I saw her, eyes bright but unguarded, just a hint of tension reflected in her own frame. Mae was by her side, with a couple of books resting atop her thighs.

I forced a smile to my face. "Doing some light reading outside?"

I felt, more than saw, Lyra still just beyond the lavender, and prayed to the Sun she would stay there.

Smelling Ada was one thing; seeing her, on the other hand...

The look they exchanged revealed they were doing a lot more than reading, but I accepted Mae's answer without letting my suspicions show. "A change of scenery helps."

"That it definitely does," I agreed, though a tightness crept into my voice as Ada's piercing jade eyes studied me. "How are you two holding up?"

Our dinner hadn't been among the most talkative ones. Days gone and still no new reference to the fragment. Even Eriyan had completely eradicated his slacking, as Dantos and Zaphine mentioned, so we were all working our butts off until our vision had blurred—then worked some more.

I shuffled from foot to foot and pushed back the wild silver strands the wind had tossed over my shoulders.

"In all honesty, if I never have to read another book about the Hazeldynes, that'll be perfectly fine with me," Mae said, then glanced at Ada who hadn't taken her eyes off me. "Though I think we're doing good—all of us, I mean—considering Chloenna had to bring some fresh blood into the librarians' teams."

That I hadn't known. The sheer shock that we were somehow more resilient than trained librarians almost made me forget this was a chat I wanted to put an end to sooner rather than later.

Almost.

So I said, "Don't let me keep you from—"

I waved a hand at the books. The two of them.

"Right." Ada's eyes narrowed even as they lost some of that unnerving focus. "You never did say what you were doing up so late. Meeting with someone?"

She scanned the surroundings, edging closer and closer to where Lyra was still standing, just far enough in the open I suspected she wouldn't go unnoticed.

"Unlike *some*," I said pointedly and moved in the opposite direction as if to walk past them, "I have no midnight appointments to meet."

Thankfully, the words had the desired effect.

Ada's gaze snapped to me. She looked so startled that the portion of me that wasn't running on self-preservation felt a little bad. "We're not— We're just..."

Maybe not *that* bad.

Seeing her flush all over—and realizing she hadn't been suspecting *me* of shady behavior earlier, but trying to conceal her own sneaking around was kind of adorable. Even Mae rolled her eyes, a silent commentary that was, in essence, not so different for my answering snicker.

"Why hide, Ada?" My gaze darted between her and Mae to further drive my point home. I really, really should be ending this conversation, but— "Or did we all get it spectacularly wrong and you two *aren't* together?"

She reached for Mae's hand and squeezed it. Her entire frame changed as she stared at Mae for one of those lovely, prolonged moments when nothing was concealed, before fixing her attention on me once more.

"We are. I just..." She huffed a frustrated breath. "I didn't know how you would take it. All of you. I mean, Mae apologized for what she had to do, but our initial encounter wasn't exactly kind to anyone."

Mae said nothing, merely kept watching Ada with silent compassion softening the corners of her eyes and mouth. As if this was a discussion Ada had bent herself backwards over more than once.

"You think we'll judge you?" I asked, unable to stave off the incredulity.

She shrugged, but she might as well have shouted "yes" for all of the Repository to hear. And seeing her like that...

I wanted to spill everything. Bring Lyra to her, then assure her that she had nothing to worry about when *I* had the person they knew as nothing less than their oppressor stashed away in my room. Her attraction, her affection towards Mae was nothing to hide. But even as I opened my mouth, the words died in my throat.

So all I did was dip my chin, then whispered, "I won't tell anyone if you don't want me to."

The gratitude burning in Ada's eyes nearly suffocated me.

I wasn't a friend. I was a liar and a deceiver.

Yet not even that was enough to change my mind.

"We should be going," Ada said softly.

We were just about to head in the opposite directions when a rustling disturbed the ground's serenity.

Both Ada and Mae whipped their heads in the direction of the swaying lavender. But where Mae's shoulders relaxed almost immediately, Ada kept scrutinizing that wretched patch.

Mae tugged on her hand. "You're jumpy, Ada. It's probably just one of the cats."

"Right." Ada rubbed her free hand across her eyes. "You're right. Sorry."

She let go of Mae who continued down the path with a parting wave.

"I'll see you tomorrow at breakfast, Ada," I said. "Try to get some rest."

With Mae or alone, she sincerely looked as if she needed it.

A brief smile flicked up her lips. "I will. And Ember,"—her jade eyes locked on mine—"thank you."

THE STRING of curses I'd been holding back flew out of my mouth the instant I released my grasp on time, snuck into the room, and set Lyra down. Mordecai looked up from where he had been reading a book on our bed, sprawled sideways across it with his back propped against the wall—precisely as I'd left him.

"What happened?"

Spewing out a few more choice words, I stalked over and sat on the edge of the bed. *Threw myself down* was more like it, given how Mordecai's entire frame jumped up when my weight hit the mattress. Lyra made herself comfortable on the blanket in the corner of the room, wanting nothing to do with my foul mood, I suspected.

The thought was sobering, though it didn't liberate me entirely from the echoes of the encounter digging into my skin like prickly thorns.

"I ran into Ada and Mae outside," I groaned, then rubbed my hands across my face. If I smeared the kohl, I didn't care. "I hate lying to them, Mordecai. I hate it."

A rustling of sheets, then Mordecai was pulling me back. He fitted me between his legs, just like that time in the bathing room, my back against his front and head resting in the nook between his neck and shoulder. Gently, he wrapped his arms around me, lying them across my abdomen. My fingers sought out his skin of their own volition.

Our breaths suffused the silence, drifting over distant chimes. I traced a curving path up his exposed forearm. "I keep waiting for Sun knows what because the right time certainly doesn't exist in this situation. It can't."

"Do you regret bringing me here?"

Driven by the caution in his voice, I twisted in his arms to peer up at him. "Never." I brought my hand to his face. "*Never*."

A ghost of a smile.

"I mean it, Mordecai," I said more forcefully and knelt before him. "I don't regret going back for you. Or bringing you here. I don't even feel guilty that I..." I swallowed. "That I feel *happy*. We still have no clue where the relic is. My family is nothing but a long line of cold-blooded killers. *And* I caused more deaths just by existing than I will ever save if we don't bring the lands back together." I'd told him about Svitanye. The madness in Somraque. Only Eira—Eira I continued to carry in the deepest, most secure vault of my heart. "But around you..." I cupped his sharp cheeks once more. "I'm happy. Despite it all, I'm happy. And it—it doesn't bother me, Mordecai."

"Until you have to deceive your friends."

"Until that, yes."

With liquid grace, he shifted our position until my back was against the mattress, his honed body towering over mine.

"You told me you had faith in them." Not a question, but not a statement either.

Or maybe my brain was too muddled by his proximity. By the way his lips were so close to mine I could feel every loving stroke of his breath. And yearned for more.

"I do," I whispered, dragging my eyes up to his magnetic gaze. "Maybe it's me that's the problem. That I don't have the guts to face them and lay myself bare like that."

Mordecai's nose brushed against mine, the caress followed by a fleeting touch of his lips. "I'm fine where I am, Ember."

The evidence of just how fine he was nudged between my legs, although I suspected that hadn't been what Mordecai had

had in mind. Heat washed over me, my breaths becoming harder. Hoarser.

"I can stay in this room for however long you need to feel comfortable speaking with the others." His mouth dipped to my ear. "But until you do—and I say this as someone who has had *ages* to ponder..."

I chuckled, though the sound came out husky. His answering smile, no more than a breeze of warmth against my ear, showed this had been his desired effect.

"Don't let things that haven't yet come to pass ravage you."

"Are you saying that just because it feels wrong to kiss a scowling girl?" I teased.

But what little air I had left in my lungs deflated when Mordecai lifted himself off me just enough to meet my gaze. For me to see the hunger making his sharp, regal features somehow even more painfully handsome.

He brushed a strand of hair off my forehead, then guided those fingers down my neck.

I shivered and arched beneath him.

"This, my dear Ember,"—his lips claimed mine—"is only the beginning of all I wish to taste."

CHAPTER FORTY-THREE

"I—"

My voice faltered under the weight of his gaze. Under the weight of my own desire. The aching, liquid heat that spread through my core, pulsing in a wild beat that matched my heart.

My fingertips skimmed his cheeks, and I breathed in the intoxicating scent of him.

This—this was the dream I hadn't allowed to take flight, kept under lock and key in the darkest corner of my soul to save myself. Because if it shattered, then so would I.

I laughed away the sting of tears and rose to meet Mordecai's lips. He hesitated, only for a moment, then responded in kind, filling me like the rapturing touch of shadowfire neither of us dared to release. I didn't know why it was now, that everything came crashing down. Why the line we had flirted with yet never crossed not only thinned—it vanished.

But I knew that for the first time since we arrived here, it felt as if it was just the two of us. Souls bared as the phantom thunder of the world rolled around us. Nothing could touch us in this room.

Not the fear I harbored, and had seen mirrored in Ada moments before.

Not the parts we had played and would still have to in the days to come.

There was only the fire. Fire that had roared even when neither of us had wanted it, still standing on opposite sides like the broken world had wanted us to.

The fire that had persevered.

Bound us.

Became a tether spawning across distances and over the imprints of past and present that should have driven us apart but only brought us closer.

The weight of his body fell on mine, and I surrendered to the taste of his lips, the strokes of his tongue. I wanted nothing more than to eliminate the barrier of clothes still separating us, but on the wings of that thought came another—

"Mordecai." I pushed him off gently, lips burning. As was my blood. "Just one problem."

He arched a dark eyebrow, wariness filtering into his gaze. I had to resist the urge to kiss it away.

"Maybe—maybe the librarians would be discreet, but I can't risk asking them for a contraceptive tonic. As much as I want to," I emphasized before he could mistake my concern for rejection.

The corners of his lips curved up, vanquishing the caution.

"I don't care how long I have to wait for you, Ember Norcross. A day. A year. I don't care. Time is not our enemy." Every word rolled across my skin like a teasing caress. "But I wouldn't want us to be anything less than who we are when I take you."

The shadowfire. Our powers merging as freely as our bodies.

No restraints.

My body writhed at the thought.

Mordecai's smile gained a decidedly devious edge.

"Besides," he whispered and raked his gaze down to my lips, "there's still a delightful number of things we can do without protection."

To further his point, he moved lower, hiking up my rose-gold dress as he knelt at the foot of the bed and drank in every inch of newly exposed skin. Stars...

Just the visual of his watching me with such reverence and hunger—

I nearly came undone.

But I couldn't look away, either.

Not when every line of his face was an exquisite, sublime brushstroke that would remain ever-changing, yet wrote every nuance, every sequence into eternity.

When his thumbs traveled up my inner thighs, all the way to the seam of my lace panties, Mordecai lifted his gaze to mine. The sheer intensity of the sapphire nearly stole away my breath, but it was his question that succeeded.

"May I?"

Reduced to a hyper-sensitive, wordless state, a nod was the only answer I could give.

Mordecai slid his hands higher, then hooked his fingers behind the thin fabric and drew it down. A soft moan rolled from my lips.

His touch never left me, even as I shimmied my legs to help speed up the process. But Mordecai was having none of that.

Intent to draw it out, he added a playful, yet firm amount of pressure to keep me in place, then proceeded with his wicked, wicked brand of torture. I cursed him at least a hundred times by the time the panties were free, the dark lace a stark contrast to the light blue sheets.

With the same breathtaking dedication, he planted himself between my spread legs.

He disappeared behind the bunched-up dress pooling around my waist, only the night-dark of his hair and the elegant arch of his brows visible, but I heard him as clearly as I felt his warm breath wash across my folds as he muttered, "Beautiful."

"Mordecai..."

The touch of his tongue, so close to where I needed him, made me forget what I wanted to say.

Heat and glorious tension blazed through me, spreading from my core and saturating my body until every last inch of it yielded to Mordecai's reign.

His fingers dug into my hips as my back arched. He held them firmly in place as he continued his slow exploration, teasing, but not yet tasting my arousal. I writhed, but was no match for his merciless grip. He flicked his tongue over the sensitive nub as if in punishment.

A whispered curse flew from my lips as I clawed at the sheets, answered by his low, taunting laugh.

The vibration of it rushed through me, and I ground against him, begging—*demanding*—more. But Mordecai retreated, his thumb replacing his tongue, and watched me from under the spill of tousled black hair. The dark, sensual edge of his smile became more prominent with every cunning circle, the ache deep in my core pronouncing the sharpening edges of pleasure until I couldn't conceal the effect he had on me from my face.

My lips parted, heat invading my cheeks as every breath became a struggle not to moan out loud. I'd woven a spell to dampen the sound escaping from our room, but I wasn't certain it would be enough for this. I sank my teeth into my lower lip, watching Mordecai watch me. A flash of ravenous hunger flared in his eyes, and he slipped his finger inside me.

"Stars," I rasped. My lids fluttered shut, head thrust back as another finger joined the first, delving into me in the rhythm of his thumb on my clit.

My body felt too tight and too vast at the same time. Pressure built under my skin, release teetering just beyond my reach.

"Please," I whispered and wetted my lips.

"Please what?" His voice was the alluring dark of the night— smooth, intimate. "What do you want, Ember?"

Any shyness I might have felt evaporated as his fingers grazed my inner walls. He wouldn't yield until I voiced my desires.

So I did.

"I want your tongue, Mordecai. On me. In me." I moved against him. "I want you to make me come with your mouth."

His lips curved into a dark smile. "With pleasure."

With an elegant hand, he flattened the fabric draped over my stomach until I could see the line of his mouth clearly as he dipped back down between my legs.

"You smell so good," he purred—and I nearly lost it.

Then truly, wholly did as he withdrew his fingers from me and granted me my wish.

The edge of his teeth, the strong, demanding flicks of his tongue... Pleasure rocked through me, and on its wings, the promised release. My fingers tangled in his hair. The resounding groan that left his lips and ricocheted straight through my core snapped the final tethers I still had to the world.

I cried out as his mouth worked through my orgasm, drawing it out until I was a panting, shuddering mess.

But even as my body wanted nothing more than to give out, so deliciously spent, a smile played upon my face as Mordecai licked away the taste of pure rapture, then sealed my lips with his.

CHAPTER FORTY-FOUR

"YOU DON'T WANT TO KEEP IVARR WAITING," MORDECAI drawled into my neck, voice husky from the too-few hours of sleep we'd both suffer the consequences for. Not that I would have changed a thing.

The softness of the covers and the warmth of his skin beckoned me to slip back into the pleasurable oblivion. I swept my nails up the arm he'd secured around my body before we'd fallen asleep—and had stayed there, an immovable, steady presence. My gaze flicked up to the gentle spelled light that illuminated the room in perfect harmony with the melody welcoming a new day. I guided my fingers back down, then closed them over Mordecai's hand.

We'd shared this bed every night since I went to Somraque for him, yet this—it was different.

More than just the tentative, gentle intimacy.

It was the kind of tranquility that reached to the very bones.

"Ember..."

I fitted my back tighter against him, finding him hard—as hard as he had been last night. *Without* allowing me to relieve any of the pressure.

This is your night, he'd said. *Let me cherish you.*

And he'd stuck with it.

But it was a new day now, which meant Mordecai's restrictions didn't apply any longer. As it was, it also meant there were other commitments I had to uphold.

Regrettably, I admitted to myself that he was right.

"Fine, fine," I half mumbled, half purred, then brought his hand up to brush a kiss across his knuckles.

His response dug into my backside, but I forced myself to climb out of bed. Though I didn't go without a fight.

Without looking at him, I padded over to the window on bare feet and pushed aside the drapes. The dawn light engulfed me, an almost tangible feeling—much like Mordecai's attention traveling up the column of my spine.

I stretched, then strode towards the en suite. But before I reached the door, before his searing gaze would leave me, I stopped and slipped off the cream-colored satin camisole and shorts, my movements wrapped into seductive innocence. Mordecai's sharp inhale was all I needed to hear. I flashed him a smile over my shoulder, pivoting my body just enough to offer him a glimpse of my bare breasts.

I could have sworn the sapphire brand on my exposed skin lingered long after I closed the door to the bathing chamber behind me.

When I walked back outside minutes later, still perfectly nude, Mordecai's gaze followed my path to the armoire. His unvoiced yet unmistakable desire imprinted on every exposed inch of me as I dressed in my running wear. Right as I finished lacing up my boots, the *swish* of sheets—and the canvas of white yet not pale skin—lured my attention.

Mordecai rose from the bed, all tousled hair and honed muscles, nothing but silken black shorts clinging to his powerful thighs. His tattoos were a taunting line up the neck I'd kissed so many times yesterday, yet felt as if it never would be enough. His gaze was smoldering as it locked on mine, but it was the roguish grin he hadn't turned around fast enough to hide that got to me.

So unburdened.

So free.

Our circumstances might not have changed, and this—this easiness, this joy between us—might be at odds with the grander picture, but it also felt natural. It felt right.

I vowed to safeguard and nourish it regardless of what the upcoming days would cast our way.

As he claimed what had become his spot by the book-strewn table, a small breakfast already set where I'd left it yesterday on one side, I dashed into the bathing room to grab the box of pins, courtesy of Mae. I perched on the edge of the bed that still carried Mordecai's scent—*our* scent, I realized—and started braiding my hair. I pinned it up into something that wouldn't unravel on the first lap, then finally allowed myself to look at Mordecai.

He wasn't bothered in the least that I caught the unguarded hunger etched into the prominent lines of his face.

A challenge.

But also a gentle check to see if I had any regrets.

As if my earlier performance hadn't been answer enough.

Driven by the need to move, I patted Lyra who was still slumbering in her makeshift cot by the wall, then walked over to place a kiss on Mordecai's lips. His hand curved around my neck, grasping the moment just for a little longer before releasing me.

"I'll see you soon," I whispered and straightened, feigning my legs weren't as weak as they felt.

A chuckle. "Another show, Ember?"

He raked his gaze down my body before meeting my eyes again. My blood heated.

"You know," I drawled, though it took a tremendous effort to weave control into my voice, "when I get back, you could join me in the bathtub."

The sapphire darkened to a dangerous shade. "I might not mind waiting, but you seem to be bent on making a mildly grating situation excruciatingly hard."

"Me? No." I glanced down at said hardness. "That's all you."

With that, I headed out the room and broke into a sprint down the winding ramp, hoping it would be enough of an excuse for my hopelessly flushed cheeks.

ANY IDEA I might have had of sharing the bathtub with Mordecai was beaten out of me a little over an hour later. My knees could barely hold my weight even when all I did was stand in place, though my mind certainly lacked no fuel conjuring up profanities to spew at Ivarr's athletic figure visible in too-fast flashes between the trees.

Every ache in my body seemed to have taken on a whole life of its own—and an agenda to make me miserable. To think I honestly believed I was improving...

To make things worse, Eriyan was grinning at me from a nearby white wood-and-iron bench, his blond hair jutting in every possible direction and sleep clinging to the corners of his squinting eyes. But though he might have looked as if he'd just rolled out of bed, his clothes—still in Svitanyian fashion he seemed to have adopted easily—were immaculate. From the sheer, dusty blue blouse and white cardigan, right down to the pastel pink high-waisted pants and shimmering loafers.

His grin only widened when he saw me appraising him during each burning, raspy pant. I narrowed my eyes.

"You." Gasp. "Woke up." Gasp. "Just to." Gasp. "Make fun of me?"

"Guilty as charged."

He brought a steaming cup of coffee to his lips. I trudged over on numb yet pain-ridden legs and snatched it from his hands. If I was his morning entertainment, fine. But I wasn't about to do it for free.

I swallowed a mouthful—a decision I regretted immediately.

"Sun, Eriyan." I grimaced, barely getting the liquid down my throat. "What did you do? Coat a cup of sugar with a splash of coffee and douse it with milk?"

He reclaimed possession of the mug. An easy smile rested on his face, though it faltered around the edges. "Sugar helps the absence of magic."

"Shit." I closed my eyes. "I'm sorry."

I'd forgotten that while we might have fallen into an almost normal rhythm here, Svitanye would never be normal for them. Because *they* weren't normal in it.

I braced a leg on the bench and started my stretching routine, peering sideways at the somber version of Eriyan I hadn't seen in a while. I was grateful he'd felt comfortable enough to drop all pretense, even as I hated that my careless comment brought it on in the first place.

He slid his thumb up and down the cup.

"How are you handling it?" I asked softly. "Aside from the nauseating amounts of sugar."

That last part earned me a smile. He sipped his coffee, still gazing into the distance where a few librarians with children on their hands strolled the paths.

I was starting to believe that was all the answer I was going to get when he startled me with his response. "I think I understand why the lands are falling apart. I feel like I am, too."

My foot slipped off the bench.

The slight wind, instead of whisking his words away, only pronounced them. And as it ruffled his messy hair, there was such a stark hollowness to his features my chest clenched.

Footsteps sounded to the right, then Ivarr materialized just beyond the rosebushes. Eriyan didn't even notice him, gaze empty yet full of desolation at the same time, but Ivarr certainly noticed Eriyan.

He slid his gaze to me, then slowly dipped his chin.

By the time I sat on the bench beside Eriyan, Ivarr was long gone.

"Eri..." I wrapped a sweaty arm around his shoulders. He leaned into the embrace. Barely. But it was there. "I'm so sorry."

Useless, inadequate words, but the unfathomable depths of the sentiment behind them translated through the touch.

"I keep reaching for a part of me that doesn't exist anymore," he said quietly. As if volume would give his admission even more of a hold over him.

"It will. It's just locked up inside."

"Still feels like it isn't there at all."

Seconds passed with nothing but the chimes ringing out around us. I wanted to silence them, erase the reminders they were, that there *was* magic in this land. But a kind he couldn't access.

"We'll find the relic," I said. The only thing I could that wasn't a petty consolation, but a truth I believed in.

Eriyan's gaze locked on mine, more green than blue, echoing the turmoil he carried inside yet refused to voice. He sucked in a shaky breath. "Whatever it takes?"

My thoughts flashed to Mordecai, poring over the tomes in our shared lodgings.

"Whatever it takes," I confirmed.

And hoped Eriyan would remember that when the time came.

WHEN I RETURNED to the room, Mordecai was studying the chronicle in front of him with such singular focus I didn't have the heart to disturb him. Especially when Eriyan's confession still lay heavily on my mind. The sooner we found the hallow, the sooner we could move on to Soltzen. And even then, they would be powerless until I reunited the fragments. *After* we spent Sun knew how long searching for the final one.

I'd never ceased being aware of the time slipping through our fingers, but now—

Now that inevitable passing carried an ominous quality etched in its structure.

Ada's words echoed through me.

I understand what my mother meant. To be forced to live like this, so empty...

It's like I'm a shell. Useless. Broken.

Telaria had had an air of resilience about her. A steely spine that, despite her resentment for a magical existence, kept her going. Ada...

She seemed better now. And I wanted to believe Eriyan carried the same quiet steel.

I peeled off my sweaty clothes, threw them in the spelled basket for cleaning, then dipped my sore body into the warm bath.

All of them had avidly avoided discussing the state this land had left them in. Even Ivarr had only assured me that he was doing fine as long as he ate regularly. But I wondered—

I wondered if it was just as bad for him when all embellishments were stripped away.

What remained when there were no distractions, no ways to cope...

I mulled over everything while I washed the sweat off my skin, and by the time my fingertips pruned slightly, cleared the topic from my mind.

The books.

The books were what I had to focus on if I truly wanted to help them.

I threw a mint-colored cardigan over my naked body and tied it at the waist. Lyra, the little hellion, darted over to lick a few stray droplets off my legs. I had to shoo her away or risk toppling over. My muscles were still burning from the run, and with the piles of books, her own cot, and the bag Mordecai had brought with him from Somraque, there was little room for maneuvering on this end of the room.

With a playful yelp, she rushed up on the bed and snuggled her slender body between the wall and the pillow, eyes all adorable innocence. I chuckled, then claimed the empty seat next to Mordecai.

EMERGENCE

His gaze fell on the curve of my breasts the cardigan's plunging neckline left exposed, but his voice was steady as he asked, "No breakfast?"

"Not today." I pulled the next book in line closer and flipped the cover open. "I'd rather work. Save my free time for you."

Gently, so, so gently, he leaned over and kissed me before leaving me to my chronicle.

If the others missed me at breakfast, they didn't come knocking to see where I was. Mordecai and I worked side by side in companionable silence, the occasional brush of our thighs offering encouragement and whispering that we were in this together. He did, however, pause his reading when I used magic to revive a memory I'd stumbled upon after two hours of skimming the paragraphs.

The sheer, fragile wonder in his sapphire gaze once I returned to the present infused every inch of my body with warmth.

How someone as extraordinary as him could look at me like that...

I managed to turn my attention to my chronicle and *not* climb into his lap. Assure him that I was his. Wholly and eternally.

But there was something unexpected about spending hours simply reading in Mordecai's presence. It was as if a bubble had knitted itself together around us and sealed us off from distractions until all that remained was an atmosphere that fed my concentration. Making it easier to work, not harder, despite being keenly aware of his proximity.

If it weren't for Lyra sinking her claws first in my thigh, then in his, I wouldn't have noticed just how much time had actually passed. And that I had weapons training to go to.

"Do you need me to bring up anything on my way back?" I asked as I moved over to the armoire and started pulling out the proper attire. Ivarr-approved tunic and formfitting pants, with undergarments that helped keep everything in place.

I'd learned the hard way during my very first run that while I might tolerate brief sprints, the kind of rounds Ivarr put me through—outside *and* indoors—weren't something my breasts handled well without support. Especially now, with just under a week until my monthlies. They were heavy and aching enough without strenuous exercise involved.

When I glanced at Mordecai, I found he'd abandoned the book in favor of watching me dress.

I couldn't help but hide a smile.

"The coffee tasted good," he said at last. I'd almost forgotten what I'd asked. "I wouldn't mind some."

The heat underlining his tone made it perfectly clear what else he wouldn't mind tasting again, but I fervently ignored it. At least until the evening.

I turned around, pulled on the tunic, then bent over to tie the laces on my boots when strong hands skimmed my waist. My hips.

I hadn't even heard him move, but when I straightened, Mordecai pressed my back against his chest. He wrapped an arm just under my breasts, the fingers of his other hand finding the perfect position between my legs. I ground against him with a curse.

His dark laugh caressed my ear. "Fight well, Savior."

"Crescent bastard," I countered, only my voice was thick, laced with more desire than my body was able to contain.

After a parting kiss on the side of my neck that sent a spill of goose bumps rushing down my skin, Mordecai moved with regal grace across the room. The dawn sky framed him beautifully as he leaned against the windowsill and watched me hurry out the door.

Unfair.

This was utterly unfair.

Though the breathless laugh that escaped me negated the bite in my mental tones I'd been angling for.

Deciding against wandering across the Repository, I took a left turn at the bottom of the curving ramp instead of a right and headed outside. It was just two short corridors from the back entrance to reach the training chamber, so Ivarr wouldn't be left waiting even if I indulged in a breath of fresh air while I took the path meandering around the sprawling castle. My flushed skin welcomed the cool kiss of wind, and my eyes thanked me for the change of scenery. I kept my gaze trained on the rustling foliage with its many shades of green—green that, according to Nyon, was the best remedy for sore eyes.

Second best. Right after magic.

But though I used my fair share of it, it still felt wrong to turn to spells and enchantments when another option existed. So I gave myself to the greenery, to the blend of soothing, exquisite aromas dominating the grounds, and observed the strain lessen with every passing minute.

The trail led me near the secluded spot where Ivarr had helped me regain my sanity that day we'd arrived at the Repository and I'd crumbled under the weight of learning just what the consequences of my birth had been. I paused, willingly sinking back into that moment. The weakness I'd felt. So similar to another, less than a week later, brought on by my family's history. Eira.

But both accounts, as wretched as they were, had fortified me, too.

I carried on to the enclosure with its stunning spell-tree where, in a way, this belief in myself had winked into existence for the first time.

I would never be the light, brilliant Savior Ada had expected. I was night and darkness. I had lethal edges someone who'd spent their lives merely posing in the sun would never see.

And it made me all that more convinced that while I couldn't be shaped into an idea—or ideal—the power to fulfill the prophecy was rooted inside me.

As I scanned the rolling shade of violet and blue streaking the sky, I thought of the survivors in Somraque, what they would think when the spell released them and they would greet the dawn for the first time. Their scars would remain, but maybe, just maybe, they would find hope in the rising sun.

Holding on to that dream, I strode away from the tree, only to find something blur in the corner of my vision.

I lifted my hand to my hair, coming away with a tiny spell-leaf the breeze must have flown over.

My gaze fell on the writing, the words resonating through my head in that peculiar double language—then their meaning registered.

Cheeks flushed, I tucked it under the tunic, right next to my heart, not wondering *how* the spell-tree knew what I required. Just grateful for its gift.

CHAPTER FORTY-FIVE

A METALLIC WHINE SWEPT THROUGH THE AIR AS I BROUGHT my sword up the split second before Ivarr's would have sliced across my face. I swore, muscles trembling and grip locked, but didn't yield.

"Good," he growled and pushed away. In the glow of the spell light, he looked more than formidable.

A honed force of nature.

I barely moved my body into a defensive position when his eyes flashed. A warning, but—

Faster than I could react, Ivarr hooked his leg around mine and toppled me backwards. Bastard.

Ignoring the pain that flared red-hot along my spine, I clenched my teeth and rolled to the side to evade his blow. *An extension of my arm.* That's what he'd told me the sword was, but as I fought to fend him off while at the same time trying to get to my feet, the weapon felt more like a limb I wanted to shed than one I could use.

Ivarr was faster. Stronger. With enviously good footwork I was years from reaching, regardless of how effective a teacher he was. There was no way I could win this fight.

When his blade sliced at me again, I did the only thing I could.

I cheated.

A tendril of pure obsidian snaked around the metal, stopping it midair. Ivarr's eyes widened and he jerked—

Then a roaring laugh rolled from his lips.

"Smart," he said as he let go of the sword that continued to hover above me, its blade encased in coiling darkness. "But if I recall correctly, this was supposed to be a fight *without* magic."

Momentarily succumbing to the pleasant rush of liberating the shadowfire from the confines of my skin, I almost drifted away when Ivarr coughed pointedly and shot a look at the obsidian. More of it than I had ever revealed in such close quarters.

The tiny vine I'd smacked him with once was nothing compared to this display of strength.

I shrugged, still sitting on the cool floor with my sword in one hand. "I'm not too keen on losing."

Ivarr's mouth curved up. He offered me his hand and yanked me up to my feet, sword and all. His blade retained its position in the air, the tendril of shadowfire extending from my body adjusting in length without as much as a conscious thought sent its way.

Ivarr's gaze flickered to the weapon again, then back at me, something akin to respect lining the half-smile. "Then I trained you well."

We moved towards the wall with its impressive array of weapons. Knives, daggers, crossbows, batons, swords, scythes, and an assortment of vicious-looking things I had no name for but seemed to be geared towards inflicting the most pain. So at odds with the peaceful, harmonious nature of the Repository.

Then again, Nyon *had* said they rarely used the training chamber, and the weapons, while well-maintained, struck me more as pieces of history than modern acquisitions.

I grabbed the empty sheath hanging on the wall and looked at Ivarr standing a few steps behind me. Unlike my own quick excursion, he hadn't let the display of weapons claim his attention.

His interest rested with one alone.

Me.

"What do you mean, you trained me well?" I slid my sword into the sheath before propping it back onto the hooks. "I don't recall you advocating cheats like the one I used…"

If anything, he'd edged to separate the fields of defense as much as possible. Precisely so I *wouldn't* rely on my magic to get me out of dangerous situations.

"If you're not keen on losing," Ivarr said, throwing my own words back at me, "you'll do everything it takes that you won't. Utilize *every* talent at your disposal, even if it means playing dirty." He huffed a laugh that matched the mirth in his eyes as he watched me approach. "I'm just glad we're on the same side."

I landed a light punch on his shoulder, but whatever comeback I might have had poised on the tip of my tongue faded as someone cleared their throat by the door. Both Ivarr and I spun as one, and a grin broke across my face when I saw Nyon standing there in his turquoise robes and blue hair pulled in a topknot with a few strands left down in the back.

I'd just taken a step forward when I noticed he wasn't looking at us, but to our right. The expression died on my face.

Even Ivarr remained rooted to the spot, though his focus was more on me than the Spellweaver who seemed unable to tear his gaze off the shadowfire coiling from me and balancing the sword within its obsidian shroud.

I yanked it beneath my skin so fast Ivarr jumped when the blade clattered to the floor.

"Forgive me," Nyon rasped softly. "I didn't mean to interrupt..." He waved a hand at the sword discarded on the ground, then brought his gaze to mine. "But..." He shook himself. "It's even more breathtaking than the books describe it."

My lips parted, but no words came out.

Of course Nyon knew what my obsidian was. Had probably read the accounts on the Ancients I was certain covered more than just what I'd seen of their end.

But what I couldn't wrap my head around was that he didn't appear to fear it.

Logically, yes. Nyon was not of Somraque where the shadowfire was synonymous with death and destruction. And the Ancients he knew of... The coiling wisps were power; they were protection. More of a shield than a weapon.

Yet for all the reasons laid out before me, actually *accepting* he didn't see the shadowfire as a threat was a whole other matter.

As if sensing my turbulent mind, Nyon strode closer, though left some room between us. As if in respect.

"The Ancients were a remarkable race," he said steadily, but his voice carried the texture of a state far from calm. "The key to all balance, created from the very essence of magic itself. It's an honor to know you, Ember. And a great privilege to witness your ancient power."

He brought a hand to his heart and bowed.

"Nyon..."

As fast as I could, I motioned him to straighten again. I didn't deserve this kind of respect. Didn't want it. But even more so, if anyone was to bow, it should have been me.

The powers within me put there purely because the right bloodlines had mixed would be next to worthless without people like him.

People who did not attempt to shape you into something you weren't, but lent the support needed for you to become who you were meant to be.

So I reached out, bridging the gap as I took his hands in mine and smiled broadly to fend off the prickle of tears. "What you said... It means more than I could ever hope to convey."

The corners of his eyes crinkled. "I meant every word."

I knew he did. It was why I was barely holding back the hug I wanted to smother him in.

"We're friends, Nyon," I said instead, needing the message to go through. "You've helped me so much, taught me so much that, if anything, the honor is mine."

"You two are adorable, you know that?" Ivarr commented from the side. "Can I join?"

I scowled at him, still holding Nyon's hands, but the amused expression on Ivarr's face quickly sent me into a tumbling fit of laughter. Damn him.

"We're being silly," I said to Nyon once I pulled myself together. "After everything..."

Nyon shrugged, dimples adorning his cheeks as he smiled. "It's always nice to appreciate friends."

I returned the expression, then let him go. The sword still lay where my shadowfire had dropped it, so I picked it up and handed it to Ivarr.

"You can always join in," I said with a wink, then turned to Nyon. "Did you need us for something? Or did word spread about Ivarr destroying me in duels and you wanted to sneak in a peek?"

Nyon echoed Ivarr's low chuckle—as good as confirming word *had* reached him—then said, "Sorry, yes. Mae sent me to fetch you." My brows rose as an eager gleam entered his eyes. "She believes they're on the verge of uncovering the fragment's location."

THE JOVIAL, buzzing atmosphere I'd expected to find when Ivarr and I, still sweaty and in our work gear, barged into the oval chamber turned out to be a headache-inducing jumble of curses, scattered books, and pacing individuals. I exchanged a weighted look with Ivarr where we'd stopped just beyond the threshold. Nobody had even noticed our arrival.

And maybe that was for the best.

The volatile charge prickled my skin, as if seeking an outlet. I'd be damned if either of us turned out to be it.

"This can't be happening," Ada snarled as she shifted a few tomes aside with such force the pile toppled over.

I cringed at the damage a few of the books had undoubtedly sustained, but one look at her face diverted my focus elsewhere. The chamber was...well, wrecked would probably be a nice way to put it.

"What can't be happening?" I muttered, though obviously not low enough.

"It isn't here!" She threw her hands up. Her intense jade eyes flashed to me, then scoured the space the next moment. "It. *Isn't.* Here."

Ivarr and I exchanged another look. He shrugged. Apparently, he had no more idea what was going on than I did.

"Give me a second," I said under my breath and, when he nodded, searched the room for someone who wouldn't bite my head off if I approached them.

Actually, Eriyan and Dantos looked more as if they were afraid of experiencing the same fate whenever Ada breezed past, and Mae—Mae was nowhere in sight.

I spied an elaborate pitch-black updo peeking from behind an armchair—then Zaphine's pinched face as she rose and dusted off her hands. I beckoned her over when she spotted me.

She cut a path across one of the few areas that were moderately free of scattered volumes. Up close, her black hair was mussed, as if she'd run her fingers through it repeatedly.

"We're missing a book," she said flatly before I even asked.

A memory stirred. "The ones you came asking about the other day? That you thought Ada might have misplaced?"

"We found them." Her lips pulled into a thin line. "All except *one.*"

Another pile crashed to the ground somewhere deeper inside the room. Zaphine winced on one eye as she glanced towards Ada who was a whirlwind ravaging the room. It was a wonder anything even survived the sheer force of her.

Silently, Ivarr stalked over and crouched beside Eriyan to help him put things in order. They stretched out their arms protectively as Ada marched by to tear into another shelf while Dantos did the same on the other side of the room. I looked but still saw no sign of Mae.

"Tell me everything," I said to Zaphine and tipped my head towards the hallway.

She opened her mouth once we were outside, but the clamor continued to pound against us, spilling into the faint, peaceful chiming. I grabbed the handle just as Zaphine rubbed the bridge of her nose, and shut the door against the onslaught of new curses —and more falling books. Zaphine's grimace mirrored mine as the ruckus dropped to manageable, almost negligible levels, but there was something else there, too. A tightness in the corners of her mouth that revealed whatever breakthrough they'd had, it hadn't been nearly enough to combat the failure afterwards.

Ada's outburst, as cringeworthy as it was, was apparently justified.

"Zaphine, what's going on? Nyon said you were close to uncovering the fragment's location..."

A full *thud* boomed from the oval chamber. Zaphine frowned at the door, then leaned against the wall beside it and sighed.

"Flander Hazeldyne had the fragment."

My heart leaped at the words—before I reminded myself this was hardly the entire story.

"He took it out of the private vaults," Zaphine went on, "wrote about it in length. Its history, how it could be used to claim total control of the world should it be somehow reunited with the other two. He—he was of the same thought as Mae's Council. Abhorred change. Feared it."

Unease coiled in my stomach. "What did he do?"

"That's just the thing." She blew out a frustrated breath and threw up her hands. "We don't know. He didn't trust his descendants to protect it, so he took it upon himself to conceal the fragment somewhere. The bloody entry ends with him leaving the estate, fragment in tow. But"—she raised a finger —"the last sentence on the last page of the book... It isn't a conclusion, exactly."

"You believe his chronicle continues in the next volume?"

A grave nod. "I do. Only the book isn't in the Hazeldyne collection." Her gaze skimmed the closed door. "Or anywhere else we've looked so far. Even the librarians we spoke to were at a loss. Their records are complete. The volume should have been there."

"Stars," I hissed. "Can't anything work in our favor?"

The smile on Zaphine's face was weak, but warm. "You sound just like one of us."

I blinked, then realized what she was referring to. I *had* been using Somraque's version of cursing along with my own. For a while now, actually.

I smiled at her and shrugged. "It rubs off on a person."

As the atmosphere between us shifted, losing the inky stains of tension, I eyed the door. "Let's go help."

Zaphine peeled off the wall. "And hopefully not die from one of Ada's books ramming into our heads."

WE WORKED without pause until dinnertime, with no luck except sore hands and backs from sifting through an entire wing of the Repository. Even with the additional help Nyon had recruited, it was daunting just to think about how many volumes we still needed to check.

None of us were willing to bet that the missing slice of history wasn't hidden behind a different binding.

So we'd taken *every* book from its shelf, leafed through it, then set it back to its rightful place.

When we were done, I was just about ready to keel over.

I filled Mordecai in as I changed from my work clothes into a lavender-tinted blue gown with full skirts, the layer of tulle above the silken fabric adorned with gold lace. It was far more lavish than anything I'd worn so far, but I was eager for the air of elegance the garment instilled. It made me feel a little bit more like myself. A touch more invincible.

The way Mordecai's gaze followed me across the room was a lovely added benefit, though I wished—I wished he could be out there with the rest of us.

Now that we knew what we were searching for, I could see that waiting idly on the sidelines gnawed at him. Even if he didn't show it.

But the intensity of his sapphire eyes chased away the somber mood of the news and my own thoughts, replacing it with a heightened awareness that was far from unpleasant. With a brilliant strand of anticipation, too.

He rose from behind the table just as I intended to leave for dinner and strode up to me.

He hesitated before speaking, as if the words he'd uttered weren't the ones initially meant to leave his lips. "You're remarkable, Ember."

A blush crept up my cheeks.

"Where's this coming from?" I guided my fingers across his chest, then up to the moon tattoos. "Not that I don't appreciate the comment."

A twitch of his lips. "Seeing you..." He sucked in a breath, then released it slowly. Somewhere in the distance, Lyra *harrumphed.* "When I told you I couldn't live with myself if I used you, I wasn't lying. I've had...partners, Ember, some I genuinely cared about. But with you—"

His fingers reached for mine.

"At first I thought it was because you were like me. When I saw your shadowfire in that alley, a part of me I'd kept sealed away cracked open. Then gained power. I learned that it wasn't what I'd thought to be impossible proven true that drew me to you. It was *you*."

He brushed away the tear tracing a scalding path down my cheek.

"You can be stubborn." His lips replaced his thumb. "Distant." Then moved to the other cheek. "But when you let someone in, there is nothing but strength and beauty. A brilliant mind coupled with a heart that is compassionate but not naive."

My breaths came out heavy as his lips nearly touched mine.

"Thank you for letting me in."

STILL RECOVERING from Mordecai's speech that left me raw yet impossibly light, my feet carried me down the winding ramp with almost no rational input. I hadn't even considered it until now, perhaps hadn't truly dared to when everything was so fragile, but I *had* let him in. Concealed no aspect of myself. But more so, I was stunned by a realization of my own.

Not once had I been bothered by Mordecai's presence.

Not once had I wished I were alone.

The chamber was by no means large, and spending my day surrounded by people should have sent me searching for solitude as soon as I got away—for time I could spend purely with myself to replenish in silence.

With Mordecai, I required no such separation.

He was more than just my calm. With him, I could coexist yet never feel drained.

Only healed.

Energized.

Whole.

As if to prove my point, a cacophony of voices and a charged atmosphere assaulted me when I entered the hall. Despite the polished armor in the form of my dress, dinner was tense enough to make every minute of it uncomfortable. Zaphine seemed to be holding up the best of all of us, but the dark circles under her eyes were nonetheless telling.

A mess, the lot of us.

The single consolation lay in the fact that even in light of the unforeseen and utterly frustrating setback, there was a unity to our group. Though I wondered just how long it would last.

The minute I could, I excused myself and slipped back upstairs. Lyra greeted me with a few seconds of furious sniffing, then, satisfied with what she'd gleaned, curled up in her cot. A long, deep exhale rippled from her. She was done for the day.

I couldn't help but smile—and admit the clever dog made a fair point.

As I padded across the room to deposit the snacks I'd brought with me from downstairs, the spell-leaf I'd stored in the nightstand's single shallow drawer rushed through my thoughts as if it had been waiting on the periphery all along but hadn't had the wings to reveal itself until now. My heartbeat sped up, and I dared a glance in Mordecai's direction.

He was resting on the bed, elbow propped up on stacked pillows, his dark shirt unbuttoned to reveal a tantalizing vee of pale white skin.

Stars, he was gorgeous.

Perfection carved from marble and night.

But not cold. Never cold when he looked at me.

"I know we talked about waiting," I said as I crossed the flimsy distance to the bed that somehow felt impossibly long, Mordecai's gaze devouring me with every step, "but..."

I smoothed the back of my dress and sat on the mattress, close, but not quite touching. Mordecai was perfectly still, just the sapphire turbulent, the color enriched with the same desire that surged through my veins.

"Do you want me?" I asked softly.

He lifted himself up and placed a strong, elegant hand to my cheek. "With my every breath."

I could have sworn the last scattered piece of me fell in place.

"Then take me."

CHAPTER FORTY-SIX

THE WAY HIS GAZE RAKED DOWN MY BODY, THEN MET MINE once more, brimming with tender yet unrestrained hunger, set my insides on fire. Mordecai's hand skimmed the column of my spine, finding the bow just beneath my shoulder blades, and tugged on it. The silken ribbons unraveled.

"How?" he asked as I arched under his touch.

Warmth invaded my cheeks. "The spell-tree. It—it offered me a gift. An enchantment that will keep me from conceiving."

Mordecai looked at me, bewildered, then laughed. The low, melodic sound slipped beneath my clothes, hardening my nipples and caressing the vee of my thighs. I leaned into the hand he'd kept just on my jaw, then touched my lips to his skin.

"Ember..."

I placed a kiss on his thumb and lightly drew it between my lips before letting go, just to erase the distance still between us. With a quiet moan, Mordecai pulled me on top of him. Our mouths met.

He was velvet, incandescence, and notoriety.

His presence ineffable.

There was no other place I wanted to be, nothing I could possibly desire more than the feel of him against me.

Without sacrificing our kiss, Mordecai shifted us farther back and leaned against the wall. I braced one hand against it, the other already undoing the rest of the buttons on his black shirt to expose his honed torso. I rocked back to take in the sight.

Glorious.

Wrought of beauty that transcended the realms of possibility.

And mine.

Mordecai was mine.

I guided my fingers along the chiseled lines of his chest, his abdomen, dipping down low before making my way up again. A smile curled on my lips as muscles flexed under my touch. His arousal pressed between my legs, and I moved my hips, reveling in the way he reacted to me.

"Tease," he whispered in a voice that was smooth and hoarse at the same time—whispered even as he reached behind me to finish what he had started earlier.

The gentle press of fabric against my sensitive skin loosened. Set me free.

But not entirely.

"We'll see how long you'll keep that up," Mordecai purred, "before you're screaming my name for the entire Repository to hear."

I bit my lip to trap the moan edging to escape. Then, shrugging one shoulder to let the dress fall partway down, ground against him as I leaned closer. "And you mine."

Mordecai didn't bother to contain his groan. He claimed my mouth, his tongue sliding against mine, an edge of teeth grazing my lips. After a slow, tantalizing exploration up my spine, he curled his fingers into the half-undone dress.

The moment I drew my arms from the sleeves, Mordecai made quick work of my brassiere. He threw it aside, carnal hunger etched in the breathtaking lines of his face, and brought his tongue to my nipple. Then flicked it over the other.

I gasped, one hand flat against the wall while I clutched his shoulder with the other, my head thrown back and breaths coming out heavy. *Stars.* His mouth worked relentlessly, pleasure cascading through me until I vibrated with it; until the ache between my legs made me grind against him harder, seeking the friction that offered at least temporary relief—and made everything that much more torturous at the same time.

"Mordecai," I rasped, "please."

He looked up at me, his smile frustratingly, deliciously smug. I tried to scowl, but the mischief and well-earned arrogance made it impossible to do anything but stare at him, completely at his mercy.

With a smirk, he snagged my nipple between his teeth again, then set a curving vine of kisses up my chest, my neck, but drew back before he reached my mouth. I groaned—much to his delight.

But he forgot that two could play at that game.

I pitched my body forward, my partially undressed form trapping him against the wall while I lifted my hips and slid a hand between us. Following the hard length of him, I stroked him through his pants then, right as he moved against me, slipped my fingers beneath the fabric. Almost there, but not quite.

Mordecai buried his face between my breasts with a groan. I chuckled—a throaty, satisfied sound—then gave him the contact he sought. He thrust his hips up as I arched my body away from him, wanting, needing to see his face as my fingers stroked his hard length.

Stars, I wanted him. Craved him.

My whole body ached and demanded and shook with the need to feel him against me, in me. Tension built up in my core as he twitched in my grip, even thicker now.

Slowly, as if I weren't barely holding myself together, I drew my hand back to undo his pants.

A knock crashed against the door.

I stilled. As did Mordecai.

Neither of us as much as breathed as a second passed. Followed by another knock. This one more forceful.

"Fuck," I whispered quietly.

Mordecai, his face caught somewhere between amusement and lust and just a hint of something deliciously predatory, let out a low laugh. Though regretting it with all my heart, I climbed off him—but couldn't resist sweeping my gaze down his partially undressed form one last time.

"This isn't over," I rasped.

The answering glint in his eyes almost had me crawling back that very instant.

I scooted off the bed instead. There wasn't time to redo the lacing in the back, so I simply kept one arm in front of my chest, as I pulled the dress up and held the loose garment in place.

Again, the knock ricocheted through the silence. Lyra's ears twitched, and she stared at the door, but a quiet, calming word from me sent her back in her restful state. Once I was certain she had no intention of moving, I undid the lock, and, through the narrow crack, found myself face-to-face with Ada.

Shit.

"I was just undressing." I infused the—perhaps a bit hasty— words with what I hoped came off as an apologetic tone. But also one that conveyed it was something I wanted to get back to. Fast.

"Sorry." She shot me a look that matched the sentiment, but didn't move.

Why of all days...

"Don't worry ab-about it," I squeezed out as Mordecai's presence washed against my back. By the Stars...

Goose bumps rushed along my skin.

He was keeping out of sight, hidden behind the door, my body.

But he was *not* idle.

I swallowed, trying not to think about those slender fingers traveling up the back of my legs and gently, so gently, taking the abundance of fabric along with them.

I clutched the dress tighter. "What brings you here?"

Not an odd question. We were all so beat we rarely saw each other after dinner, and tonight I definitely got the impression we were all eager to head in.

Mordecai's palm skimmed the curve of my hips.

Then ventured lower.

Ada rubbed the corners of her eyes, smudging the kohl. "Mae thought we all needed to unwind. We're meeting her in the training chamber in fifteen minutes, and she'll work one of her spells on us, boosting our energy while taking some of the edge off."

An edge I was certain no magic could save me from as

Mordecai's fingers concluded their journey right below the apex of my thighs. I clenched them tighter together. Which only made things worse, with Mordecai's hand trapped there.

"Do you want to come?"

It took everything to keep a neutral face. "Thanks for the invitation, Ada, but I think I'll stay in. Climbing under the covers is all I need right now."

Just a hint of disappointment flashed in the stark jade, but the smile she offered was sincere. "Mae said you might prefer that." Warmth softened her eyes, though faint shadows crept along the edges. "That exploring your magic and attuning to it has been different for you than it had been for us when we first started honing our skills. I just wanted to make sure solitude was what you wanted."

"Thank you. Really. And—it is."

Liar, liar.

Ada tapped her fingers on the doorframe, and some of the tiredness she'd kept at bay seeped to the surface. "I'll see you tomorrow, then." She let out a soft laugh. "Hopefully in a better mood. Today was...not good."

"But understandable," I said and meant it.

With a quick, parting smile, Ada strode towards the landing.

The instant I closed the door, Mordecai spun me around and rammed me against it, my body pinned between his arms. The guilt that had started to erode me from the inside out during my brief, lie-ridden conversation with Ada stood no chance against the Crescent Prince. As if knowing exactly what I needed, his lips caressed my neck.

My dress slid down as I brought my hand to his waist, wanting to continue where we'd left off, but Mordecai ground against me until there wasn't even a sliver of space left between our heated bodies.

"This is why we have to wait." His gaze darted past me to the door, then he leaned in and whispered into my ear, "When I drive into you, Ember, I want no distractions."

He pushed away, leaving me gasping and more than a little flustered. I was still standing there when Mordecai dropped into his usual seat by the window and stretched his legs over the second chair, looking every inch the man who intended to sleep there.

"What are you doing?" My question came out perfectly flat. Angry even.

I didn't care how ridiculous I must have looked, with my dress hanging off my hips and hair disheveled.

Mordecai's lips twitched. "My resolve can only take so much, Ember. You in bed beside me..." He raked his hand through his dark, tousled strands as his gaze seared the exposed parts of me. His voice was a velvet purr. "Too much of a temptation."

When I opened my mouth, Mordecai drawled, the sapphire a dark demand. "And I will *not* settle for anything less but the entirety of you, Ember." He cocked his head to the side. "Regardless of what undoubtedly pleasing proposition you were about to offer."

Try as I might, I couldn't deny that he was right. But that didn't mean I was looking forward to huddling under the covers alone. Actually, that was one thing I refused to accept.

I shimmied all the way out of the dress, then, with a strand of shadowfire, captured his wrist and yanked him to me.

AFTER A NIGHT OF SLEEPING, and *only* sleeping, next to Mordecai, I was glad to find the group in better spirits. Whatever magic Mae had worked on them had done wonders. While no one was thrilled to comb through the seemingly endless Cognizance Repository, at least the danger of receiving a book to the back of the head had subsided. Which also made it possible to appreciate the beauty of their collection, as daunting as it was.

Mordecai kept reviewing the tomes in our room, searching for any other mention of the fragment, though we both knew chances of that were slim. I paired up with Ivarr—scouring the shelves in the very same chamber that had produced the Norcross chronicle. I hoped it was a good sign. That the library would offer up another key piece of information.

Although a part of me wondered if I had ended up in that room just for the essence of my ancestors to gloat over our continuous failure.

As long hours passed, the latter sounded more and more like the truth. Thousands of volumes, not one the missing tome we sought.

When evening arrived, exhausted was too mild a word for the state I was in. I leaned against a plum tree in one of the more hidden corners on the Repository grounds, mulling over everything as Lyra did her customary sniffing. Quite a few librarians strolled in the distance, but I wasn't worried about anyone seeing her. Not anymore. Lyra and I had fallen into a steady routine and had formed a silent pact to trust one another I had absolute faith in.

I scanned the shadows for the telltale gleam of her obsidian skin. Her wagging tail as she apparently found her company for the moment—a tiny black bird with a blue belly—made me forget about the lack of progress. At least for a heartbeat.

The bird's sonorous chirping cut off abruptly. It took to the skies, wings streaked with blue flapping wildly—as if it couldn't get away fast enough. Lyra's ears perked up, and her lean muscles went still.

As did my entire body.

She'd grown accustomed to the presence of the many living souls occupying the Repository and never reacted to them beyond mild curiosity that disappeared as quickly as it manifested. Which could only mean—

The blood in my veins froze. I ran over to Lyra in a half-crouch as I caught a spill of pitch-black and vivid blue hair among the greenery, far too close for comfort.

Tana.

The councilor strode towards the Repository with single-minded purpose. I grabbed Lyra and drew on the pendant's power. Time stilled. We ran. A single look at Tana's confident posture and cold expression told me she hadn't come alone.

I hurtled towards the safety of the Repository's walls at breakneck speed, away from the main path. Away from the areas that suddenly seemed too exposed. Yes, I had training, and more faith in my abilities, physical and magical alike, than ever before, but a confrontation with the guards should they discover me would draw more attention than we needed.

No risks. We could afford no risks.

The mere fact that Tana was here—

Keeping an eye out for any sign of the councilor's entourage, I sprinted along the blooming bushes, around the corner, then slipped through the open doors of a side entrance that would take me to the kitchens. The magic dispelled right as I crossed the threshold.

I scanned the small, dusky space for danger—

And found it.

Only not in the form I had expected to.

My heart leaped in my throat.

Eriyan was there, munching on a pie, and beside him—Ada. Ada, whose cheerful, conspiratorial laugh died down, her gaze now fixed on Lyra in my arms.

On the truth I couldn't conceal any longer.

CHAPTER FORTY-SEVEN

A SECOND POUNDED AGAINST THE CANVAS OF TIME THAT
seemed to have stilled despite my pendant's power resting
dormant.

Another. Its oily wings stretched taut—a vast shadow that
blocked all light from my mind.

The third. The third shattered the paralysis.

Anything I could have said would only serve to make matters
worse. So I set Lyra down first and let her reunite with Ada—
hopefully, hopefully cushioning the blow that was about to
come.

As Ada dropped down into a crouch and Lyra rushed
straight into her lap, Eriyan studied me with stark wariness in
his eyes, the pie in his hand forgotten. He didn't flinch even
when Lyra scurried over and pressed her front paws to his leg,
demanding attention he clearly had no intention of giving. She
dropped down on all fours and turned to me. My heart almost
broke as she rushed over to bop her heat against me, her

gratitude pure and palpable, before she skipped back into Ada's embrace.

I have faith in them. I have faith in their determination. I reminded myself of what I'd told Mordecai. Of what I believed in.

But the conviction fell short, doubt settling in my chest instead as Eriyan continued to stare at me and tears glistened in Ada's eyes—almost masking that undertone of suspicion I wasn't certain she was even aware of.

"I returned to Somraque," I said into the silence disrupted only by the skittering of Lyra's claws.

Ada shot up as if I'd yanked a string. Suspicion overpowered every last gentle, fragile nuance that had shaped her face. "What?"

I bit the inside of my lip. It was a topic I knew would have come hurtling my way once Ada came to question *how* Lyra was here. I merely wanted to be the one to speak up first.

But the way that single word cut through the space, sharp and demanding, made me pause.

Lyra glanced between the two of us, clearly picking up on the charge building in the air.

"When I—" I sucked in a breath to dislodge the words from my throat. "When I found out that my ancestors were responsible for shattering the worlds, when I saw what they did..."

My father, bent over my newborn sister. Ekelyon slaying Mordecai's parents with nothing but greed guiding his wretched sword.

"I had to get out," I confessed, loosening my shoulders. "I had to see what was left of Somraque."

Silence.

431

"You went back." Ada's voice came out flat, a hint of what might have been trepidation staining the edges.

But it wasn't her I was looking at any longer. On the wings of beating footsteps, four shapes filled the hallway leading to the antechamber we were in—Mae in front. Like a coward, I turned my full attention to her, immensely glad when Eriyan and Ada followed suit.

But not only because it took the heat off me. Mae was fuming, and that could only mean Tana had gotten the face-to-face she came here for.

"The Council wants me back."

Ada was beside her in an instant, reaching for Mae's hand without caring who saw. Whatever part of me wasn't frozen solid with indecision and fear warmed at the sight.

"What happened?" she asked. "Are you all right?"

"Tana—she came to deliver their message personally. I'm fine," Mae added, though the hardness in her gray eyes spoke otherwise.

Ivarr's presence crept towards me like a shadow. It was written clearly on his face, that he knew they had walked in on something. But instead of pushing me for answers, he simply stood beside me by the still-open door, gaze on Mae—though he hadn't let me out of his peripheral vision.

"Is she gone now?" Ada's words were so soft they hardly carried across the chamber.

Mae clenched her jaw. "For now."

She addressed all of us. "They're demanding I return to Ausrine. And they're starting to suspect I'm not here for a spell."

Zaphine tensed, inching closer to Dantos. They might have arrived together, but Mae had clearly waited to share that disturbing detail. "You think they know about us?"

"There wouldn't have been any proof of your death in the Waste, and with the Repository a force unto itself, there's no definite way for them to know I hadn't fulfilled the execution order. But even if they didn't so far, they *will* connect the events eventually. The longer we stay here..."

"You think they'll come in numbers?" Ivarr crossed his arms and leaned against the wall between me and the door. He looked ready to hack down anyone who stood in our way. Not that it would make a difference. In a struggle between blades and magic, the latter would always win.

"Let's not linger long enough to find out," Dantos offered to the room, then looked to Ada—or, rather, *behind* her. His entire demeanor shifted in a heartbeat, and a stream of curses exploded in my head.

"Lyra?" Zaphine's brows knitted together as she followed Dantos's gaze. "How?"

The drop in temperature that ravaged the atmosphere matched the one in my veins. Ada rose, releasing Mae's hand.

Her jade gaze locked on mine. "Ember went to Somraque."

"Stars." Zaphine took a step forward, then thought better of it. "Is—is there anything left?"

"Nysa is..." How could I tell them the majority of the town had fallen? Their homes? Their lives? The people they cared about and loved?

With a glance up at the ceiling, I pulled together the threads of my composure. This was as good a place as any to have this conversation. All of it. If the worst happened, at least I could run out into the gardens—which, of course, depended on whether I could suspend time faster than Ivarr reacted, every inch of his body on high alert.

Fingernails digging into my palms, I exhaled and tried again. "Magic claimed most of Nysa. As well as some of its people."

I counted the seconds in my head. Forty-three. Forty-three seconds spent in utter silence before Ivarr muttered, "Fuck."

The rest, however, merely kept staring at me, though the subtle shift in their focus let me know that I could carry on. That they had at least processed the information, if not accepted it.

"The destruction was the worst around the palace and spread outwards. The survivors fled to Saros. I don't know how many, and I don't know who..." I shook my head. "But the havoc magic wrought on Nysa didn't extend beyond the town."

Because Mordecai had stopped it. Because he had been ready to give everything to preserve Somraque.

"Where did you find Lyra? *How* did you find her?" Zaphine asked. She moved past Mae and Ada, past Eriyan who continued to look at me with that same wariness, and crouched to greet Lyra whose tail had begun to swish. Slowly. Then faster.

"Actually, *she* found *me*. When I was walking through"—*the rubble*—"Nysa, she sought me out. She was there the whole time. Well taken care of," I added.

"My mother?" I barely heard Ada's voice, though I didn't miss the hope in it. "Lyra was with her?"

"No." I braced myself. "She was with Mordecai."

CHAPTER FORTY-EIGHT

"YOU WENT TO THE CRESCENT PRINCE?" ADA HISSED. FOR once, I was glad she didn't have her magic.

There was nothing but spitting fire in her gaze. Nothing but hate. And I didn't miss how her hand went to her waist, to the dagger she kept there.

"He saved Somraque," I yelled as the others, save Mae, tensed, each in their own way falling into the mood Ada had set. One that was decidedly against me. "If it weren't for his interference, Somraque wouldn't exist anymore. Not before, and certainly not now. Stars, don't you dare say you didn't feel your home falling apart before he cast us all out of Nysa!"

The words gave them pause, but I didn't wait to see how long the reprieve would last.

"When Mordecai told me what happened after we left, what could *still* happen if he lost even a breath of control, I cast a spell. Submerged Somraque in stasis that will hold until we set the world right." I raised my voice, emotions getting the better of me. "I'm *done* with innocent people dying. Fucking *done*."

Mae looked at me with open appreciation, but that was the extent of it. The hostile atmosphere pressed against my skin, its vile toxins filling my lungs until breathing became a struggle. Even with the open door, the room was too small, too saturated and charged. A threat. I reached for the shadowfire inside me, sought its comfort, but didn't let it breach the layer of my skin. There would be no coming back from that.

"Mordecai will help us," I carried on, calmer. "He's *been* helping us, reading through the books—"

"You mean to tell me," Ada growled and prowled halfway across the space, punctuating every word as if it were a blade she wanted to bury deep, "that all this time you were *working* up in your room, he was there with you?"

"Yes."

The hatred, disgust, and betrayal that contorted her features were mirrored on Eriyan's and Zaphine's as well. Even Dantos stared at me as if I were a snake who'd lied and cheated her way to their trust. Mae remained watching me, that brilliant brain of hers working behind unreadable gray eyes. But what surprised me the most—or rather *who*—was Ivarr.

He hadn't moved from my side. But while tense, none of that was directed at me.

A man who hated the Crescent Prince.

Sticking up for me when no one else would.

"We could use someone powerful on our side," Ivarr said carefully, gauging everyone's reaction. Ready to fight if push came to shove. My breath caught in my throat as he angled his body ever so slightly between me and the others. "Only Ember and Mae have magic right now, unless we recruit the librarians for more than just searching the books. And once we cross to Soltzen, Ember *alone* will stand against whatever we have to face. Like it or not, the Crescent Prince is an asset."

Ada opened her mouth, but it was Mae who said, "I agree with Ivarr."

Ada whirled on her, but didn't turn her back to me entirely.

As if I'd attack her.

As if that was the kind of person I was.

"You *agree?*" she seethed.

"Ada…" Mae's voice was gentle, but also stern. "When we find the location of the fragment, I suspect we'll need all the power we can gather to make the travel with the Council breathing down my neck. That Tana came here… It's not a good sign." She lifted her chin higher, her posture that of a sovereign who wouldn't let stubbornness overpower reason.

My insides were still jittery, suspected they would remain so long after this conversation was over, but even I couldn't overlook the beauty she irradiated.

She folded her hands in her lap, the contours of her face exquisite, unyielding, despite the softness they still carried. "Ada, you know I'll do everything I can, but if the worst happens—the Ancients' magic just might make the difference between failure and success."

"The man *burned* the magic from my mother," Ada exploded. She cast an arm in my direction, her eyes glistening as if she was barely holding back her tears. "He's a tyrant and a murderer. Sharing the same goal isn't enough. I won't have him anywhere near us. No matter what the damn risks."

But I saw it in the others, the indecision. They knew, deep down, that Ivarr and Mae were right.

We weren't sufficient.

Especially now that the Council made it clear they had it out for Mae. My personal feelings for Mordecai aside, he *was* an asset, precisely as Ivarr had said.

"You recruited me," Ivarr offered as the silence neared its boiling point, the words spoken not in mockery, but to point out the naked truth. "My list of kills is long enough to fill a chronicle. The Crescent Prince claimed lives from a position of power while I did from the lowly shadows, but my hands bear no less blood than his. Of course, you knew that already."

The way he delivered the statement, so calm, so matter-of-factly...

This was the unrepentant assassin.

And I sensed where this was headed long before he said, "You knew of my reputation. You knew all deaths weren't deserved, let alone justified. And yet you sought me out. What makes him so different—aside from your personal connection?"

I couldn't bring myself to look at Ada. As much as I was grateful for Ivarr's intervention, I also understood who Mordecai was to her. Or rather, what the Crescent Prince embodied.

But my compassion could only reach so far. And it hurt, damn it. It hurt that in the blink of an eye, she made me her enemy. Even if she was only venting.

"I'm sorry I sprang this on you like this. All of you," I said with enough steel in my voice to draw everyone's attention. "I wanted to tell you before, but this, exactly what's happening now, was why I didn't. I understand you don't condone what I did, and I don't expect you to." A lie, the latter, yet it rolled easily off my tongue. "But what matters above all is getting that Sun-damned fragment. Every second we waste arguing is a blow against us that we can't afford."

Out of the corner of my eye, I noticed Ivarr and Mae lock

gazes. At least the two of them knew where I was coming from. And, apparently, mercifully, agreed. But we still had four more people to convince—and I suspected *that* wouldn't happen anytime soon.

I peeled away from the wall, claiming the space. "We won't get anywhere like this. Not right now." I forced myself to meet all their gazes one after the other, my face devoid of emotion except for the exhaustion that wanted to drag me under and bury me there. "It's been a long day. I'm headed to bed, and I think all of you should do the same. We'll talk more in the morning, I swear."

"To bed?" Ada sneered. "Where *he* is?"

The lock on my temper snapped.

"I had to hide him somewhere." I threw the words at her, not entirely sure why I was even defending my actions. It was a lost cause tonight.

"Well, you're not hiding him now," she parried, one eyebrow arched high and her arms crossed. "He can have his own room. Unless you'll miss snuggling with the tyrant."

"You don't have to do this," I said to Mordecai as I slumped on the edge of the bed and rubbed my temples. Unsurprisingly, the headache didn't lessen.

Mordecai swept down in a crouch before me. He replaced my fingers with his. "Yes, Ember, I do."

I didn't bother to mask the hurt.

Not the one pounding in my head. Not the one clawing at my chest.

Mordecai could see the rawness.

He lowered his hands, one on my shoulder, the other gently tilting up my chin. There were depths to his sapphire no words could adequately convey. Yet even as I embraced them all, the weighted hollowness in me didn't stop spreading.

"Right now, you need to stand together." A brush of his fingers against my jaw. "If staying in another room helps calm the tension, then I'll do it. We *both* will."

Denying he was right would make me no better than Ada or Eriyan, who'd opposed Mordecai's presence the loudest. Echoes of the repetitive arguments we'd had before we parted right as the pressure in my head threatened to cleave my skull in two played through my mind. Or maybe they had never subsided. But I couldn't ignore the reality they highlighted.

Doing something for the greater good didn't mean we had to like it.

The only thing that mattered was acknowledging the truth and coming through.

"I'll miss you," I whispered.

Not just the proximity of his body, but his presence. The way his features sharpened into concentration as he studied the chronicles and softened whenever he looked at me, elegant fingers splayed across the page. I'd miss the sound of his voice, with those small comments we shared throughout the day that had become a lifeline. His steady breaths, lulling me to sleep.

But most of all, I'd miss the way my very soul seemed fulfilled whenever we were together, free of restrictions and shields.

A sting built at the back of my eyes.

Mordecai would only be across the hall, not a world away. Not gone. But why was it that I felt I was losing so much?

"I'll miss you, too, my love," he murmured against my lips

and claimed them with such tenderness it was a struggle not to shatter. "I won't lie and tell you this is easy for me. I've spent so many ages in solitude it became a natural state—one I didn't think I could, or would even want to, part from. These past days...

"I abhor the thought of willingly walking away from something that still feels more like a dream than reality. But I believe I've made my intentions clear. Eternity. With you. I don't care how long it takes, Ember, or the obstacles we have to suffer. When we rejoin the worlds, there will be nothing left to keep us apart. Nothing."

A tear slipped down my cheek. Mordecai stole it with a kiss.

"I love you, Ember Norcross." He smiled, and my heart broke all over, though the ache was not one of pain. "My soothing dark of the night."

CHAPTER FORTY-NINE

Wʜᴇɴ ɪᴛ ᴄᴀᴍᴇ ᴛᴏ ᴛʜᴇ ᴀᴄᴛᴜᴀʟ ɴɪɢʜᴛ, ᴛʜᴇʀᴇ ᴡᴀs ɴᴏᴛʜɪɴɢ soothing to be found in the glaring emptiness and silence even the ever-gentle chiming failed to infuse with life.

Without Mordecai, without Lyra's adorable slumbering sounds, I'd stared at the ceiling, begging sleep to whisk me into oblivion at long last.

The morning was hardly better—made worse by the fact that there was no run with Ivarr to give me purpose. Though I couldn't pretend he *hadn't* been right when he said I'd need the extra time.

The confrontation yesterday had left me drained. I wouldn't have done my body any favors if I pushed it even further.

I dressed in my version of armor—a silver-gray dress with a sheer bodice and sleeves that glistened with white and dark gray gemstones, several trails of them spilling down the floor-length flowing skirts. The cosmetics hardly covered the dark circles under my eyes, though with the abundance of kohl and with my hair pinned in a half updo, I didn't quite look as wrecked as I felt.

Another day, another battle.

With one final look in the mirror, I was as ready as I could possibly be.

I sensed him long before I slipped out of the room.

Lingering in the hallway, a shoulder braced against the wall and his posture casual yet unmistakably regal, Mordecai didn't move as I closed the door behind me. Only his eyes locked on mine, entire worlds of intensity and emotion contained in the sapphire.

Out here, I didn't know what we were.

But my fingers itched to trace the lines of his face, to curl into the black fabric of his shirt and draw him to me so I could capture his full lips with mine.

Only the distance between us didn't change.

Each on our own side of the corridor, we let seconds slip by. Waiting for some interruption to break the moment.

None came.

Chatter wove from Dantos's room, a female voice—Zaphine, no doubt—laughing at something he'd said. But the sound was distant. An entire realm apart from our silent hallway.

A disbelieving, wretched part of me crooned it was a trap. Surely after separating us, they wouldn't stand for stolen moments like this, even if they remained unaware of the true depths of our relationship that had existed within the intimacy of four walls.

But the rest of me couldn't think beyond using the gifted opportunity.

I sucked in a breath and stepped forward. Closer. But not quite there.

Mordecai, however, didn't hesitate.

In a ripple of elegance, he was towering over me, then drawing me to him, a force I didn't want to stop. Only surrender to.

His kiss was searing. Ravenous. His mouth worked against mine as he curved an arm around my back until our bodies rested flush against one another. I had to stifle a groan as his taste exploded on my tongue—had to hold on to the present, to reality, before I'd let myself go completely pliant in his arms. Unleash the shadowfire that burned for him.

Again, Mordecai took control. With a soft brush of his lips, he left me standing alone in the middle of the hallway, my cheeks flushed and breathing ragged. He resumed his position by the wall. So infuriatingly casual. As if he hadn't just stripped me of everything with a kiss.

But in the contours of his features, in the too-perfect lines, I noticed the artificial composure.

Such fragile, fragile ground we treaded.

"How did you sleep?" His voice rolled across my skin.

I snorted halfheartedly. "What do you think?"

His lips pulled up in a smile, but the sapphire, a vibrant, darker shade now, revealed he hadn't enjoyed the lone hours any more than I had.

It had been an effort not to sneak into his room during the worst, most desperate minutes in that wretched emptiness. As if anyone would have even known when I could wrap it in the same sound-muffling spell I'd placed on mine. But for better or for worse, I didn't want to breach the agreement between us.

A door opened down the hall. Zaphine emerged, dressed in high-waisted pleated culottes and a halter-neck top that showed off the straight line of her shoulders—even more prominent with her dark hair pinned up. Her eyes darted between Mordecai and me before she found whatever it was that Dantos was still doing inside far more interesting. To her credit, she remained rooted to the spot, though I could see it in the tightness of her posture that her instincts were telling her to bolt.

For that alone, I wanted to make things easier for her.

I glanced at Mordecai. "Want to grab some breakfast?"

I half expected him to decline, but Mordecai did a little half-bow that was so endearing I almost forgot why I'd rather we skipped the meal altogether.

"After you." He swept his hand towards the landing. "I—I remember this place, but not well enough to navigate it."

"You've been here before?" My eyebrows rose.

The Repository was ancient, but somehow I hadn't even considered it was one of the places Mordecai might know. He'd certainly never mentioned it before now.

He inclined his head. "It wasn't called the Cognizance Repository back then." He swept his gaze across the landing. "It took some time for me to connect these scattered, half-buried impressions with the name, and even then, I wasn't certain."

Not until he left the room. But—

"You didn't sleep, did you?"

"A little." A corner of his mouth twitched. "But I didn't wander too long or too far, either."

The image of his walking the halls alone at night awakened something in me. Not only the wish that I could have been there with him, but...understanding.

The kind capable of existing only between souls made of the same stardust.

As we descended the ramp, Mordecai's face turned more pensive with every step. I didn't press him. If last night had roused recognition, I could see in the way he seemed to be drinking in the surroundings that he was attempting to overlay them with whatever memories were rising from the depths.

I guided my gaze along the windows, the ornaments adorning the smooth stones, all covered with elegant, small scripture, and wondered if I would someday be in a similar position. Unearthing memories of this day when the people surrounding me would be long reduced to dust and remembrances.

A chill snaked through me.

At least I would have Mordecai.

He... He'd braved all of that on his own.

In such a light, eternity seemed more of a cruel punishment than a gift.

"I had visited the Archivum Vive often with my family. Especially my mother," he said as we reached the bottom, and I veered towards the dining hall, eager to escape my thoughts. I had to slow to match his pace. "It's...hazy. I was just a child."

Just a child when my ancestor had slain his parents and fractured the world, too.

I hid away my wince.

Because Mordecai's expression... It wasn't one filled with regret for all that had been taken from him. It was the gentle warmth of reviving, at least in memory, something he'd loved. I would have hated to tarnish that kernel of light.

"My mother worked closely with the librarians." A whisper of a smile ghosted across his lips. "It always irked me when the doors to their meeting chamber closed, sealing me out while they discussed matters not suitable for my ears. I remember *that* quite well."

I placed my hand on his arm. Even if the entire world saw, I refused to curtail the tender marvel of this moment. Of *him*.

"What did you do?" I asked.

"Rebelled at first. Hid from her when she was done—as if she didn't always know precisely where I was." His smile grew, turning into a thing of such beauty my breath hitched. "A librarian found me sulking in my hiding spot once. The meeting took longer than usual, and I was so stubborn, I refused to reveal myself even when my legs had begun to cramp and my stomach growled.

"The librarian coaxed me out with the promise of food and drink, then introduced me to his colleagues. They made me their apprentice." He drew away from my arm when the clamor of the dining hall became more prominent. "So every time my mother was occupied, I had a task, too. Cataloging. Rearranging shelves..."

"Sounds lovely," I said, choking a little on the words.

"It was."

He looked at me, the warmth still lingering on his features, and tipped his head slightly towards the hall. Right. I had stopped just far enough away so the others couldn't see us. And while I *had* been entranced by the sliver of the past he'd shared, I was also stalling.

Speaking of Mordecai was one thing. Him coming to face them...

I chewed on my lip, but the calm conviction in Mordecai's eyes carried enough strength to fortify me, too. I smoothed down the dress, then my hair.

Only one thing left to do.

Attuning to my shadowfire as if it billowed in a dark corona around me, I exchanged one last look with Mordecai.

Ancient to Ancient.

Past to present.

And strode into the hall.

The contraction into stiffened was immediate, palpable—but not absolute. If the librarians knew or sensed who Mordecai was, they didn't react in any way aside from the casual, welcoming acknowledgments I'd come to associate with them. The easiness wafting from them as they chatted softly over breakfast didn't shift, which only made the glaring stillness of our part of the table starker. A carved-out hole as empty yet potent as the Void.

I imagined what we must have looked like, approaching the table with steady, measured steps.

Mordecai a slash of darkness against my glimmering silver.

We didn't need to hold hands to present the unified front we were. A statement we—*I*—needed to make.

Even apart, we stood together.

Nothing could change that. But it didn't mean that no one could join our side.

A decision that was theirs to make.

Stillness turned to throbbing, oily tension the less distance separated us from the table, but the emotions their reaction should have elicited never came. This went beyond friendship. Beyond stains and pain that, while undeniably real, had no place in the expanse of eternity we were fighting for.

Mae now observed Eriyan and Ada more than she did us, a kind of casualness to her demeanor I hadn't expected regardless of her taking my side. I didn't doubt for a second that Ada, who was shooting venomous daggers our way, had detailed every dark aspect of the Crescent Prince. Eriyan looked somber, stirring his sugar-filled coffee so harshly the spoon *clanked* against the ceramic. But where Ada was all hatred and long-burning vengeance, Eriyan veered towards fear. If one that was hidden under a thick layer of disdain for the person who brought the monster into their midst.

My gaze slid to Ivarr next. I couldn't quite place the guarded emotion on his handsome face, but his gaze met mine before dipping down to the empty seat beside him.

A tendril of emotion cracked my calm.

He'd moved.

Ivarr had moved to claim my old spot on Mae's right so that Mordecai and I could sit together right beside him.

The weight that seemed to have borne down on me the hardest, the only one that had remained even when I'd let all else go, evaporated. I'd been afraid to even admit it to myself, but Ivarr's reaction mattered. Stars, it mattered.

Not only because I knew that he would lose if he were to challenge Mordecai, but because there was hope for us still. Hope that I could still call him a friend. Family, even.

I dipped my chin then sat beside him. The gesture could never encompass the gratitude I was unable to put into words, but I had a feeling Ivarr understood. He winked discreetly, then swept his gaze over Mordecai who claimed the seat on my right.

Almost the very next second, Zaphine and Dantos entered the hall. Eriyan sped up his *clanking*. I wondered if they had been lingering in the background this entire time, refusing to pass us on the way down here. Zaphine chirped a quick greeting—one that encompassed the entire group. Including Mordecai.

He returned it without hesitation, a perfect model of cordiality. I directed my attention to the food before the strangeness of everything had a chance to mess with my mind. Something, I suspected, the others were struggling with, too, regardless of the tone we'd all set earlier.

Even the texture of Ada's hostility had shifted, though it

persisted to be a vitriolic tang in the air the aromatic coffee steaming from the pitchers hardly countered. I munched on my still-warm chocolate pocket. At least my appetite hadn't seemed to suffer.

I grabbed another from the plate, briefly meeting Zaphine's gaze across the table as she reached for one herself. Her lips quirked—a movement so quick, so discreet I almost thought I'd imagined it. Probably would have, if the change in her posture, the fluidity of her movements, hadn't followed.

Mae didn't miss it, either. She looked at me behind Ivarr's back over her cup of coffee, then set the mug down and addressed the entire table. "I spoke with a few more librarians last night."

With how Ada stiffened, I suspected it hadn't been after our argument in that wretched antechamber, but one of their own. One Mae had more than likely cut short to visit the librarians.

"They agreed to help with the search, and Chloenna gave her blessing, so we should be able to cover even more ground."

I hated to even ask, but this wasn't the time to skirt around the subject, however unpleasant. "Do you believe we truly have a chance at finding it? What if—what if someone took it? What if it isn't here at all?"

Mordecai and Ivarr's interest sharpened on either side of me —as if I'd just voiced a truth they had fended off from rooting. *Clank. Clank. Clank.*

"I already asked Chloenna if she could prepare records of all visitations." Mae pursed her lips, expression solemn. "Unless someone managed to get past the wards preventing anyone from sneaking a tome off premises, a borrow should be noted. *Somewhere.*"

"So we only have, what, three hundred years of records to cover?" Zaphine's eyebrows rose.

"Something like that, yes."

Zaphine sighed, muttered something under her breath, then said to Mae, "If you need a volunteer, I'll do it. I already had to keep records for my shop, and while it never failed to feel like a painful death, I taught myself how to scan them quickly without missing anything."

"I'll help as well," Dantos pitched in, then shrugged when Eriyan shot him a questioning look, the spoon in his hand temporarily still. "Sowhl orders. Can't run a brewery if you aren't proficient in these sorts of things."

Mae bobbed her head. "Excellent. I'll take you straight to Chloenna after breakfast, and she'll show you around the records."

"Mordecai and I can take whichever sector you were assigned for today," I said to Zaphine and Dantos, then turned to Ivarr. "If you don't mind me skipping out on you."

A smile tugged up a single corner of his lips, but before he could reply, Ada's sharp voice sliced through the space. "No."

"Ada," Mae warned, but fell short.

"No." She dropped the piece of bread she'd all but squished onto her plate. The black cherry marmalade smeared like blood across the ceramic. "I won't allow two people with shadowfire to work together."

Eriyan's spoon *clanked* against his cup one last time.

Actually, it clattered, his attention now completely on Ada— as was everyone else's. Even the librarians passing by gave our end of the long table wide berth.

I stuffed down the impulse to point out Mordecai and I had

had *days* to do something nefarious, if that was what she was worried about. We were hardly a threat *now*...

Whatever rushed through his mind, Mordecai didn't react outwardly—giving me the space to handle the situation in whichever way I saw fit. I touched my knee to his even as my entire *visible* focus rested with Ada.

"Ada, Mordecai needs someone to show him the ropes," I said with lethal calm, leashing the anger and trying to convey the meaning beneath my words without saying it outright. I knew Ada wasn't as far gone as to not realize that whoever worked with Mordecai would actually have to work *with* him.

His memories alone weren't enough to get him around the Repository, and while he'd been sifting through the tomes in our room, the system we'd developed for scourging the many halls wasn't quite so straightforward. Sun, even *I* had to check the schedule over and over to refresh my memory of which sections fell under my daily task.

"Not you," Ada replied in a tone that made it clear she wasn't about to budge on the matter.

Stars, she really was her mother's daughter sometimes.

My composure fraying, I opened my mouth to say that *I* didn't trust *them* to be around Mordecai when Ivarr stirred in his seat.

"I'll team up with him." Though he was looking fixedly at Ada, his presence, his intentions—they crashed into me in waves, as if I'd experienced the full weight of his gaze. He said to Ada, "Is that acceptable to you?"

When Ada nodded, he turned to me, and the warmth, the steadiness of his brown-speckled green eyes matched what I'd felt earlier precisely.

"Ember, you take over Zaphine's sector, and the Crescent

Prince—Mordecai," he corrected, "can fill your role beside me. If you don't mind working alone."

In the background, Ada was fuming despite her earlier concession, but it was Ivarr who held my attention. The open expression that revealed how implicitly he trusted me.

And, by extent, the person I put my faith in.

I lay my hand atop his. "Thank you."

"We're all in it for the same thing," he said to the table, then gave me a hard stare that was all masked mischief and affection. "Though working away from me doesn't mean you can skip training. This morning was all the rest you get, Savior. If you don't show up, I *will* hunt you down and make you pay for it."

Despite myself, I laughed. The sound crashed against the stains still marring the atmosphere, broke them into smaller, though resilient pieces. Mordecai's fingers skimmed my thigh, and Ivarr curved up a corner of his lips, gaze challenging.

I smirked at him. "Keep talking like that, and I'll be tempted to skip out on you just to see if you'll uphold your promise."

UNABLE TO STEAL a moment for ourselves, I resolved to watching Mordecai leave the hall with Ivarr. Both dressed in black with black hair to match, they struck me as two shadows that had uncurled from darkness to become their own entity. Somewhere, a voice told me I should be worried, letting two enemies go off alone, but as they exchanged one comment, then another, I shoved that ridiculous thought away.

They were dangerous, yes. But not to each other.

Not anymore.

I nibbled on one last bite of the...fourth—or maybe it was

the fifth—chocolate pocket and sighed. How Ada was fine with the two most lethal individuals of Somraque working together when she had so much to say against *me* teaming up with Mordecai burned my curiosity. But it was also an unpleasant topic I had no desire to delve into right now. The morning had been strenuous enough already, and we had a long day ahead of us.

"She'll come around," Mae said softly when just the two of us remained among the librarians. Her gaze slid to where Ada had been sitting before she'd taken off without as much as another word, her coffee only half drunk. "Just give her time until the hurt wears off."

I wondered if she was following her own advice, too. Had no choice *but* to.

I refilled my cup, savoring the brew's aroma. "I presume she told you everything?"

"She was very...vocal about who your Crescent Prince is." Mae lifted her hand before a tumble of explanations could spill from my mouth. "But don't forget that I grew up here." She encompassed the Repository with a sweeping glance. "There are always more sides to history than we're aware of. I expect theirs is the same."

"I think Mordecai would disagree with you." I laughed dryly. "He's done everything Ada told you, even if his reasons were different from the ones she believes in."

Mae shrugged and wiped her hands on a napkin. "We've all done things we wouldn't have had circumstances been different. While a small thing, perhaps, our initial run-in is no different."

I blew on the lip of my cup to cool the coffee before taking a sip. Still a touch too hot, but I needed the boost.

With a whispered command, Mae floated what had remained of our glasses and plates to the table by the kitchen's entrance.

"I understand," she went on when everything was neatly stacked to take up the least room, "why you went for him. Brought him here. You hid his presence well, but the light in your eyes—"

"Wait." My fingers curled around the hot mug. "You *knew*? That Mordecai was here?"

Mae chuckled, her upswept gray eyes gaining an even lovelier spark. "I sensed the presence of another Ancient. And echoes of Somraque still clung to you. It wasn't difficult to put two and two together."

I gaped at her as all those small moments, so easily dismissed as coincidences, rushed through my mind.

How she'd suggested it was sometimes a person who helped calm an overactive mind; how she'd excused me from their group unwinding, though that hadn't stopped Ada from coming up to my room; the glances during our shared meals...

Even the way she'd reacted when I'd told everyone of Mordecai's presence here.

I'd thought it was because she didn't share the others' history with him, but...

All this time, Mae had *known*.

"Why keep my secret?" I asked at last.

Mae folded her hands in her lap, the gold bracelet glinting. She drew a loving finger along its smooth surface. "Ada and I had a fight before we went to Nebla."

Surprise swept through me. The two of them always seemed thick as thieves—at least had been, until Mordecai.

"I'm sorry to hear that," I said sincerely.

"It was...unexpected, I admit." Her lips quirked a sad, distant smile that was gone within a blink of an eye. "She didn't condone my view on shadowfire—that it could be used to protect us if we encountered any difficulties." She dropped her gaze for a moment, brows furrowed. "I hadn't known shadowfire was a threat her entire life. I've only ever respected it. Saw it as greatness, not—"

"Destruction?"

"Precisely." Her voice was soft, eyes warm as they locked on mine. "She cares for you, Ember, very much, but reconciling the person she grew attached to and the wielder of power that had scarred her reality... She's struggling. But she's also driven to succeed. Keeping your Ancient's presence a secret gave her at least a little more time to adjust."

"Unfortunately not enough," I said and gained a compassionate look from Mae.

One that morphed into a tender smile as silence engulfed us.

I sipped my coffee and waited until two librarians strolled by before asking, "What's that expression about?"

"I know that you went for him because you love him. But for the sake of everyone else"—her smile turned sly—"let's just say that having a true Ancient on our side can only be an advantage."

I bit my lip. "Mae, are you sure?"

Her gaze seemed to pierce right through the very heart of me. "Do you have faith in your Crescent Prince?"

"I do."

"Then there's your answer," she said simply, then, with a whisper, tucked the scattered chairs in and guided her own away. "We need to get going if we don't want to be late."

Her prompt was gentle, but efficient.

I finished my coffee and rose to carry it to the table with the rest of the dirty dishes. I didn't trust myself to float it over with magic right now. Everything inside me was...soft from our conversation. From hearing and voicing truths I never thought I would.

Already a step past Mae, I turned to find her looking at me— as if she'd sensed there was something more I wanted to ask.

"You don't..." I brushed my thumb over the cup and blew out a breath. "You really don't think the shadowfire is evil?"

"No." Mae smiled. "Just powerful. Though the two are often perceived the same."

CHAPTER FIFTY

I WORKED SIDE BY SIDE WITH NYON, MORE THAN A LITTLE relieved that he'd switched positions to be on my team, even if our communication was limited thanks to the endless shelves of books we had to sift through. But just having him there—it was more than I could have asked for. Eight other librarians helped with our sector, and by the time I had to leave for my session with Ivarr, we were all desperate for a break. I made a mental reminder to treat them to some coffee—or something stronger —for the afternoon and evening portion of our search when I returned.

Detouring through the gardens with a book on the Hazeldynes I wanted to skim through again after my training tucked under one arm, I reveled in the breeze that cooled my heated skin and gave the wide-legged, high-waisted pants I'd changed into a life of their own. The dress I'd worn this morning would have almost been better. If I was already learning proficiency in hand-to-hand combat in any attire, I wasn't all that averse to doing the same while handling weapons.

Climbing ladders in it, however, had proven to be a pain I'd been eager to eliminate.

Not *everything* had to be a struggle. The pants would have to do.

Though as I lifted my gaze from the copse of birches to the Repository's towering walls, I contemplated hurrying back inside to slip into the dress.

Once we made it to Soltzen, a perfect, polished exterior would be the best camouflage for whatever I would have to do to obtain that last fragment.

I didn't doubt for a second either the Rosegraves, the Brynes, or my own father had it locked away somewhere. I let my fingers skim a thorny stem of the rosebushes extending along the path. There were still old corners within me that shivered at the thought of coming face-to-face with them, my father in particular, but—

I looked forward to seeing them fall.

Caught up in the thought of tearing their vile, gilded lives apart, I hadn't noticed a bleary-eyed Briar until we all but collided head-on. The Hazeldyne chronicle flew from my hand, and he hurried to pick it up, muttering apologies the entire time.

"Briar, it's fine." I laughed. "I was just as preoccupied."

I took the book from him, and he ran a hand through his disheveled blue-and-white hair. His dark, cool brown skin had a sheen of sweat to it.

"Are you all right?" I frowned.

He looked at me, opened his mouth, then closed it firmly before he shook his head. "No, no, you've got enough problems of your own."

"Doesn't mean I can't listen to yours, Briar. I still have some time before I have to show up for training."

For a moment, I almost thought his stubbornness might win, but in the end, he said, "I'll walk with you."

We carried on down the path. Several librarians were out and about—some tending to the gardens, others simply enjoying a breath of fresh air.

I didn't miss the way Briar looked at them.

"What's on your mind?" I prompted softly.

He stared down at the path. "I think I want to leave."

The omnipresent chimes wrapped around his words, but instead of burying them, they only gifted them a starker ring.

"The Repository?"

He nodded.

When Nyon had told me it was a common occurrence for librarians to find other work, I hadn't received the impression the decision was quite so difficult. After all, Nyon made it sound as if they were following their dreams.

I took us down a curving pathway around one of the small ponds, gravel crunching softly and filling the silence before I asked, "What do you want to do?"

Briar stopped when the track almost touched the bright water. Small rainbow-colored fish swam over the scriptured stones. A few drifted closer—curious or expecting food, I couldn't tell.

"I want to create," Briar said, lifting his gaze from the fish. "I've—I've always had this idea of merging fiction and fashion. To design living stories people can wear."

"Briar, that sounds amazing."

A timid smile graced his lips, then faltered. "I was doing okay before, found time to work on the side, but..." He rubbed his eyes. "Chloenna promoted me to senior librarian."

I held back the congratulations the persistent ghosts of my upbringing wanted me to say. Briar moved down the gravel, and I fell in step with him.

It wasn't until we crossed to the stone path that would take us to the back entrance that I said, "If designing is what you want, what's keeping you here?"

He paused beneath a cherry tree, back to the Repository—as if merely looking at it would be too much. "I'm scared."

I hugged the chronicle to my chest, but didn't say anything. The way Briar tipped his head back and closed his eyes—he wasn't done.

"I'm a child of two librarians." He stared at the sky. "I grew up here. Lived here my entire life. I'm—"

A groan spilled from his lips and he shook himself. But as the moment passed and his gaze locked on mine, there was something different there. Stronger.

Perhaps a touch angry, too.

"I'm afraid. I'm afraid of being out there on my own. I've read so much about Svitanye, *know* so much, but actually experiencing it, navigating a life beyond these walls... It terrifies me."

My heart ached for him.

I'd always wanted to see more, *live* more. I couldn't imagine what it must have been like to be afraid of your own wishes. Not when it came to shaping the life you desired to lead.

But I also sensed comfort wasn't what Briar needed.

"Wait a while longer." When his expression turned puzzled, I went on. "Wait for us to bring the lands together. The world will be old and new and as familiar as it will be something else entirely. An unknown we'll enter together."

Though I'd been skeptical if my meaning would come true, Briar nodded as if he understood perfectly.

"And," I continued, "if you'll take orders, I'd very much like to wear a fiction-dress."

He chuckled and peered at me with glassy, but hopeful eyes. "For you, no charge."

After making sure Briar would truly be all right, I hurried into the Repository—just a little late for training, as the spelled vines and roses telling time on the stone wall revealed.

The hallway I traveled down was dim, and my eyes needed a moment to adjust to the brightness of the training chamber when I burst inside, already shouting my apology.

Ivarr came into focus first, examining the impressive wall of weapons, as if picking what my punishment for tardiness would be. But to his right—

I halted by the door.

Mordecai.

What was he—

A low chuckle uncurled from Ivarr when he finally turned around and saw me staring. He twirled a throwing knife around his finger, then waved it towards Mordecai who smirked. "The more the merrier."

I gave Ivarr a grateful look, though his grin was positively dangerous.

"Don't think," he crooned, "this is a boon, Savior." He

stalked over and draped an arm over my shoulder then guided me into the center of the room. He shoved the knife in my hands. "It only means you'll have to go against the both of us."

CHAPTER FIFTY-ONE

THE LESSON PROVED TO BE A CONTEST OF HOW MANY CURSES I could squeeze through gritted teeth while the two men did everything in their power to make it impossible to even suck in a full measure of air lest I wanted to end up on my ass.

It had started off well enough. A quick warmup and a few rounds of letting the balanced dagger fly from my hands during which Ivarr and Mordecai sparred.

I had to admit, I might have missed a couple of targets, watching them move instead of focusing on my own task. Their skill and dexterity drew the eye, both of them elegant, graceful, as if wrought of silent, lithe steel that was as beautiful as it was deadly. And seeing Mordecai like that—it was a sight I never wanted to let go.

But even more so than the alluring visual, it was Ivarr's advice to study my opponents whenever I got the chance that had been responsible for the occasional off-beat throw.

Unfortunately, they were so far above my level that even with the bits and pieces of information I'd gleaned, I'd known sparring with them would be brutal long before Ivarr had beckoned me to join them.

Sometimes, it would be nice to be proven wrong.

But today wasn't that day.

My muscles burned from the weight of the sword I wielded again and again, blocking Mordecai's advances while Ivarr attacked from the sidelines and tried to force his way through the shadowfire. He understood the power would never harm him, merely create a protective shield.

And he fought like it, too.

But that was what I needed.

Though all three of us agreed the obsidian would be the last line of defense since tipping any opponent off to the full scope of what I could do would more likely hurt than help my cause in the long run, I still had to know *how* to use it in the heat of battle.

Outright killing my imaginary enemies would have been the easier way, but it was also the absolute last resort. If anything, I'd much rather have blood on my blade than death clinging to the coiling obsidian.

Panting, sweating, and swearing, I kept awareness of my shadowfire in my heart while training all my other senses on Mordecai and his relentless attacks. He was holding back—I knew that without a doubt—though I was surprised that it wasn't nearly to the extent I'd expected when we first began.

Surprised.

And glad.

I didn't want any special treatment, even if my arms *had* begun to shake so badly it was only a matter of time before I couldn't hold my sword up any longer.

Gritting my teeth, I did the one thing neither of them expected.

My shadowfire surged through the room, encasing Mordecai while I directed my physical assault at Ivarr. He swore and ducked out of the way, but the split second of hesitation had cost him. When he recovered to make his stance, the tip of my sword touched his chest.

After a heartbeat of stunned silence, he laughed, pride brimming in his eyes, but...

The rush of this small victory made me forget about Mordecai.

His previously contained shadowfire rubbed against mine, powerful and seductive, a silken caress that purred of everything he would have done to me had we been alone.

"Shit," I hissed and yanked away the coiling obsidian strands.

Shivering, I drew them under my skin, but couldn't stop the flush undoubtedly making my face even redder. The bastard... I composed myself in time to see Ivarr's gaze on the breathtaking silver of Mordecai's shadowfire the instant before he reeled it back inside.

I braced myself for the hate, the outrage...

But all Ivarr did was laugh again, his head tipped back and entire body shaking.

Stars...

As relieved as I was, I also wanted to smack him. I gripped the sword tighter with my calloused fingers.

"And *that* is why you can't drop your guard even when you believe you've already won," Ivarr said to me, eyebrows arched high, then faced Mordecai. "Whatever it is you did to Miss Savior here,"—a knowing smirk—"I applaud your tactic."

A sensual chuckle grazed my ears. "She's not the only one who can play dirty."

I scowled at him, at them both, then strode off to the corner where we kept our water and, thanks to Ivarr's foresight, some towels. The sword nearly slipped from my hand as I set it down, then all but collapsed onto the ground. After a quick exchange that was too low for me to hear—not that I even had the strength in me to *resonate* on their conversation—both men strode over. Mordecai claimed the spot on my left, his back against a wall and an easy, content smile on his lips, while Ivarr sprawled across the floor before us.

He ran a towel over his face, then set it aside and grabbed the pitcher of water I slid his way. "Any luck upstairs?"

"As if we'd be sweating here otherwise..." I swallowed a mouthful from my own pitcher and shook my head. "If the Council comes for Mae—"

"Now that's *precisely* why we're sweating here," Ivarr teased, though the truth beneath his tone was as sharp as the blades we'd handled earlier. "If the librarians are open to it, you and Mordecai could probably ward off any attack on the Repository with your shadowfire."

I frowned, even as surprise at his view on our Ancient power whisked through me again. "I don't know if I could stretch mine out that far. I never really tested my limits. But Mordecai..."

I glanced at him, only Mordecai wasn't paying attention to our conversation at all.

He was staring at the Hazeldyne crest embossed on the book I'd brought along with me, so engrossed in whatever was taking place in his mind I wasn't even sure he was breathing. I exchanged a look with Ivarr who arched an eyebrow, just as in the dark. I set my pitcher down and curled one leg beneath me, facing Mordecai.

Gently, carefully to not startle him, I touched his arm—skin to skin.

"Mordecai? Are you all right?"

"I remember..." He shook his head and pressed his eyes shut, then exhaled. As if he'd brought himself back to the here and now with the released air, his gaze drifted between Ivarr and me. "I don't know if the librarians are hiding them or if time made them forget, but... There's one more place you haven't searched. Once more place that could hold the book."

Ivarr went on alert just as I breathed, "What?"

"The catacombs."

CHAPTER FIFTY-TWO

"I'LL COVER FOR YOU," IVARR SAID BEFORE I COULD EVEN react to the massive news Mordecai had sprung on us. "I'll cover for you," he repeated and climbed to his feet to pace the room, "in case the librarians *are* concealing the catacombs' existence from us." His gaze slid to Mordecai who picked up the Hazeldyne book in one hand, the fingers of the other resting on the embossed crest. "How much time do you need?"

I saw Mordecai's mind working behind the sapphire, sifting through whatever shards of past he fought to extract from the fog.

I grabbed a towel and thoroughly wiped away any remnants of sweat just to have something to do.

The librarians lying to us—it didn't feel like the truth. They had not only given, but risked a lot by offering us a safe haven. An action like that went beyond merely being at odds with the Council. It signified a direct, blatant defiance.

Keeping these catacombs a secret didn't fit with the larger

image. But it also made me wonder how something like that could be forgotten in a place where all was remembered.

I tossed my towel aside and rose to join Ivarr.

Mordecai was still submerged in thought, his concentration a thing of stark beauty that struck me as unbreakable—yet I didn't want to risk the ripples of my fidgeting to disturb the utter stillness just in case it wasn't as adamantine as it seemed.

I angled my head towards the distant corner of the chamber where knives and daggers hung on the wall. Ivarr fell in step with me without a single word. Only once we had put enough distance between us and Mordecai did we speak.

"I'm thinking..." He glanced at Mordecai and leaned closer. I tilted forward. "I'm thinking your boyfriend's old age is showing."

I froze, the breath knocked out of me as my brain, expecting something else entirely, struggled to process just what had left his mouth.

"I'm sure the librarians have some herbs or nifty magic to help stimulate an elder's mind."

I jabbed him in the stomach with a harmless strand of shadowfire even as I fought to hold back a laugh.

Ivarr, of course, wasn't deterred. "You're lucky he's got the moves of a young man—"

"Shut up." I choked on my laughter, and Ivarr's eyes gleamed. "But thank you."

How he always knew precisely what I needed to unwind was still beyond me, but I was grateful for it. I needed a clear head, not get swept up in coiled, volatile anticipation that would serve no one.

Only Ivarr went on, surprising me further. "For all the clusterfuck these past two weeks have been, I'm glad you two found each other." Something distant entered his gaze. "We would have run ourselves into the ground."

Whether he meant our group or Somraque before my arrival, I didn't know. Both, if I were to venture a guess.

I reeled the vine of shadowfire back in and stepped beside him, my shoulder against his. "You think the book will be in these catacombs?"

Ivarr took a long while to answer.

"I think it definitely isn't in any of the rooms we're searching." He turned his head towards me. "And I think whatever your boyfriend is digging from the depths"—I stifled a chuckle at the brief twitch of his mouth—"pertains to more than just the layout of the catacombs."

"Stars, I hope you're right."

We said nothing more, merely stood in our corner, the vastness of the chamber stretching between us and Mordecai who kept tracing the crest on the cover absentmindedly. I had no idea how much time had passed—enough that I startled when Mordecai's voice rang out.

"Two hours."

We hurried over.

Mordecai fixed his gaze on Ivarr. "Two hours. Can you give us that?"

Either the catacombs weren't as grand as their name implied, or he had thought of something. Something, perhaps, he'd seen while he'd been hiding to taunt his mother for leaving him behind closed doors.

Ivarr had been right.

"You want to go now?" I knelt beside Mordecai and asked softly right as Ivarr dipped his chin in confirmation.

"Either we'll come back with the missing book and move on

from here." His fingers entwined with mine. "Or we'll know to keep searching upstairs."

"Then let's move."

I HAD no idea what kind of excuse Ivarr had come up with to cover our absence, but I hoped he hadn't been serious when he said he'd tell them we were becoming impossible to train with so he ordered us to just go have sex and return somewhat saner. If we weren't in such a hurry, I would have wrapped him in obsidian for the smug grin he flashed while delivering that particular statement.

Though those pieces of me that had still retained the earlier light, almost cheerful, mood amused themselves with imagining how that would have played out. Probably because deep down, I knew Ivarr would never truly put Mordecai and me in a compromised position—even if he did joke about another type of it.

As we neared signs of life after leaving the training hall behind, I took Mordecai's hand in mine and wrapped the other around the pendant. While slow, merely a languid river, the power came to me. I wouldn't be able to hold it for long, but whatever minutes, even seconds, it might shave off our absence while keeping us hidden from the many eyes within the Repository, I'd take it.

Mordecai and I ran at full speed down the corridors, and I was immensely grateful for all the morning laps Ivarr had put me through. Mordecai, after all the days he'd spent cooped up in our room, seemed more than happy to embrace the physical effort. His hand was steady in mine as we delved deeper and deeper into the bowels of the Cognizance Repository, his steps confident, unwavering.

He hadn't told me where, exactly, we were going, how we were to enter the catacombs, but it wouldn't have made a difference anyway.

Or maybe it would only serve to make matters worse.

Sometimes it was best not to know the path ahead.

Easier to focus on every split second of the present than worry about the turns and long stretches yet to come.

I trusted his guidance. *And* needed the entirety of my focus as sweat prickled at my temples and my hold on time slipped inch after painful inch. I clutched it harder with my ethereal hands.

If the magic dissipated now, we'd burst into existence in the middle of at least thirteen librarians headed in a cluster towards the east wing and—

And Eriyan.

He was frozen, like the rest, Lyra resting by his feet which meant Ada had to be nearby as well.

No, we *couldn't* manifest right in front of their eyes.

Clenching my jaw, I focused on holding the magic that sifted like sand through my fingers. I maintained barely enough awareness of my body so I didn't stumble when Mordecai made a sharp turn. My vision swam as I fought against the inevitable.

We stopped in front of a door. Mordecai reached for the handle.

The magic slipped.

He lunged, his fingers a blur as I struggled with the whiplash. All the while my ears sifted through the terrifying amount of nearby sounds. If they came just a little closer...

The lock clicked open.

I swayed on my feet. Mordecai caught me and ushered us both inside. He locked the door behind us, then wrapped me in his arms and simply held me until I returned the embrace, letting him know I was all right. Still, he didn't release me entirely.

His hands cupped my face—a moment snatched in the rush of time as he leaned over and kissed me.

"Soon," he whispered when our lips parted, and my entire being seemed to echo the word.

Soon.

He traced a finger down my jaw, then led me to a rustic-looking cabinet fixed to the wall.

"What—"

The wicked gleam in his eyes silenced me.

Wait and see. That's what the look conveyed.

So I stood close by, but didn't get in the way as Mordecai hooked his fingers through the twin, ring-shaped iron handles.

One by one, he pulled out the drawers filled with various papers I was fairly certain no one had touched in decades. The small room became saturated with the heady fragrance of times long past, sprinkled with ink. I shuffled a few drawers aside to make more space. Once everything was out, Mordecai crouched to examine the back.

The flex of his shoulder was the only indication he'd found what he was looking for before the wood gave way with a loud *snap*.

A nervous laugh fluttered from my lips, and I couldn't do a damn thing about it.

Mordecai looked up at me over his shoulder. "Ember?"

"We're going through *there*?" I eyed the opening gaping just beyond him.

Mordecai glanced at the cabinet-sized passageway, then me, a frown shaping his brow line. "Are tight places a problem?"

No sign of mockery in his voice, only curiosity with a touch of concern hidden beneath the words.

I swallowed. "Not too fond of them, no." Especially when nothing but pitch-black waited beyond the too-narrow entrance. "But I'll manage. We should—"

Get a torch, I'd wanted to say, not trusting my control to hold the *illuminate* command when Mordecai sliced his palm on one of the daggers we'd taken from the training room. An orb of light manifested, then another.

"It's as much as I can risk," he said almost apologetically.

I stared at him. I hadn't even considered that the blood magic, *his* blood magic, would work beyond Somraque's borders. Then again, why shouldn't it? He *was* an Ancient. I'd seen him open portals, too, when it should have been an impossibility.

Mordecai might have been trapped in Somraque, but he wasn't a Somraquian.

And while everybody believed I wasn't limited to using only native powers because I was *the One*, I had a suspicion it had much more to do with being a descendant of the very same people Mordecai belonged to. The protectors of *all* magic. My heritage only granted me an even wider, grander scope.

Still stunned, I motioned him to carry on. The twin lights bobbing in the air helped, but that didn't make me any more inclined to head into the catacombs first.

I crouched when Mordecai started to crawl through the hole —wondering if his frame would even fit. Those damn talons closed around my throat as I watched him fill the passageway.

He wouldn't get stuck. He wouldn't get stuck. He wouldn't get stuck.

But regardless of how many times I told myself that, the scene was still one wrought of those nightmares that always left me drenched in sweat.

"I was," he grunted, gaining another inch, "much smaller the last time I went through here."

The gentle exasperation in his tone coaxed a chuckle from me. Imagining Mordecai as a curious, if a little insulted, child wasn't the easiest thing—although my heart warmed every time I did. It was...

Not exactly like seeing a reflection. But it was more common ground we shared.

More insight that explained why I had been so drawn to him even when I hadn't known him at all. As if my soul had sensed a kindred spirit and refused to let him go.

When he finally emerged on the other side, dusty but whole, if his words were to be believed, I shoved my fears in a tight, locked box, and followed him.

The entrance was kinder to my smaller frame but not any more pleasant than I imagined. I swallowed deeply and, reassuring myself I would be fine, crawled on through the short tunnel carved into the thick stone wall.

Mordecai's light illusions cast a soft glow across the scriptures that weren't quite as neat as I'd become used to—as if new words had formed wherever the stone had crumbled. I tried to keep my focus on these manifestations, but in the dance of light and shadows and grooves, my head was beginning to spin.

Shit, shit, shit.

The lack of breaths only made things worse, I knew, but the end of the tunnel was right there and—

Air replaced the rough-hewn walls.

I would have collapsed on the damp ground had Mordecai

not offered his hand immediately. He lifted me to my feet. A stairwell made of time-licked stone delved farther into the darkness, but at least the rock-hewn ceiling here was high enough for us to stand.

"Are you all right?" he asked.

The orbs' gentle light cast an intricate canvas of shadows across his face, turning the sapphire a dark but vibrant shade.

This time, the speed of my heart had nothing to do with the uncomfortable setting.

Mordecai seemed to sense what I needed, giving me time to anchor myself through him. A faint tremor still tingled my fingers, but the nausea had died down entirely by the time I said, "I'm fine now."

He gazed at me for a moment longer, then turned around. His boots scraped the stones, the sound starker than it should have been.

The chimes, I realized.

They were barely audible here, as if the dark swallowed them, refusing to let anything disrupt the silence of times long past.

I kept my hands on Mordecai's back as we descended the slick steps, not leaning on him, just craving the comfort of the touch that eased the growing tightness in my chest. Neither of us spoke as the walls breathed then closed in again, as we moved deeper underground where the stale air turned cold and humid, sending chills all the way to my bones.

When the ground beneath our feet leveled at last, Mordecai stopped to see how I was faring. The smile I gave him was a weak consolation—something his expression made perfectly clear—so I lifted myself on my toes and brushed a quick kiss across his lips.

"Let's keep going," I whispered, though just the sight of the narrow corridor with grooves I was fairly certain were actually bones that stretched ahead dried out my mouth.

Mordecai turned his back to me, but didn't start walking until my palms found their place on his shoulder blades. Despite my pounding heartbeat, I couldn't help but smile at that.

With the two glowing orbs softening the darkness, we progressed across the uneven ground. I fought to keep my gaze trained on Mordecai's black tunic, on the familiarity of his dark strands grazing the collar, but my treacherous eyes seemed adamant to wander.

Dust and cobwebs stirred whenever our hands or shoulders accidentally brushed the ancient rocks and—there was no doubt about it now—the bones clutched in their harsh, everlasting embrace.

The macabre sight wouldn't have bothered me so much if I hadn't *felt* the skin-prickling ethereal presence of all those buried here. As if they had become a part of the Repository in death, pouring their last breaths of magic into the library where it would live on for as long as the structure stood. Perhaps even transcended its end.

A beautiful sentiment, but—

I could see now, why the catacombs had been forgotten.

This was no place for the living to disturb.

Eventually, the eerie, rough-hewn walls gave way to polished, if worn stone. Shadowed alcoves opened up on both sides at irregular intervals. I refused to look at what was inside them. More remains was the most likely answer.

"Not much farther now," Mordecai said, as if he'd felt me tense.

Though given how desperately I was clutching onto him, he probably did.

"I find it hard to believe," I whispered, just to find a touch of normalcy, "that you hid down *here* just because you were upset."

"Not upset," Mordecai corrected, and I could almost hear the smile on his lips. "Insulted. I'm certain you have a fair few stories to share yourself..."

I did, probably enough to fill an entire chronicle, but that was beside the point. Still, the chill pressing in on me had subsided at the remark.

Just as I directed my gaze up ahead, noticing the ceiling was becoming higher, Mordecai turned to face me. His hands came to my waist, and he hoisted me off my feet in a twisting blur of movement that spun my surroundings around.

"What—"

The splash of his boots hitting water cut off my words. I glanced over his back as he waded forward.

A shallow, inky pool stretched from wall to wall, the ripples revealing there was a source of water streaming through the catacombs. Not *all* was dead here, at least.

Gently, Mordecai set me back on the ground, the corridor here wide enough for us to stand side by side. Only his gaze wasn't on me. It rested on an alcove to the right, larger than all those we'd passed before, its edges illuminated by the light Mordecai had sent forward.

The discomfort, the uneasiness—it all fled from me as we both rushed ahead and I saw the seal dominating the middle of what looked like a small stone gate making up the innermost wall.

Not just a seal.

The Hazeldyne crest.

CHAPTER FIFTY-THREE

"This is it," I breathed and threw my arms around Mordecai's neck.

He hesitated, just for a heartbeat, as my lips found his, then returned the kiss with the same kind of fire that roared within me.

Grinning, I pulled back. "I'm sorry, it's just..."

But no words existed, adequate to hold the worlds of wonder and joy and relief that bloomed within me.

So I kissed him again. Conveyed it all through the contact of our skin. The purest of conduits.

An unguarded smile graced Mordecai's face as we drew apart, his expression bright—brighter than I'd ever seen except in those moments of teasing within the privacy of my room. He looked younger somehow.

No, not younger.

Hopeful.

I cupped his cheek, wishing I could capture him like this.

He kissed the palm of my hand. "Ember..."

"Right." I huffed out a laugh but couldn't resist bringing my lips to his one last time before I turned to the crest—to the tomb, the vault, it guarded.

The words were out of my mouth before I was even aware of them vying to escape. "Handsome bastard."

Mordecai's blithe amusement trailed behind me then gradually abated as he examined the stone-carved door. I traced my fingers gingerly along the chiseled stone. A thin seam indicated that the wall was, in fact, a door, but there was no latch or lever, no hint at all, how to open it.

Fortunately, there was more than one way to get into a locked place.

Mordecai must have come to the same conclusion, because he drew a familiar-looking bone-handle dagger I hadn't spotted on him during our training.

The past pulsed between us. Those fragile moments when the animosity that should have been unbreakable had weakened and the truth that lay beneath, the truth neither one of us had wanted to admit at that point, had seeped through.

I lifted my gaze to Mordecai's. "Even then, I couldn't hate you."

Among the stones, my words seemed to resonate with a life of their own.

"I always wanted magic. To be allowed to use it, though I knew I never could. That Soltzen would never let me. But you... You gave it to me freely. I was supposed to be your prisoner, and yet I had more, *was* more. It was..." I laughed to fend off the emotion threatening to choke off my voice. "It was confusing."

"When I brought you to the palace... I didn't know what I

was doing half the time," he said simply, but his gaze burned in the dim light. "I'm only grateful I didn't fight it."

With that, he readjusted his grip on the blade, and I stepped aside to give him some additional room. That primal part of me that had always been attuned to magic deriving from objects of power immediately recognized the inception of a portal as the dagger carved air.

But where I had expected it to bloom, the spark of life died.

Mordecai's brow furrowed. Not in frustration, but...

"You try." He handed me the blade. "I might be a full-blooded Ancient, but you're stronger than me, Ember."

Instinctively, I wanted to argue but snapped my mouth shut instead. Progress.

Even Mordecai seemed briefly surprised my stubbornness didn't make its usual appearance.

I dealt him a quick look that was both warning and mirth, then focused on the feel of the dagger, on the destination I wanted to reach. It didn't matter that I had no idea *what* lay on the other side of the stone barrier. My desire to be there was enough.

Air shimmered in the split second a crack sliced through reality. I willed it to spread, become a passage. The power obeyed.

It had grown large enough to squeeze through, only—

"What?" I gasped, staring at the sheer wrongness of what I'd created.

Mordecai's expression was thoughtful. "A dead-end portal."

The wording felt right for the oddity hovering in the air before us, even if I didn't know what, precisely, it meant. The only thing I did know for certain was that the phenomenon wasn't something I'd ever considered to even be possible. Portals either worked, or collapsed. There was no in-between.

Yet this one...

I leaned towards it and scrutinized every inch of the structure.

This one held while leading nowhere. Just a wall of pitch darkness that—

I dared probe it with a finger. "It's solid."

"And warded," Mordecai pointed out.

Still, that thoughtful expression of his didn't falter. He stepped closer, examining the useless portal as if he saw something I couldn't. Most likely he truly did.

"There are old wards," he explained, gaze drifting to me. I could have sworn that was an undercurrent of amusement I sensed in his tone. "Few people could master them, but they are an excellent deterrent. Beyond them, a portal cannot find purchase."

"Great," I grumbled. Then, noticing he was far less annoyed by the prospect than I had expected him to be, asked, "But you know of another way to get us in, don't you?"

A corner of his lips flicked up. "Mm-hm."

Oh, yes, he was definitely too cheery.

"What?"

"You."

"Me?" I frowned. "In case you haven't noticed"—I gestured towards the failed attempt at a portal before willing it out of existence completely—"this was hardly successful."

Mordecai accepted the bone-handle dagger I handed back to him, then leaned against the dusty wall of the alcove. The orbs streaked his face in light and shadows as he turned his profile to me, observing the sealed door.

"Do you see the inscription just above the crest?"

I narrowed my eyes at him, then did as told. With the entire world built on words, I hadn't been paying all that much attention to the fine lettering surrounding me at every step. I took in the chiseled, curved line of text—and nearly stumbled when the double-voice in my mind lay out its meaning.

"By the Stars..."

While not a spell by itself, the magic of the one it referred to must have leaked into the words written in the ancient tongue, allowing only Spellweavers to read them. But that meant—

I whirled towards Mordecai. "You're a Spellweaver? Why didn't you say anything when I told you about me? When we used the spell in Somraque?"

"My mother was," Mordecai said simply, though emotion brightened his eyes. "The world fractured before she could teach me how to use the power. But"—he nudged his chin towards the inscription—"I can read it just fine."

It hit me in that moment, why the prophesized Savior had to be a child born of all three worlds. Were the Ancients, the true protectors of magic, truly extinct, then we were the closest manifestation of their all-encompassing power. I braced one hand against the cold stone.

He'd told me he could only open portals within Somraque when I'd confronted him on the wings of my then-failures. But...

Had Mordecai truly tried opening one to another world?

Had he considered that, whatever the Somraquian prophecy said, he had the very same predispositions required to *be* the Savior? The magic of all three worlds?

I hadn't been successful until the memory of that cell had dislodged from the suppressed crevices of my mind. The blood required to cut a passage through the veil separating our lands.

Were he to replicate the process, could he, too, be able to create such a gateway?

Unless...

"Ember?"

The stone's grooves dug into my skin, but the churning of theories didn't cease.

Maybe it *had* to be someone like me. Not just with one variation of the three main branches of power embedded in them, but someone who possessed every single one of them?

My head throbbed as thought after thought crashed and rolled through my mind.

If Mordecai were only a Spellweaver and not an Enchanter, then I *was* stronger. Which also meant my lineage was far more complex than anyone had dared to predict.

"Ember?" His voice, though still tender, now carried a demand. A call.

I shook my head and looked at him. This wasn't the time for the conversation, but I filed it away for later. Finally, *finally*, things were starting to make sense in their own, although still confusing, way.

There was one pressing issue, however, that even my revelation couldn't solve.

"All three powers." I released the stones, fingertips aching, and squared my shoulders. "All three powers to get into the chamber." I glanced at the inscription, then Mordecai. "But I don't know how to use blood magic. *Any* blood magic..."

Mordecai peeled away from the wall and cupped my cheek. "The blood *is* magic. A raw, unshaped force. But it's there."

As his words resonated within me, my thoughts flashed back to the Norcross chronicle—how the crimson had seeped into the page, leaving nothing but new chapters behind. It wasn't an illusion to trick the body or mind, but whatever process had sprung to life and transcribed my memories into the book, my blood *had* triggered it.

As it had been my blood that had ripped open a portal through worlds.

I lifted my gaze to Mordecai's as the pieces fell together.

The magic I had seen in Somraque was refined, a tool of perfection. But perfection wasn't part of my vocabulary.

It hadn't been when I had defied my parents, time and time again. It hadn't been when I'd refused to fashion myself into the image of the Savior everyone had expected.

I'd already broken so many rules, I shouldn't have been so surprised that the same would apply to my power.

"Three magics," I whispered, then unsheathed the blade I'd strapped to my waist and stepped back.

Separate in their existence as were the lands, yet within me, integral parts of a whole.

I *was* magic.

I was the hallow unbroken.

Mordecai became the epitome of stillness as I guided the sharp edge across my palm. When the brilliant crimson welled, I extended my hand towards him. He passed the dagger imbued with Soltzenian power.

I could have used it to slice open my palm, but I didn't want shortcuts. Every step was a release of magic unto itself. Threads I could then twine together. Threads that *would* twine together, as was in their—*my*—nature.

I smeared the cool metal with my blood.

Only one thing left.

Straightening my spine, I poised the blade to slash through the air, and murmured, "*Unveil.*"

CHAPTER FIFTY-FOUR

IN THE MERGING OF MAGIC, THE GATEWAY OPENED.

A portal like any other at first glance, but connected to it as I was, there was no mistaking its singularity—a barrier crafted of a power that had somehow survived the passing of time; a field that extended *beyond* the utterly stable, hovering seam connecting two locations.

It wouldn't tolerate any other magic but mine.

A person, yes, as Mordecai proved by stepping through the portal with me, but only as long as he kept his power leashed. I didn't dare think what the consequences would be if he'd attempted a display.

The ominous presence of the rule pooling within me like an inky black lake suggested enough.

Unfortunately, that also left me at a disadvantage.

I couldn't call up light—it was too precise, too polished an illusion for the wild nature of what coursed through my veins— and my mind wasn't sufficiently focused for an enchantment. So only the two illuminated orbs, bobbing just on the other side of the portal, struggled to keep the darkness at bay. Barely, but they did. How long they would last, however, deprived of Mordecai's direct influence, was another matter.

I would have asked, but my throat seemed incapable of creating sound as my eyes adjusted and I took in the chamber. The *tomb*.

Mordecai's knuckles brushed against mine.

A sarcophagus dominated the very center of the square-shaped space, a resting statue fashioned after whichever member of the Hazeldyne family deserved the honor carved atop it. I didn't recall her lovely profile from any of the remembrances, but the serenity it exuded... An encouragement.

What little I could make of the walls encompassing us revealed chiseled reliefs, marking the various resting places in the everlasting stone. Not all of the Hazeldynes were buried here. The chamber was too small, the sigils and names too few to encompass all those people I'd read about. And I had only touched a small portion of their bloodline in my research. Even more so—the bones buried here...

They reached farther into the past than those chronicles. I brushed a trembling finger along one of the names.

Flimsy cobweb strings adhered to my skin, but I hardly paid them any attention as the sheer age of this place filled my heart. It might have been no more than my imagination, but I could have sworn I *felt* the essence of the world before the break stirring along with the motes of dust.

An ancient resting place left in peaceful seclusion achieved through, perhaps intended, oblivion, but one Flander Hazeldyne —or whoever it had been who had concealed the volume mapping out his journey—hadn't forgotten.

Mordecai's palm bled warmth on the small of my back, and I noticed he, too, trembled faintly. But whether it was due to the atmosphere that felt so much grander than us or the object secured atop the resting sculpture, I couldn't tell.

My steps bounced off the stones as I approached the sarcophagus. Mordecai remained where he was, so still he would have blended with the crypt had it not been for his rhythmical breaths echoing my own.

I cast him a look over my shoulder, seeking that burning sapphire alight with hope, then reached for the uncharacteristically thin tome placed atop the statue's chest, just above the arms folded across its abdomen. A trail of dust rose through the air as I took the leather-bound book in my hands. More of a journal than a chronicle, as if it had been written with the intent to conceal it all along; no more than a sliver of past too small for anyone to notice its absence—unless they were looking for it.

Almost afraid of what I would find, I cracked open the book. The groan of three centuries reverberated through the crypt, and a puff of dust rose before me, but the age-speckled pages—they weren't fragile.

I angled the book towards the faint light seeping through the portal.

Mordecai was no more than a shadow in the periphery of my vision, though his presence saturated the air and pressed up against me as if there weren't all these steps separating us.

Line upon line of handwritten text I recognized as Flander's...

My fingers sifted through the pages, trembling slightly as they followed some inexplicable call urging me on and on until—

"You found it," I whispered, then looked at Mordecai, my

heart thundering against my ribs. "You..." I erased the distance between us, presenting the book like an offering. "It's here. The location is here."

Not lost.

Not even inaccessible.

The fragment was hidden in a place called La Clau—an actual place in Svitanye we could go to.

If it weren't for Mordecai and his memories...

It was all I could do to keep myself from flying into his arms and letting my lips convey the gratitude words never could. But we had already spent too much time down here, and our path back wasn't exactly the quickest.

"We both did," Mordecai said softly. It took me a moment to remember what he was referring to. My gaze followed his to the portal. "We both did."

With a smile on his half-parted lips, Mordecai cupped my cheek and tilted my head towards him. There was something hauntingly beautiful in the texture of his gaze—the longing and intent and restraint I felt was about to break.

I inched closer, his breath a caress—

A vicious skittering set me jerking back.

I snapped shut the book and glanced around the tomb only to realize the sound was coming from the other side of the portal.

The twin orbs of light hovering ahead blinded me, but Mordecai said, "Rats, perhaps."

I shuddered as more skittering ensued.

Claws on stone. A swish of a tail.

There were definitely small animals out there.

Then silence.

"We should probably leave." I placed the book in Mordecai's hands then ushered him through the rip in reality.

Nothing came at us. No shadows slinked along the walls.

I had no desire to linger and see if the occurrence would repeat itself.

Dispelling the portal required no more than a thought, and with the twin lights bobbing around us, we rushed into the musty dark of the catacombs. We followed the ever-louder chiming all the way up the slick steps and through the too-narrow opening. I'd hardly noticed the press of walls.

But the skin-crawling wrongness that wrapped around me the instant we emerged—that, I didn't miss.

CHAPTER FIFTY-FIVE

"WHAT DID YOU DO?" ADA'S VOICE BELLOWED OVER THE painfully loud chiming as we sprinted out the door—straight into the chaos that had overcome the Repository.

The blunt force of the question hit me like a wall of solid air.

I stopped in my tracks, frozen, Mordecai a tense presence beside me amidst the discordant chimes; chimes that couldn't truly reach me when I beheld the fury on Ada's face.

She skirted around a mound of rubble—part of the ceiling that had fractured and collapsed, dusting the floor with debris. A blur of black and white streaked across the background. Lyra, thankfully unharmed. As was Eriyan, who scooped her in his arms and made room for three librarians, all locked in granite concentration.

"What. Have. You. Done."

I dragged my attention back to the fiery storm that was Ada, almost upon us now.

Just behind her, Mae rolled her chair forward—using hands,

not magic, I noted—but while she was following Ada's path over to us, her gaze was distant, focused on something only she could see.

I pressed myself closer to Mordecai, but held my ground as I told Ada, "We found the missing book."

It was hard to keep my voice leveled when all I wanted to do was beg her to tell me what had gone wrong. But the accusation in her jade eyes—

The timing was too much of a coincidence for me to even hope Mordecai and I weren't the reason for whatever had transpired up here. Yet I knew that even if it weren't true, she would blame us first nonetheless. While not unexpected, the thought stung.

Librarians rushed past us in a gust of sweat and dust, tending to the destroyed parts of the Repository—again, not using magic, but supplies and their own hands, fixing whatever they could. Discordant chimes assaulted my ears, and on their jagged wings something softer followed.

"We have the book, Ada," I repeated, willing the message to get past the thick veil of hatred. "What—what happened here?"

Ada's gaze dropped to the tome in Mordecai's hands, but it was Mae who asked, "You used magic to retrieve it?"

Not an accusation. Not from her.

I nodded. "Mordecai remembered the catacombs, the Hazeldyne tomb." Surprise flicked across her features, but she quickly filed it away as I went on. "It was warded, coded so that only someone who could wield all the magics at once could pass through."

"Ignorant bastards," she muttered, the remark aimed at the Hazeldynes, not us.

As the softer, harmonious chiming overpowered its

cacophonous twin, I ventured a guess: "The power disrupted the balance?"

"It caused a shift *within* the library," Ada spat.

Mae reached for her hand. "Almost. It *almost* caused it. No one got hurt, and nothing was lost." She said to me, "I was able to contain the damage, smooth over the natural protections of the focus point..."

"But the crack remains." Mordecai looked at Mae, his knuckles white as he gripped the book. "How long will the seam hold?"

"A year. A month." She shrugged, but the simple gesture only emphasized the weight, the gravity of her answer. "I can't say for certain. It all depends on how much more volatile Svitanye gets."

The words permeated the melody of magic, fused with it somehow.

This was too familiar.

A heavy silence suffused the air between us before I faced Ada and spoke as the Savior to the one who had once been a leader. "We can't waste any more time, then. We retrieve the fragment and move on to Soltzen as soon as we can."

This time, Ada didn't argue.

I DIDN'T KNOW whether it had been the command in my voice, laying out the truth, the promise of the fragment, or the explanation that without Mordecai's help, we would never have found the relevant book, but some of the tension dissipated when we gathered in the dining hall—one of the few parts of the Repository that had come through the incident completely unscathed.

The usual pleasant, bubbly atmosphere, however... It was more of a low buzz comprised of so many notes I entertained the idea of moving us onto the patio. The conversation we were about to have was too monumental yet fragile to have anything but our full attention. But before I could voice my suggestion, Zaphine squeezed past Dantos and Ada. She unrolled a map marking Svitanye's focus point—including La Clef, the small town built around a temple Flander Hazeldyne had known by its old name, La Clau.

Clutching my coffee, I leaned over the intricately painted map. Zaphine, her dark hair escaping from the bun she'd twisted it in, dutifully pointed out the relevant spot. I needed just a second to orient myself as I was seeing the map upside down—right as Dantos said, "This is it. This is truly it."

Zaphine's answering smile was all warmth, a beautiful thing to behold in the healing but still ravaged atmosphere. I let the moment whisk through me, then focused on the map once more.

La Clef was situated closer to the Repository than Ausrine and, thankfully, lay in the *opposite* direction of the capital. While distance meant little when the Council could control shifts, I nonetheless hoped the advantage it would give us once we left the Repository behind would be enough. Enough to get there. Retrieve the fragment from the temple. Then escape through the portal to Soltzen.

Because if the Council suspected Mae, if they knew she had chosen us over them...

I sank back into my chair and slid my gaze to her, but she was too busy wolfing down food to replenish the energy she'd lost to notice. Dark circles shadowed her eyes, but as she looked up, done with her quiche, there was a glimmer of hope in them.

With the map still occupying the center of the table and becoming a kind of focus point of its own, Eriyan flipped through, then passed on the Hazeldyne journal. Not for the first time.

Nor, I suspected, the last.

I knew the impulse to re-read that entry over and over—the need to verify that this wasn't some dream wrought of our collective wish. Of all of us, only Mae hadn't touched it yet since Ada had refused to let her do *anything* but focus on herself.

The fact that Mae didn't fight it revealed a lot about her state.

"Don't you wish people would believe you two went off to fuck instead of wreaking havoc with your Savior magic?" Ivarr drawled from beside me as everyone else was too busy to pay attention.

I stared at him, slightly openmouthed and a whole lot unsure whether to laugh at the joke or smack him for it.

Mordecai hid his laugh behind a cough.

Incorrigible.

Before I could devise a clever comeback, the journal made its way back over to us, Dantos's large hands dwarfing the thin volume as he extended it towards me.

"Can I see it?" Mae asked and wiped her hands.

Ada slid a plate loaded with pastries in her direction without missing a beat.

I reached around Ivarr and gave her the book. Unlike most of us who jumped straight to the fragment's final destination, Mae flipped it open at the beginning and started to make her way towards the relevant entry.

"We rest tonight, replenish our strength, then set out first thing tomorrow." Ada rose, embracing the leadership I'd hoped she would reclaim. The sharpness in her jade eyes was a welcome sight. Even when she looked at me, then swept her gaze along the rest, her stance didn't change.

This. This was what I had hoped for. What I'd told Mordecai I had faith in.

And I could have sworn all of us, save for Mae, engrossed in her book, sat up straighter.

"Pack what provisions you need, not only for the trip to La Clef, but Soltzen."

A series of nods and anticipatory inhales at the sound of the final land we had to scour. Mordecai's fingers brushed against my thigh. I caught them in mine.

"I doubt we'll get a chance to linger, so we all need to be prepared for the path forward," Ada went on. "And we'll need to work fast, possibly even organize smaller groups to cover more ground at the temple since we still don't know *where* in La Clau the fragment is—"

Mae dropped the chocolate pastry she'd been holding, her face gaunt as she stared at the book.

Tension coiled around the table and suffocated all light.

"Mae, what's wrong?" Ada's voice was laced with urgency I suspected had more to do with Mae than whatever had caused her reaction. But the rest of us...

Eriyan looked at me over the table, desperation clear in one of those rare unguarded moments before he closed off again.

"We won't be going to La Clef," Mae whispered, her turquoise eyebrows drawn and jaw hard. Her gaze flicked to the map. "Not that one."

I tightened my grip on Mordecai's hand, but he drew away—to wrap his arm around my shoulders. No one reacted. No one cared for the blunt display of affection.

Not when Mae closed her eyes and swore, fear etched clearly in the somber lines of her face. Whatever it was, it shook her more than the threat of the Council. More than anything—

"La Clef used to be called La Clau, yes." Her words trembled, and she touched her fingers to the silver ring but didn't twist it.

Didn't do anything but lift her gaze, revealing her haunted eyes. The hint of anger.

But mostly terror.

Primal, chilling terror.

"There was another before it. The *original* temple, not the one that had been rebuilt in a more stable environment after we lost the old one."

"Lost?" Zaphine asked, voice small, the wretched word an echo of the many times we'd already faced it. Yet there was something different about it now.

Ivarr reached out and silently took my hand.

"I can get us there." Shadows burdened Mae's gray eyes. "But it won't be easy. La Clau, the first La Clau, where Flander Hazeldyne hid the fragment—it's the most volatile geographical point in all of Svitanye. Worse even than the Waste. A labyrinth of shifts supposedly impossible to cross. To escape. And he..." She pressed her lips together. "He *made* it."

CHAPTER FIFTY-SIX

FLANDER HAZELDYNE WAS A BASTARD—AN INGENIOUS, CLEVER bastard who had twisted the truth so masterfully even history had recorded it as fact.

But he couldn't fool Mae.

Between the wards on the tomb designed so that only someone with the three magics alive within them could enter, and the timing of his visit coinciding with the sudden manifestations of the temperamental shifts that had swallowed the old La Clau temple and were next to impossible to cross, Mae realized he hadn't feared *all* change.

Just the kind someone who would use the fragment for their own nefarious purposes could bring upon his world.

Everything he'd done, the stage he'd set up... It was waiting for us.

For *me*.

But Flander Hazeldyne had obviously harbored no desire to make it easy.

The many layers of protection he'd employed, I understood, regardless of how unsettled Mae's reaction to La Clau had left me. But he had also taken a massive, massive risk, hiding the journal in the Hazeldyne tomb. If it weren't for Mordecai and his memories, we would never have found it.

So unless Flander Hazeldyne had had a way of spying into the future and was aware of my involvement with someone who had been around for ages...

That part of his plan had relied on pure luck. Maybe fate, if you were inclined to believe in such things.

Then again, I suspected Flander hadn't anticipated the Cognizance Repository would seal off the catacombs entirely, bury the *dead* history they represented compared to the one in their books—the one they considered to be alive.

Even Chloenna, once we reported everything, had been shaken that the catacombs had never crossed her mind. Almost as if a spell had made sure they lay dormant.

But luck or some grand design, it truly didn't matter.

As I trudged towards Nyon's room, I thanked the Stars, the Sun, the Dawn, anything and everything for the individual stones coming together to form the path that had led us to the tomb.

And hoped with all my heart that same good-luck streak would last us through to the end.

I rapped my knuckles against the wood. If we were to leave tomorrow, I didn't want to do so without a proper goodbye.

We'd see each other again, of that I was certain, when the world was whole again, but our last encounter in the halls of the Repository had been too brief, too distracted to sit well with me.

As seconds passed with nothing but silence on the other side of the door, I cut a path towards the storytelling room. While the hour was late and the librarians had undoubtedly kept their children well away from the scars marring the Repository, I figured the solace of books that carried the essence of a carefree childhood just might tempt the Spellweaver.

I knew that was where I would have ended up had our places been switched.

Gentle, harmonic chimes accompanied my footsteps as I crossed from the moderately undamaged part of the Repository to the maze of rubble. Pieces of scripture-adorned statues littered the wide hallway branching off the landing, smaller debris crunching beneath my feet. My chest tightened involuntarily.

Using all three magics to get into that tomb had been a necessity, but the price...

I wanted to console myself that no one got hurt, that none of the tomes were damaged, and that the Repository was still standing, but I'd grown beyond softening the razor-sharp edges of reality.

So while my heart bled for the Repository, I accepted the full scope of the consequences—but refused to carry the remorse that trailed behind them.

Gradually, the rubble the librarians had gathered gave way to cleaner floors and only slightly cracked walls. I ran my fingers along them, savoring the silent strength and wishing it would last until we reunited the fragments.

The storytelling chamber was empty. Disappointment slithered through me, but I strode inside—right to the bookcase containing the thin tomes and titles I recognized, my childhood spread before me.

I didn't pull a single one off the shelf.

I just stood there, marveling at the small point of

convergence between worlds that cherished the lore of past times and one that wanted nothing more than to silence it forever.

I PACKED my provisions while I still had the energy left in me. I'd spent more time than was probably wise in the storytelling chamber, but the solitude and revival of memories derived from times that had shaped me into who I was turned my spine to steel and my determination into a diamond that would cut through Soltzen's power-hungry deceit. And if I was to face the people who murdered my sister, their own *daughter*, to eradicate the very magic I carried in my very essence, I needed every ounce of strength I could get.

I shuffled over to the bed and the half-full travel pack the librarians had provided resting atop it. The bottom was already filled with spare clothes, several knives—all Ivarr's pick—tucked up against the sides in slots designed specifically to hold weapons, and a pouch of coins Chloenna had given every one of us to ease our transition to Soltzenian ways. In a small, separate compartment, I stashed the Spellweavers' diary entries Nyon had given me, unable to part from the book for some reason.

Maybe I just wanted something of Nyon's with me.

Maybe instinct hinted my Spellweaver side would come in handy yet.

I also threw in some sanitary pads since my monthly bleeding was only a few days away. Mae had taught me an enchantment and Nyon a spell—depending on which suited me better at the time—that made them redundant, but if Soltzen weakened my Svitanyian magic, I wanted to be on the safe side.

With the usual heaviness of my flow, two layers of protection were just the right amount.

Wouldn't want to scandalize any of our wholesome, genteel High Masters or heirs by having a bloody stain on my dress.

Lastly, I moved the fragment, wrapped protectively in a cloth Mordecai procured, from the drawer to the top of the bag. I'd decide tomorrow whether I would wear it on my person. It all depended on what I would be more at risk of losing. The bag. Or my skin.

I snorted and glanced around the chamber as I closed the pack.

The Norcross chronicle I left on the desk. I wanted the librarians to have it. Wanted what my father had done to Eira to remain a permanent stain on our already tarnished history.

Ekelyon had searched for sadistic glory through documenting his actions.

My father buried his, tweaked parts of his past Soltzen was all too eager to help erase.

I would be the Norcross to put the festering rot up for display—right as I ended it. My blood would feed the chronicle. My actions write the only end our line deserved before the beauty of a new world took root.

And I would hide nothing.

Once I was certain I had everything I needed, I made quick use of the bathing chamber. I washed my hair and twisted the still wet silver strands into a tight braid that snaked down from the top of my head. I needed this small bit of comfort. If we succeeded and pushed through to Soltzen, I wasn't certain when we would have the luxury of fresh, warm water again.

There weren't many inns in the country, as far as I knew, and the larger settlements, always near estates, were too risky for us to venture into blindly when High Masters and heirs visited them more often than was safe for us. It wasn't as if I could just show my face to someone who might recognize me.

Not until the time was right.

I toweled my body and slipped on the nightgown, but when I reentered my room and saw the gaping emptiness of the bed, I couldn't bring myself to climb into it.

On bare feet, I strode into the slumbering hallway, and with a whispered command, let myself into Mordecai's chamber.

He was lying on his bed, hands tucked behind his head and gaze focused on the ceiling gently illuminated by the perpetual light of dawn. The rose-patterned duvet reached just above his hips, revealing his flat abdomen and lean, muscled torso. His eyes drifted to me as I approached.

He didn't say anything, simply shifted on his side and made room for me on the mattress.

Our legs entwined as I joined him under the covers. I pressed my face into the warmth of his chest, and as his arm curved around my back, the touch secure, fulfilling, I let sleep claim me.

THERE WAS no morning run with Ivarr for me that day, and the breakfast we'd shared, long before any of the librarians woke up, was bathed in silence.

Grim-faced but determined, we went through our meal, then returned to our respective chambers for that last moment of solitude before we'd set off. For better or for worse, another step towards the future would be decided today.

I shouldered my pack, now heavier with carefully chosen

nutritious snacks that would last us a few days, and said my goodbye to the space but not the memories I would take with me.

As I closed the door, my gaze fell on Mordecai. No one else was in the hallway, though faint sounds carried through the walls. His gaze swept across my braided hair, then down, past the pendant to the formfitting black tunic and skintight pants, so at odds with the native fashion I wondered if the librarians hadn't sewn them precisely for this task.

Slowly, his attention drifted back up, heat following in its wake.

"You look exquisite," he said in a sinful whisper.

"As do you." In attire of the same deep black shade that matched the tattoos on his neck and the stark fall of his hair.

Just a barely perceptible twitch of his mouth accompanied the flash of desire in his eyes, and then Mordecai was kissing me, his lips moving against my mouth in whispers of hope and comfort that I hoped would carry me through whatever we would face at La Clau.

As voices rang louder, hinting the others would soon join us, we stepped apart, but didn't force any additional distance between us. While, with the exception of Ivarr and Mae, they remained unaware of the depths of our relationship, this familiarity was one they had all seen before. In light of what still waited for us, it seemed futile to pretend it wasn't there. Especially when I suspected I would seek it out again long before we stepped through another portal.

Ada's jade gaze seared my skin as she exited Mae's room at the far end of the hallway, Lyra darting around her feet, but the intensity died down when the others trickled out. Lyra used the moment to sprint up to us, and, to my relief, Ada didn't call her back when she touched her front paws to Mordecai's legs. With a gentle, huffing laugh, he ran his fingers through her white hairs. Her tongue flicked over his hand before she dropped back down and, after bestowing an adorable greeting upon me, wove among the bodies that had filled the corridor.

I swept my gaze across the formidable image we presented.

Perhaps it was overkill, gearing up as we had, but I couldn't deny that it also wove a powerful atmosphere I suspected we all siphoned strength from.

We didn't plan to encounter anyone, and if we would—those wouldn't be friendly faces who'd greet us with open arms. And in Soltzen...

I welcomed every blade.

Ivarr approached Mordecai and me, handsome and dangerous in a tailored tunic and pants brandishing an assortment of daggers. A sword ran across his back, the hilt I recognized from our training downstairs peeking over his shoulder. He smiled broadly and clasped hands with Mordecai while I exchanged an appreciative look with Zaphine. It was unusual, seeing her in battle gear, but her trademark elegance remained untouched.

She walked up to me, then slid one of her slender, lethal pins into my braided hair.

"I think it will serve you far better than me," she said softly.

At a loss for words, I merely dipped my chin, but Zaphine understood. A smile graced her features before she motioned Dantos forward. Ada, Mae, and Eriyan brought up the rear with Lyra beside them.

We marched down the curved ramp together, the animosity left behind. For now.

"We should reach the outer perimeter of La Clau in two

hours," Mae said once we turned left and crossed the open, empty space towards the front doors.

I fell back to walk by her side while Eriyan—*Eriyan* joined Mordecai and Ivarr in the front. There was distance between them, but the gesture still spoke volumes.

"Are you sure you want to expand so much magic?" I asked Mae. "We could just follow the focus points."

Ada cast her a concerned look and added, "Especially with what you expect La Clau to be like…"

"Conserving magic won't do us any good if we waste time on the road." Mae sighed. "Anything more than two hours and we risk the Council tracking us to La Clau before we can even tackle the land."

"I think it's too late to worry about that." Eriyan stilled so suddenly Dantos barreled straight into him.

We all halted, waiting for the ominous words to be some sort of misplaced joke but—

I hurried up to Eriyan, then past him—to the large domed windows overlooking the Repository gardens on either side of the door. Cold sweat licked up my neck.

No, we didn't have to worry about the Council tracking us to La Clau.

They were already here.

CHAPTER FIFTY-SEVEN

"Shit," Dantos said just as Mordecai stepped beside me.

My fingers tightened around his. Not in fear but preparation.

He returned the gesture, though his jaw was set tight, indicating readiness but not willingness. I couldn't help but echo the sentiment as more shapes filtered through the trees, the greenery, the telltale clothing of the Council's guard a discordant presence beneath the dawn sky.

At least forty of them were covertly making their way towards the Repository, creating a damn perimeter next to impossible to breach, yet even as the sight demanded my attention, it was the view of blue, lavender, gold, and red that sent my shadowfire roaring.

I looked at Mae who joined our battle line, her face drawn as she stared at her fellow councilors, the people who were supposed to be her family, now coming to retrieve her by force. Perhaps even claim the Repository if we resisted.

There was no mistaking this for a friendly visit—or even a benign one.

Not when their timing meant most, if not all, librarians were still sleeping.

Not when they had brought such numbers.

Not when Tana, Annora, Rienne, and Iesha formed a unanimous wall that made it clear it was them against Mae.

Whether they knew Mae was harboring us or merely suspected she was up to something that went against their wishes, they weren't about to let her betrayal slip even if it meant leaving their base at Ausrine.

The thought sent a wave of shivers down my spine.

"Could they have felt what happened yesterday?" Ivarr asked from behind.

Mordecai's touch was a lifeline as Mae gave voice to my fears.

"There had never been a fracture in a natural focus point before. We stitched it together but... I don't know if it's contained. Or if magic leaks."

"So they could know what we've done? That we're here?" Zaphine touched a hand to Eriyan's shoulder, and Dantos wrapped an arm around her waist.

Beyond the glass, the four councilors approached as if they had all the time in the world. A diversion while their guards found positions that would allow them to cover the most ground.

We weren't getting to the gate.

Not through the front door.

"Can you push them back with shadowfire?" I whispered to Mordecai right as Mae confirmed the answer to both of Zaphine's questions was more than likely *yes*.

"The Repository is too weak to withstand the amount of

power that would take." His thumb brushed my clammy skin. "A few, yes, but not all of them."

A whole discussion must have taken place during our own exchange because the shift in the atmosphere was distinct— action, not resignation.

Zaphine met my slightly confused gaze. "We'll circle around them. Wait them out when they press in." Her gaze slid to Mae, locked in a hushed, fast exchange with Ada. "Mae said they'll only leave a few guards by the gates."

I nodded. "That Mordecai and I can handle."

"Good." A tight-lipped smile. "Then I can tell Ada to cool it off."

I didn't want to think about the lengths Mae had been prepared to push her body to take out the guards.

With one last look at the approaching Council, the snare they were setting up, we retreated from the window and made our way towards the dining room, the kitchens beyond.

"Shouldn't we warn the librarians?" Eriyan asked no one in particular.

I flinched. I hadn't even considered raising the alarm, prepare them for what was coming.

"We already know," a voice said from the hallway we'd just passed.

My body jerked at the unexpected sound, but when I saw it was Nyon, motioning us to follow him down the hall, relief broke through the tension.

"Come. I can get you out," he prompted, then hurried down the rubble-filled corridor when we reacted at last, his turquoise robes billowing behind him. "The back and side entrances are monitored, but we're not without our tricks."

The path he took us down was familiar—too familiar. I

glanced at Mordecai, but he only shook his head once. He didn't know any more than I did how Nyon intended to get us out unseen. However well Mordecai might have explored the Repository while hiding from his mother, he obviously hadn't found out all of its secrets.

Once we reached his private quarters, Nyon flung open the door and ushered us towards the bookcase showcasing his Spellweaver tomes. I frowned as he dropped into a crouch and removed the bottom two shelves, so focused on what he was doing I hardly registered the too-many bodies crammed in a too-small space. The books trembled as he set them aside, but didn't scatter, Nyon's work precise, as if he'd gone through the motion countless times before. Darkness gaped where the shelves had been moments ago.

If my heart weren't racing, I would have laughed.

A tunnel.

Another damn tunnel.

"I—I won't fit through there," Mae started to say when Ada swept her up in her arms so suddenly she couldn't even protest. They edged through the small space in a series of small, visibly uncomfortable moves, but the sigh of relief that drifted into the room hinted our path onward wouldn't be so nauseatingly crammed.

Ivarr snatched the pack Ada had dropped, then grabbed Mae's chair, flipped it sideways, and eased it through with barely a scrape. He slipped through next, Lyra fast on his heels.

As I walked up to the bookcase, Nyon's hand caught mine. "Good luck, little wolf."

"We'll see each other soon," I said around the tightness in my throat, then, with a sharp inhale, ducked under the book-laden shelf.

"Illuminate." The whispered command flew from my lips and cast a soft spill of glowing white across the stones as I was able to rise to full height again.

Mae, once more in her chair, dispelled her own light, wisely conserving her power. Between us, I was the one who would pay the smaller price for pushing myself.

Ada shot me a grateful look over Mae's head, then pressed herself against the wall beside Ivarr as I went ahead to investigate the tunnel.

After running parallel to Nyon's rooms, it sloped down at a sharp, though thankfully not breakneck, angle. I strengthened my mental hold on the *illuminate* command as light flickered in response to my emotions, then backtracked and waited for Eriyan and Mordecai to come through. Zaphine and Dantos had already made the crossing.

"Everybody all right?" Ada asked.

When a round of affirmatives sounded, she locked gazes with me and dipped her chin.

I took the front with Mae close behind me, while Mordecai brought up the rear. The three of us were the only barrier we had in case things went south. As I glanced over my shoulder to check how they were faring, I noted the distinct glint of Ada's dagger and Ivarr's sword.

Well, maybe not the *only* line of defense.

If we could keep the Council and guards from using magic on us. Or at least lure their attention where we needed it for the two of them to strike unseen.

After we must have crossed an entire length of the Repository's shorter wall, the incline leveled. A door etched into stone rested ahead. I snuffed out the light at the same time Mae cracked open the door from a distance with a whisper. The hazy dawn light speared the dark and gifted the large green leaves sticking over the edge an ethereal glow.

Camouflage.

No wonder I hadn't noticed another way into the Repository. The thick greenery shielded the entry better than any spell.

I pushed the door all the way aside when the secluded corner of the garden up ahead proved empty, but made no more than three steps when I felt it. Heard it.

Something sinister entwined with the chiming of the land.

Something human.

The shadowfire still contained within my body rolled and coiled.

I looked to Mae who flattened her mouth in a tense line and raised a hand in warning just as a low growl from Lyra overpowered the dichotomous chiming.

CHAPTER FIFTY-EIGHT

LYRA LAUNCHED HERSELF INTO MY ARMS.

"Grab onto me," I snarled just as a guard pushed through the shrub. I shifted Lyra into my right arm and held her so I could still reach the pendant. My left I offered to Mae. "*Now.*"

We hadn't counted on needing my temporal power, hadn't practiced moving as a group, but for whatever lack of preparation we might have had, our survival instincts took over as if we'd honed them to perfection. Even the bags we all carried were hardly an obstacle.

Fingers wrapped around my arms, my shoulders, my waist.

No discomfort stirred within me, only the sharp steel of protectiveness and determination to get us out.

The guard opened his mouth, now free of the shrub—

I didn't look to see where everyone was, just felt them, all of us coming together like pieces of a puzzle before I drew on the pendant's magic so fiercely its power exploded across the grounds.

"Can you shift the land once we get beyond the Repository's wall?" I asked Mae as we cut a diagonal path past the guard caught mid-enchantment, then shifted direction to maneuver around a whole bloody cluster of them frozen in their sprint to block our path. Had we taken only a few seconds longer...

I scowled and shoved aside useless thoughts just as Mae said, "Yes, I can shift the land as soon as you let go."

Her answer sounded from slightly behind me, and although I knew she was struggling to keep pace despite Ada's help while holding my outstretched hand at the same time, her chair never snagged my foot, and her grip never faltered. Much like the unwavering conviction in her voice.

We didn't speak again.

The beautiful gardens were a hindrance, the narrow paths on this side of the Repository nothing more than snares designed to entrap us. But for once, with no ravine lying between us, our group progressed without fault.

I couldn't tell whether it was my need or the magic I had worked yesterday in the catacombs, but my control over time was stronger. It *had* to be. Because when we rounded the bend and saw more of the Council's reinforcements the sprawling gardens had concealed from us before, I knew that a single mistake or weakness would cost us our lives.

My heart went out for the Repository, what we'd brought to them, but maybe once they realized we weren't here, the Council would have no cause to attack the librarians. A paper-thin version of events, but...*we* were the enemy.

A Savior who they believed would doom them.

I held Mae's hand tighter.

A deserter who had committed the worst crime.

All of us, whether rich with magic or devoid of it—we didn't belong in their reality. And like a stain, needed to be erased.

Even the frozen threads of time couldn't hide the animosity oozing from them.

We might have had death perched on our shoulders from the moment our presence had first disrupted the land, but that had been a product of—however misguided—necessity. This...

There was fire feeding them now.

Dantos swore under his breath just as Zaphine let out a gasp, but the sound barely registered as the sight slammed into me.

The gates. The men standing tall before them, cutting off our access.

Not just a few, no.

Positioned from bush to bush across the light gray stones with Sylo at the very center, they formed a wall of hardened expressions and sharp eyes without a single sliver of space for us to slip through.

Right as my gaze fell on the somewhat more sparsely planted rosebushes to the guards' left and I opened my mouth to ask Mae if her magic worked, the telltale chime caressed my ears. I heaved a breath of relief.

The absence of resistance as Mae's chair hovered in the air propelled my feet forward. I guided us off the path, onto the bright green grass, and straight towards the opening. Fabric ripped as the rosebushes shifted and swayed when Ivarr, Ada, Dantos, and Mordecai brushed against them, but no one complained about the cuts and scrapes. I held Mae's hand more securely.

Two more bushes. Just two more and we could veer back onto the path, then out the open gates.

The denser layout demanded an adjustment to our

formation. Small alterations we tackled in a tense silence devoid of breaths. Of anything but the shifting of feet.

Perspiration coated the palms laid upon me.

Coated my own.

And as we progressed, my awareness of time stirred. Beads of sweat rolled down my temples and wetted the hairs at the back of my neck.

Not yet not yet not yet.

I ground my teeth, refusing to let go even as my vision swam.

"Ground yourself, Ember." Mordecai's words swept away the pain beating against my skull and extended a tether.

I trusted Zaphine walking in front of me to lead the way and found my anchor in Mordecai's touch on my arm; in that soothing silver presence, invisible to the eye yet so stark and majestic to my soul, as if the entire world burned with it.

I drew on it, let it reinforce the sharp talons of my mind as they held the power I now felt with my entire body—and commanded it not as a foreign entity, but something that came from within.

I was time.

And I refused to lose even the slightest part of me.

"Ember, you did it." Mordecai's voice was thick with adoration. "We're clear."

Lyra flicked her tongue up my chin, picking up on the relief that surged around me, in me—

But I didn't let go. Didn't dispel my control. Not until Mae's magic rose, infusing the still frozen terrain.

As the two powers met, I released my hold.

And Mae increased hers.

A shout, then another—the guards by the gate, noticing our sudden appearance behind them. They rushed after us, but before Sylo, who had been the fastest of them all, could set foot on the patch of land Mae now commanded, we were swept away and thrown amidst gnarled olive trees and vivid fields of poppies.

Only faintly I realized everyone save Mae was still holding on to me.

It wasn't until she urged us to move off the land and cross onto the next sector that the hands fell away, one after the other, until nothing but Mordecai's grip remained. I placed Lyra on the ground with slightly trembling hands, and, when I rose, Mordecai slid his arm around my back in support. Support—but also acknowledgment.

He knew how much it had taken to refuse time's desire to slip away.

If not for the exhaustion and pressing need to reach La Clau, I would have wondered how such a thing was even possible, extending magic beyond its limits.

I leaned on Mordecai, and together we followed the group across the terrain. As drained as I was at the moment, I wouldn't be of any use in our pre-arranged positions. But being with him just might help replenish my reserves faster.

His lips brushed my sweat-streaked temple as he muttered, "You were astonishing."

A weak smile was all I could muster, but it was sincere.

Up ahead, I heard Zaphine say, "I understand yesterday weakened the Repository and possibly allowed our presence to escape the confines of the focus point. But didn't you say the river would keep us safe? How could the Council feel us beyond it, if they truly came as a result?"

The answer rang through my very bones, but the glance Mae shot me over the shoulder, masked in casual concern to see where the rest of our entourage was, told me she wasn't about to cause a rift in our group. Even for the truth.

The magic I unleashed yesterday had done more than harm the Repository's focus point. It broke past the natural barrier of the Cuer River.

"Wait." Eriyan sped his steps until he was walking by Ada on Mae's left. "Something doesn't add up."

Mordecai held me closer, as if sensing my relief at Eriyan's interjection. Though it wasn't a guarantee the following subject would be any more pleasant.

Ada placed a protective hand on Mae's shoulder. "What."

"The Council," Eriyan elaborated. "Let's say the magic did alert them to our presence at the Repository..." He glanced down at Mae, frowning. "Don't you think they were a little *too* organized? Too fast in their response?"

I couldn't see Mae's face as she dropped her gaze to her lap where Lyra had taken up residence, but the rigidness of her shoulders—that I didn't miss.

But Eriyan was right. The attack seemed too well-formed for something done on a whim, and that all four councilors had left Ausrine...

From what Mae had told me, their tasks were carefully delegated, their devotion to magic complete. They would have had to devise a tactic to honor their duties and travel at the same time.

"My guess is they were preparing for a while," Mae said after we crossed onto a reddish stretch of barren land. "They didn't believe me last time, and, like I said, it wasn't a question of *if* they would realize what I'd done, but *when*. Yesterday was merely their cue. We were lucky we were on our way out."

"They have to be tired from the trip," Dantos pitched in,

though the lack of conviction in his tone was jarring. "They won't be able to keep with our pace, right?"

Zaphine brushed her hand across his back. "But they *will* be able to track us..."

As Mae's solemn "Yes" rode the chiming air, my gaze slipped to Ivarr. He was watching me with the blunt concern of a friend written all over his face and keeping his distance more than likely to not overwhelm me. While I appreciated the gesture, I waved him over as Mordecai and I kicked it up a notch to keep with the rest of the group.

Ivarr fell in step with us and produced a bread roll from his satchel. "It isn't much, but it might help."

"Stars, I could kiss you right now." I shot him a grateful smile and snatched the food from his hands as he muttered, "And lose my balls to shadowfire?"

Mordecai commented something that made Ivarr laugh, but I was swept up in a memory of a different time, a different role —when it had been me who'd offered food after Ada had burned through her power to get us to Nysa under a veil of invisibility.

I looked ahead to her braided, fiery hair and the proud line of her back, Lyra once more trotting beside her. As if sensing my thoughts, she glanced over her shoulder.

Although it felt like a lot more, it must have been only a second that we stared at each other before she dipped her chin, then resumed her conversation with Mae. But the acknowledgment... It was more than enough.

THERE WERE no signs of the Council of Words or their guards, but the landscape issued us an abundance of warnings that we were headed into dangerous territory.

The magic felt charged here—a sizzling undercurrent that became more prominent the nearer to La Clau we came. As if the old temple was an epicenter, sending out ripples in concentric circles of, from our perspective, increasing magnitude. The focus points were sparser here, too.

Without Mae, I wasn't even sure we would have been able to cross the distances—like the land itself wanted to cast us away. Back to where the echoes of the lost temple didn't exist.

"What will happen once we get to La Clau?" Dantos spoke into the chimes, gaze trained on the tall grass ahead and blond hair still tousled from the vicious wind we'd encountered a few shifts earlier.

A dry laugh left Ivarr's lips. "Search for the fucking fragment."

Unfortunately, he wasn't wrong. The journal made it seem as if Flander Hazeldyne had merely placed the hallow within the temple—a much smaller version of the one I had seen Mordecai's parents make their last stand in—and left, letting nothing but the magic he'd commanded to make the land impenetrable guard the piece.

Somehow, I doubted it would be quite as easy as just walking through a ring of shifting land.

Chimes rose and fell, another patch of Svitanye that would bring us closer to La Clau manifesting in front of us, courtesy of Mae. She appeared to be holding up well, but from the way she had remained silent throughout the journey, it was also clear she was conserving her power. She'd even asked Ada to push her chair, refusing to expand magic save for when the ground was too uneven for the slender wheels.

When the chiming became a cacophony that grated against my ears, Mae told us to stop. This was the last break—the only one we would have. No more focus points, however sparse and eerily devoid of life they had been. No more masses of terrain for Mae to bring to us.

Only the core of Flander Hazeldyne's grand design.

We passed around skeins of water, re-fastened whatever supplies we had, and recomposed ourselves, fully aware we had no idea what waited for us the instant we crossed into the unnerving, chaotic melody of change.

We couldn't even *see* the patches of land surrounding La Clau.

They blurred, shifting so fast it was impossible to catch even a single impression. My mind reeled whenever I tried to focus, and instincts screamed to avert my gaze. Pack up and head in the other direction.

What Flander had created—it was an affront to Svitanye.

An abuse of magic that disturbed my shadowfire.

But Mae believed she could command the magic once we were inside.

And for better or for worse, nobody doubted her.

As the others finished with their preparations, Mordecai snuck a quick kiss and took my hand. My fears and hopes were reflected in the brilliant sapphire, in the line of his mouth, caught between concern and a smile.

"I'm glad you're here with me," I said.

"It's an honor." Mordecai winked, but there was a seriousness in his words the mirth in his eyes couldn't mask.

My obsidian rose beneath my skin, aching to embrace him—

"*Fuck*," Ivarr's voice exploded from behind.

I tore myself from Mordecai, but didn't let go of his hand as I scanned the general direction Ivarr was looking in.

Trees and shrubs and—

A lone Council guard ran across the dry grass. The texture of my shadowfire changed, hardened within the confines of my body, and Mae whirled her chair towards the man, ready to strike. The metallic whine of steel unsheathing cut through the chimes. Ivarr, I presumed, but couldn't tell for certain, my gaze on the guard.

He veered to the side to skirt around the massive oak standing sentry in front of us.

I readied my shadowfire.

Felt Mordecai hone his.

To capture and restrain, not kill, as it was only one man. The magic in him was inconsequential. My fingers flexed around Mordecai's.

Together, we were stronger.

The guard opened his mouth, almost clear of the tree—and stumbled on a protruding root.

Hands careening, he fought to regain balance. His torso tipped sideways, towards the blurred ring and its violent chiming.

Into it.

I wasn't the only one who screamed when the shifts wrenched his body apart.

CHAPTER FIFTY-NINE

I DIDN'T CARE ABOUT MY RESOLVES, DIDN'T CARE WHAT anyone would think as I buried my head in Mordecai's chest and let him hold me. The way the land had ripped that guard apart...

My stomach roiled.

That was what happened when I had been born. How Mae's parents and countless others had died at the whim of power rooted inside me. I choked on a sob.

"Breathe," Mordecai whispered. His fingers stroked my hair, arms caging me in a protective circle.

Someone retched in the background, but the violent chiming swept away the sound as effortlessly as it had that man's life. Stars. I didn't want to turn around. Didn't want to look at that severed leg and spilled entrails, the pool of blood the earth gulped up greedily.

But if we didn't move, the Council of Words *would* catch up with us. Yet another death sentence. Only I didn't know where we could go from here.

Against such a force, we were powerless.

"Flander Hazeldyne did this," Mae said. Her voice was laced with too many emotions to be as sharp as it was, and yet the steel prevailed. "He *broke* the land to protect the fragment."

"Or the fragment's presence furthered the imbalance," Ivarr offered.

"You didn't know?" Zaphine.

Mordecai only stroked my hair again as I shivered.

"The Council's spells and enchantments cover the entirety of Svitanye." Mae's tone was a mixture of fear and bewilderment. "The shifts... They shouldn't be like this."

Bile scorched the back of my throat, and I leaned away from Mordecai's warmth, just a little, and looked at him. Noticing my attention, he drew his gaze from Mae and the others, the sapphire tumultuous yet soft.

"So your magic doesn't even work here?" Eriyan rasped.

"Eriyan," Ada warned, but Mae said, so quietly I barely heard her over the foul chimes, "Apparently not."

Throughout the exchange, Mordecai kept his focus on me, feeding me with silent strength I, perhaps, would have had, too, if images of what had transpired across the entire land eighteen years ago weren't corroding my mind.

How Mae could face this and not crumble—

I steeled myself. Fortified my shaken body with those imaginary scales of adamant that felt so real. That muted the turmoil. Shaped me into who I needed to be.

A slight shift in Mordecai's eyes revealed he sensed the change in me.

His fingers traveled down my braided hair one last time, then curved a gentle path along the line of my jaw. When he concluded his caress with a final brush of his thumb across my lips, I wiped away the tears and turned to face our group.

Mae, Ivarr, and Ada were staring at the blurred ring of death, while Zaphine, Eriyan, and Dantos, their skin a sickly hue and eyes haunted, clung to one another, gazes fixed firmly on the ground. I couldn't blame them. I fitted my back against Mordecai's chest and willed the last of the tremors from my body.

I almost succeeded when Mae said, "I can hold it. If I use everything I have,"—she looked to us—"I can hold the land long enough for one of you to get the fragment."

"No." Ada dropped to her knees before her. "*No.*"

Mae's smile was filled with sorrow. "It's the only way."

"It will *kill* you," Ada countered, but Mae...

She had already made up her mind.

"The Council might kill me, too," she said with warm resignation, then placed her hand against Ada's cheek. "And even if they don't, *you* won't survive another sentence. It won't be the Waste they'll send you to this time."

Ada opened her mouth, then closed it, her jade eyes lined with unshed tears. She wrenched away from Mae and turned to me.

"Open a portal to Somraque. We go there. Evade the Council and find a way to get through this,"—she waved her hand at the blurred wall—"this bullshit."

The force of her urgency, her plea masked in a command—the single form I knew she could manage right now—squeezed the air from my chest. I didn't think we would find another solution to Flander's malignant protection. Not in a dormant world where even records of Svitanye were nearly nonexistent, let alone insights into this particular branch of magic.

Perhaps the Council as a whole, working together directly on La Clau, could make a difference—a safer version of what Mae had proposed. But that was a utopic dream best left untouched.

People never listened to reason when they desperately clung to their own beliefs.

We would receive no help from them. But maybe—

Maybe if Mae and I could join powers, somehow blend her enchantment with my temporal magic, perhaps through a spell, then it just might be enough to overcome this lethal storm.

"What do you think?" I stepped away from Mordecai, wanting to hear his opinion on the matter. He released me, but it didn't seem like he even registered the movement as he studied the volatile land, gaze distant. Pensive.

Hope leaped against my ribs. The last time I saw him like this, we'd ended up in the catacombs—

"Shadowfire," he murmured, then looked at me from beneath his dark lashes. "We use shadowfire to get through."

My brows knitted together, confusion gripping my mind on the backdrop of cacophonous chimes...

Realization burst to life within me.

"Protection." I wound my fingers around his arm. "Of course. If we weave it around ourselves, the shifts shouldn't touch us. But do you think it will work? We won't have any solid ground..."

Any solid *anything*, really.

Mordecai tipped his head to the side, wavering for just a moment—but the hesitation, however brief, spoke volumes. We were firmly in the realm of untested theory.

"It should," he said, gaze sliding to the shifts. "But I'm not certain of the effect it would have on the land. It might...fracture it further."

Meaning we might not return.

Meaning we might wreck Svitanye entirely.

"What are you talking about?" Ada snapped, but I sensed a thread of something vulnerable underneath her sharp tone, beneath the hardened expression when our eyes met.

I glanced at Mordecai, who only gave me a slight nod, then faced the others once more. "Can you trust us?"

CHAPTER SIXTY

SILVER AND OBSIDIAN KNITTED TOGETHER. A MINIATURE model of the cage Mordecai and I would ensconce ourselves in if his hypothesis proved right.

The group fanned out in a semicircle behind us—protective, yes, but I was keenly aware of their attention on our shadowfire. Keenly aware that something as intimate as the joining of our power had an audience.

I never thought I'd welcome trepidation with open arms, but the edge of uncertainty and fear... It dulled my body's responses to the inevitable caresses of Mordecai's power against mine as we wove the cage shut.

"What if it doesn't work?" I muttered, too low for the others to note the tremor I couldn't keep from my voice.

The second that passed before Mordecai's reply came was answer enough, even if he tried to soften the blow with his gentle tone. "Then we lose a small part of ourselves."

I wasn't ashamed to admit the thought scared me to my very bones.

With the memory of Ekelyon's portals ripping away the shadowfire Mordecai's parents had sent at him...

Maybe our existence truly was inseparable from the past. As if kernels of it had planted seeds that grew vines, determined to wrap around our lives.

Mordecai's fingers found mine.

"Together, Ember. We'll go through it together. Whatever comes."

I nodded, but didn't trust myself to speak again beyond a single word that felt all too much as if I were sealing my fate.

"Okay."

Tense anticipation licked at my back as Mordecai and I stepped closer to the demarcation line.

We wouldn't enter, not yet. But the proximity offered a false reassurance we both needed. As if the closer we kept our shadowfire, the safer it would be.

I'd given up on pretty lies—just not this one.

What little space still remained between the silver and obsidian vanished. Even in the face of pain, of loss and doubt, the touch seared me with heat. I held on to it, drawing on that strength as my will echoed Mordecai's and carried our tightly interwoven power towards the seam.

Breath was beyond me.

Even my heart stilled as our silver-and-black construction passed into the blur.

Chaotic, violent magic scraped the sides of the cage. Gnawed and tore and ripped at them with an unparalleled desire to shred the construction apart.

Though I could hardly see anything beyond the braided rope of power diving into the whirlwind of shifts, I felt *everything*.

Our shadowfire against the land. Against reality itself.

The cage...

The cage held.

I let out a weak cry of relief, and Mordecai's fingers tightened around mine. A shudder rippled through his body as if he hadn't allowed himself to experience the full weight of what could have gone wrong until now. As if he, too, had at the same time refused to believe we would succeed.

There was no need for words as we drew our power back. The way we had merged our shadowfire created a link through which we understood each other perfectly.

Still, I didn't allow myself to breathe properly until the Ancient magic was safely on our side of the line. Before Mordecai could unravel the cage completely, I infused the coiling, parting wisps with love, my obsidian caressing his silver in a way that was far more passionate, far purer than anything should rightfully exist under such circumstances.

Mordecai's eyes flared as he returned the caress, but when he turned to face the others once I withdrew my strands, his features were nothing but unyielding, resolute marble.

"Stay vigilant." His gaze drifted to the pack, *my pack*, Zaphine was holding in her hands. "If anything happens, protect that fragment." He met their hardened, grim expressions—Ivarr's the longest. "Protect Somraque."

It was only a theory that my stasis spell would last beyond my death should the worst happen, but there was no doubt that in the destruction of the fragment lay the destruction of Somraque, too.

We couldn't take it with us.

Even if there was no way for the Somraquians to return home, they could still guard their land from here through the broken relic. And, maybe, if time was so inclined, pass it down through the generations until a new Savior arrived.

Zaphine's eyes glistened.

"If the Council arrives," Mordecai went on, the calmness and authority of an Ancient ruling his voice, "and we haven't yet returned, you run."

No one countered his directive. No one as much as flinched at the idea of accepting it from the person who had been their enemy—although I could have sworn that was gratitude deepening the green hue of Ada's eyes as she took Mae's hand.

"Good luck," she said, and the others echoed the sentiment.

My gaze locked on Ivarr's, his blades ready in his hands should another guard arrive, and in that moment, I didn't doubt he would send the blade flying long before a whisper could spur magic into effect. He flashed me a dark, wild smile—one I couldn't help returning even as a part of me still wanted to shy away from what Mordecai and I were about to do.

We were one mistake from ending up shredded into pieces.

But this wasn't goodbye.

I had to trust in that, regardless of Mordecai's instructions.

They had been a necessity. Not a premonition.

With a steadying breath, I looked up at Mordecai and unleashed my shadowfire. His argent unfurled not a moment later, and I couldn't resist admiring the magnificence of the sight. I doubted there would ever be a time I wouldn't.

We faced one another, Mordecai now holding both my hands in his, his gaze flickering between my face and the obsidian rising behind me.

A single corner of his lips curled up. "Beautiful."

His voice infused my veins, my chest, and I lifted myself on my toes to bring my lips to his as our surroundings became nothing but an inseparable blend of silver and black. The shadowfire curved above us, beneath us, encased us from all sides until the power and the two of us, cocooned protectively within it, were the only reality that existed.

Just for a heartbeat, I allowed wonder at what we had created to swell within me before my mind sharpened, honed to focus on nothing but the task at hand.

"You truly are remarkable," Mordecai purred. "My soothing dark of the night."

The scraps of doubt and trepidation that had clung to me dissolved. "As are you, my eternal light."

As if the words liberated our Ancient hearts, our souls, the shadowfire fortified—shone, somehow. Power in its purest form.

As it had always been intended to exist.

"Just one question," I whispered as we stood side by side again, fingers interlaced. "If the cage is impenetrable, how will we see the fragment? Retrieve it?"

A corner of his lips curled up—not a smile, exactly, but reassurance. "I'll command the threads to let it pass. And only it."

I nodded, understanding what he meant on a level that wasn't logical or rational, but derived from some deeply coded instinct.

"I'm ready."

"Yes." Mordecai's voice was tender. Loving. "Yes, you are."

I squared my shoulders and, with my unwavering faith in Mordecai reinforcing my skin like armor, strode into the cursed heart of the volatile land.

CHAPTER SIXTY-ONE

I'D LOST SENSE OF DIRECTION FASTER THAN I WAS comfortable admitting.

How attuned I was to my shadowfire was irrelevant. I might as well have been cast into a tumbling chamber, blindfolded and with nothing to orient myself by.

The tug I'd felt in Ausrine...

I'd give anything for right now.

Mordecai's gentle guidance, however, never faltered. He sensed something I couldn't beyond the unyielding tapestry of our power and led me like a fledgling through the storm.

Beneath the soles of my feet, the shadowfire felt solid, stationary even, though I knew it moved across the shifting land. The pressure of our footsteps against the power might have been nonexistent, but there was no such mercy when it came to the whipping and bashing we received from outside.

Lash after lash.

Blow after blow.

A violation.

That's what it felt like.

Everything I was cried out as the shadowfire relayed the painful details of the incessant assault—a clawing so fast, so forceful, my mind could hardly comprehend how the cage managed to resist. The dead guard speared into my thoughts.

He'd only *touched* the whipping circle of land and had faced a fate I wouldn't wish on anyone.

In here...

I focused on moving forward. That was all that mattered.

While Mordecai's features were drawn into a mask of perfect concentration, one that only sharpened the longer we walked, awareness didn't cease to flow between us. Where my senses failed, his filled the gap. So I knew—I knew, even as nothing seemingly changed inside our airtight power-cage, when we neared the eye of the storm.

The lashings increased in intensity. Every rake of phantom claws became agony. I pressed a hand to my heart as ghostly thunder cracked and rolled around us.

"We're breaking the land, aren't we?" I said over the ominous sound.

Mordecai clenched his jaw. "The pieces should maintain their orbit. Whatever force made the concentric rings around the temple shouldn't suffer the effects."

Nothing more than guesses, but I grabbed onto them, willing them to be the truth. I didn't dare think of an alternative outcome.

We slowed when the thunder became near-deafening, but didn't stop. Inch by inch, our entwined shadowfire crept forward. Mordecai's fingers held mine in a death grip as he focused on a point up ahead where I presumed the temple's ground should be—perhaps was, reduced to a remnant that had survived the destruction, but one we couldn't see.

In the roaring thunder, I stopped entirely when Mordecai did, and gathered as much information as the power could feed me. But beyond the land's endless attacks, I gleaned nothing.

So I stared at roughly the same spot in the argent-and-obsidian web as Mordecai and read his body instead.

A twitch.

A tremor.

The faint perspiration forming between our joined hands.

Then a stirring that did not originate from him but—

A jagged tip appeared through the shadowfire.

Then the rounded edge of what had once been a whole disk.

I sucked in a sharp breath, unable to tear my gaze from the fragment as it rested, now entirely, on the bed of silver and black strands. The fragment. Svitanye's fragment.

Lightheaded, I laughed.

We'd done it.

We had the second of the three pieces.

With a look that was wonder and relief and admiration fused into something of unparalleled beauty, Mordecai released my hand and crouched before the hallow.

"I've waited so long for this," he muttered.

The longing, the pain—it pulsed from him in crashing waves that nearly choked me. Even if I'd been prepared for the swift change in his emotions, the magnitude in which they pulsed from him would have overpowered me.

Ages of shaping himself into a monster, into a nightmare, searching, then hunting as his need deepened, for the one who could bring salvation.

Our paths could have ended in so many ways, all ensnared in

thorns and loss and death. But we found each other in the darkness, and shaped it not into an enemy, but a friend.

"Mordecai," I said softly.

If he heard me, he didn't respond.

He traced a finger along the disk, and I couldn't help but wonder if he had *seen* it fracture. He must have. He had known it was a Norcross who had slain his family. And now he was holding in his hands a part of what his parents had given their lives for.

Mordecai straightened, sapphire eyes turbulent, and offered me the relic. "This belongs to you."

I swallowed past the tightness in my throat, past the tears I was barely keeping at bay, and secured the piece in the small satchel I'd strapped around my waist.

The feral shifts slashed at our cage as if they knew what we had taken, but I hardly noticed the pain as Mordecai pressed his hands to my cheeks and kissed me.

Through the shadowfire, through the fervent movement of his mouth against mine, he bared his depths, leaving not a crevice concealed. Tears streamed down my cheeks as everything he was flowed into me, and I returned the gesture, pledging myself to him through my flesh, my soul, and the obsidian that had always called to him.

We shared no words when we parted.

Anything we might have said would have been redundant, a pale imitation of the truth.

Mordecai simply bent down and pressed his forehead to mine, his dark strands framing us for a moment longer, then took my hand and led me away. Back to our people.

We made it three steps when his fingers clenched around mine—clenched and held on as harrowing agony unlike anything I'd ever experienced ripped through me.

Mordecai's scream preceded mine.

I staggered and slammed my hand against the brutal hollowness in my chest. Mordecai, roaring now, held me upright.

I barely pushed down the nausea when another vicious swipe slashed my very being apart.

I didn't need an explanation. Not when Mordecai's haunted gaze fell on mine.

The land had claimed our shadowfire.

CHAPTER SIXTY-TWO

My ENTIRE SHREDDED EXISTENCE NARROWED DOWN TO THE feel of Mordecai's hand in mine, the strength that seemed to pool there in our defiance to let the land rip us apart.

I held the cage of shadowfire with all I had as the raging shifts wanted to devour more.

Payment for the fractures we'd caused with our rebellion.

A price only Ancients could pay.

Flander Hazeldyne had been clever, but not wise. He hadn't considered his protections would turn into a death trap in the centuries the fragment had been here. And the wounded, aching part of me hated him for it.

A mere Savior couldn't survive this on their own; and even with Mordecai's aid, even with my own Ancient abilities, the cost was one I wasn't certain how we could recover from.

But I didn't think about the jarring slash of emptiness within me where the torn obsidian had been. Only moved. Pushed forward until the harrowing pressure lessened, then disappeared so abruptly Mordecai and I crashed onto the ground of our own knitted cage, his fingers slipping from mine.

Tears marred my cheeks.

"It's over," Mordecai whispered. His muscles trembled as he braced himself on his arms. "We made it out, Ember. We made it out."

But not whole.

I lay on my back, one hand on my heaving chest, the other around his wrist. Mordecai looked at me and I knew. I knew that, however impossible it seemed to me right now, we'd get past this.

Not regain our previous existence, no, but craft a new one with what had remained.

He rose and offered me a hand up, then, with a slow dip of his chin, began dispelling the shadowfire. I followed his example, but not before my fingers skimmed the full pouch, reminding me that this was real. That the sacrifice...

I reached into the damaged core within me.

The sacrifice was worth it.

Six pairs of eyes stared at us when the silver and obsidian threads retreated. The cacophonous chimes blasted from behind us, its weaker, but no less abusive brethren ringing all around— but it was our companions' silence that reigned. Their stillness.

As if Mordecai and I were an illusion that would dispel with something as insubstantial as a single breath.

I touched my fingers to the pouch and said, "We have it."

But the weak smile that barely found purchase on my face died as shapes manifested in the background.

Mordecai tensed.

No.

Too caught up, we had all been too caught up in the magnitude of the moment to notice the texture of the chimes. The second, human quality now entwined with them.

Ivarr, reading my expression far faster than anyone else save for Mordecai, responded first.

He whirled towards the guards closing in on us from the northern side. He unsheathed his throwing knives and took up a defensive stance—

More forms emerged.

Mae's soft whispers echoed amidst the chimes. In every possible direction not ruled by La Clau's blurring shifts, the Council's trained warriors battled the terrain that did not yield quite as easily to Mae's wishes as it should have. I could almost feel her pour more power into her whispers and send the shifting land harboring the guards as far away as she could.

But it was of no use.

The land resisted.

When the four women emerged, I didn't have to wonder why.

Mae let out a furious grunt between her whispered commands, her magic grappling and clawing to subjugate the terrain the Council of Words had claimed for their own.

Ivarr's throwing knives speared for the guards who had come the closest. Eriyan, Ada, and Dantos formed a protective circle around Mae—and Zaphine, who still had the first fragment. Who held a blade of her own.

Mordecai remained beside me, silver shadowfire poised to strike. I'd almost brought out my own—we hadn't just reached the point of using what we had agreed was a last resort, we were beyond it. But—

Shouts rose on both sides. More whispers. More chimes.

But amidst the flurry of activity, it became clear what I needed to do.

"Cover me," I said to Mordecai, then I extracted Mordecai's Soltzenian dagger—my dagger now—from its sheath and slashed its edge across my palm. I clutched the pendant with my bloody hand, willing the portal into existence—

"Do you have *any* idea what you have done?" one of the women snarled. Tana or Iesha, it made no difference.

The portal struggled.

"A part of Ausrine *broke* because you abandoned us, Maelynn. Because you chose their lives over ours."

I gritted my teeth, flooding the rip in reality with my will and magic.

"I chose Svitanye," Mae bellowed. "I chose to give it a future." Whispers, then— "Look around you. Stasis won't save something that's in constant flux!"

The portal pushed against the land that protested its existence.

"Svitanye has held until they showed up," the same female voice said just as another sneered, "You betrayed us!"

"Don't. It will only make it worse." Ada. To Mordecai. His shadowfire retreated to shielding me, not attacking the Council, the guard—something I felt more than saw, although the sensation was nothing but an afterthought as my head pounded and bile burned at the back of my throat.

Chiming. Wretched chiming.

I fought against the Council's hold on our surroundings, as did Mae, all the while protecting us from the vines of spells edging to ensnare us and bring us down. We would run ourselves ragged if we didn't escape.

We would end up depleted. Dead.

With a cry, I threw everything I had, everything the feral landscape hadn't stolen from me, at the portal.

The window to Soltzen expanded.

Then collapsed.

CHAPTER SIXTY-THREE

"STAY CLOSE," MAE BELLOWED, THEN BROKE INTO A SERIES OF rapid murmurs.

Her command wrenched me from the talons of horror that had snapped around my neck like a collar.

I turned to her, noting Lyra in her lap, the others gathered in formation around her, and yelled, "The Council's power is constricting the portal. I can't open it like this."

"Don't stop." Her gray eyes locked on mine, weary but sharp.

I dipped my chin.

Whatever it took.

We would both do whatever it took.

A guard slipped through the defenses Mae's whispers crafted, but was met by Ivarr's blades long before his magic struck.

He couldn't have that many left.

Instinctively, I skimmed the sheaths, an alarming amount of them empty.

I reopened the wound on my palm.

When the second and third guard pushed through the cracks of whatever power Mae was twisting into a barrier to not only hold them back, but fend off the Council's hold over the land, Dantos and Ada joined the fight.

Blood gushed down my skin and spilled across my wrist, saturating the sleeve of my tunic as I brought my hand up.

Zaphine and Eriyan stayed back—not covering, but forming the last line of defense shielding Mae if the others went down. Zaphine, I noted, had also given my pack, the Somraquian fragment within it, to Mae.

Nausea knotted my stomach, but now wasn't the time to yield to its demands.

Even at a disadvantage, the others revealed no weaknesses. I'd be damned if I would be the one to lack that strength.

As I wrapped my fingers around the pendant and gathered my own power—pure power, not overrun with fear or the treacherous urgency that birthed mistakes—I turned my back to the battle. Chimes and whispers and shouts crashed against me.

I cast a pleading look at Mordecai over my shoulder, urging him to help the others. The resolve etched in his face, however, made it clear my wish would go unanswered.

I was vulnerable when I worked.

And there wasn't a damn thing in all three lands that could make him leave my side.

I didn't argue. Not when I would have done the same had our roles been reversed.

Not when the battle at my back gained momentum with every wasted moment.

I saturated the pendant with my blood until not a single glimpse of silver or the three obsidian stones remained.

I was power. I was the hallow unbroken.

No single magic could contain me.

Because I was made of all.

"Stay close," Mae warned again just as the first flicker of the portal materialized in front of me. Tethering. Growing. Reaching through the veil and struggling to solidify—

A battle cry spilled through my clenched teeth.

More, more, more—

Mae yelled, "Ivarr, *no!*"

I whipped around. Ivarr's gaze fell on mine even as he sprinted towards the outer rim of Mae's power.

Towards the councilors who were refusing the portal its anchor.

"I know you'll find me," he called over the chimes.

And threw himself at the enemy.

The instant his blades flew towards the four women, I felt it. The slip in their power. I screamed as magic poured through me and blinding sunlight bathed my skin—a ray, then more. As the edges of the portal fanned out—

"*NOW!*" My voice swept across the chimes and vicious whispers.

Air whooshed past me as Zaphine and Eriyan, pushing Mae's chair with Lyra and my bag in her lap, rushed into the portal. Then Dantos. Ada.

Mordecai.

He said something to me, the sharp cut of his frame haloed by daylight and black hair gleaming, but I couldn't hear him past the roaring of blood in my ears.

The portal took everything. And I had to *give* everything to keep it stable.

I undid the satchel containing the fragment and flung it through.

If the power drained me, they could still reunite the lands. I wanted to be there with them, wanted to see the world as it had been by Mordecai's side, but this...

Knowing *they* could was enough.

Hot streaks scalded my cheeks as I tried, one desperate last time, to move.

But my legs refused to obey. Refused to move off the volatile land holding me hostage.

Beyond the portal, turquoise shimmered.

Kinder, warmer, but no weaker whispers combatted the ones spearing at me from behind.

Nyon's wide eyes found mine as the rest of the librarians fanned out, Chloenna a formidable force I felt with all my crumbling being.

Dizzy and nauseous, I closed my eyes and prepared to seal off the portal with the final breaths of power still in me.

They were through.

I didn't matter.

And the librarians—this could spare them.

The Council would cease their attack. A truth I felt through their magic. Through the repairs they were already bestowing upon the land even as they kept lashing out in desperate, futile attempts to retrieve the future standing on the other side of the portal.

Giving up my life for theirs, for *all* of theirs, didn't seem so bad at all.

Claim me, I said.

Wrought of magic from the world, I would return to it.

I sensed the edges of the portal site as I offered the land all I still encompassed.

They folded inward, slowly, knitting together the bridge—

Strong fingers wrapped around my wrist.

Fingers and something smoother. Powerful.

Something that called me off the ledge.

The argent shadowfire and Mordecai's grip wrested me from the land and yanked me forward, through the seam of two realities and into the sunlight.

I fell on all fours, Mordecai's arm around my waist. His hand on my back.

"Release it," his smooth, familiar voice begged. "Ember, let it go."

I did.

Not myself. Not here, where there was no price. No instability, no hunger to feed off me.

The only thing I let go was my hold.

As the portal sealed shut within the span of a single heartbeat, the storm within me died.

Shivering, I pushed back onto my heels and lifted my gaze from the dark winter grass. Mordecai held me close as pale blue sky streaked with sunlight greeted my arrival. But its beauty, the very beauty painting something akin to rapture on our companions' faces, couldn't blind us—blind *me*—to Soltzen's festering core.

It only highlighted the rot.

BONUS CHAPTER ONE

The Crescent Prince

He felt her. Past the music, past the illusions.

He couldn't *stop* feeling her even if he wanted to.

The pulse that had sprung to life right before the celebrations and burned bright as a star as they'd ridden down the terror-laced avenue hadn't subsided, only grew. She was a beacon calling to him with a force that went beyond the threads of magic forming the veins of this world.

Mordecai didn't dare examine the strand of luminous darkness luring him across Nysa, simply followed it. His guards trailed behind him, then fanned out at his command to create a perimeter he hadn't even been aware of giving.

He'd never experienced such...loss of control.

Never had moments pass by like strands of night that slipped through his fingers. But—

So long. He had waited so long in this declining world,

fueling fear and hatred to preserve the balance built on lives his shadowfire had consumed.

They thought to keep her from him.

But no more.

He didn't care who he had to ensnare in silver to ensure Somraque's salvation. Ensure the safety of the people who would rip into him without second thought and cheer when the light in his eyes dimmed.

He was inconsequential in this. Had accepted that role ages ago and upheld it with no remorse when he learned it was the only way.

The present always bled for the future.

The people's stillness when he passed the stalls and illuminated shops was absolute. They didn't know what he truly was, couldn't. Yet some primal, subconscious part reacted to the presence of an Ancient, not merely the tyrant they despised.

Though the latter—it always prevailed.

Even the illusions seemed to have paused, though Mordecai sensed them. As he always did. Their brightness and life a song the Void never failed to answer. The solstice celebrations demanded his utter control and fast responses from his guards to put out any unordained displays of magic. A risk, the festivities, but one he knew he had to take to curb the bloodshed.

Maybe for the last time.

Answering the draw of that obsidian thread, Mordecai left the silent crowds behind and dismounted. He strode along the backstreet past a tavern brimming with Somraquians drunk on sowhl, then slowed as he neared the alley the pull originated from.

A ripple of disbelief shot through him. Within his reach.

She was within his reach.

Their salvation. His end.

It was only fitting that it would be a descendant of the bastards who had started it all to bring the story full circle. As if fate itself wanted the Norcross line to suffer for what they'd done.

Unbidden, memories of the temple surged.

The burning sun with a blade running down its center emblazoned on the man's tunic as he approached Mordecai's parents as if he had the right. As if they hadn't spent their lives protecting the very magic that he, too, carried.

He'd never forgotten the thread of power within that man—a thread he sensed in *her*, too—but it had taken Mordecai a long time to unravel the horrors he'd seen that day. To recognize *what* had driven the scum to slaughter his parents—as his cronies and guards had slaughtered the children Mordecai had grown up with, leaving nothing but a bloody sword behind. Like a calling card. A final slap.

Sneering, Mordecai shoved away the past, thought somewhere in the depths of his mind that boy who had hidden behind a statue and watched not only his world but reality itself fracture remained.

Sometimes, he wondered if people were even worth saving.

And yet saving them was all that mattered.

It was the reason behind his magic. The reason behind his existence.

But once he fulfilled his duty, the Norcross line would pay. Too much blood marred their filthy hands. He didn't doubt the stain was still there, even after all this time.

The narrow alley opened up before him as he rounded the corner. Shadowfire coiled beneath his skin, at attention—

He stilled.

Wisps of obsidian.

Wisps of pure obsidian licked the blue-tinted air. A silver-haired girl—*the* girl—stood with her back flush against the wall, barely visible behind the growing veil of darkness that poured from her and crawled up the man keeping her pinned against the stones.

Mordecai's vision flashed silver with rage.

Even if their position weren't telling enough, the girl's face said it all. Norcross or not, he wanted nothing more than to rip into the worthless swine who'd cornered her, but his body refused to obey, mesmerized by the shadowfire—like his, yet different. Beautiful.

And deadly.

The man screamed.

Or tried to.

The girl's shadowfire wrapped around his life-force, something Mordecai didn't see, but *felt*, snuffing it out with every breathtaking flicker of lustrous black. The man staggered back, just a silhouette now, ensconced in untamed obsidian. Mordecai's own shadowfire broke through his skin of its own volition, drawn by the sight of her. The feel of her.

Like him.

He'd been wrong.

Blinded perhaps, by her Norcross lineage. By his own need for what she represented.

Though he—he had sent his mother's pendant across the veil without true cause, but an action wrought of a primal desire he'd refused to acknowledge for eighteen years.

Now, he had no choice.

She was not just a child of three worlds, but a descendant of the people Mordecai didn't allow himself to think about despite the spearing shafts of memories that dug into him every solstice.

It had only ever been him. For *ages* it had only been him.

He was unable to move, unable to do anything but brace himself against the wild thrashing in his chest. The illuminated thread within the tapestry of Somraque's magic burned bright with the silver and obsidian shadowfire free in the air. Mordecai watched hers retreat, an elegant wave of darkness that seeped back into her and left nothing behind but a husk of a man sprawled on the alley floor.

Horror lined her beautiful face as she stared at the corpse, but beneath it, Mordecai saw something unyielding. A deep, endless pool of strength. A greatness he wanted to kneel before.

Faintly, he remembered the role he was supposed to play. The reason for him being here.

But as much as those talons rapped at his mind, they couldn't break the wonder, the reverence—

Her gaze found his—a striking pale blue that seemed to reach right to his very soul.

Mordecai waited for her to scream. To run.

Needed her to react to the monster wrought of nightmares he was.

But she only looked at him.

As if she saw something wonderful too.

BONUS CHAPTER TWO

Enemies

Mordecai always knew he would come face-to-face with Somraque's best Magician eventually.

They were both too large a force, too magnetic in their power to coexist without colliding—like stars of a binary pair spiraling inward.

This meeting, this...supernova was inevitable.

But Mordecai had believed it would end with an explosion only one of them would walk away from.

Not sifting through books side by side, with hands that had seen so much blood it was almost sacrilege to place them upon the old tomes.

Then again, if Somraque had been their barycenter, it stood to reason that in Svitanye, their gravitational waves would differ. Cause a merger, not a collision. But with so many unknowns in play, Mordecai didn't dare presume anything reached beyond the sphere of speculation.

His gaze skimmed Ivarr Revere's dark wavy hair that concealed his face from this angle, then, balancing on the tall ladder, surveyed the large room with its floor-to-ceiling shelves. The librarians worked in moderate silence on their own partitions, only an occasional whisper breaking up the rustle of pages.

The Archivum Vive.

It might have changed its name, but its essence—Mordecai could feel the past and present fusing. The kindness of the librarians then mirrored in the hearts of those surrounding him now.

Perhaps when all of this was over...

Perhaps he would ask them for the chronicles pertaining to that time. Not the end, not what Ember had seen, but *before*. If one of them could extend a remembrance—

He would like to see his parents one more time.

A hushed laugh from the other side of the chamber brought him back. Mordecai descended the ladder, shifted it farther left, then climbed back up to reach the top row. None of the spines bore the Hazeldyne crest, but that was expected. Everybody was not just presuming but *hoping* the volume had been hidden behind a different binding. But with the Repository's beyond-vast collection, the hope also bore a bitter undertone.

A gargantuan task.

With no guaranteed outcome.

Volume after volume, he picked out the books, sifted through them, then placed them back on their rightful place.

Beneath him, crouching as he tackled the lower shelves, Ivarr Revere did the same.

As Mordecai took on another row, repeating the motions, he observed the Magician out of the corner of his eye.

Revere's reputation was almost as bad as his. The man had never hidden his hatred for him, but even more so, he'd never hid that, for the right price, his services could be bought by anyone—except those loyal to Mordecai.

Not that they were many in that camp.

The single reason Revere hadn't ended up in a cell was that for all his blatant opposing, the use of magic beyond limits Mordecai allowed, the Magician... He was an integral part of Somraque.

Like Ada Aldane, like her mother had been, before she had cast that impossible spell eighteen years ago.

The latter he'd contained the only way he could—hoped that by taking Telaria Aldane's magic, he would dissolve the spell. Or at least glean how to.

But the others...

They were flames to monitor, curb. Not extinguish.

Mordecai returned his attention to the books before the Magician would notice him staring.

But as hard as he tried, he couldn't figure Revere out. Nor could he stop the endless roll of thoughts.

Ember had told him that the Magician had taken her side when everyone else, save for the gray-eyed Maelynn, wanted to tear her apart for the choice she'd made. Bringing him here. And when Revere had offered to partner up...

He had been...cordial. Not uptight. Not curt or brisk in his explanation of the system they'd set up to search the Cognizance Repository. Different land or not, Mordecai burned to know the true reasons behind Revere's change of heart. Why the man hadn't attempted to kill him on sight.

He set the last book back on its shelf. Another segment covered. Still no missing Hazeldyne chronicle. He placed his left foot one rung lower when Ivarr clasped a hand around the side rail.

Mordecai hadn't even noticed him stand.

"I can do that for you," Revere said.

Mordecai arched an eyebrow, but before he could ask, the Magician patted the side rail. "You don't have to climb down every time. Just let me know when you're ready and I'll slide you a little farther. It looks like we're going through the books at about the same pace, anyway."

"Thank you," he said, but the caution in his words must have been more evident than he thought, because Revere laughed, then ran a hand through his dark hair.

"I'm not going to send you flying off the fucking thing."

This time, a laugh burst out of Mordecai, too, surprising him. He pulled himself together enough to say, "Don't blame me, Revere, for not blindly trusting someone who wouldn't mind stopping my heart less than a month ago."

"Call me Ivarr," he said and shrugged. "Ember explained who you are. Seemed petty to cling to old beliefs."

"Such as?" Mordecai climbed all the way down.

Ivarr glanced around the room, then at Mordecai. "Come on. I think we earned a break."

Need it was what the unvoiced undercurrent said.

Mordecai didn't argue. He wanted those answers, and...he, perhaps, found himself compelled to speak with Ivarr.

The librarians spared no more than a glance in their direction as they walked out into the corridor, then up the ramp to the topmost floor. Faint flashes of memories surged through Mordecai's mind. Wisps and impressions of a time that seemed so long ago, he would have thought were a figment of his imagination were he not seeing the same walls, the same terrace once more.

Lounge chairs were set haphazardly around a low table, as if someone had forgotten to straighten them. Or perhaps the casual nature of the site was deliberate. Nothing about the Cognizance Repository he'd seen so far felt rigid.

Ivarr grabbed a bottle from a cabinet pressed up against the building, then stalked over and threw himself in one of the armchairs. He motioned Mordecai to join him.

"Eriyan keeps this place stocked up." He waved the bottle in his hands before uncorking it and taking a long sip. He passed it on to Mordecai. "I'd prefer something stronger, but this stuff isn't half bad."

Mordecai eyed the bottle then tipped it to his mouth. The drink went down easily.

"What is this?" He handed it back to Ivarr.

"Local stuff. Lumi." Another long sip. "Want more?"

There was just one answer to that. As he indulged in a little more of the drink, Ivarr reclined in the chair, fingers interlocked atop his stomach.

"When Ada and Zaphine showed up on my doorstep, one with fire in her eyes, the other startled like a doe, albeit a pissed-off one," Ivarr said. "I almost laughed in their faces. It was so damn clear they wanted nothing to do with a murderous prick, and still, they were there, babbling about Saviors and reunited worlds and"—the faint smile on his face turned wicked—"infiltrating your palace. I indulged them for that alone."

"I can imagine," Mordecai commented flatly, but let a tentative edge of humor seep through.

The latter wasn't lost on Ivarr.

He huffed a laugh and scraped the heel of his boot across the floor. "It was no better when I met Dantos and Eriyan. I thought they were a bunch of zealous kids—"

"As if you're that much older than them..."

Ivarr shrugged and took the bottle Mordecai offered. "You take the crown, of course, but... It didn't feel like there was just six, seven years between us. They were so...untested. Not exactly unfamiliar with the darker side of life, but not—*shaped* by them, either." He tipped the bottle and drank deeply, then returned it to Mordecai. "Though I'm not dismissing the possibility I was just an annoyed, pretentious ass. Either way, once we started working together, I realized they weren't overly ambitious dreamers.

"They still treated me like I was a stain that would leech on their souls and mostly just avoided me as much as they could, but... Their will, the fact that they constantly pushed through their fears—I began to admire them."

Mordecai slid his fingertips along the curve of the bottle. "Life has a way of surprising us, doesn't it?"

Ivarr nodded, then turned his gaze to the dawn sky.

Beats of silence passed, the clouds shedding hues and taking on new nuances as they drifted by.

"I never even knew this existed," Ivarr said after a while. "Just as I didn't know what you were doing to hold Somraque together. I fucking hated the restrictions of magic you forced on us."

"You weren't the only one," Mordecai noted dryly.

Ivarr tipped his head back and laughed. When he looked at Mordecai again, the mirth was gone. But not the familiarity. "I have nothing against you."

"Nor I you." He passed the bottle of lumi back to the Magician who accepted it with a curve to his lips.

Ivarr returned his attention to the sky, though Mordecai doubted it was the dawn he was perusing. A hint of a frown rested upon his brows. "Ember—do you love her?"

Had the question come from anyone else, Mordecai wouldn't have answered. His feelings towards Ember were his own, not a discussion.

But there was something in the way Ivarr had asked that made him reconsider keeping his silence.

"I do."

The Magician met his gaze—then slowly gave an approving nod. "Good."

ACKNOWLEDGMENTS

This book was the longest, most difficult, yet at the same time most beautiful one we've ever worked on. But it wouldn't be what it is without the amazing individuals sharing this journey.

Lindsey R. Loucks and Michelle Rascon. Our word-wizards, librarians, and indispensable Savior team. Thank you so much for giving Emergence the shape and shine it would never have had on its own. You are absolutely incredible, and we're humbled to have you on our side.

Merwild, once again, your cover art blew us away. Your rendition of Mordecai is nothing short of perfection. Our gratitude for bringing him to life reaches through the veil across all three worlds.

Leeroy and Merkaba, our barking, adorable pups who always know how to walk a thin line between giving us a reprieve from work and annoying us by making it impossible to work. You two really are devils in a super cute casing, but we wouldn't have it any other way.

To all the wonderful, beautiful bookstagrammers, bloggers, booktubers, and reviewers who were with us right from the very start. You do such amazing work, spreading bookish love and building a welcoming, kind, and inspiring community. Special thanks go out to Georgia (thebookishgurl), Areli (offaerietalesandbooks), Nuša (coyoteswillguideyou), Leslie (acourt_ofbooks), Amy (zanybibliophile), Briony (acourtofbriony), Jessy (zeilenmagie), Esmay (paradiseofpages), Tahnee (readingismybliss), Martha (martha_lostinpages)—just to name a few. A huge thank-you also goes to FaeCrate for featuring *Evenfall* in one of their lovely boxes!

Last but not least, our heartfelt thank-yous go to you, our readers. You breathe life into stories and make this profession one of absolute magic. We love you!

ALSO BY GAJA J. KOS & BORIS KOS

SHADOWFIRE TRILOGY

Upper YA fantasy

Evenfall

Emergence

FORGED IN FLAMES

Dark epic fantasy

THE IRON HEAD TRILOGY

YA epic fantasy

The Fox

The Heart

The Bird

ALSO BY GAJA J. KOS

KOLOVRAT UNIVERSE

PRESENT

BLACK WEREWOLVES SERIES

Urban fantasy

Novels:

The Dark Ones

The 24hourlies

The Shift

The Ascension

Novellas:

Never Forgotten

Chased

Black Werewolves: Books 1–4

NIGHTWRAITH SERIES

Paranormal romance

Windstorm

Blackstorm

Nightstorm

Nightwraith: The Complete Series

SUCC

Open relationship standalone paranormal romance

FUTURE

PARADISE OF SHADOWS AND DEVOTION

Standalone paranormal romance

LOTTE FREUNDENBERGER SERIES

Urban fantasy

Shadow Moon

Darkening Moon

Transient Moon

SHADE ASSASSIN

Urban fantasy

Shadow World

Shadow Lies

DAWN OF KOLOVRAT

Urban fantasy standalone novellas

Destiny Reclaimed

ROMANCE

SILVER FOX CLUB

Steamy May December standalone novellas

Cotton Candy